THE
CONSULATE

ALLISON CARR WAECHTER

THE WORLD OF THE
ORPHIUM MAERE

Ebook ISBN: 978-1-963134-14-8

Paperback ISBN: 978-1-963134-13-1

Hardcover ISBN: 978-1-963134-12-4

Book Cover by Robert Kraiza

Editing by Kenna Kettrick

Interior Illustrations by Charlie Arpie

First edition 2024

CONTENT GUIDELINES

THE WORLD OF THE ORPHIUM MAERE

THE AUTHORITY

The human-led government that has ruled Kraitos for the past two thousand years.

THE CONSULATE

The shadow organization on Kraitos that mediates between parapsychs (those with paranormal abilities) and humans. Formed to protect parapsychs as the Authority came to power.

THE TRINITY

The three main groups of parapsychs, ruled by three dynastic "families" across the Three Cities.

THE NECROLINE DYNASTY

Those who interact with the dead.

THE COGNOSCENTI DYNASTY

Those who see outside the parameters of reality.

THE THAUMAS DYNASTY

Those who perform miracles.

THE MAERE

Fifteen immortal warriors who stand between the Consulate, the Trinity and the Authority.

THE THREE CITIES

Three huge city-states that make up the known population of Kraitos, as much of the world, is covered in monster-inhabited oceans. Between each of the Three Cities sits the "Wastelands," vast, dangerous areas of wild land that is best avoided.

Orphium *(City of the Dead)*
Aradios *(City of Miracles)*
Palladiere *(City of Foresight)*

THE SAINTS

St. Amarante *(immortality)*
St. Paloma *(miracles)*
St. Tanith *(death)*
St. Cassandra *(foresight)*
St. Ekate *(magic/the underworld/Hel)*
St. Irys *(tricksters/Fate)*

CHAPTER 1

EMBER

Skyscrapers were slippery bitches in a storm. I had just enough room on my ledge to keep watch as rain pummeled into the building, blown sideways by the wind. I was soaked through and shivering. It would have been nice to look nice, but it isn't as though Lara Achilles has ever cared much about how I look.

But maybe I wouldn't see her tonight. I'd been here every night for a month, after catching wind that her release had been approved, but so far, waiting had been a bust. Cautiously, I leaned against the glass, watching fog roll through the streets below. The fog meant the rain was about to let up. That didn't stop the next lightning strike and its subsequent roll of thunder from shaking the glass-clad building.

A few offices down from where I stood, a light was still on. Someone was burning the midnight oil at O-Tex. Someone always was, though—the Corps never slept. I closed my eyes against the last of the rain, breathing evenly to tamp down the growing impatience building in my chest.

It took me nearly a decade to understand why Lara stayed in the Asylum when she could've walked out at any time—and another to reconcile my guilt at not having stopped this to begin with. I'd been so preoccupied with finding our swords and regaining our honor that I forgot to be vigilant with my people. My lack of foresight got us here.

It had been long enough. If Lara was getting out, I was going to get her and the rest of the Orphium Maere back. Movement below caught my attention. A tall, lean figure pushed open the heavily carved metal door to the Asylum and slipped outside, lighting a cigarette as she went. Tonight was the night, then. I'd recognize the swagger in Lara Achilles' step in any decade, any lifetime. I stepped forward, into the rain and off the ledge of the O-Tex corporate headquarters, falling nearly forty stories, clean into a crouch at Lara's feet.

"Fucking Hel, Verona," she said, without so much as a flinch.

"Good to see you too," I sniped back.

And it was. She looked fantastic—like she'd adopted one of those seventeen-step skincare routines while she was in, meditating every day and shit. Really, it was just the immortality, but it was a lark to imagine it the other way. Easier than thinking about what it was really like in there. I shuddered to think of the conditions in the Asylum. No one knew much, because almost no one ever got out. And those who did rarely spoke about what it was like inside.

Rain hit us both square in the face as the wind shifted, sending the fog rolling towards us in ominous, billowing clouds. In Orphium's midnight glow, Lara looked like the anti-hero of a comic. Her dark hair, though shorn poorly, was damp from the rain. It fell into her narrowed ice-blue eyes as she raised her chin defiantly at me, taking a long drag from the cigarette in her bony fingers before turning away from me.

She tossed the cig and looked both ways before crossing the street, which was an old habit—there'd been a time when being clocked as an immortal would have meant torture, or worse. Lara knew better than most what "worse" entailed. Even now, we adapted to the ways mortals moved through the world, despite the Consulate's progress with the Authority.

Looking both ways wasn't necessary, though. This time of night, the streets surrounding the Asylum were clear. No one wanted to hear the inmates' screams.

"Fuck off," Lara said as she strode into the wet intersection, fog swirling around her feet. "I'm out."

There was no getting out of the Maere. She knew it. I knew it. This was all bluster and fuss. And I couldn't blame her for it —but I did, anyway. Whatever the reason she'd had for staying in that abominable pit, I wasn't interested in hearing about it anymore.

Her stunning lack of loyalty to me after hundreds of years of friendship fucked me up on a personal level, and fucked me over on a professional one. The bitch stayed in, refused every lawyer I sent her way, and wouldn't see me or the rest of our sistren, no matter how we begged.

It ruined us. Scattered us to the winds. I hadn't seen Rhi, Max, or Sera in almost eighteen years. Barely heard from them, either. It had just been me standing between the parapsychs of Orphium, the Authority, and the Consulate for twenty years and I was sick to death of the balancing act. Lara was supposed to be the one I could trust. My ride or die. The one I depended on. And she left me to fend for myself without so much as an explanation.

I had every right to be angry, but I chose something closer to begging, since we both knew I wasn't too proud for such measures. "Come on." I grabbed the sleeve of her tuxedo jacket. We'd been to a posh Consulate function the night she was taken in—as if I could have forgotten. "I've got a new place. You'll like it."

Lara twisted out of my grip. "The old place is fine."

"It burned to the ground after you left," I shot back, swallowing the acid that rose in my throat at the thought of the fire. "Necroline ghouls." I practically choked over my next words: "Without you—everything's gone to shit."

For a moment I thought she might relent, might finally tell

me what went down the night they took her, *why* they took her. But Lara Achilles was a stubborn little git, and she just shook her head, fury building on the sharply carved planes of her face. I wanted to punch her till she did things my way. But we'd agreed to stop solving problems that way centuries ago, and unlike her, I kept my promises.

The rain hadn't stopped yet, and it soaked us both through as it fell harder, banishing the creep of the city's notorious fog. We were a mess. But when Lara reached out for me, I made the mistake of thinking she meant to embrace me. Instead, she gripped my chin in her fingers, her ragged nails digging into my skin as she yanked me towards her.

"It was always going to shit, Verona. Don't you see that? We're useless. Always have been, always will be. Go live your life."

As if I had a life to live without the Maere. As if any of us did.

She let me go with a hard shove. I stumbled backwards, stung by the violence in her eyes, but not surprised. I stood on the corner, watching as she crossed the street, heading downtown.

"Don't follow me," she called over her shoulder. "Forget you ever knew me, Verona. I'm sure as Hel going to forget I know you."

CHAPTER 2

EMBER

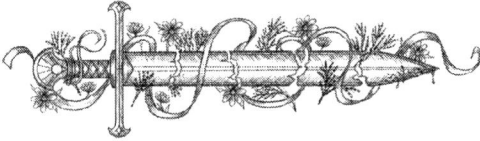

SACCHARINE PINK WALLS contrasted with acid green gutters and wood trim. If the color combination wasn't enough to give me a headache, the noise certainly was. The sound of balls rolling down the polished wood lanes and pins being knocked down filled my ears. Everything smelled of cigar smoke and aged leather. Oldies played on the overhead speakers, as Lourdes Thaumas poured champagne out of a pink plastic pitcher, into the mug I held out for her.

It said #1 Boss on it, which I assume was Lourdes' attempt at a joke. I wasn't laughing. Lourdes wasn't either, though the miracle worker was dressed as a ray of sunshine. Her perfectly tailored three-piece suit was a nearly blinding shade of neon yellow that contrasted with her dark brown skin. Today, her tiny box braids were pulled back in a thick bun at the base of her neck.

"Drink up," she suggested, clinking her teddy bear mug to mine. "Before you puke your guts out."

I rolled my eyes, but I threw back the champagne and directly poured myself another. My head still throbbed painfully. A little hair of the dog wouldn't hurt. Lourdes sat across from me, kicking her feet up on the bench seat. Both of us wore rented bowling shoes, but neither of us bothered with a ball. It wasn't like we were going to play.

"Why do we have to meet here?" Lourdes sidestepped how obviously hungover I was to talk about something else. Avoidance was practically her middle name. We never talked about the things that mattered. Only the ones that didn't. Maybe life was easier that way. "We've got all the money in the world. Why can't we get a nice steak at The Rack, or even see the girls at The Odyssey? At least that place has class."

I shrugged and even the tiniest movement of my shoulders felt like it might send me into the spins again. Immortality like mine was a terrible joke. I couldn't get sick or die, but I still got hungover. One of St. Irys, the Trickster's, greatest jokes, though folks naturally attributed it to St. Amarante. "Neutral ground. You know the drill. Consulate rules."

Lourdes shook her head. "Next month we're meeting at the Automat. The food here is wretched."

She said the same thing every month, and every month we met at the ThunderBowl, same as always. Same time, same day, same bullshit. And we'd keep doing it for-fucking-ever. Literally.

"Ain't that the truth," Lux Medios drawled as she appeared out of nowhere, long cherry-red hair grazing my shoulder as she kissed my cheek, her Saints-charms tinkling like bells around her wrist. It took me a moment to realize she was talking about the food, not my inner monologue of doom. "Good to see you, honey. Sorry about the bad luck with Lara."

So they'd heard about that already. It hadn't even been twelve hours. I gritted my teeth. The last thing I needed was their pity—and Ares Necroline was going to find a way to use this against me somehow. The scary motherfucker nearly always had something up his sleeve, and he'd had it out for me for decades.

As though thinking of the necromancer called him forth, he

appeared behind Lux. Today, he was a head shorter than her, but that was only because Lux's platforms added at least six inches to her already staggering height. They were a lesson in contrasts, Lux's muscular frame draped in a lush ice blue velvet track suit that brought out the warmth of her light brown skin, while Ares Necroline, pale as death and tattooed to high heaven, wore a gray three-piece suit that looked like it came straight off the set of a gangster flick. The leader of the Cognoscenti was over-the-top luxury mixed with something vaguely metaphysical, while the Necroline asshole was a nightmare waiting to happen.

Both came to sit around the pink molded-plastic table—Ares sat directly across from me, an irritating smirk playing on his perfectly sculpted lips as he draped his long, muscular body on the bench seat. It was maddening that someone I disliked so much was packaged in such a delectable way, but Saint Irys loved to tease me.

Lux pulled a champagne flute out of her handbag, cut from pink crystal that matched the walls. Of course, she'd brought her own champagne flute. Why wouldn't she? No one took these meetings seriously.

I was a joke to them. Every month we met was painful.

"Fill me up, Daddy," Lux purred at Ares.

He obliged with a smile, though he did not drink himself. I snatched the bottle from his grip and filled my mug again.

"I was sorry to hear Lara refused your offer of sanctuary," Ares said, his voice low, as though he were keeping a secret for me.

"Don't use that tone with me," I snarled, unable to keep my temper leashed.

One eyebrow arched at me. The man had no right to have such alluring eyebrows. "How does someone who *looks* as elegant as you manage to be so… What's the word I'm looking for, Lux?"

Lux rolled her brown eyes, the expression made more exaggerated by the false lashes she wore. Today's had bright blue glitter dusted over them, and I envied her ability to get them glued on just right. Any time I tried falsies, I got them stuck all over my eyelids and looked utterly deranged. "Divine. Ember always looks divine."

Ares rolled his eyes. "I thought we weren't going to coddle her."

"Just look at her." Lux chucked me under the chin. She smelled incredible, her perfume some mix of earthy woods and rich amber. "She's pathetic. Her eyes are puffy and red. She probably cried herself to sleep, but she still looks like one of those drugged out models we all wanted to be like twenty years ago. I said what I meant—Ember Verona is *divine*."

"Gods above and below," Lourdes swore, throwing her hands in the air, her gold rings sparkling in the hot-pink neon lights. "Can we just get to business? I'd like to get out of here before dinner."

It was barely noon. There was no chance of us being here another ten minutes now that everyone was here. They never bothered reporting in anymore. When Lara broke up the Maere, Orphium's Trinity stopped respecting my authority. None of these parapsych bosses gave two shits about what I thought, what I wanted, or what I did with my time.

I was a glorified messenger girl, a Consulate stooge. Nothing more. My head pounded.

Each of them took out an envelope of cash and passed it to me. Tithes to the Consulate were due, and I was in charge of the drop. It was the only reason I showed up here every month. I secreted the envelopes away in my bag and leaned back, snuggling into my oversized leather jacket. The red lining was silky and felt good against my skin. "That's done. Can we go?"

Lourdes glared at me. "The point is to share relevant information with one another, is it not?"

I shrugged. *Now* she wanted to do what we were supposed

to? *Fishy, fishy, fishy.* I shook my head. It was because Lara was back. The brat wasn't even *here*, and Lourdes wanted to act better to impress her. They'd had a thing once, maybe Lourdes wanted to revive it. Or maybe she just respected Lara more than me. Couldn't blame her there.

Finally, I sighed—she was right, after all. This was how we'd always survived. Parapsych abilities weren't exactly illegal anymore, but they certainly weren't accepted. We were in murky territory with the Authority, serving a purpose for many of the Corps, as our abilities gave our capitalist overlords an edge. But as far as society at large was concerned, we were not to be trusted, and our people often remained outsiders. It's why we needed the Consulate, vicious as it could be. Our world ran on secrets, and I was supposed to be keeping the three of them, and their dynasties, in line.

I just didn't feel like it today.

I hadn't felt like it in nearly twenty years, but that was the curse of immortal life. The curse all of us bore. The years came and went, mortals going about their mundane lives around us, while we lived in opulent shadow—only important when they needed a miracle.

The only miracle I needed today was a nap. My eyes weren't red from crying, but I had been up all night pacing—and drinking. I was ready to go home, sleep my hangover off and start again tomorrow.

"I heard something," Ares said after a long silence between the four of us. Apparently, Lourdes didn't have anything to actually tell us, she just wanted to bring it up to get a gold star. "Something that might interest you, Verona."

I quit glaring at Lourdes in order to glower at Ares Necro-line—everything about his tone irritated me. Too much history I couldn't forgive, and now everything he did drove me wild. "What's that?"

"The National Gallery has a new exhibit for the Auction this year," he said, his words slow and careful.

9

"It has a new exhibit for the Auction every year," I said with a sigh. "It's the event it is *because* they have a new exhibit to showcase. That is hardly news."

"It's 'Weapons of the Ancient World' this year. There are *swords*," Ares said as he rose. "And they're going to be part of the Auction."

My heart dropped into my stomach. There was only one set of swords Ares Necroline might think I'd be interested in. Cold sweat broke out on my back at the thought of seeing them again. My mouth went bone dry as the world turned on its axis.

Ares shook Lourdes' hand with a curt nod, brushed a kiss to Lux's hand, and then bent close to my face. "You might want to check out lot A342," he murmured. His breath caressed the sensitive shell of my ear, sending a delicious chill through me. "See you next month."

Lux drained her champagne glass, then placed it on the tray and rose from the table, looking worried. "Do you want to come shopping with me, LouLou?"

Lourdes sighed. "Only if we can go downtown to your guy for imports."

Lux grinned. "But of course, my love. Ember?"

She sounded like she meant it. The offer was genuine, which I appreciated. As much as they were pains in my ass, Lux and Lourdes had been good friends when the rest of the Maere split on me. Lux might side with Necroline too many times for my liking, but she always made it up to me later. Long brunches on the river, girl-talk at the salon. She'd been the one to help me decorate when I moved into the new place on my own. Now, she stretched a hand out to me, her elegant nails shining with iridescent polish as she waved them at me.

I shook my head as I squeezed Lux's hand. "Thank you, but I have things to do."

As the acting head of the Maere, I was required to maintain some semblance of respectability these days—especially with all my people scattered to the wind. I was a walking target. Not that I could die, but it was a pain in the ass to heal from the efforts of those who wanted to test the theory. Besides, I had to get home, change my clothes, and get downtown. It was time to find Lara and end this. The chickens were long past due to come home to roost.

CHAPTER 3

ARES

I UNBUTTONED my jacket as I opened the back door of the sleek black sedan waiting for me outside of the bowling alley. A news station was playing on the radio. One of the better stations, but Saints, if the shit they let go on the air wasn't a bunch of utter drivel. The public radio hosts were interviewing an influencer, trying to ask her questions about whether or not she *really liked* the things she hawked on her platform.

"Shut that shit off," I scolded as I slid into the back seat, not wanting to hear the answer. Everyone was selling something all the time now. There was no trick to it. No art. We were all just selling our souls to the Authority. To the Corps. And, much as I hated it, the Consulate.

Avaline and my brother were waiting, sitting in companionable silence in the front seat. Eryx read the newspaper. He preferred a fresh hard copy each morning to using the app that came on his phone, and the car smelled faintly of leather and fresh ink.

Eryx flipped the switch on the radio, but not before the host announced that they'd be interviewing freshman Senator Cromvale next. I grimaced at the name. The Three-Cities Senate was as corrupt as the rest of them.

Avaline's favorite little Poltergeist was consuming something disgusting in the back seat. "Out," I commanded.

It gave me its hellish version of puppy dog eyes, to which I glared. Av looked in the rearview at her pet and shook her head. The thing was about to throw the disemboweled rat at me in protest.

"That would be an unwise choice," I murmured, twisting the family ring on my right index finger. "You know what I can do."

The Poltergeist disappeared, not wanting to be blasted out of existence, I suppose. "I do not enjoy that thing," I remarked, checking for signs of rat detritus before I moved over.

More likely than not, the rat hadn't been real, just an illusion to disgust me. Poltergeists were like that—they mostly wanted to irritate the fuck out of their victims.

"His name is Stanley," Eryx reminded me, voice dry as a bone.

Not a hint of humor whatsoever. My brother was not joking. The cursed Poltergeist had a *name*. I gritted my teeth, suppressing the urge to give a lecture about respecting spirits' essential nature and not treating them like pets.

For her part, Avaline was, as ever, the picture of perpetual calm—alert and deadly. My crew joked that the necromancer never slept, and I couldn't deny she had a kind of otherworldly air about her. She'd been that way since we were children. Of course, that was so long ago at this juncture, that it was practically irrelevant.

"Did you give her the information?" Av asked.

"Yes," I replied tersely.

She'd never felt good about what happened twenty years ago. Av's sense of honor made it difficult to reconcile that what we'd looked into hadn't caused Lara's capture—though I couldn't deny it had been relevant to the scenario, if she'd been taken for the reasons we suspected.

Destroying the Maere's old place made an enemy of Ember

Verona, but we couldn't risk anyone finding out what we knew —and all the answers had been in that ramshackle old mansion, if anyone had known what to look for. And someone had been closing in on us. Burning it down had been the only answer— but we'd thought they'd all been out.

We'd *seen* Serafine Duval just an hour before. Or at least Av was told we had, by one of her best informants. But we'd been wrong. And while the Maere couldn't die, they could be gravely injured. It took Sera years to recover. It's what broke Orphium's Maere. *We* broke them.

And much as I hated to admit it, the Trinity needed strong Maere to keep the balance between us, the Consulate, and the mundane world. The Authority and the Corps pulled too much power these days—they were practically one and the same, having bought one another off so many times that anyone who bothered to pay attention had lost count. It had only made them both worse, and more powerful.

The Consulate was nothing like my adoptive father, Roman Necroline, had intended for it to be anymore. They had lost their way long before his untimely death, but things got worse all the time. The nominal power the Trinity used to hold within the organization had dissolved, and as I wasn't Roman's biological child, I had no claim to his Founder's Seat on the high council.

We took a calculated risk by tipping Verona off to the swords. I could only hope it was worth it. The Consulate ruled us more directly, but they were not a sovereign entity. Despite everything, on some level, they still answered to the Authority. We all did—there was no use in longing for the ancient past.

I shoved the threat of nostalgia for a time that never was to the back of my mind, drumming my fingers on my knee. Av took a sip of her coffee, then put the car into gear. As she pulled out of the alley, I leaned back in my seat, breathing deeply. Trying to get the scent of Ember Verona's perfume out of my nose.

Typically, I hated the smell of roses, but she smelled like something else as well, something rich, musky, with a hint of spice. Peppercorn, perhaps? That had to be it. The perfume's unexpected allure was the reason I couldn't stop thinking about how she smelled when I dropped the tip.

She'd been hungover, keeping her oval sunglasses on the entire meeting, but she never went out without earrings, a slick of lipgloss, and smelling good enough to devour. Today there'd been a slump in her shoulders that made me uneasy. I'd had the bizarre urge to ask her if she wanted my macaroni and cheese recipe, but blessed be the Saints, I'd kept that to myself. I tried to tell myself I was just happy she hadn't vomited in public.

"What's the word on Lara Achilles?" I worked hard to banish thoughts of the way Verona's leggings hugged every luscious curve of her thighs, or the odd surge of jealousy I felt seeing her oversized leather jacket. Six of one, half dozen the other she was going for style, but the mere thought that it might have been a lover's irritated me.

Eryx folded his newspaper and pushed a lock of hair away from his face. People said we looked alike, but my brother had at least twenty-five pounds of muscle on me and a good five inches. Other than that, sure, we were alike. Dark hair, somewhere between brown and black, pale tattooed skin, and our mom's crystalline green eyes.

Eryx turned slightly in his seat. "Achilles paid a visit to Aqualand last night."

Inwardly, I swore. How did she know we were on to her? "Did she talk to Bubbles?"

"They were the only one in last night," Av said as she turned uptown.

"Hang a left on Park," I said with a sigh. "Let's go see about a fish."

CHAPTER 4

EMBER

THE SMELL of chlorine hit me in the face as I breezed into the Mega-Dome Swim Center. The yellow structure ballooned over the green water of the half-dozen pools, glowing like some cheap version of the sun. It was the closest we were going to get to a sunny day this time of year, and though the chlorine made me sneeze, the wet, warm air was welcome enough.

There wasn't much use in searching for Lara. I knew exactly where she'd be today as soon as the pool opened. I waved to little Eden Philips, who wasn't a kid anymore but always would be to me, then swiped my card at the reader and found a seat in the bleachers.

My phone buzzed with notifications. I glanced through them. My monthly work from the Consulate was wrapping up. It was mostly administrative tasks right now—more glorified errand-girl shit that I hated. It had been a while since I had a bigger job. The last had been guarding the Aradios Trinity leaders at their annual meeting with their Orphium counterparts three months ago. Without my sistren, real jobs—like the ones the Maere in the other territories got frequently—were fewer and farther between all the time.

I resisted the urge to fuck with my phone and doomscroll

through all the bad news and weirdos hawking pyramid schemes. Nothing on socials was entertaining anymore—even the cute cats were selling something these days.

At any rate, my situation was anxiety-producing enough without all the extra stimulus, so I stashed my phone. My knee bounced erratically while I waited, my hands itching for something to do. I'd never been good at sitting still. Lara was in the furthest lane from me, zooming through the water like a damn porpoise, and twice as mean.

When she finally popped out of the water, I stood up. She caught the movement as she pulled herself up on the ladder, rivulets of the chlorine-packed stuff streaming off her. Lara was just as handsome as she'd ever been, and she'd built up an impressive rack of muscles in the Asylum.

"Fuck," I saw her say, rather than hearing her, because Eden Philips was blasting some wailing lounge singer over the speakers. But Lara didn't bolt on me, which I took as an invitation to talk.

I picked my way between puddles on the tile floor and cut right to the quick of it. "Someone's got our swords and they're going to auction them off at the National Gallery Gala."

Lara didn't so much as act surprised. The smug bitch pulled a towel off a red plastic lounger and asked, "You know this for certain?"

There was no use in lying to Lara. We'd known each other for too long. "No. I thought we could check it out together. But the intel came from Ares Necroline, so…"

Lara rolled her eyes. "So it's just as likely a goose chase as real intel?"

I crossed my arms, not disagreeing, but not wanting to talk it out either. "Don't you want to find out?"

She squinted as she thought it over. "Meet me in the parking lot in ten."

I moved to follow her, and she glared at me. "If you follow

me to the showers, Verona, I'll kick your skinny ass six ways from Sunday and twice on Tuesday."

"Bitch," I breathed with a smile.

"Cunt." No smile, but there was a glimmer in her eyes that gave me hope.

I waved to Eden, told her to tell her mom to ring me up—that it had been too long since we played euchre—and headed out the back door. The woman would never call. She never did, but I still offered.

Outside, Lara's midnight blue Dodger was in the parking lot, shiny and looking like it just got a wax. I heavily doubted she'd ghost me. She loved the car too damn much. I didn't dare lean on it, so I crossed my arms against the cold and waited. Autumn had been especially frigid.

In exactly ten minutes, Lara came out. Her raven hair was damp, and she wore a swipe of lip balm, a decades-old ThunderBowl t-shirt, and a blue satin bomber jacket with a rising sun on the back. The jacket used to be mine, but I could let that go if I knew where she'd had it stashed. She wore her Saints medallions as well, the gold charms clicking together as she fished a box of Luckies out of the jacket's inner pocket. She hadn't had them on the night she was arrested.

The vast majority of our stuff had burned up in the fire. I'd taken the Dodger to Bubbles for safekeeping. They were close, and I knew they'd take care of the car, but where had these clothes and her jewelry been? Suspicion gnawed at me.

Lara lit a cig, and I hadn't the heart to smack it out of her lips. What did it matter if it gave her lung cancer? She'd never know it. Never sick, never injured, never dead. That was us. The other parapsychs—members of the Trinity dynasties—were different. Their lives played out much like the mortals' did. They could get ill, hurt, and even die. So long as they didn't, they'd live forever, as far as anyone knew.

But the five of us and the rest of our kind? We were eternal. Hurt us badly enough and it would take a while to recover, but we always *did* recover. So what did it matter if Lara Achilles smoked a pack a day, or two or three.

"Give me one," I said as she unlocked her car.

She threw the gold and white box so hard it smacked me in the face. "Light it yourself."

They were the expensive ones that smelled like whisky and creamy vanilla. Lara slid into the front seat and reached over to unlock my door for me. The inside of the car was oxblood leather and plush carpet.

I used the car lighter as Lara started the Dodger. A mixtape I made her thirty years ago came on, playing at full blast, and I grinned. "You still love me."

The only answer was Lara flinging the volume knob all the way to the right before peeling out of her parking spot. While she didn't say a word, a smirk curled the left corner of her full lips. Neither of us spoke as she headed uptown, an old habit on car rides. I couldn't remember which of us decided it wasn't something we liked, but among the five of us, we never chatted idly in the car.

Instead, we sang. At the top of our lungs. Lara drove like a maniac and the rest of us were required to sing as loud as we could. As we crossed the bridge into uptown, Lara wove through traffic, barely missing the other cars as the city sped by, rain pelting the front window. But it was just me and Lara now, singing twenty-year-old top 30 songs and dying inside. Metaphorically, of course—there was nothing in this Saints-forsaken world for us but time.

Lara turned the music off a block away from the National Gallery's main offices and archives. They weren't located in the museum proper, but two blocks away in a secure building. It'd been a while since we had dealings with the Gallery, but we'd done jobs for them before. Ones on the up and up. As liaisons between the Consulate and the Authority, we often had to deal with the National Gallery in cases of haunted objects.

"How do you want to play this?" Lara asked. "Go right in

and introduce ourselves to the new curators, or try to get a look at the swords another way first?"

Neither of us was dressed for a meeting with the curators. This kind of thing had to be handled delicately. But I was fine to stop by the visitors' center. "I'll hit up the front desk."

I pulled out my wallet and flashed my membership card at Lara. "They put out these exclusive brochures before an auction."

"For members only, I assume," Lara said, examining my card before rolling her eyes.

I pushed open the car door. "You got it. Back in a flash."

CHAPTER 5

ARES

THE DAY HAD TURNED DARKER than usual, despite the fact that it was past lunchtime. Orphium was like that. Clouds combined with the perpetual smog that covered the city—evidence of our corporate overlords' never-ending toil. Gray and more gray, but today everything was murkier. It made the red and gold leaves that fell to the ground stand out more, their jeweled tones the only thing that broke through the dismal cityscape—besides the endless neon lights in the stygian atmosphere.

This far downtown, people rushed back and forth between shifts. The sidewalks were full of people, and the spirits they attracted. Most mortals couldn't see them. But a few wanted to be recognized and were willing to drain the energy of the living to be seen. Those spirits were visible islands in the stream of people we passed, showcasing the ways they died, or lived, as was sometimes their way. It didn't matter what they did. Mortals and parapsychs alike avoided them downtown. The nebulous prejudice against parapsychism always applied more down here than uptown, where the Trinity mixed with the upper crust regularly. I hated the way it worked.

"Bad weather rolling in," Eryx commented, glancing back at me as Av veered towards the curb.

It was obvious he was talking about more than the rain. My brother was a poetic soul, as he'd always felt the shifts in tides of power more acutely than I could. I took his statement for what it was—valuable insight—and nodded to show I understood. We'd never needed many words, often communicating in just such a shorthand.

There was a rare parking spot right outside Aqualand. My brother punched Av in the arm, light with his touch. "Rockstar," he said in a tone that let me know it was some kind of inside joke between them.

She stuck out her tongue and shook her head, shaking her black hair so that it undulated like a sheet of silk. Definitely an inside joke then. Anyone who didn't actually know them would say they were the most serious in my crew—the most ruthless— but here in the car, when it was just the three of us, we were kids again.

I wasn't privy to all their secret jokes. In some ways, they were a closed circle. But I was allowed to be here, and they were comfortable showing their true selves around me, which was something anyway. A small stab of envy over the intimacy between them hit me in the chest. An unusual reaction for me, as I believed in holding myself apart.

As I got out of the car, an elderly couple came out of Aqualand, holding hands. He carried a pair of goldfish in a plastic bag and held them up to her. The old woman smiled and said, "They're perfect. Just like us."

Eryx raised an incredulous eyebrow at Av, as if to say, "What a trip." But the lonely ache in my chest deepened. I blew out a long breath, trying to banish the feeling. There was nothing for it. This was the life.

As the leader of the Necroline, I had to be on at all times, detached and logical, always in control. There was no room in my life for companionship or inside jokes. I had to make do with the fumes of better relationships. I should count myself lucky that I was even allowed on the periphery of Eryx and Av's friendship.

After the elderly couple made their way down the street, Eryx pushed open the shop door for me. I was immediately struck by the singular smell of fish tanks. The shop was dark, but for the lights in the tanks, glowing neon teal. Bubbles had the radio onto one of the local talk shows. These days, they were little more than gossip, hosts trying to get the inside scoop from the endless who's-who of Orphium.

And there was always a new rising star. Always a fresh face, just waiting to be crushed by the city's unreasonable expectations. If you believed what you heard or read, there was just one solution for such a feeling: buy more shit. At the back of the shop, Bubbles sat behind a cash register, embroidering a pillow that appeared to read "Sounds fishy."

"Still listening to this bullshit?" I asked as I approached, but my tone was friendly. I loved Bubbles dearly, though they seemed committed to making me worry about them.

Bubbles was an impressive figure, with a round belly and muscular arms the size of tree trunks. Their brown skin glowed in the neon light of the tanks, and their bright floral shirt was unbuttoned halfway down their hairy chest. When they saw me, they grinned one of their signature sparkling grins. There was very little in the world as charming as Bubbles smiling.

"Hey, Bub," they said in a soft voice, their round, handsome face pleasant in the teal glow. They lowered their embroidery as Av and Eryx followed me into the shop.

I couldn't remember when Bubbles started calling me Bub. About thirty years back, maybe. They didn't have nicknames for many people, so I took it as a deep compliment. I nodded once to them, waiting for the okay to approach. Bubbles wasn't fond of folks who came in looking solely for info, but knew I couldn't keep a fish alive to save my life.

They glanced down past my knee. A lone goldfish floated belly-up at the top of the tank. Bubbles shook their head, closing their eyes. When they opened them, the fish twitched a few times, righted itself, then began swimming slowly in an awkward circle. It was missing most of its fins.

"Poor little guy got attacked," Bubbles explained. "Keeps giving up on me, but I just can't seem to let him go."

I sighed, knowing there was no use in chiding the necromancer about the dangers of bringing dead fish back to life because you liked them. This was the kind of shit that got our people in trouble with the Authority, but the idea bounced off Bubbles like rubber. There was no use in saying anything when I could do nothing to protect them. Bubbles knew the rules as well as I did. If they disregarded them, that was none of my business.

Bubbles glanced up at Eryx and waved a finger at a tank just behind him. "You ought to check out the Black Oranda I just got in. She's a beaut."

Eryx raised an eyebrow, but went to look at the fish. Av joined him. The two of them were unusually entranced by the creature. They stood in twin postures, hands shoved in their suit pockets as they bent to stare at the fish. There was no predicting them.

Bubbles crooked a finger at me, then resumed work on their embroidery. "You want to know what Lara Achilles asked after, yeah?"

I nodded, approaching the register slowly. Bubbles didn't like fast movements. "What can you tell me?"

Bubbles shook their head. "Nothing much. Other than that she bought a piranha. Cute little guy. Last of the fry. Ate all his sibs."

I cleared my throat. The image was unpleasant. "No conversation?"

Bubbles shrugged. "She wanted to know if the Pizza Queen on 88th was still in business."

Av shifted her luminous brown eyes towards me at the mention of the pizza joint. Neon fish reflected in them, giving her the look of the gods of old, before all our deities turned to Saints. I shook off the image. The Pizza Queen was one of the Cognoscenti's spots, run by some of Lux's favorite girls. I didn't remember it being particularly important, but that didn't mean it wasn't.

"You getting that fish?" I asked my brother. This conversation was obviously over.

Eryx didn't smile with his mouth—ever. But his eyes smiled, crinkling up as he nodded. "Yeah. Cute little guy."

Av kicked up her left foot, grinning for Eryx. "The *cutest*."

The sigh that came out of me rose from ancient depths. I pulled my wallet out of the breast pocket in my wool overcoat. "How much?"

Bubbles raised an eyebrow. "Two thou."

"For the fish?" I asked, incredulous.

"For the information," Bubbles replied. "The fish is free to a good home, you know that, Bub."

I leaned on the counter, blinking my long lashes at Bubbles, giving them my best *I'm-so-patient* smile. "But you haven't *given* me any information."

"Booth 7," Bubbles replied. "That's where she sat."

I forked out two thousand. Steep for what might yield nothing more than a pepperoni pie. But it might be worth it if it turned out to be more. "Bag up the Black Oranda, please?"

"Of course," Bubbles said with a smile. "You need a tank, Eryx?"

My brother nodded. We were going to be here all day.

CHAPTER 6

EMBER

I COULDN'T EXAMINE the brochure until I was back in the car with Lara. I'd flipped through it, of course, just to make sure there were photos. But I hadn't been able to look. There was no way in Hel I'd admit I needed Lara's support, but I did.

By the time I got back into the car, it was dumping rain and Lara had reclined her seat. Blessed heat seeped out of the Dodger's vents. Lara barely spared a glance for me when I slammed my door shut. I waited, stretching my fingers towards the vents to warm my frozen fingers, but she didn't sit up.

"Don't you want to look?" I asked, fidgeting impatiently with the Saints medallions around my neck. Tanith and Amarante clinked together. I liked to imagine they were kissing in moments like these.

Lara was silent for a long moment. She never gave the silent treatment, so this was something else. I craned my neck to look back at her. Her eyes were squeezed shut, her jaw tight.

"If I hadn't fallen asleep on watch—"

We'd been through this a thousand times.

"You'd just ascended," I said with a sigh. "And you dozed off. They got the jump on all of us, Lara. It wouldn't have mattered if you'd heard them. They were just *better* than us."

"But if I'd heard them sooner—I'd have had hold of *my* sword."

It was tempting to sigh again. We'd been over this countless times. "And you'd have done what? They might as well have been ghosts, Lara. They had the swords so fast none of us had time to do *anything*."

It was true. We'd made camp, and the four of us had fallen asleep easily, with Lara on watch. Back in those days, the life was traipsing around the wastelands on a horse. Humans had a lot of weird nostalgia about the medieval period, but I didn't miss it. I wouldn't miss whatever the historians would call this wretched era either.

Back then, sleeping outside was cleaner and safer than the desperate little wasteland inns. The five of us had woken in time to realize something was wrong, and then the swords were just gone. It wasn't that we didn't see the thieves. Technically, we *did* see them.

We all saw the same thing—a blur of movement, and then *nothing*. They didn't even have to attack us. They moved faster than they should have been able to, obviously fueled by a miracle, though the Thaumas in the area admitted to nothing. With our swords gone, the Consulate felt it necessary to give us the worst assignments. It had been almost eleven hundred years of this shit. But none of us had ever blamed Lara for falling asleep. We blamed ourselves for letting the youngest of us, ascended only a few months, keep watch overnight.

We were all hundreds of years older than Lara and we'd forgotten what it was like to be habitually ruled by mortal urges like unelected sleepiness. The loss of our swords and honor had been devastating, making us the weakest of the Maere and the least respected. We still had our immortality, but the things most Maere could do, we couldn't. The swords acted as a conduit for power we couldn't access otherwise. We'd had to get scrappy since we lost them.

Lara never answered me about what she would have done.

Whenever the subject came up, it always went the same. She beat herself up, wouldn't let anyone talk her out of her stance, and then she went silent and depressed for weeks. We didn't have time for nonsense like that—not if these actually *were* our swords and we had a chance to get them back.

"Just look and tell me if it's them," she said, sounding depressed already.

I suppressed the urge to snap back at her that she was the fucking expert about swords, having been a blacksmith, a swordsmith, and a rare weapons dealer. Instead, I flipped through the brochure's expensive, heavy pages until I found them. Five swords with identically crafted blades, each with a different hilt. The photos were not clear enough for *me* to positively identify them, but they looked real enough that my breath caught.

Lara's seat went up in a flash and her chin rested on my shoulder. "Fuck."

I tapped the brochure. "There's an online viewer. They have videos. We need to go look."

"Okay," Lara agreed. "Where's the new place?"

"I lied a little last night."

"About having a new place?"

I bit my lip. "No. About you liking it."

Lara glared at me. "Where is it?"

"It's at the Carlyle."

"Ember," Lara snarled before the word had even left my throat.

I knew she would react this way. She'd hated everything the Consulate stood for since the swords were stolen. It's why we'd lived elsewhere before she was taken. "Why the fuck would you live there? The Consulate's given us short shrift for hundreds of years. Why are you so fucking loyal?"

Who was she to talk about loyalty? I was loyal to my sistren, my cohort. Who the Hel had she been loyal to all these years? "Where else was I supposed to go, Lara? You all left.

The Consulate is all I've got, and the apartment is free and safe."

"Nothing that comes from the Consulate is ever free." Lara shook her head, her jaw clenched tight as she revved the Dodger to life. The truth stung. "I'll come in for a few, but I'm not staying."

"There's actually room for everyone. It's a penthouse—"

"Stuff it, Verona." Lara pulled into traffic without another word.

Forty-five minutes later we were in the wood-paneled office in my apartment, *our* apartment, pulling up the National Gallery's auction website on my giant monitor. The Carlyle was an all-purpose building owned by the Consulate, with offices in one sector, and residences in another.

Plenty of the city's most dangerous parapsychs lived and worked here. I got why Lara hated it, but I had no idea what she expected from me. Where did she think I'd be living? Some shoebox downtown, probably. Crying into my Happy-Os every morning with only the rats to talk to… *No thank you very much.*

Lara spun around in the chair I'd picked out for her. "So you just decorated this place all on your own? With our money?"

I glared at her. "It's not 'our' money, it's the Orphium Maere's money. It is not my fault that the four of you refused to do the job."

This wasn't the time to have a fight about why she hadn't let me help her, but I'd have it if she was going to get shitty with me about spending money on this place. It wasn't as though I'd bought crap. I'd done my best to make things ready for my cohort to return. And maybe that had been foolish, but I wasn't the one who abandoned her family.

29

Now it was Lara's turn to glare. "Just log into the website. Let's get this over with."

I turned back to my computer and did as she asked. It took the video of the first sword forever to load, and in my head, I justified spending the money. We were all rich as royalty after centuries on this cursed plane of existence, but the designated Maere in any city got a stipend from the Consulate to help run their outfit. Typically, that stipend was easily spent between five ancient warriors who liked new toys for running their territories.

Without my sistren, I'd struggled to spend the money. I'd even asked the Consulate to send less, but they wouldn't, purely as a reminder of how meaningless I was to them, I assumed. So I spent it on my people, anyway. Furnishing this space, kitting it out with all the best stuff. Waiting, like some pathetic little girl for her best friends to *please come home*.

How many times had I sent that exact message? In texts, emails, postcards, and at least one telegram. But no one came. And for a while, I was mad about it. Now I just wanted to stop fighting and be a family again. I needed them to come home, now more than ever. There was a good chance that these swords coming up for auction was an epic trap. That whoever stole them in the first place was playing a long game with us. We wouldn't know til we looked, though.

The video finally played. It was Rhiannon's sword. Lara leaned towards the screen as the camera panned down the blade and tapped the screen as a tiny nick glinted in the light. "She got that at the Vale of Lovane."

"I remember." I pulled up the next sword.

A choking noise came out of Lara as the hilt came into focus, still wrapped with the scarf of the mortal girl Lara had loved—and lost—when she ascended. The Maere were the only parapsychs that were not born. Not exactly, anyway. We grew up mundane, and when we reached twenty-eight, our aging slowed, just as all parapsychs did. The difference was that we gained preternatural strength, agility, and other talents… and knowledge. Everything about us sharpened as we regained all that had been lost—we called this ascending.

I closed the window and loaded the third sword in the lot, holding my breath as the camera panned down its pristine blade. Deep inside me, I felt the comfortable grip of the hilt, the way it felt to run my thumb over the scales of the snakes. My stomach turned, and I was dizzy. There was no doubt in my mind that it was my sword.

I opened the fourth and fifth videos simultaneously, desperately needing this to be over. But something was wrong. Lara stared blankly at the wall, still lost in her grief. I hit her leg with my hand. "This is wrong. They look like Max and Sera's swords, but…"

Slowly, she dragged her eyes away from the wall to my monitor. First she frowned as the videos played, then she shook her head. "They're good replicas, but those aren't their swords."

"What does this mean?" I breathed, resting my elbows on the desk. I didn't expect an answer.

"Who's the seller?" Lara asked, picking up the brochure. That had been the first thing and only thing I'd read, before I even left the National Gallery offices.

"It doesn't say."

"You need to call Rhiannon." Lara leaned back in her chair. She crossed her arms over her chest. Before I could protest, she grinned, wicked and smug at the same time. "Better you than me."

CHAPTER 7

ARES

WE MADE it halfway to the Pizza Queen before Eryx got the call. I was reading the cast off sections of his paper in the backseat when his phone rang. Av's eyes went serious in the rearview mirror as she sensed something I couldn't about his changing countenance. She saw the shifts in him better than almost anyone.

On St. Tanith's grave, and not for the first time, I wished for Eryx's sake that he and Av could find romantic love together. It would take a special person to love Eryx the way he deserved, to know him as deeply as it would take to love him, and Av already knew him that way. But alas, it was not meant to be. I worried less about Avaline. She'd told me a thousand times that romantic love was not for her. That being with us was what she wanted most in the world.

And so I had to accept that this was yet another thing I could not control. That they were happy as they were. It didn't stop me from wishing I could wrap them both up and make them safe, though safety was not meant for those such as us. This was the best I could give them, and maybe the best any of us could hope for.

When Eryx hung up, he glanced at Av, shaking his head.

"We've got a problem. Spirit possession on 88th and Vine. Kid murdered someone."

"Are they registered associates?" I asked. "The family. Are they registered with the Consulate?"

It wasn't a requirement that parapsychs register with the Consulate. But to be recommended by them, to get the benefits of all the ways the Consulate had twisted into the Authority, registration was a necessary evil. A double-edged sword that most definitely cut both ugly ways.

Eryx turned to face me. "No. Does that mean you won't help them?"

This was one of myriad things I hated about the corruption of every system we lived under. There was no way to lead with honor. No way to serve my people without feeding systems that had been created solely to harm us.

I swore, tossing the Finance pages aside. "Of course I'll help. I have to ask, Eryx." I always had to ask. Always had to know where my people stood in the complex webs of power that governed not just Orphium, but the Three Cities as a whole. It was exhausting because it was meant to be.

If Eryx's face softened, even a little, I couldn't see it. He waited for further orders. Waited to find out if I would live up to his expectations of me. My heart beat faster. The Consulate's rules said we weren't supposed to help unregistered parapsychs. We were supposed to call situations like these into the Authority, who would send a shitty, low-level exorcist who'd get rid of the spirit, but would probably break the kid's brain in the process.

"Divert the Authority for as long as you can," I said. "They'll still want to take the kid in, but we'll do our best to stop them." Eryx nodded, then immediately unlocked his phone. He shot off a series of texts.

"Get us to 88th and Vine," I said, answering the question in Av's eyes. "I'll handle this myself."

She nodded. When Eryx's fingers slowed, I put my hand on my brother's thick shoulder. "Call Lola Carmichael at the

Consulate, tell her I'm calling in my favor and to get paperwork started to register an underage medium." I couldn't fix the world, but I could make one kid a little safer.

Eryx nodded, scrolled through his contacts list, then paused, and turned back, his green eyes open and expression earnest. "Thank you, Ares."

He shouldn't have to thank me. Things shouldn't be this way. Eryx was right. A storm was coming, one I no longer wanted to stop. While I'd lived long enough to know that change wouldn't come easily or quickly, some measure of balance had to return to Orphium. This one small act wouldn't solve anything, but as Lux always told me, there was no way to know what would ripple. Sometimes we had to operate on instinct, and instinct told me this was the right move.

I didn't answer Eryx, but leaned back in my seat and closed my eyes, searching for my earplugs in my coat pocket. "I need to prepare. Give me a few." I located my earplugs, took them out of their case, and shoved them in my ears.

When we got to the ramshackle tenement building at 88th and Vine, there was a small crowd gathered outside as rain came and went in frustrated spurts. Local Authority stooges loaded an ambulance up with a body bag. A woman sat on the tailgate of one of the Authority SUVs, wrapped in a blanket.

"Get these people out of here," I murmured to Av, as I got out of the car. Eryx followed me, a heavy presence at my back that would stop anyone who didn't know exactly who I was from questioning me.

I needn't have asked to have the area cleared. People saw me and scurried off, shooting fearful looks at one another as I moved towards the SUV. A memory of the way people gravitated to Roman haunted me. People loved my father as much as they feared him. They only feared me.

There was an Authority rep already here, a thin, pale man I recognized from a few other such scenes. He wasn't the worst sort, but anyone who voluntarily worked for the Authority was bad news. "Mike Fairchild, right?"

The Authority rep nodded, his lips pressing into a grim line as I approached. "Mr. Necroline, your talents aren't needed here. I've called in an exorcist. Be on about your day."

It was a little too much like a command. I arched one eyebrow, sinking into my weight and physical presence, using my power to manipulate auric energy to strengthen my aura. As a human, Fairchild wouldn't see it, but he would feel it.

Fairchild blanched a touch as my aura's vibration increased in frequency, apparently remembering who he was speaking to. His attitude was odd. Most humans feared me, feared my power over the dead, and what folks said about me in backroom whispers. Why wasn't Fairchild afraid of me?

I put a little more power into my aura, just for good measure. "There's no need for your exorcist, Fairchild. It's no trouble at all."

The woman shook her head, a sour look twisting her face. "No, not him."

Who in this Saints-forsaken city *wouldn't* want me to perform the exorcism? Maybe I was an insufferable prick, but I was also the best. My hackles went up for about a hundred reasons. "Who is this?"

Behind me, Eryx tensed. Something *was* up with the woman. My brother was never wrong about people and if I could sense his discomfort without even looking at him, then something was off with *her*.

"The mother," Fairchild said. "What she says goes, Necroline."

Something dropped in my stomach. Fear meeting anger. The disrespect coming off this motherfucker was going to get him killed. I would see to fixing his attitude later. Right now, my concern was the kid—and whatever'd sent that shot of fear through me.

"She's not the child's mother," Eryx said, his voice low and lethal. I glanced behind me. The spirit of a dark-haired postal worker with kind eyes leaned towards my brother. Eryx was the kind of clairsentient who attracted good spiritual energy. He and Av were a lot alike in that way, though their essential talents were quite different. "She's the *step*mother, and has no legal authority over the girl. The father's the one that got killed."

Gravel and a tumble of dried leaves crunched under my shoe as I shifted my weight, raising an eyebrow at Fairchild as I swiped what I assumed was the woman's identification key out of his grip. Sure enough, she had no dependents listed. The kid wasn't hers. I tossed the key back at Fairchild, who scrambled to pick it back up.

A couple drops of rain spit out of the overcast sky. The clouds hung lower now, the air thick with the coming downpour. If we stood out here much longer, we were going to get soaked.

"That hellion *murdered* him," the woman screeched. "She murdered her father—my husband. Channeled a spirit to help her do it."

Every word out of the woman's mouth sounded like a lie. I watched Fairchild as she spoke, rather than her. I knew the woman's sort well enough. What I wanted to understand was what Fairchild knew. From the way he nodded as she rambled on, he knew full well what she was up to, and he endorsed it somehow. This was a part of a bigger picture. I'd been right about the ripples.

Av appeared beside me, as though out of thin air, spritely and terrifyingly sharp. "That one is registered, Ares," she said, pointing an accusatory finger at the stepmother. "Pretty talented little medium herself, actually. She's got a whole list of jobs with the Authority."

A picture of what might be happening here formed in my

mind. I liked this situation less by the second. Ripples indeed. "Why hasn't anyone registered the girl?"

The woman sputtered. "How was I to know she was a medium?"

Av laughed, a terrifying sound in this instance. She sprang forward, caging the woman with her thin arms, getting right in her face. "It's people like you who keep us down, you little..."

The woman drew back, appropriately afraid.

So she knew who we were, and she was afraid of us. *My people were never afraid of me, Eryx or Av*, unless they had good reason to be. Humans were, but no one in my own dynasty had anything to fear from me. Which meant she was one of the rare types that was registered, but not loyal to the Trinity or even the Consulate. That explained all the Authority jobs, at least, and how Fairchild got an exorcist ordered to the scene so quickly. They were trying to pull a cover-up here.

I glanced at Fairchild again, who had the sense to look deeply uncomfortable. He hadn't expected us to show up. Because typically, we wouldn't have. I'd have sent someone else. Guilt ate at me, even though rationality reminded me that I couldn't be everywhere at once.

I was spread too thin. The Trinity's power had been waning for years. Especially the last twenty. Inwardly, I swore. If this all came back to the Maere, back to Lara Achilles and what we'd done, I'd never forgive myself. The pattern here pulled in too many of the wrong directions. I fucking hated this shit.

"Av," Eryx said softly, bringing me back to the moment. "The kid."

Av backed off.

"Where is the girl?" I asked.

Fairchild hesitated. The kill order formed in my head. Not now, not this week or this month. Six months from now, he was going to meet a bad end, after experiencing a tragic run of bad luck. Fucking with me when I wanted something was poor decision making at its finest, and I liked a long game.

"The girl," I insisted, my voice taking on a menacing tone.

"Apartment 44," Fairchild finally answered.

"No!" the stepmother screamed.

"Building cleared otherwise?" I asked Av, ignoring the step-mother's wails.

She nodded, her angular eyes narrowed dangerously as she stared at the kid's stepmother.

"Don't let that one get spirited away," I remarked as I walked away from the SUV. "I want her investigated."

"Of course," Av answered.

I gripped Eryx's elbow. "No one goes in until I get this done."

My brother nodded. "Got it. Call if you need me—if it goes bad, don't let her die in pain."

I squeezed Eryx's arm. "I won't need you, and she'll be fine."

He looked into my eyes, his expression never changing. "Good luck."

The tiny apartment was dark when I entered, all the shades drawn. But it didn't hide the blood spattered everywhere, or the fact that while the furniture had been nice at some point, it hadn't been well taken care of. The place was the kind of mess that didn't happen overnight. My chest ached. Much as I resented the woman outside for the way she was clearly targeting her stepdaughter, everyone had a story.

A shaking form huddled in a corner of the kitchen, near the ancient refrigerator, snarling. That was the story I cared about most. The one that got a teenager into this mess. And frankly, the one that got her out of it. I needed to help this child find another ending than the one that waited for her outside, or in whatever cracked facility the Authority would disappear her into.

"Hi," I said, keeping my voice gentle as I crouched down, reaching towards her. "This is going to hurt real bad for a second, but don't fight it, okay?"

The girl looked up, and even in the dim light I could see her red-rimmed eyes, and the opalescent cast to her irises that told me she was possessed. She snarled at me again and then lunged. Calmly, I stood, pushing back at the spirit's aura as the girl moved towards me with supernatural speed.

The spirit within her stopped, sensing my authority.

"I am not going to banish you," I said. "Come out right away and I'll let you go."

The girl let out an otherworldly howl of rage. I closed my fist, catching hold of the aura as it projected just enough to grip onto. "I will pull you out of there, if necessary, but let's do this the easy way."

The girl hissed at me, the spirit, really, but at this point the difference didn't much matter. "The stepmother locked me in," the girl growled, sending chills down my spine. I'd done this for centuries, and the voice of a Rider coming from a medium's throat still shot fear through me. It was pure instinct. Proof that despite the parapsychism and relative immortality, I was still human. "Yank all you want, Necroline King." *The spirit knew who I was, who Roman had been to this city.* "Use violence and you'll only hurt the child."

This was exactly what the stepmother wanted—why she didn't want me to perform the exorcism. She'd doomed the child to death with another exorcist. She *meant* to kill her step-daughter. All my empathy went out the window, rage replacing it. I added her to my list, right after Fairchild. Child-killers would find no mercy with me.

I didn't have any salt, or anything else I needed to make this easier, and we didn't have much time. Fairchild would, no doubt, send the Authority's team of "experts" up as soon as they got here. Even my name wouldn't stop them.

We would have to do this the hard way. It was going to hurt the kid, but there wasn't much use in warning her again. "Hold on a minute—I'll get you free."

I fished my phone out of my pocket and texted Eryx with one hand. We needed my best team on this. The girl was going to need help after this, and only the Phoenixes would do. Each of them had gone through something similar as kids, and now they were the team I called for anything remotely sensitive. Eryx typically handled their business these days. When my brother responded that he'd be up in five, I put my phone back in my pocket.

"Don't hurt her," I said, pulling at the spirit's aura.

"I have no desire to," the spirit wailed from within the girl. She was probably fifteen or sixteen, and a tiny slip of a thing. Looked like she didn't get enough to eat.

"Why did you kill the man?" I asked as I picked apart the knot in the spirit's aura. Now that I knew what had happened, it was more apparent. The spirit was cooperating; apparently it had some respect for my power, and the fact that it didn't want to hurt the girl helped.

"The woman. The stepmother," the spirit within the girl ground out. It was having trouble communicating. The step-mother had known what to do to lock the spirit inside the girl, but she hadn't done it well. The girl wasn't screaming, and showed no signs of distress. I thanked Saint Tanith profusely—the spirit had her locked down tight. It was keeping her from feeling me pull her aura from the spirit's.

Now I saw it. The way the knot had been tied told me all I needed to know, confirmed every one of my suspicions. I pulled it free, and the girl screamed, no longer protected by the spirit's aura. I rushed forward to keep her from falling when the spirit released her.

Eryx burst through the door.

"Take her," I said, passing the child off to him. "Don't let her out of your sight. Have Elias look her over when the Phoenixes get her. She'll need medical attention."

Eryx hugged the frail child to his chest, nodding. Elias was the medtech of the Phoenixes—had made it all the way through school and everything, though the Authority had denied him his degree. He'd take care of the kid's injuries, and the rest of the team would get her shored up and safe until we could figure out what to do with her.

Eryx's eyes closed as he took in whatever the spirit wanted him to know. I could speak to spirits, but what Eryx did was a more complicated, deeper form of communication. "She's in no danger. She was weak to begin with—the spirit tried to help her. Tried to get her more food."

The shadow in the corner nodded. *I tried my best.*

A vision, from the girl's perspective, of her stealing food from the local grocery filled my second sight. The spirit wanted me to see this moment and had the strength to project it through my brother. We would both be exhausted tonight.

"Go," I said to Eryx. "I'll take care of this. Fairchild doesn't come near her."

"Got it," my brother agreed as he passed through the door.

I sat down on the arm of the ratty couch that wasn't covered in blood and stared at the diaphanous form of the Rider. "Tell me what happened here. Every bit of it, and I'll let you go."

CHAPTER 8

EMBER

THE SOUND of my molars grinding against one another was sickening. I had to stop this or I'd be forced to grow new teeth and that was annoying and painful. But Lara's attitude was just that grating. It was impossible, sometimes, to understand how I could love her so fucking much and also want to punch her face so, so badly.

But then, that was the gist of spending an eternal life together. Not that any of my cursed cohort showed signs of comprehending that kind of nuanced perspective. From what I could tell, they preferred to cut and run.

Rhiannon Brontë hadn't just left me. She'd gone to work for the Consulate itself. After what happened with Lara and Sera, she'd very calmly stated that she'd had a better offer and would leave. Two very long lifetimes of friendship, and she'd just up and left.

The audacity of these women never ceased to amaze me. Though I was tempted to argue with Lara, she was right about calling Rhi. "Fine. I'll call her."

Lara sighed. "Do whatever you want."

I closed my eyes, searching for some semblance of patience. "It would be nice if you could at least *pretend* like this matters."

Lara stood up. "I don't need this shit from you. It's not like we have a way to get the swords, anyway. We'd need a lot more talent than you've got access to."

I just about lost it, pushing my chair back so hard as I stood that it flew across the room. "And why is that, Lara? Whose fucking fault is it that the five of us split up?"

She stepped to me, glaring. "Go ahead and say it, Verona. You know you want to. You're just itching to blame me for the fact that we lost the swords to begin with."

"No," I breathed, all the vim and vigor gone out of me. Having this argument again was infuriating. Why couldn't any of them ever focus on what and who our *real* enemies were? "No. I am not. I don't know how many times I have to say it. What happened is on all of us."

We stared at each other for a long moment. She shook her head, her dark hair falling into her eyes. "I need to take a walk. Blow off some steam."

At least she wasn't threatening to disappear again. Blowing off steam was probably a healthy choice. It was one I never felt as though I got to make, but I was happy for her to. "Yeah," I agreed. "There's key cards by the door. Grab one before you go. I'll get your DNA coded in tomorrow."

"Fine." She sighed. "Okay if I bring the rest of my stuff back from storage?"

So, she had a storage unit somewhere. That's how she'd gotten her Saint's-charms and my jacket back. At least that was one mystery cleared up. Just twenty-three thousand left to unravel, but I had all the time in the world.

"Of course," I murmured, worried that I might scare her off entirely if I so much as spoke too loud.

"Get a grip while I'm gone, Verona," Lara said as she stalked out the door.

I stifled the urge to snap back at her. If we stood here scrapping over the last word, I'd never get a call into Rhi. I retrieved my errant chair and sat back down at my desk, to the sound of the front door opening and closing. I pulled up the security footage on the floor, watching Lara go for the elevator.

I don't know what made me do it, but I accessed the CCTV for the whole block through the Consulate feed, and watched Lara leave. She headed back downtown, towards where the old storage units were. I had no reason not to believe Lara, but it had been twenty years. It wasn't long in the scheme of things, but there was a lot I still didn't know.

There was nothing more in the world I wanted than to trust my sistren. The trouble was, not a single one of them was actually trustworthy by any standard. Perseverating over the fact wasn't going to make it any better, or any less true. I picked up the heavy receiver of the black phone on my desk and dialed. It took forever to hammer out the numbers individually, a massive pain in the ass. I rarely used this phone, but it was a completely secure line.

It barely rang before she picked up.

"You've seen the swords," a low, breathy voice said by way of hello. Same old Rhiannon. Right to the point.

"Hello to you too, Rhi," I said, mocking a tone of cheery friendliness that I certainly didn't feel. "How *are* you? What's life like in Aradios? Still have that dog?"

"I *had* a cat," Rhiannon replied, her tone curt. "And I don't relish catching up. I don't know who the seller is, and yes, I've already used all the leverage I have to find out."

I noticed she didn't tell me what happened to the cat. That made me sad for about a second. Before I remembered how irritated I was with her, anyway. "But you didn't call me," I said, unable to keep the edge of resentment out of my voice. "Ares Fucking Necroline told me about this shit. Do you have any idea how bad that makes me look?"

Rhiannon was quiet for a moment before asking, "Is Lara with you?"

I glanced at the CCTV. She'd disappeared from my immediate sight. "Yes. Well, not right this second. She's gone to her storage unit."

Rhi made a noncommittal sound. This whole call was annoying, but now I was getting angry. I'd never sanctioned any of them for leaving. I could have filed complaints with the Consulate, with the Authority—and worse. For Rhiannon, Sera and Max, at least. I could have had them raked across whatever coals I liked for abandoning their posts, and no one in this gods-forsaken world would have batted an eye.

But I didn't. I'd asked nicely. I'd begged. I'd made an ass of myself for twenty years for the whole lot of them, and I was beyond exhausted. Yes, I'd made my fair share of mistakes. We all had. But this was unacceptable.

"What do you know?" I asked.

I stared at my nails while I waited for whatever bullshit Rhiannon came up with next. I needed to re-paint them, maybe oxblood this time to emphasize my ragey interior landscape. Something that screamed "slaughter" might be nice.

"Nothing," she replied.

My lip curled in response. She was lying. I could tell because I knew the way Rhiannon Brontë spoke, and the little lilt up in the way she said "nothing" was a tell.

A tell that she knew full well that I knew. We had dozens of such tricks. Having multiple and various ways to communicate indirectly had kept us on top of things for a very long time. Until, of course, it hadn't. But still. Perhaps this line wasn't as secure as I'd thought.

"Damn," I said, drawing the word out a little as I worked through what to say next. "Well, that's a shame. It's my birthday next week. Did you remember?"

"Of course," she breathed, her interest obviously piqued.

Good, good. We were back on the same page.

We didn't celebrate birthdays. Ever. It wasn't a Maere thing; it was an us thing. We'd always celebrated other milestones, but none of us wanted to remember our mundane lives before ascension and our birthdays were ugly reminders of those lives.

"Are you coming to my brunch?" I asked, sure to inject a heavy dose of irritation into my voice for whoever might be listening in. Was it the Consulate, or… *No.* I didn't want to think about the possibility of the island's involvement—that would be the cherry on top of this shit sundae.

"Are you finally inviting me?" she snapped back. Now I was sure she knew the line wasn't secure. When Rhiannon was actually angry, she never got snappy. She got infuriatingly calm.

This was a ruse. She knew more than she was letting on and she wanted me to know. We were in trouble. "Yes," I replied, keeping my voice full of barely leashed irritation. "Maybe it's been long enough."

"Fine," she said. "But you'll never get Max and Sera to come. They're well and truly done with us."

"I don't know," I mused, thinking my words over carefully. "I think there's still something real there."

"There isn't," she said. "They're out."

So they already knew about the swords, knew theirs weren't among this lot, and had already refused to help retrieve them. It pissed me off that no one had thought to call and tell me anything, but I was going to have to keep trucking right on past that point. "Fine, I'll skip a call, then."

"Probably wise," she said, without a hint of a lie. "Sera's trying another treatment. I'll see you soon."

She hung up before we could set a time or location. Just as well—she could surprise me. The crafty little minx loved to sneak up on people, and I loved how much easier she was to get along with when she got her way. I stood up and walked into the living room, crossing my arms tightly around me as I watched the afternoon light change.

A storm was rolling in, and it was dark as twilight, clouds descending over the city as rain spattered the streets below. I watched the ads on all the digiscreens change, flashing garish lights that rivaled the neon that dared to peek through the gloom. In the distance, lightning flashed over the Erydanos River that cut through the city, lighting it up for the briefest of moments, thunder rolling across the city. My heart beat in a low, slow thump as the little information I had about what was going on spun round and round in my mind.

Rhiannon had never felt the need to make it clear to me why she took the Consulate job after we split up. But I'd known there was something she wasn't saying. Something more than trying to get better help for Sera, though that was part of it, of course. And I was grateful as fuck for that.

Sera was years ahead in her recovery because of Rhi's Consulate connections. But there had to have been another reason for Rhi to go so far into the belly of the beast. She hated the way the Consulate was run. Hated the Trinity and the way the Consulate had made puppets of us all.

Whatever she thought she could gain by going so deep in had to be pretty important. I wracked my brain through the weeks before Lara was taken. I couldn't remember anything particularly special that was going on. The days after she'd gone to the Asylum had been hard, especially with the Necrolines setting fire to the house and Sera being so injured.

Anger lit a fire in my gut—same as the day Sera got hurt. The lingering shock of those events made it difficult to remember much about what had happened. Rain pelted the windows, blowing sideways now. I tilted my head to match the angle, squinting a little so that my view of Orphium turned to nothing more than a blur of gray clouds and neon lights. Ares Necroline had never bothered to explain to me *why* his people burned our house down. Just that *he* hadn't meant to hurt Sera.

All that had sounded hollow at the time. But it felt odd now. We hadn't had issues with the Necrolines before that. As far as their dynasty went, Ares kept his house clean as a whistle—he was a breath of fresh air after his horror show of an uncle. Roman Necroline had been a piece of work, heavy-handed, but noble in many ways. His younger brother was a monster. Rumor had it that Magnus killed Roman and Ares killed Magnus.

When Ares took over, it had been a relief. Until the fire, anyway. The more I turned the events over, the stranger they seemed. I'd held a grudge against Ares for the better part of two decades, but when Sera had been hurt, Ares left a trail of bodies and fear that had reminded Orphium not to fuck with him.

Magnus had been cruel, and for that, people had feared him, but showed him very little real respect. By contrast, Ares was more like Roman. Terrifyingly smug and violent with the kind of horrific precision that made people cross the street to avoid pissing him off.

The way he'd whispered that information in my ear at the ThunderBowl had sent shivers through me. When everything went down with the fire, he'd been angry that Sera had been hurt, not defensive. Which meant burning our house down *hadn't* been some petty vendetta.

My heart raced at the thought. This was huge, and I'd missed it. If someone had betrayed Ares to fuck with us, did he know why? *And why hadn't I gotten more curious about this sooner?*

Shame filled me as I blew out a long sigh. Because I'd been reeling for years after those few short months when everything fell apart. And when everyone scattered, I shut down. I stopped being me. I stopped caring about anything except keeping the bare minimum going. Having a shitty attitude covered up the disgraceful mess that I'd become. I let resentment get the better of me for far too long.

Eternal life was far, far too long, but I'd been in an especially deep rut. It was long past time to get out of it. I hunted down my phone and shot off a message to Ares Necroline. Might as well start now. If he wanted to pass tips along about the swords, then maybe he'd answer my questions about the fire as well.

CHAPTER 9

ARES

I SAT on the stoop of the girl's apartment building, mulling over what the Rider had told me. The stepmother was resentful of her husband's child. Feared he loved the girl more than he did her, her jealousy twisting a father's love into something sick in her mind. She'd meant to kill him and have the girl tortured in the Asylum.

But the stepmother hadn't been particular about the Rider she summoned. All she wanted was a vicious, murderous spirit. She hadn't even bothered to ask what motivated the Rider. And it had turned out to be her undoing. The spirit she summoned was vengeful because her own children had been killed.

My husband's mistress killed them, the Rider had whispered. *She killed my babies to have him to herself.*

I strongly suspected the mistress had killed the Rider as well, but it was rude to ask such things. Besides, I knew what I needed to. A long life of talking to the dead had taught me one thing for certain: you did not fuck with a spirit whose children had been murdered. If the girl's stepmother had any sense, she would've created wards to prevent such a thing from happening. She ought to have anticipated just such a problem.

The inexperienced believed like called to like, but the truth of the matter was that evil often attracted its counterpart when it came to spirits. Riders were often vengeful creatures, and they looked for opportunities to exact revenge on just the types of people who wronged them in life. Unfortunately, the child's father had been complicit in his wife's abuse, though not so evil as his new wife had assumed.

The Rider had no issue killing him, and had fully planned to kill the stepmother as well. Before I let it go, I promised the girl would be taken care of, and the Rider promised to haunt my dreams if I didn't. It was a fair enough trade. The spirit of the postal worker sat down next to me when the Rider had gone.

"This neighborhood's not what it used to be, Necroline." Her accent was from somewhere north, an outpost near Palladiere, probably.

"How long have you been here?" I asked, fiddling with the rings on my left hand. I didn't mean Orphium and she knew it.

The spirit smiled. "I don't know anymore. Sixty, seventy years maybe. This used to be a nice place to live. Now, people are afraid. The Trinity doesn't help anymore and the Consulate's been trash since the start."

I nodded at the chastisement. "You're right."

The Consulate was supposed to help parapsychs, but more often it seemed like they were lining their own pockets. No better than the human mafia or other organized crime. Everyone knew it, but few said it so candidly.

"The Angel helped. Twenty years ago. But then she disappeared, and we were left alone again." The postal worker lost form, fading between.

I hadn't heard anyone mention someone named the Angel before. It was as though a curtain had been pulled back on something significant. Spirits, especially Shades, didn't give out information like this often, unless they wanted it passed along in some way. I pulled my notebook out of the interior breast pocket of my coat, along with my pen, and jotted down all I could recall about the encounter, including the conversation with the postal worker. Might come in handy later.

Av and Eryx were long gone. I'd promised I could see myself home after Fairchild left with the stepmother, and I might as well get going. I stood, stretching my legs as it started to rain, heading toward the nearest metro tunnel. The streets were busy, folks trying to escape the storm before getting soaked.

The emerald green tiles on the walls of the metro tunnel gleamed in contrast to the faux-terrazzo tile floors. Elegance mixed with cheap solutions to complicated problems. That was Orphium in a nutshell. I swiped my metro card and headed down to the platform. A busker played a violin—a cover of an old school rap song, eerie as it echoed through the metro station. A couple of kids on the platform knew all the words. I slumped onto a bench, pulling a beanie out of my coat pocket, yanking it down over my eyes.

I didn't want to be recognized. The postal worker's words wormed into me. Nothing I did was enough. My people were still suffering and it seemed like there was nothing I could do. Guilt oozed through me, right into the meat of my burdened heart. The fact that I even had the audacity to think of myself as burdened made me an ass of the first order. My jaw clenched tight, my chest constricting.

The spirits in the tunnel sensed my distress. Their stirring caused something that resembled a chill breeze, cold spots flaring throughout the platform. A few people whispered to the rapping kids, obviously worried the unquiet spirits were attracted to the noise they were making. I hissed through my teeth, sending aura out in waves, pushing the spirits back.

Though the humans on the platform couldn't see them, they sensed their retreat. Relief was tangible as the spirits retreated. All but one. A skinny kid that looked a lot like the girl I helped earlier. For a second, I thought he might be an Echo, the way he seemed to glitch out, then reappear in the same spot. But he made clear eye contact with me.

Echoes didn't see anything. They just replayed some important moment of their life, stuck in a loop for eternity, unless someone like me came along and untangled them. But this kid watched me, unaffected by my power that still repelled spirits from the platform. He wore clothes from long, long ago, the kind of loose tunics and fur boots Eryx and I wore as children, which explained why looking at him felt like a memory.

I stood, watching the kid. A train screamed around the bend in the tunnel, its lights flashing high and bright as it came into view. I blinked, averting my eyes. When I looked back up, the kid was gone. There weren't many spirits who could resist my authority, but there were some.

I didn't want it to mean anything. My phone buzzed in my pocket. I sucked freezing cold air in at the sight of the name that flashed on my screen. I glanced sidelong as I exhaled. The spirit I hadn't managed to banish stood next to me. His eyes were hollowed out, two black holes.

"If you've got something to say, say it," I cautioned. "Or I'll send you somewhere you won't like."

"You abandoned us, Ares Necroline," the kid said, before pushing me hard towards the tracks. I stumbled backwards to avoid him, but he didn't have the power to actually move me. Still, as he went through me, the bittersweet taste of death burned my tongue.

"Traitor," the spirit hissed as it dissipated.

Some Shades were like that, attracted to strong emotions, skimming thoughts off the top of your conscious mind to use against you. But the kid's words ricocheted through me. He called me a traitor. I hadn't been thinking that about myself. That was the Shade's thought.

I shook off the encounter as best I could, but my guilt lingered. It always did when it came to how little I could actually do for my people. The Authority had beaten us into submission a thousand years ago, and now they didn't even have to use egregious shows of violence. Now it was just the knowledge that we were constantly surveilled, and the frequent disappearance of anyone who dared to make their thoughts about the state of things too known.

That was all it took for the Trinity to cease fighting back, content to be relegated to the shadows forever if it meant we survived. It wasn't that humans had it any better. They didn't. We were all the same amount of fucked, the flavor was just different.

My phone buzzed again. The spirit had distracted me from Ember's message. She wanted to meet. *Laundromat between 5th and Newport. 40 minutes. Come alone.*

Another text came through from her as the train screeched into the station. *Preferably with laundry, so you don't look like a dick.*

I gave her last message one of those ugly thumbs up emojis to annoy her, then checked my watch. There was just enough time for me to get home and to the laundromat. I got onto the train just before the last door closed. The spirit who'd burned through me stood on the platform as the train pulled away, menace in his hollow glare.

⚜

The laundromat between Fifth and Newport was a hole in the wall I'd never been to before. From the outside it was almost invisible, just a simple black and white sign that said "Laundromat" on frosted glass windows. Inside, there were so many potted plants growing on shelves between the rows of washers that the fluorescents made the silver machines appear green.

A friendly Shade in the corner pointed to the back, where Ember Verona stood folding her laundry. My throat went dry at the unguarded glimpse of her. Her shiny brown hair was piled on top of her head, and a brightly patterned silk scarf held it back like a headband. I'd never seen her look quite so comfortable, though she'd showed up hungover to our monthly tithe handovers plenty of times.

Now, she looked at ease in a pair of loose, wide-legged jeans and a slouchy, emerald green sweater that fell off one shoulder. She looked like she belonged at the laundromat, comfortable and cozy, all her usual rough edges smoothed out somehow. My heart thumped louder as I watched her move.

The Shade arched an eyebrow at me, as though to say, "You like her?"

I shook my head, but even the motion felt like a lie. I *didn't* like Ember Verona. She was unnecessarily rude, gave up too easily, and was quite possibly the most beautiful person I'd ever met. But that was beside the point. Beside all points that could possibly be made.

What was going on with me? I'd been sappy over her all day. I tried to tell myself it was the guilt over what had happened to Sera. But it was more than that and I knew it. The Shade pointed to the magazine on the table next to her. It was a gossip rag from at least two years ago. I turned the page for the spirit and then lugged my basket of laundry back to where Ember stood.

"Hey," she said, her voice softer than usual. There was something vulnerable about her right now. Like she was having a particularly rough day. There was my fucking heart again, with that slow, hard thump that seemed reserved for her.

"Hey," I replied, taking my laundry detergent out.

We loaded our washers at the same time, quiet, just working together in peace for a while. When that was done, she hopped up on the bulky metal folding table, pulling a sleeve of caramel corn out of her big, slouchy leather bag.

"Want some?" she asked, offering the bag to me as she popped a kernel between her glossy lips, then sucked sugar off her fingertips.

Watching her pull her long, lacquered nails from her soft, wet mouth made me want to leave. The thoughts that threatened in the back of my mind were like emotional blackmail. I couldn't have them. Couldn't have anything that had to do with her, so I counted backwards from one hundred and thought of dirty gym socks.

This was not at all the way I thought this was going to go. Ember Verona hated me, and for good reason, but she was being almost nice. It was odd, but not uncomfortable. As I held out my hand for some caramel corn, it occurred to me that perhaps Ember's usual bad attitude had more to do with being forced to mediate between the Trinity and the Consulate, not with hating me.

"Why'd you burn my house down?" The question felt like it came out of nowhere, but was twenty years in the making. Her tone wasn't exactly calm. It was more like she was tired. Exhausted, really.

I could relate. Deeply. That too was dangerous. Relating to Ember Verona, when I needed to be so careful around her, was going to fuck one or both of us over. But I needed to own up to my mistakes, and with Lara back, she certainly needed to know what she was dealing with. I owed Ember that much—for what I did to Sera, and the effect it had on her life.

Honesty it was, then. "Twenty years ago, there was someone killing parapsychs."

Ember nodded, a deep line forming on her eternally lineless forehead. It was like her skin knew it should be wrinkled after so many years of life, but couldn't quite get there unless given a chance. "I remember."

"We investigated, after three of our own were taken," I continued. "Av got hold of the Consulate's findings."

"The special investigators' stuff?" Ember asked. She looked impressed when I nodded.

"Av's got a talent with information. I try to use it sparingly. Not many people know."

Ember's face smoothed out, immortal youth and ancient crone all at the same time. I wondered if she saw a similar dichotomy in me. "No one will ever hear about it from me."

The thought that she might be the closest thing I'd ever see to a goddess crossed my mind in a flash, disappearing before I could shove it down somewhere. Dangerous. This was a dangerous line. Lying to myself, but being honest with her. Part of me wanted to run, to just leave my clothes and walk out of here. What I'd been keeping from her all these years was going to ruin this shred of goodwill between us.

"Thank you," I replied, before continuing. "We knew from the files we'd gotten a hold of that trying to investigate the killer would be a dead end. The SIs hadn't had a lick of luck. So we investigated the victims instead."

Ember drew a breath in, nodding, but didn't say a word. I liked the way she leaned toward me, her slender shoulder bumping against mine. I liked it too much. The temptation to jerk away from her was strong, but my affection starved body won out. I let her touch me, talking to keep from thinking about what it might feel like to let her touch me more, in other places… what her fingers might feel like moving over my bare skin.

No. This was not acceptable. I barreled through to my next revelation. "The victims were, to make a very long story short, terrible people. Parapsychs using their abilities to hurt people and keep it under wraps."

"Shit," Ember muttered.

I waited to see if she'd say more, but she didn't. She didn't have to. Parapsychs had to be perfect. If one of us did something wrong, it painted the rest of our community in a bad light. The Authority constantly looked for ways to tear us down. This was the kind of thing the Consulate had worked hard to conceal, their shady dealings for once benefiting the greater good for all of us. I still wasn't sure how they'd done it, but I was grateful all the same.

"The only trace of evidence we found led back to Lara Achilles. She'd been seen in each of the victims' neighborhoods in the month before they died."

Ember went completely still, then pulled away from me. It was a small movement, but my entire body ached for her warmth. "Who else knew what you found out?"

I shook my head, as much to banish the feeling of missing her, when she sat right next to me. I knew this would happen. That there was no chance for so much as an alliance between us. "Nobody. Or at least I thought so at first. I wasn't as careful with my inner circle as I am now. We had a break-in, and though nothing was taken…"

"They took Lara anyway," Ember finished. Her voice snapped with fury, every syllable sharp and halting. "So, why'd you set fire to my house?"

I sighed, shame filling me for how the whole thing had gone down. "To protect her. Av got word that the SIs had gotten permission to raid you. They weren't getting anywhere questioning Lara. So we burned the house down to eliminate whatever evidence might have been there."

Ember rolled her eyes. "You could have just *talked* to me."

I knew that now, but at the time, relations had been bad between the Necrolines and the Orphium Maere. Magnus had been a shitbag, nothing like my adoptive father. At the time of the fire, I had only been a decade into turning the Necroline Dynasty around, and I hadn't known who to trust.

Ember seemed to recall all this and shrugged before I could think up some bullshit answer. It was one of the few things I liked about her. She was quick to put things together, smarter than just about anyone I knew. "All right. You probably couldn't have. But I still don't know why you did it."

I stared up at the styrofoam-tiled ceiling, glowing green in the neons. For all her intelligence, she couldn't fathom why I'd done it? "Because if it *was* Lara, she did us a favor. The vics in those cases were monsters, Ember. If anyone had ever found out who they were and what they were doing, the Authority would have come down on parapsychs so hard it might have destroyed us all."

The awful noise of Ember's molars grinding together set *my* teeth on edge, but I made every effort to keep my face neutral. "So that's why you decided to tell me about the swords. You feel guilty about Sera and grateful for what you think Lara *might* have done."

Her tone was sharp, the cadence of her voice pregnant with accusation. She didn't like my answer. I didn't much like my answer. I nodded. "Yeah." My phone buzzed in the pocket of my sweatpants. I pulled it out and answered. "Hey."

Eryx's voice was grim on the other line. "The girl's stepmom got let out, nearly as soon as Fairchild took her in. The dick didn't even book her." I was about to order one of our people to go pick her up to ensure she stayed away from the girl, but my brother kept talking. "The stepmother is already dead, Ares. Somebody murdered her."

I shook my head. The pieces lined up all too conveniently, but we were going to have to look into it, either way. "Send me what you've got."

"Sure thing," Eryx replied before hanging up.

My phone vibrated as Eryx's photos came through. I grimaced. They were terrible, and familiar. The stepmother had been decapitated from a kneeling position. I turned my phone to Ember. "Do you know where Lara is right now? This is exactly what the bodies looked like twenty years ago."

Ember took one look at the photo and went completely gray. I couldn't parse out why, though. There was no way she was squeamish. Not after her long lifetime of violence. The world was different now, but once the Maere were thought of as butchers. Mercenaries in the early days of the Consulate.

"I'll find her," Ember promised, sliding off the table. "Right after my dry cycle."

CHAPTER 10

EMBER

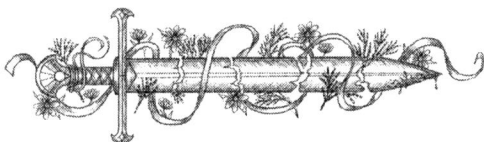

THE PHOTOS of the beheaded woman were all too familiar. I choked so hard on fury, I thought I might asphyxiate. Fuck Lara Achilles. Fuck her straight to whatever hellish afterlife awaited us if we ever did die. If it weren't completely futile, I'd hunt her down right this very minute and murder the foolishness right out of her.

I allowed myself twenty full seconds of imagining how nice it would feel to backhand her so hard she just fell the fuck over, before moving on to brooding. All these years, I'd told her that what happened with the swords wasn't her fault. And it wasn't.

But also, it so obviously *was*. Before the SIs, the Consulate had us to do their dirty work for them. We investigated crimes they couldn't sweep under the rug. And we'd been tasked to hunt down a serial killer who only went after parapsychs and stop them.

It had been her all along.

Lara had been the killer we were looking for.

This clarity opened up a terrifying host of possibilities both about who'd stolen the swords, and why. And the little bitch wasn't going to tell me. She was going to let me just walk into what very well might be a trap without all the information.

59

Twenty more seconds of fantasizing about punching her really hit the spot.

"Easy," Ares said. "You'll tear your clothes."

I came out of what could only be described as a mild fugue state to discover how angrily I'd been moving my clothes into the dryer. A long, deep breath helped to bring me back to the moment. The empty laundromat hummed with the sound of our washers and dryers. The spirit who haunted the little old woman who owned this place peeked around the corner. I couldn't exactly see the Shade, but I could sense her presence.

"I'm fine," I assured her.

Ares glanced at me, then the spirit, frowning. "Can you see that spirit?"

I shrugged. "Not exactly." I didn't add, *not without my sword*, because I couldn't bear to articulate just how much I'd lost when the blades had been stolen.

Ares' fingers brushed my arm. I jerked back from him. My anger with Lara, and all the loss of the past two hundred years, infected every part of me. He stepped back from me like I had smacked him. "Sorry," I growled. "It's just all a lot to take in."

The wounded look in Ares' eyes haunted me, and I could *feel* the spirit rolling her eyes at me. A sick, aching feeling twisted my gut as he turned from me to tend to his own laundry. My attention focused all too narrowly on the way his black sweater hung off his broad shoulders, the delicious hollow of his sharp cheekbones, and the tantalizingly casual air of his gray sweatpants.

I'd never seen Ares Necroline in anything but a suit, but Saints alive, he looked good in sweats. Elegant still, and deadly as ever, with all those tattoos and dark brooding eyes, but delicious all the same. He pushed the unruly hair that had fallen onto his sculpted brow out of his eyes, glancing sidelong at me.

That twisting in my gut heated, pooling lower as it deepened into something richer and bittersweet. The way those dark lashes brushed his pale skin was utterly unfair. I swallowed hard.

We weren't here on a date. We weren't even friends. *Couldn't* be friends.

The best Ares and I could ever hope for was to be cordial associates. However well-meaning his intentions had been, he still burned my fucking house down, and grievously injured Sera. I could follow the logic of it all and forgive him, but there couldn't be more between us.

What was I trying to convince myself of? Of course, there couldn't be—*wouldn't* be—more between us. Ares had his role to play, and I had mine. Neither of us had room for even one ounce of trust for another creature.

"What?" He pushed the sleeves of his sweater up, revealing more of his gorgeous floral tattoos. "You're staring."

"Your tattoos are beautiful," I replied, the words sliding out of my mouth like traitorous drops of poison.

A small smile quirked the corners of Ares' mouth. He was like a work of art, from the tattoos to the sharp lines of his body, every bit of him carefully constructed. "Thanks," he said, softly. "Do you know much about the language of flowers?"

I tore my eyes away from him and shook my head. This felt like dangerous territory. "Never had much time for gardening."

He made a thoughtful noise. I thought he might explain more about the language of flowers, but he stayed quiet for long enough that it was clear he wasn't going to say more. It stirred something in me. Something torrid and wild that I was going to interpret as anger, rather than lust. That was better for me. If I couldn't fuck him, and truly, I *couldn't*, it was better to be angry with him, to try to hate him.

I let the rage build in me, mix with my natural irritability when it came to how long Ares Necroline felt was acceptable to keep me waiting, and then set it loose within my heart. My emotions created a scorched plane within me, room for me to breathe.

When Ares finally spoke, he asked, "What are we going to do about Lara?"

All that fury had to go somewhere. "We? *We* are not going to do anything, Necroline." He started to say more, but I shook my head. "I mean it, Ares. Leave it." I turned towards him. He'd crossed his arms over his chest and was positively glowering at me. I stepped forward, hating that in my comfortable clogs, I still had to look up at him to make eye contact. "Forget this, or I'll find a way to make you sorry."

His arms fell to his sides, relaxed, but clearly ready for anything. "Oh?" he asked, tilting his head to the size, quizzical. "And how do you reckon you'll manage *that*?"

"Believe me," I hissed through my teeth. "I can be very creative when I want to be."

Ares Necroline's gaze iced over. His breath came in short, furious inhalations. I couldn't tell if he wanted to hit me or screw me, though that disloyal little sliver of my mind hoped it was the latter. Could I piss him off enough to get him to fuck me right here on the folding table?

My thighs clenched together like a vise at the thought. Hollow and empty. *I was hollow and empty.* I forced my hands to stay down, to keep from grabbing him. My skin burned, craving his touch.

It was wrong.

It was all I wanted.

I had to do something to make this stop.

Luckily, Ares shook his head, turning from me, then pulled all his laundry from the machines. The wet fabric slapped against his round plastic laundry basket. Each piece of clothing that fell in—the dry and sopping wet bleeding into one another —was a barb to my heart, but I couldn't tell why.

I didn't *want* to tell why—that there was more to all this than the slick desire heating between my legs. Doing laundry with Ares Necroline had felt like the most blissfully average forty-eight minutes of the past twenty years, and I didn't want to admit that it felt good to be comfortable with someone.

To trust that the things they said were true.

Because the one thing I knew for sure about Ares Necroline was that he chose his words carefully, and when he spoke, he spoke the truth. If he wanted to hide something, he simply didn't say anything. The fact that he felt like the only person in Orphium I could trust, and I'd pissed him off enough that he was busily combining soapy, wet shirts with dry, fluffy towels felt like a metaphor.

The part of me that wanted something—anything, really—to feel true screamed at me to apologize. To grit my teeth and just bang out a sincere apology. But that wasn't in my best interests, nor was it in Necroline's. Neither of us could afford to trust anyone in this vipers' nest of a city, especially not each other.

CHAPTER 11

ARES

"SHE WANTS TO APOLOGIZE," the spirit said, as I pushed past Ember with my mess of a laundry basket. "She just doesn't know how."

I glared at the spirit, then noticed something familiar about her. Her eyes. They were the same shape and color as Ember's. "Are you *related* to her?" I whispered, hoping that Ember, with her preternatural Maere hearing, couldn't pick out the sound of my voice over the washing machine and dryer that were still going.

The spirit appeared to sigh, and nodded. I paused at the door to the laundromat, waiting as she spoke. I was curious to know the answer. "Distantly. She's taken care of our family for centuries. I can't understand why. From everything I could tell when I researched her history, my ancestors treated her terribly."

I smiled at the spirit. The answer was easy. It was one I was quite familiar with. "Devotion."

Not love. Love was not for people like Ember Verona and me. But devotion? Devotion was a concept we both knew all too well. I pushed the door open with my shoulder, turning to look back. Ember stood under the cascading foliage of a spider

64

plant, her hazel eyes wide and glassy, teeth sunk into her full bottom lip.

I could practically hear those molars grinding together from here. She should quit it with that or she was going to need one Hel of a dentist. The thought almost made me laugh. *Almost.*

But almost was enough to remind me why I came in the first place. Why I'd burned her ridiculous house down all those years ago, misguided as it was. The Maere were the parapsychs' best hope, the only force in the three territories that could genuinely stand between us and the Authority's horrors. In Aradios and Palladiere, the Maere had made things better—made the Trinity better there as well. The difference was the swords... And the fact that the Palladiere and Aradios Maere hadn't been shattered to pieces. Guilt gnawed at me.

"I'll call you if I find anything else out, Verona." I don't know why I said it. Maybe I believed she could make things better if she had her swords back. Maybe I wanted to accept the apology in her eyes. Or maybe I just didn't want to leave mad. My guts were twisted up with unfamiliar emotions. Ones I couldn't afford, but I wanted her to know she could trust me all the same. "What we talked about stays here."

Her teeth sank deeper into her lip. If she drew blood, I might drop everything to try and fix it. I had to leave. Whatever this was flooding me, I had to get away from Ember Verona before she crept into my heart. I pushed out of the laundromat, infuriated that I'd let my feelings take me over.

Outside, rain poured down. I crossed the street, towards the metro tunnel, and as I made it to the other side, I made the mistake of looking back. Ember stood on the sidewalk in the pouring rain. She'd followed me out of the laundromat. It was raining hard enough that she was already soaked, and freezing from the looks of things.

Her sweater clung to her body, revealing the shape of her breasts. Desire raged through me, an inferno I had no business allowing to burn. Every base instinct in me told me to drop the basket, cross the street, and kiss that look right off her face. Push her up against the brick building the laundromat was in and warm every bit of that cold, wet skin with my hands, my body, my mouth.

We stared at each other for far too long. Her lips parted, and hard as it was raining, I could see from here that her chest was heaving as hard as mine was with the labor of her breath. The labor it took to stay in place, when all it seemed either of us wanted to do was cross the street.

Years of eyeing each other silently had come to this. Less than an hour alone in a hole-in-the-wall laundromat, and I was tempted to throw all my principles away to get inside her. To feel that long, pliant body wrapped around mine. To be the person she trusted.

Fuck. What was wrong with me? I willed myself to move first, to take the power back and show her I didn't want anything from her. Her mouth moved. She was saying something. Two words, over and over. *I can't.*

Whether she spoke to herself, or meant for me to understand, it didn't matter. She couldn't, and neither could I. We had people to worry about, two factions that weren't exactly opposed, but also had never bothered to work together. That's not how the Trinity worked, and it certainly wasn't how the Consulate worked.

Despite my pie in the sky dreams about a better future, the Maere were bought and paid for. They were Consulate creatures through and through, and the Consulate could not be trusted. That was the truth and it should be reason enough to walk away. But those words on her lips. They were the only ones that mattered to me. *She couldn't.* Couldn't turn away from what she felt.

I'd known Ember Verona for so long, it was hard to remember a time when I didn't know her. And though we weren't close, I knew her nature. Impulsive. Chaotic. Reckless.

She was doing everything she could to rein that in right now. If I had a shred of decency left in me, I'd fix this for her.

In one horrifically painful moment, I tore my eyes away. Time, which seemed to have slowed while I hesitated, moved at its normal pace again. If I wanted it to continue, I would have to keep my attention focused on my own business. I moved towards the metro tunnel, and much as it pained me, I didn't look back.

Two days later, and no one had heard a word about Lara Achilles. Nor had Ember been spotted at any of her usual haunts. My desk chair felt like a part of my body, but I was determined to know if the two of them were all right. And more than that, I wanted to know what Ember planned to do to stop Lara from getting herself, and all of us, into trouble again.

Because if she was the killer, and the Authority found proof, they could take us down with them. We'd covered up what she'd done. I glanced over at Eryx and Av, who were simultaneously playing a game of chess while each of them watched a screen of their own.

Av had a chat box open in a corner of the dark web that I didn't particularly want to know more about, while Eryx scoured less shady parts of the internet for mention of "the Angel." I'd be a fool not to think that moniker referred to Lara Achilles.

I glanced at my phone for the tenth time in as many minutes. None of my contacts had gotten back to me. Reluctantly, I opened a spreadsheet. Waiting was not my forte, but spreadsheets I could handle.

Though being the head of the Orphium Necroline dynasty

seemed like a fairly glamorous job from the outside, the truth of the matter was that it was a lot of paperwork and analyzing data. The business of keeping my people safe in a world that wasn't built for them was boring a lot of the time, but usually I was willing to put in the hours. Right now, the columns swam before my eyes, practically meaningless while other thoughts clamored for attention.

The three of us sat quietly for a while, with only the sound of tapping keyboards and marble chess pieces moving in the background. When this was Roman Necroline's office, the paneled woodwork on the walls had gleamed with precious oil, and the chesterfield furniture had been soft and supple. Under Magnus, things had slipped into disrepair.

I'd done my best to restore things to the way Roman had kept them, but I could never quite measure up to his nobility. The wood never had the same luster, and the leather in all the furniture bore scars. Still, our offices, high in the bureaucratic wing of the Carlyle, were nicer than many of our people's homes. That thought grounded me, drove me to focus. I slipped into a flow state, my fingers flying over my keyboard as I calculated a projected budget for the fourth quarter.

"Ares?" Av's voice broke through my focus.

I glanced up to find her next to me, laptop in hand. Her Poltergeist, Stanley, wove around her feet, taking the shape of a rather adorable sewer rat. When I almost smiled at him, he grinned back, revealing a mouth of human teeth.

"Revolting," I said, refusing to react further.

Av smiled. "He doesn't know any other way to behave, Ares. He's a good boy."

I swallowed hard, not wanting to argue with Avaline. If she was happy with her ghostly little pet, who was I to argue? Eryx covered his mouth to keep from laughing. We were both humoring her, apparently. She held up her laptop as Stanley disappeared.

Her screen showed grainy footage of the Pizza Queen. Lara

Achilles walked in, sat down at a booth, and picked up the phone to order. Only, instead of ordering, Lara was quiet. She nodded several times, then hung up.

"What are we looking at?" I asked. "Is there sound on this?"

Av shook her head. "No, but look." She pressed a key and the video sped up. At the video's twenty minute mark, someone brought Lara a pizza box. She opened it, took out a slice of pepperoni mushroom, bit into it, and walked out.

"She never said a word," Av remarked as she closed her laptop. "So what did whoever was on the other end of that call tell her?"

Eryx shook his head, his brow furrowed. "You'll never find out unless she tells one of us." His phone pinged several times on the table. My brother leaned forward. "We've got them. Verona's at the Automat, and Achilles is four blocks away, closing in on her. Should we intercept?"

I shook my head. "No, if they've been avoiding each other, they need to catch up. Let them." I glanced at my watch. It was nearly eight o'clock at night. "But we're going to follow. See what they do."

Eryx nodded to Av, who stowed her laptop in the safe. I slid mine in after hers. We didn't have desktops anymore, and the safe was built as a Varaday cage—a shielding device against EMF and other surveillance tech. Each of us had similar pockets built into every jacket we owned for our phones. Our secrets were locked up tight these days, and would stay that way.

"Bring your phones, but make sure they stay in your pocket unless we need them," I cautioned. "I don't want anyone to know what we're up to."

Av nodded. "I'll call Stanley in, as well."

I nodded. This was why I let Av keep the disgusting creature. Poltergeists were incredibly effective at repelling tracking tech, but it took a rare medium to befriend the contentious creatures. Av was my secret weapon in more than one way.

"Let's find out what our girls are up to," I murmured as I followed Eryx and Av out of my office. The more we knew about what was going on, the safer everyone would be.

CHAPTER 12

EMBER

MY KEY LIME pie was the best I'd ever had. The soft light of the filtered neons was a soothing silver tone that bled out from behind the hundreds of compartments that held food. The Automat really was better than the ThunderBowl in about three thousand ways. It was also blessedly quiet, just the hum of the neons to keep me company.

But the best damn thing about the Automat was all the spirit activity. It scrambled any kind of listening devices, and because the place was so haunted, the owners had made it fully automated. The spirits didn't make much trouble, as such things went, but the volume of their presence often repelled humans. There wasn't a living soul in the entire building.

Because of the spirit activity, typically people didn't linger here to eat. They came, got their food and left. But when I arrived, a human couple, two men in their early sixties, were enjoying pie—blissfully unaware of the spirits hovering around them as they devoured their lemon meringue. Some humans were more attuned to spirit activity than others. Typically, the happier, and more oblivious to others' suffering that humans were, the less they seemed to sense spirit activity.

These two were both blissfully happy and completely oblivious of anything but themselves. It was sort of sweet, actually. Oddly enough, it was comforting to sit and listen to them talk about their children visiting for the winter holy days.

The spirits liked it too, I guess. They quieted, as though listening to the wholesome conversation. The couple couldn't see the spirits, obviously, but they also ignored me. That was the thing about humans. They had a refined sense about parapsychs. Something in them recognized what we were, even if they didn't know us.

I'd been one of Orphium's Maere for so long it was nearly impossible not to be recognized at this point. But it wasn't just that. I wore a hat, and had dressed purposely to blend in. Neither man had looked at me for more than a moment when I'd busied myself selecting my pie, my back to them.

They recognized *what* I was, and their instinct was to completely ignore me.

Long ago, it hurt to be treated this way and worse. Now, it was more of a fact of life than anything else. If it bothered me, I no longer registered my distress. When Lara walked in, out of the pouring rain, wet through and stunning as a black hole, the couple looked up, startled by her appearance.

She pushed her dark hair back, water flying everywhere, like she moved in slow motion. While we'd never been attracted to one another in that way, I'd have to be numb not to feel her magnetism. The lethality in every move she made—the wicked tilt to her grin—had the humans staring at the meringue left on their plates and deciding it wasn't worth it to finish eating.

They pushed past her, leaving their plates on the table. She shrugged, clearing them herself, then selected a grilled cheese sandwich from the bank of compartments labeled "Hot Sandwiches." When she had a cup of black coffee and a grilled cheese with bacon, she sat down with me.

I shook my head, stealing a fry from her plate. "You did that on purpose."

Lara's eyes narrowed, her long, straight lashes obscuring my view of her light green eyes. She was the embodiment of every brooding hero in a romance novel in her leather jacket and heavy combat-style boots. A voice in the back of my head said, *and Ares Necroline is the sexy villain you wish the heroine would pick instead.* What the Hel was *wrong* with me? This obsession with Ares had to end.

"Why don't you ever get your own fries?" Lara asked.

I rolled my eyes. "They taste better off your plate."

"How long's it going to take you to ask?" My heart pounded. How could she know why I'd been looking for her? She sighed when I froze. "I'm sorry I didn't come back to the Carlyle. That place gives me the creeps."

I sniffed a little. One of the humans had been wearing cologne that made my nose itch and it lingered. "You should have called."

Lara swallowed a bite of her grilled cheese, the sandwich dangling from her tattooed fingers. "Probably."

My heart raced, but I had to push through this. "Are you going to keep acting like a petulant child, or are we going to talk about all the beheadings?"

The sandwich fell to Lara's plate, but there wasn't a hint of surprise on her face. "How did you find out?"

I laughed, shaking my head. "Did you think you could take the head off someone in Necroline's territory without me finding out? You haven't even been out a week. What the fuck were you thinking, Lara?"

Now, Lara looked confused. "What are you talking about?"

After the laundromat, I'd dug into what I could get out of the reports. "That woman at 88th and Vine. The medium with the stepdaughter. Don't play the fool, Lara."

Lara brushed crumbs off her fingers. "I haven't killed anyone since I got out."

"She hasn't," a low voice said.

Both of us turned, whipping around lightning fast, ready to

fight if need be. But there was no need, even though the voice belonged to the most dangerous creature in the three cities.

Rhiannon Brontë stood by the pastry section, perusing like she'd been here all along. She was completely dry, her blonde hair set in waves that cascaded just past her collarbone. A long, black trench coat hung over her shoulders like a cape, and as she turned towards us, I saw she was dressed to the nines, as usual. Aubergine velvet suit with no waistcoat or top of any kind underneath, just some kind of sheer, plunging lingerie.

Every generous curve of her body was perfectly accentuated. Her makeup was flawless and minimal, but expertly applied. And the enormous umbrella sitting by the door explained why she was dry, but nothing could ever explain the way such a statuesque woman of substantial proportions could sneak up on you the way Rhi could.

"How the *fuck* do you do that?" Lara asked, grinning, her whole face lighting up at the sight of our assassin. "You've gotta teach me."

"Never," Rhi replied with a delicate purse to her lips, which hollowed out her cheekbones.

She paid, then prepared herself a cuppa from the tea station before making her way to our table. Lara pulled a chair out for her, and I shook my head. She was so rude to me, but chivalrous with Rhiannon. I stifled the urge to make a snotty comment. Rhi inspired this behavior in many people, but especially Lara. She was elegance embodied, and the true lethal element among us. All of us were killers, but Rhiannon could eliminate victims in silence. It didn't matter if she used poison, a weapon, or her bare hands. She never left a mess, not even a throw pillow out of place.

She held out her hand to me when she was seated. Her oval nails were painted an opalescent beige that shifted color in the light. I took her hand and squeezed. Despite the circumstances, it was good to be together again. When she squeezed back, I saw the concern in her dark blue eyes.

"Someone else was sent for the stepmother," she said without preamble, gazing straight into Lara's face.

Lara nodded. "I went to the Pizza Queen for orders, but they said I had a month to recover from the Asylum."

I itched to ask questions. To demand answers. Hel, I practically seethed with the desire to force the truth out of the two of them. But it was better to give them plenty of room to talk, to let little bits and pieces out that they might not otherwise. I had to bite my tongue, but I was used to that.

Rhiannon turned to me. "*This* is why I went to the Consulate. This is why I left you. I am sorry, Ember."

Her voice was even, devoid of any real emotion, but her expression was open. Rhiannon's version of candor didn't always register with people, but I knew it for what it was. She loved us, even if it was sometimes difficult to tell.

But even that love could not excuse the secrets she hinted at. The flagrant disrespect she'd shown me as her superior officer. Before I could say a word, she was talking again. Again, I bit my tongue. This time for real, drawing a hint of blood, metallic resentment clouding my mouth.

"Have you explained to her?" Rhi asked, directing her question to Lara as her hand slipped out of mine.

Lara shook her head. "Didn't figure Miss Company-Line would care."

"That's not fair," Rhi said, her voice dangerously soft. "Ember stayed. When we all left, she *stayed*." My eyes fell to my lap. It was the first time any of them had acknowledged what I'd done. Lara opened her mouth, as though she might argue, but Rhiannon shook her head. "I know exactly how hard it was for you in the Asylum, Lara. But you could have left at any time. I made that clear to you. You chose to stay in. How many did you get?"

Lara's answering smile was so dangerous that a chill slipped down my spine. "All of them. I got the whole damn bunch of them."

My stomach nearly dropped out of my body. Who had she killed in the Asylum?

Rhiannon nodded. "Good. She'll be pleased."

My blood ran completely cold at Rhi's reaction. This was not at all what I expected. I couldn't bite my bloody tongue a moment longer. "What the *fuck* is going on?"

Rhiannon took a deep breath. "The Automat was a good choice. The spirits here keep this place safe."

Every atom of my being stilled. The air was saturated with secrets. The look that passed between them enraged me. It was all so obvious now—I'd been kept on the outside of something bigger than me, bigger than my sistren. The betrayal cut deep, but even while bleeding out, I wanted back in. I wanted *us* back, and if letting the hurt of this moment go was the way, I'd let it go.

"Yes, yes." I pushed all my frustrations into a tiny box inside my heart. "Get to the part where you tell me, *in detail*, what has been going on behind my back." The two of them shared that *look* again. Like they were considering the wisdom of coming clean with me. I practically threw myself backwards in my chair. "For fuck's sake. How long has this been going on?" Rage churned within me in waves, a rising tide, tight pressure mounting in my chest.

Lara finally had the decency to act worried. "It wasn't like that, Ember. We had to keep this small. So small that you, Sera, and Max would stay safe."

Rhiannon stared into her cup of tea. "And Sera still got hurt. That was a message."

I shook my head, crossing my arms tight across my chest, the crisp fabric of my navy three-piece suit crinkling under the pressure. "Start explaining or I'll start making calls about the two of you."

Rhi pried one of my hands out of the pretzel I'd formed across my chest. "You wouldn't. I know you wouldn't, Em."

I snatched my hand back from her. I hated being called Em, and she knew it. "Then explain. Now."

Rhiannon sipped from her teacup, her lipstick leaving a mauve stain on the porcelain. When the cup clinked on its saucer, she closed her eyes for a half-second, her impossibly long lashes fluttering. "Since the Consulate formed, there have been Authority moles."

I nodded. This was a well-known fact, and frankly, even if it wasn't, it would be easy to believe from a strategic standpoint. "Just as we have people inside their institutions as well."

Rhiannon sighed. "Not in the same way, Ember. The humans' ability to sense us has kept us out of their inner circles. They have our own spying on us—changing the course of our operations."

I swallowed hard. It wasn't that I couldn't believe that our people would do such a thing. Everyone had their price. It was the way Rhi's shoulders sagged when she spoke, like knowing these things was unbearable.

"The Authority has infiltrated the Consulate at the highest levels."

If she thought I would react with shock, she was wrong. All I felt was numb—a dull feeling of acceptance washing over me. *Yes, that made sense.* The way things had moved around just enough to give us the impression progress was being made, but nothing really changed. Circumstances simply shifted.

The names humans once called us were no longer acceptable in polite society, but it was rare for a parapsych and a human to become friends—or for average parapsychs to hold high-paying jobs, or positions of power at all—at least in wider society. Our mere existence was no longer considered a blight on humanity, but neither were we allowed to operate in the open. Instead, our people were relegated to the shadowy bits of society. There when humans needed us, but otherwise pushed to the edges.

"And what does this have to do with Lara and the murders?" I asked, hoping to get to the point sooner.

Lara answered this time, crossing her arms over her chest. "The Authority has been weaponizing parapsychs against one another. They have a powerful Cognoscenti in their employ, who has predicted some of the most powerful parapsychs the world has ever seen. Mediums who can walk in the netherworld, thaumaturges with the ability to do actual magic, seers who don't need divination tools…"

I shook my head as she trailed off. "No one like that exists. We would hear about it." Lara and Rhi shook their heads, in almost perfect unison. Understanding dawned on me, like fog clearing in my mind. How had I missed this? "They hire other parapsychs to kill them—or frame them for crimes so perverse they end up in the Asylum…" My stomach turned as reality crystallized—as all of the experience my long life had afforded came to a fine point. "Where they are…"

I couldn't say it, but Lara could. "*Studied*."

The things they might learn chilled me to the marrow in my bones. If they learned the truth of what and who we were… would any of us ever be safe again?

Rhi's eyes closed, as though she was warding off some horrific knowledge. "There is one who would help us—who has always helped us when she could. No one knows who she is. We call her Mother."

Lara and I both leaned towards Rhiannon now. In this moment, we felt like us again. Centuries ago, before our swords were stolen, we were more than just good at our work as mediators between the Trinity and the Consulate—we protected our people better than the Maere in any other territory. I'd never been surprised that someone had tried to eliminate us—they hadn't been the first to attempt it—only the first to succeed.

Rhiannon continued, lowering her voice, as though by instinct. "Mother has many operatives. Lara is one of them. She takes out as many of the killers as she can, before they're able to destroy promising parapsychs."

A lump formed in my throat. That was all well and good, but it didn't make what I'd said before any less true. The kinds of parapsych talent Rhiannon described just didn't exist. "And what happens to the people she's saved?"

Rhi and Lara shared another look, but Lara answered me. "We don't know."

CHAPTER 13

ARES

THE CAR WINDOWS had fogged up, and Eryx's eyes were still milky white from the spirit he channeled inside the Automat. We sat in a nondescript town car over a block away, watching the three women talk, listening to their conversation emanate from Eryx like he was a radio. It was an unnerving talent. Rare and special, like Av's ability to bond with spirits, or my exceptional talent for exorcism and auric manipulation.

The three of us had always flown as far under the radar as we possibly could, downplaying our abilities since we were children. There was a pervasive ethos in parapsych communities around how much of your talent you displayed. The less humans knew about what you could do, the better off you were.

From the back seat, I reached forward and shook Eryx's shoulder. "I've heard enough."

Av frowned, twisting in her seat to argue with me, her brows raising into the thick fringe of her dark bangs. "But Ares—"

"The girl from 88th and Vine," I interrupted. "Where did she end up?"

Av's eyebrows shot higher as Eryx's eyes cleared. "She's one of them. One of the talented they were talking about..." The wheels in Av's head turned before my eyes as she came to the same conclusion I had. If what we'd heard the Maere discuss was true, that girl was in grave danger.

Eryx licked his lips a few times. His mouth was always dry after he channeled a spirit. I handed him a glass bottle full of electrolyte infused water from the stash we kept stored in the console of the back seat. He gulped some down, and then asked, "If Lara didn't kill the stepmother, could it have been a frame job?"

I threw my hands up in frustration. "You heard what they said. This Mother, whoever she is, has multiple operatives. If the girl is in some kind of danger, do you want to find out the hard way?"

From the front seat, Eryx shook his head. The three of us knew all too well what it meant to be just a *little* more talented than the average parapsych. If the girl fit into the category the Maere discussed, then she wasn't safe, even with my best team watching her.

Av started the car as Eryx rattled off the address. I whipped out my phone, pulling up the number for one of the few people in Trinity leadership that I trusted besides Lux. The phone rang before I could change my mind. As Av wove through the dark city streets, rain spattered on the windshield.

Eli Cabot answered after just three rings. Unusually fast for his grumpy ass. "Lux said you'd call."

I wasn't surprised she'd known I'd call Eli. She was more in tune with me than most, and it made her predisposed to seeing into my immediate future. Lux, Eli and I were old friends. Aside from Eryx and Av, they were some of the few people in this cursed world I actually related to—because like my brother and Avaline, they were both just a little too talented for their own good.

We held common ground and a long history that made it easier to place faith in them. That made it easier than with other people who had less to risk. *You trust Ember too*, that pesky voice at the back of my mind taunted me. I pushed it aside, not wanting to consider the particulars of why I had so much confidence in her.

"I need a favor," I said, hoping Eli wouldn't be too much trouble. He could be rather prickly.

"And I owe you one," Eli said. "*One*, Necroline."

There was the prickliness, and the reminder that our long years of friendship didn't extend so far as un-owed favors. That was fine. It was enough. Eryx showed me his phone, and the address we were headed to. I nodded. "I need to move fast and the ability to make a teenage girl disappear."

Eli didn't ask for more information. The thaumaturge knew how this worked. The less any of us knew about what the others did, the safer we all remained. With that safety came loss. The less the Trinity trusted each other, the less likely it was that we'd ever get out from under the Authority's—or even the Consulate's—thumb.

And that, of course, was the point of hunting us for centuries—leaving just enough of us alive that we could still do the humans some good, but shattering our ability to trust one another so thoroughly that they could rule us by sheer force of their numbers against ours. It wasn't as if any of this was a surprise, but if the girl had some kind of hidden talent, she was important.

Saving her life meant pushing back. It meant showing the tangled knots of power, where the Authority and the Consulate intersected, that we were more than just pawns in their unending quest for control.

Though Eli did not respond, I heard the unmistakable noise of a struck match, of a spirit candle sizzling to life, and of the low hum of the thaumaturge speaking to the universe... or whatever it was that he did. That was another of the problems with the way things were—the secrets of parapsych talents were locked down by each of the dynasties in the Trinity.

We didn't share knowledge about how our power worked. Ever. Very few things were even written down anymore. There were just too many ways for what we could do to be used against us.

"One hour," Eli said after a long moment of silence. "You, Eryx, and Av have one hour to do what you need to. You should be able to move with speed, though to do the three of you, I can't make you invisible."

"What about the girl?" I asked.

"When you find her, tell her 'the Angel hears your plea' and she will become invisible until you reach safety."

My heartbeat slowed, sounding for all the world like the drums of old inside my mind. "Where did you pull that phrase from?"

Eli made a noncommittal noise before delivering a sham of an answer. "You know I can't say."

"Right," I replied, doing my best to suppress the snarl of frustration caught in my throat. "Thanks."

"My debt is cleared." Eli's tone was suddenly formal.

"Sure," I replied absently. "If that makes you feel better."

"What's going on?" Eli asked. "*Really?*"

The fact that he had the gall to ask after telling me his debt was cleared was grating. If Eli Cabot wanted to be a curmudgeon that was his business, but I couldn't handle the emotional whiplash right now.

"Ask Lux, since she knows so much." My tone was clipped as I hung up. I'd lost my patience. "We have an hour to get the girl somewhere safe."

Av looked back at the Automat, watching the three ancient warriors with their heads bent towards one another. "Do you think they can do it?" she whispered.

"What?" I asked, annoyed that she hadn't started the car yet. I tried to tell myself that it was talking to Eli that got me worked up, but the thorn in my side was Ember Verona. The damn woman put me off my equilibrium.

"Get their swords back—become who they were meant to be again," Av replied, her voice harboring a wistfully soft note.

Eryx watched her, his eyes narrowing slightly as his brow furrowed. He was worried about her. Whatever that emotion she displayed was, it concerned my brother. And thus should concern me. It did, but we were out of time.

"Av." I leaned forward, touching her arm as gently as I could. "We don't have much time. Get us to where you stashed the girl."

What was this longing she had for the Maere? Av had been like this ever since she discovered what the auction's theme would be. I tried to make eye contact with Eryx, but he wouldn't look my way.

She nodded, but her gaze stayed on the Automat. "We should ask them to help us."

I sighed. If only we could. In another version of this world, perhaps. But the Trinity and the Maere had been at delicate odds for centuries. The Consulate was a necessary evil, one we could not forego if we wanted to survive the Authority. But it was hard to ignore how much damage it had done, how sometimes it felt like the Consulate was working against us as much as the Authority was. I followed Av's gaze. The three women in the Automat were different somehow. They always had been.

When they had their swords, they had been better. Things had been better for all of us. I hadn't realized it til they broke apart. Til the five Orphium Maere had turned to one lonely, desperate woman. The feeling that I'd played a part in fucking all that up chased me down, eliciting a lump in my throat I could hardly swallow.

"We can't," I murmured, feeling distracted. If only we could band together, we would be an even match for the Authority and the sheer numbers the humans had against us.

That kernel of hope wormed its way into my heart, but I dug it out, tossing it aside before it had the chance to germinate. Hope was fickle—dangerous. "Drive, please."

Av nodded, starting the car. Eryx glanced back at me in the rearview mirror. He knew as well as I did that underneath Av's icy exterior beat the heart of an idealist—that our girl held out hope for a better world, even when the rest of us could not. She pulled away from the curb, and I could feel her disappointment, heavy and desperate.

For all the times she'd been right about things and I hadn't been able to listen, surreptitiously, I slid my phone out of my pocket. I found Ember Verona's phone number and sent a single text: *Could use some help*.

Then I pulled the pin on our geolocation for the girl and sent it to Ember as well. If Av was right and we needed them, then I didn't want to make another mistake. When it came to Orphium's Maere, I'd failed to listen to Av one too many times. It sent dread through me to ask them for anything, but I convinced myself I was doing this for Av.

Because if it was for me, then I was too far gone. If I let myself need Ember Verona, I was lost.

CHAPTER 14

EMBER

A STREAM of human teenagers flowed into the Automat. They were children, raucous and clearly having fun, but my heart sank at the way they shrank away from us. The way their joy stopped the moment they clocked who, and what, we were.

I got up from the table and deposited my tray in the return window before staring pointedly at Lara and Rhi. Lara shook her head and Rhi sighed, but they followed suit as I stepped out into the night. Rhi stared down the street for a long moment as a black town car rounded the corner a block away. Her eyes narrowed for a second, but when she turned back towards me, her face was schooled into its usual mask of calm.

"We should check out the Auction Gallery," she said, keeping her voice low as we made our way down the wet street. It had stopped raining, and fog drifted through the streets, thick and soupy. "Tonight. There's a special exhibit in another gallery and we should be able to walk right by the swords."

I bit back all my arguments and my desire to ask about a hundred more questions when Lara nodded. Wasn't this what I wanted? My sistren back, to work together again? I could bite my tongue. Keep my mouth shut and just listen for a while. Not everything had to be a fight.

Rhiannon explained that there was an evening showing of some bioluminescent art installations at the National Gallery, and it would make good cover for checking out the space where the Gala and auction would be held. Casual enough that we didn't need to change clothes and a popular enough event that it made sense that we'd attend.

If this was a trap, and we had to assume it was, then whoever wanted to catch us out would be expecting us. The trick was to behave as though we hadn't considered we might be set up. To be as arrogant as many assumed the Maere were. Just walk right in and case the joint. Why the fuck not?

I glanced to my left at Rhiannon, who looked serene as ever as we strode down the dark sidewalk. What went on behind her perpetually halcyon exterior had always been a mystery to me. To my right, Lara practically vibrated with nerves. They glanced at each other, as though looking right through me. It had been nearly a century since they were together, but there were still times I felt that spark of connection between them.

The one that practically screamed, "if we'd tried harder, could we have made it work?" They knew the answer was no. I knew the answer was no. Anyone who'd spent even ten minutes around them knew. They were volatile as romantic partners. Great as friends, devious as colleagues, and completely miserable as lovers.

I sighed as my phone buzzed in my jacket pocket. As soon as I saw the name on the notification, I slid it back where it came from. After the night I'd had so far, I couldn't stand the thought of hearing from Ares Necroline. Whatever had passed between us at the laundromat was dangerous. The connection I felt to him was messy. There was no way for us to act on whatever these feelings were without trouble.

"Fine," I said, if only to interrupt any further rumination over the Necroline leader. I stepped out into the street, raising a hand to hail a taxi. "Let's go."

I nside the National Gallery, the special exhibit was crowded. We wandered through it first, putting on quite a show of being interested in the bioluminescent art. Several humans snapped photos of us—of Rhi and Lara. No one was that interested in me anymore. But the humans liked to keep track of our whereabouts, treating us like curiosities rather than people, and neither of them had been sighted in Orphium in years.

That was the odd thing about the Asylum. People just disappeared. No one ever confirmed, publicly, that parapsychs went in or got out. I don't know why I hadn't wondered why that was before.

When the Authority was so gleeful about publishing our every individual transgression as evidence against us, why hadn't I questioned why they weren't equally as forthcoming about who was kept in the Asylum? It all made sense now, but in the wake of this evening's revelations, I was frustrated with myself for not clocking all of this sooner.

Rhiannon's heels clicked gently on the marble floors of the gallery, just ahead of me. She and Lara walked arm in arm, as I trailed behind them, turning my thoughts over time and time again. It would be all over message boards and gossip sites within the hour that we were here. I assumed this was what Rhiannon banked on. That interest in the fact that the three of us were together again might flush out some piece of information on whoever had our swords.

Rhiannon glanced back at me. We'd been in the special exhibit for a half hour, seen all the glowing sculptures made from various mosses, lichens, and fungi. It was time to slip out and make our way to where the swords would be displayed during the Gala.

I followed close behind. My phone buzzed again, the

reminder notification that Ares had texted me earlier. I pulled it out of my pocket, took a deep breath, and unlocked my phone. I'm not sure what I expected, but a request for help wasn't it.

I quickened my pace behind Rhi and Lara, my fingers flying over the keyboard. *Still need help?* I watched my phone as we exited the special exhibit, but there was no sign he'd seen my text.

As we wound our way through the Antiquities wing, I checked my phone again. In doing so, I failed to see that Lara and Rhi had stopped. The smaller gallery where the auction goods were displayed each year was directly ahead of us. It looked as though they'd already set up extensive security measures, which was no surprise.

I could just make out the spirit traps from my vantage point, and my mouth went dry. Spirit traps weren't illegal, but in the last fifty years or so, there'd been enough of an outcry about them that legitimate organizations like the National Gallery no longer used them. This would make things harder, for sure.

Spirit traps were cruel, but they were extremely effective in cases like these. The spirits were never allowed rest, and when caught inside the trap, they were forced to do the trap owner's bidding. A bit of bile rose in my throat.

Rhiannon turned, her eyes full of rage. "We are leaving."

Technically, she didn't get to make a decision like that, but sometimes Rhiannon forgot that I was her superior officer, not the other way around. I craned my neck to look around her, my stomach lurching as I caught sight of the spirits themselves—or rather the auric energy they emitted. I froze, gooseflesh raising on my arms as my heart beat faster than it should.

"How?" I breathed. My fists clenched, nails digging viciously into my palms. Without my sword, it was hard to see aura, but something about the way these traps had been programmed intensified it enough that I could read the souls' auras clearly. "How…"

Lara glanced at me. "Rhi, she's going to lose it."

Rhiannon grabbed hold of my arm. "We can't do anything about it now, love. We have to go."

But I couldn't turn. My eyes were locked on the five souls the Authority had guarding the gallery. Five younglings, none of them yet twenty-eight. They'd all died so young. And yet, I *knew*. Each of them had been destined to be Maere—one of *us*. It was evident in their aura as spirits, the same thread that connected the rest of us. My teeth gritted.

Was this the Authority's doing? Were the talents they were snuffing out potential Maere? How was that even possible? My mind spun with possibilities, tumbling through horrific scenario after scenario. I'd lived too long, seen too much.

They knew. They knew we'd come. This wasn't just a trap, it was something else. Something bigger. Whoever had our swords didn't just want to bait us into stealing them back, they wanted to *hurt* us. This was *personal*.

"We'll never get past them," Lara growled under her breath as they got me moving towards the exit. She was right. Those spirits were a failsafe. Any ideas we'd had about an easy in and out on the night of the Gala evaporated.

"We are *so* fucked," Rhi breathed.

In my pocket, my phone buzzed. Again and again as we made it out of the National Gallery and onto the street. Finally, I pulled it out of my pocket. "Hail a cab," I said, calming as I read the return text from Ares Necroline. "I have a plan."

They glanced at one another for a moment before remembering that I was still their commanding officer—that even after everything, I was actually still in charge. Rhi stepped out into traffic, her long, elegant arm hailing a taxi.

"What are you up to, Verona?" Lara asked, her dark brows furrowing.

"We're going to upset the apple cart," I snarled. "Do something they won't expect."

A block away, a cab sighted Rhi and turned its blinker on. She stepped back onto the curb. "An alliance?"

I nodded. "With the Necrolines."

She shook her head. "They'll never agree to that."

I smirked. "Oh, but they will." I turned my phone to show them both the message Ares Necroline had sent: *In over our heads. Please come.*

CHAPTER 15

ARES

As Av ROUNDED the narrow city corner, it was apparent the safe house was already compromised. This was what the humans considered a bad neighborhood. Tall brownstones, covered in ivy, lined the tight, poorly lit streets. Curtains were drawn against the night. There were no flourishing gardens, just lush trees and ivy. Not a clue given that these houses were occupied by parapsychs with talents that could aid plants in their growth, or who could get a message to a dead loved one.

It was the perfect place to hide a teenage girl with burgeoning power. I had safe houses all over the city, in neighborhoods just like this one. None had ever been breached before now. My muscles coiled as Av slowed the car.

My best team of fighters lay dead, lined up against the wrought iron garden gate like trophy kills—a message to the entire neighborhood. Unbridled rage boiled in my gut as my attention narrowed onto the figure I could just make out from three blocks away. Mike Fairchild sat on the front stoop, casually smoking a cigarette. The front door to the house was open, giving me a full on view of the man inside the brownstone, beating the ever-loving shit out of the girl.

Eryx's hand shot into the backseat of the car. He shoved me, hard, back into my seat. "Don't," he hissed. "It's what he wants."

I gritted my teeth, feeling for a moment, like Ember. Like leashed lightning, about to strike. I wanted to tear into that house and stop what was happening. Eryx's grip on me tightened. He felt the same as I did. He was holding himself back, as much as he was me.

Av turned off the headlights as she pulled into an alley, cutting off my view of the safe house. She shook her head at Eryx, but he didn't let me go, so she tried to diffuse the situation by talking. "How'd he kill the Phoenixes? They're the best."

"*Were*," Eryx muttered as he released his hold on me. "They *were* the best."

Av gulped, covering her tiny face with her hands. Her eyes shone with glassy disbelief above her short, manicured nails. "Mike Fairchild is a nobody… I looked into him. Sorted him up and down. There was nothing suggesting he, or any team he is a part of, are capable of this."

Eryx placed a hand on her arm. It was shaking. She let him touch her, let him grip her arm for a long moment before she nodded, giving him a small half-smile.

My brother reassured her. "If anyone could have known who he truly was, or how resourced he was, it would've been you, Av." To me, he said. "Fairchild isn't who he appears to be. We need to start from the beginning and sort out what's going on."

I gritted my teeth, but nodded. "Nothing going on right now is what it appears to be. We're in over our heads."

I already had my phone out when Av said, "Maybe we should call Ember Verona."

"On it," I said as I typed out a second request for help.

Whatever Mike Fairchild was capable of, I couldn't afford to just rush in. Not with my best team dead. My organization was large. Orphium was the City of the Dead, after all—and there were still more necromancers here than any other parapsychs.

Even with all that, in times like these, the pool of people I could trust always shrank to the three of us.

I hated having to ask for help—and worse—having to wait for it. The image of that child, strapped to a chair, being beaten by a grown adult, was more than I could live with. Fire lashed through my veins.

Eryx turned again, shaking his head, his gaze darkening. "I know what you're thinking, big brother... You can't rush in there."

My jaw clenched tighter, my neck aching with the effort of it. "If Roman Necroline hadn't risked himself in just the same way, we wouldn't be here now."

I could hear the sound of my brother's jaw clicking. Watched as he shut his eyes against the memory. Fury rose up in me. I was the one who took the beating. I was the one some Authority bastard with too little oversight and too much audacity had nearly killed, just for the fun of it.

Our adoptive father had rushed in with a team, like a legion of avenging angels, and everything changed. I swore to myself, on that very day, that I'd never let that debt go unpaid. The child on the metro's accusation ricocheted through me. I'd let my people down too many times. Maybe I *was* a traitor. Too comfortable in my seat of power for my own good.

I took a deep breath and nodded. "You're right," I agreed. "We'll wait for the Maere."

Eryx sighed with relief. He was just doing what he did best, protecting me from myself. From the terrible temper that lurked beneath my typically stoic exterior. "Thank you."

I nodded, solemn. "Of course."

As soon as he turned back around, I was out of the car. I strode towards the safe house, the power of the nether-realms crackling at my fingertips, and called every spirit in a six-block radius to me. Fairchild had fucked with the wrong Necroline. There were at least a dozen Poltergeists in the vicinity, which was some real luck, and a handful of Shades.

The Poltergeists went in first, screaming as they swept through the garden gate so hard it hung off its black hinges. Mike Fairchild was knocked aside by their passing, and I was up the steps and had him by the collar before I saw what became of the spirits. They still screamed, but this time, their auras were pulled apart. Exterminated. Not sent back to the netherworld, but eliminated.

It was as though going through the door had eradicated them. There wasn't so much as an auric signature left of them. The middle-aged man beating the girl had stopped to watch what happened outside the front door. He was a tall, pale man, with colorless hair and a burly musculature. Recognition dawned on me. The man inside, alone with a helpless teenage girl, was one of the Authority's most notorious torturers.

I'd only ever seen him once, right before my adoptive father died, and he'd aged since then, but I recognized him all the same. The memory of Roman Necroline jerking me away from my favorite ice cream vendor when I was twelve played like a movie at the back of my mind. "That man tortures people like us to see what we're made of," Roman had warned me. "Memorize his face. And if you ever see him again, you *run*."

Roman Necroline had been a good father. Grief caught in my throat, replacing a child's fear with a grown man's desire to eliminate the threat the man before me posed. Now that it was quiet, a slow smile spread over the torturer's face.

Still in my grip, Mike Fairchild began to laugh. "You have no authority here, Necroline."

I shook him. "I have *all* the authority here, Fairchild."

The smarmy little bastard smirked up at me, so smug I wanted to rip his face off. "There is only one Authority, Necroline, and it will never include abominations like you. *All hail the Authority, under whose benevolence we flourish.*"

The words were old. Ugly. From the days when our gods were relegated to Sainthood, and the Authority was declared the one and only spiritual force. A false front for worshiping greed. Under the Authority, there was no god but capital. No salvation without money. Fairchild smiled at me, his plain, nondescript, pale face a mask of mediocrity. What lurked behind the mask was something far more dangerous. A zealot.

His words told me he believed something that not many humans still did: That the Authority was led by a god. A god that called on his people to trample one another to get ahead, and worse, that people like me were abominations of humanity, evil at our core, and that the world would be better off without us. Not many still believed this, though the remnants of the old ways clung to humanity like a stain. What had we stumbled into?

Eryx and Av stalked towards us, guns drawn. A tinny noise in my ear, like the whine of a mosquito, grew louder by the moment. Still gripping Fairchild, I looked inside the house again. A shimmer of something I hadn't seen in years revealed itself in the doorway, just as Eryx approached. I threw Fairchild aside, leaping for my brother.

I caught hold of him just before he stepped over the threshold, yanking him backwards so hard that we tumbled down the stairs. "Hex boxes," I hissed. "Look at the door."

Eryx looked at the silvery glimmer in the threshold, then snarled as he rose, seeing what I did: two iron devices, clipped to the bottom of the doorway, that generated a bastardized version of a necromancer's power. There was only one way to reverse-engineer the power of bringing what once was dead back to life, to concentrate it into pure death, instead of a cyclical life force. It was a bastardization of all that necromancers believed about the holy cycle of life and death.

Hex boxes were invented about a hundred years ago, their inception a horrifying tale of parapsych death that twisted necromancers' power into something evil. Something with no respect for the soul, because, in general, as an organization the Authority did not believe in such "tall tales."

The only thing that had stopped the production of hex

boxes going mainstream was the general population's mass hysteria that parapsychs would manufacture their own to use against humanity. That had been a brilliant rumor for the Consulate to conjure up, but it had done nearly as much harm as it had good.

For Fairchild to have the use of not one, but two hex boxes, confirmed he was not what he appeared to be. Who was he? Before I could ponder it further, an Authority guard appeared from the slender alley that separated the safe house from its neighbor, bully club in hand. Two more rushed out behind the first, their own guns drawn, equipped with silencers.

"You're not leaving here alive, Necroline." Fairchild laughed again. "And neither is that girl. I just wish I could make you sit and watch."

Eryx launched himself at the guards. I turned back to Fairchild, but he squirmed out of my grip. Without thinking, I reached for his aura, whispering a prayer to St. Tanith for forgiveness. A necromancer should never touch the aura of the living, but I couldn't let him get away.

But Mike Fairchild slipped away, without a hint of auric energy for me to grasp onto. And then he blinked out of reality in much the way a spirit might. My gaze darted around me, but I couldn't find him until laughter coming from inside the house caught my attention. Fairchild was inside, with the girl and the torturer, and I was stuck outside. I rushed up the steps, gripping the doorframe, trying desperately to remember if there were any tricks to disabling a hex box.

"Get the car ready," Fairchild told the torturer. "I'll bring her out in a minute." He drew a switchblade from the pocket of his tweed jacket. "Would you like to keep a little piece of her, Necroline? A pinky perhaps, or an ear?"

I snarled with rage, pounding the door frame with my fist. There was no time in recent memory that I had felt so helpless.

Fingers closed around my shoulder. I flinched, ready to

fight, but when I turned, I came face to face with an ice-cold stare. Lara Achilles.

"Move," she said, her voice deadly soft. Then she stared at Fairchild. "I'd run, if I were you."

Fairchild just smiled. The expression faltered when Lara Achilles walked through the force-field of death the hex boxes generated, completely unscathed. In fact, her skin seemed to glow, having absorbed some essential power from the force field. She glanced back over her shoulder, her icy eyes glowing with an almost neon light. "Get to the back."

I didn't hesitate. I sprinted down the steps, moving impossibly fast towards the narrow alley, my legs pumping as hard as I could, with only a glance to spare for my brother and Av. They both stood in the garden, surrounded by bodies, mouths gaping open at a statuesque blonde woman, who frowned at the speck of blood on her gorgeous wool coat. Rhiannon Brontë was back, and she'd dispatched the Authority guards in the blink of an eye.

Even Eli Cabot's miracle was no match for one of the Maere, swordless as she might be. A flurry of movement rushed by me, Ember Verona's familiar scent filling my nostrils. I put more energy into my miracle-fueled speed and reached the back of the house at the same time Ember did.

Without a word of hello for me, she burst through the kitchen door, a dagger flashing in her hand as she slit the torturer's throat and tossed him out the back. The movement was so quick and clean, I barely saw it. In only a moment, she'd dispatched a man so evil he'd haunted my dreams since I was a child.

We raced through the kitchen and through the narrow hall towards the front room. The old wallpaper in the hall was peeling, revealing layers upon layers of other patterns, other choices made and rejected over the years. Dimly lit sconces flickered angrily as we moved through the house. The safe house's spirit guardians were furious. They'd been shut out of the front room, unable to help the Phoenixes, or the girl.

Ember reached the parlor door and pressed a hand to it. "More hex boxes," she muttered, then glanced at me. "Stay put."

I nodded as she pushed through the door, ripping the hex boxes from the door frame as she went, crushing them in her delicate fingers. It had been ages since I saw the Maere for what they truly were: lethal weapons.

I stepped into the parlor, not knowing what I would find, but Lara Achilles had the teenage medium in her arms. Fairchild was gone. The girl had lost consciousness. I could do nothing more than stand and watch as Achilles nodded to Verona, who reached down and pulled the hex boxes from the front door frame.

Her voice was so soft, I almost didn't hear her, but Lara whispered to the girl, her dark head bent over the child's, "The Angel hears your plea."

The child's eyes fluttered open, a faint smile on her lips. "My guardians said you'd come for me."

"And I did," Lara murmured back. "You are safe now, sleep."

The girl relaxed in Lara's arms, her head nestled against the Maere's broad shoulder as she disappeared from sight. Lara looked back at me, a tenderness in those icy eyes that defied everything I thought I understood about what she did. She didn't kill those parapsychs out of rage; she did it for the same reason I did anything. For the same reason Verona did: devotion.

Her devotion was just bigger than mine or Verona's. Lara Achilles saw a vision of what we could be, not what we were. The hope in her eyes nearly choked me. I tore my eyes away from the Angel, shame roiling within me for all I could not be for my people.

"Clear," Ember said, before glancing back at me. Outside,

Eryx had pulled a van around to the front of the house. There was no way this hadn't all been caught on CCTV, but he and Av piled the bodies of the guards and the torturer into the van. Rhiannon Brontë pulled our people off the garden gate, gently closing their eyes, her lips moving in silent prayer to Tanith.

These Maere surprised me. I knew I'd been wrong not to talk with Ember all those years ago when we suspected Lara of the murders. But now I saw that I'd underestimated them all. That I'd seen them as Authority collaborators, when what they truly were was the hairline between us and the entities of power that wanted nothing more than to suck our people dry and discard them.

Ember Verona had held that line alone for twenty years.

No wonder she was tired.

Lara Achilles walked out of the safe house, the little medium in her arms. As she walked down the steps, I knew why they called her the Angel. There was a nobility in her countenance I hadn't seen in centuries. I stood next to Ember as Lara spoke to Rhiannon in the garden.

"Thank you," I murmured, watching the two warrior women speak to one another.

My brother stepped forward, and vaguely I heard him ask how Lara had known what to say to make the girl invisible. Lara's tight smile told me the words were a secret she'd kept for a long time. "I have always said it to the ones I helped. I did not realize it would make her invisible tonight."

Lux. She'd known that Lara would be here, that they would come. I cursed the Seer silently, but it wasn't her fault. Visions were tricky things. Sometimes, if the subject knew what was to happen, it changed things too quickly. All too often, a Seer's visions were useless.

Av and Eryx stared at the Maere the spirits had called the Angel with awe in their eyes. For the briefest of moments, I understood what the world had once been, what the Maere and the Trinity were before the Authority—and before the Consulate.

There was no way for me to say if it was better. I hadn't lived quite so long as all that. The Consulate was formed hundreds of years before my birth. History told us that those had been dark days. But history was written by the Authority. Written by those who hated us. Roman's accounting of it had been that those were halcyon days, but I knew better than to wholly believe in his nostalgia for the days he was King.

Ember's frown interrupted my rumination. I was far too attuned to her moods and when she spoke, all other thoughts flew out of my mind. "Don't thank me just yet. We need your help." My heart beat faster as she held out a hand to me, her back straightening and her shoulders rolling back, as she spoke the simple ancient words. "You are called, Ares Necroline. Will you answer?"

The past I'd just been imagining melted into the present, the days of knights and kings reborn. My hand went around her forearm as I sank to one knee in front of her, a chill going through me as I bent my head. The feel of her long fingers wrapping around my forearm was so delicious as to be distracting, but took nothing from the solemnity of this moment.

Whatever happened here tonight, it was bigger than anything the Necroline Dynasty could handle on its own. I knew what Ember Verona would ask, and I would gladly pledge all my aid. Orphium needed its Maere back.

So I spoke the ancient response without hesitation. "Your call is answered. The Necroline Dynasty pledges fealty to the Orphium Maere. Use us as you will."

CHAPTER 16

EMBER

ARES NECROLINE's hand slipped from my forearm so slowly it sent heat lashing through my veins. His pledge felt as though it wasn't just to the Orphium Maere's leader, but to me, personally. The thought was ridiculous. Of course, he hadn't pledged a thing to *me*. I was, technically, above him in the chain of command.

He was simply doing what he was required to.

Obeying me.

Not that he had ever done so, in all the years I'd known him. I brushed the thought aside, trying to calm the breath that pushed through my lungs, which threatened to heave as evidence of the desire that mounted inappropriately at the base of my spine, seeping into lower, more intimate places.

Rhiannon walked towards the bottom of the garden gate. She held her phone to her ear. I hadn't heard it ring or vibrate, but somehow, she'd known to answer it. Her face was grave. *The Consulate.*

She called up to us. "We need to go. The Authority is sending a team for cleanup."

"Was this sanctioned?" I asked. It was frustrating that the

Consulate called her and not me, but that was the way of things.

Rhiannon shook her head first, then shrugged. "They say no, but…"

I nodded. We were never going to get an honest answer about that. It had been a silly question. All I wanted was one hundred years of sleep and a thousand percent less bullshit. But here we were, right back in the thick of things.

Ares held an arm out, indicating that I should pass by him to get to the front door. As I slipped past him, my fingers grazed his, unintentionally, but time slowed regardless of my intention. The world stopped as his hand flexed, as though to open for mine. As though he might lace his fingers through my own, and bring them to his lips. Like a knight kissing his Lady's hand.

My breath shuddered through me as those pale green eyes bored into mine, intense with the heat of the stalled moment. When I passed safely out of his orbit and through the front door, I looked back. The slightest hint of color flushed Ares Necroline's pale cheeks, his razor sharp cheekbones hollowing out further as he swallowed down the moment between us.

The look he gave me might have been interpreted as a glare. But the heat that undercut it drove through me, coursing through my veins like wildfire. If he hated me, the way I did him, then it was because I'd cracked him open like an egg, just as he had done to me. Now, both our messy yolks were spilling out for all the world to see. Down in the garden, our people stared up at us, waiting for orders.

I sucked air through my teeth to get my bearings. "The Carlyle is the safest place for all of us," I finally said, without so much as a glance back at Ares Necroline. The sound of the door locking told me he was right behind me. "You don't keep residence there, do you?"

"No," he said, his voice soft in my ear as he came to stand next to me. "Do you have room for the three of us?"

I nodded, handing him one of my cards. "Address is on the back."

He tucked it into the inner pocket of his overcoat and nodded to his brother, who was openly staring at Rhiannon. I frowned at him, and catching my gaze, he averted his eyes. That particular Necroline brother could blush fully, his cheeks going bright red. Rhi barely seemed to notice, or perhaps it was her perpetual mask of unbothered righteousness.

I sighed, knowing how unfair that was. She was doing her best, just like I had been. Both of us caring for the people we loved most in the world the best way we saw fit. She should have led us, not me. Her deep emerald eyes met mine, the faintest of smiles on her full lips.

Rhi nodded once, her face apprehensive, as though she was contemplating saying one thing, then changed her mind. She turned to Avaline Reyes. "Can you give us a lift? We need to get the girl home."

As Avaline nodded, Ares swept past me on the stairs. "I'll go with Eryx to dump the van, and we'll meet you back at yours as soon as we're done."

Rhiannon sucked in an uncharacteristically loud breath. "Actually…" She averted her eyes from mine, focusing narrowly on Ares. She was about to say something I wouldn't like—I'd bet money on it. "They've called you in." She didn't have to say who "they" were. The way she emphasized it made it clear. The Consulate bigwigs wanted someone to have a word. Rhiannon glanced up at me. "Both of you."

Ares nodded, as my jaw clenched painfully. There was nothing I hated more than visiting the home office.

Avaline raised a hand. "Could you get my laptop from the office? If you're going in, I mean."

Ares nodded, all seriousness and focus once more, but as he passed her, he brushed a kiss to her cheek. "Stay safe."

She nodded at him, adoration in her eyes. Eryx Necroline took the tiny necromancer's hand and squeezed it tight. There was deep affection on their faces, but not romantic attraction. The three of them were unusually close for the Necroline Dynasty, which was as cutthroat as they came in this city. Why hadn't I ever noticed it before?

Had I even been paying attention?

"I called you a car," Avaline said. "They'll be here in just a moment."

Ares and I nodded in unison, like two oddly shaped little peas in a pod. We glanced at each other, and then both shook our heads. Part of me wanted to laugh, but the part that didn't like the way we were gelling so easily scowled instead. Apparently, he felt the same, as he mirrored my expression.

For her part, Avaline looked as though she couldn't wait to escape the two of us as she retreated with the rest of our people. I moved back to the steps of the house, watching as Ares stared at his dead people, whispering the words I assumed would send them safely to the other side. Wherever it was the restful dead went.

Jealousy washed over me. Wherever Ares' Phoenixes had gone, it was a place I'd never see. My eyes squeezed shut against the thought. Knowing there was no rest in my future, no promise of quiet respite, was too much to acknowledge—too much to bear—so I didn't.

CHAPTER 17

ARES

THE SUZERAIN WAS BUILT over the burial mound of Orphium's feudal lords, making it almost unbearably haunted and a seat of Necroline power—a reminder that Roman's dynasty once ruled this city, wholesale, as kings. Before the Authority. Before the Trinity. Before the Consulate.

The flatiron building now sat in deep shadow, skyscrapers towering over its meager heights, still stately in spite of it all. Ember and I checked in at the concierge, checking both our coats and weapons. No violence was allowed in the Suzerain. All grudges between parapsychs were to be left at the door to the main building, above which read *oderint dum metuant*, "let them hate, so long as they fear."

Ember's lip curled as her eyes ran over the words carved into the rough marble. "As though their fear has ever brought us anything but pain," she muttered as we walked through the doors to the Consulate's seat in Orphium. She glanced back at me. "Sorry, that was Roman's motto, wasn't it?"

I nodded. He'd said it the day he gave over his crown, and joined the newly formed Consulate. The motto was meant to be a comfort for his people. We could not stop humans from hating us, but we could cloak ourselves in what they feared most: death. In death, was safety. Roman had believed in the Consulate's power to protect all parapsychs, not just those under our care.

He'd been wrong about that. We all had. I couldn't deny the truth in Ember's words, and I didn't want to. I believed differently than he had, but I wasn't certain I acted any better. Various parapsychs sat drinking various beverages in the Suzerain's luxurious velvet-clad lobby. Some of my midtown vassals waved at me, beckoning me over to them, but I shook my head and held up a hand in greeting as Ember and I made our way to the block of elevators at the center of the building.

A text came through on Ember's phone. She glanced at it. "Rhi got us transferred to Lola Carmichael." Her eyes flickered over the screen. "She says you have a connection with her?"

I nodded, knowing Eryx must have fixed this for us. "She's good with kids."

Now Ember nodded. "Good. We need someone who is. I don't think that girl should go back into protective custody." She looked up at me, her eyes narrowing for a brief moment. "I don't mean that as a slight, Ares…"

I filled the void in her words. "I know. The Phoenixes were one of my best teams. If they were defeated so easily, we need another solution."

Ember took a deep breath, nodding once. We both stood in alert silence, absorbing the conversations happening around us, every move the high-level Consulate parapsychs surrounding us made. Her eyes slid to mine and held my answering gaze. Neither of us trusted anyone in this building, that much was clear.

When our car came, we rode to the subterranean offices in silence. Whoever decided to locate the more bureaucratic aspects of the Consulate in the basement knew what they were doing. There was very little I hated more than coming down here. When the elevator reached level 13B, the doors opened on a waiting room.

Ember let out a long breath as we got out and waved to the admin at the window, who gestured for us to take a seat. We were expected. The temperature in the windowless, wood-paneled waiting room was several degrees too cold for comfort, likely due to all the spirit activity in the passages beneath the city.

Golden oldies played over the fabric-covered speakers affixed to each corner of the room. Ember slumped next to me in an uncomfortable chair that looked to have been manufactured sixty years ago, or yesterday, it was hard to tell. The scowl she'd worn since we left the safe house seemed stuck to her face. I had no real issue with that. We were in an uncomfortable truce.

What was interesting to me was the fact that she sat so close to me. Not just right next to me in her chair, but her shoulder actually bumped against mine, like it had in the laundromat. I could smell her perfume acutely, that black peppercorn note standing out to me more now that I'd determined what it was. Sharp, spicy, alluring.

"Why do you think they decided green shag carpeting went with these orange chairs?" she grumbled, almost under her breath.

I raised an eyebrow. "I'd call them 'burnt sienna,' personally."

The faintest snicker slipped out of her, harsh and sweet at the same time. My low laugh joined her, and before I knew it, we were both chuckling. The admin, who sat behind a thick glass window, looked up. He peered out at us through thick-rimmed glasses, shaking his head as he picked up a hand-held speaker.

"Quiet in the waiting room," he said.

Ember rolled her eyes. "C'mon, Jackie. It's not like anyone is *out* here."

The admin's name tag read "Jonathan." He shook his head and pointed to the brass placard affixed to the wall next to his window. It read, *SILENCE BUT FOR THE SCREAMING*. It was my turn to shake my head as "Jackie" went back to typing. Indeed, there were enough Poltergeists on this level of the building to warrant the exception. Likely, there was quite a bit of screaming from time to time. I tried not to think too hard about that, lest I attract them.

I leaned over to whisper to Ember. She tensed for a moment, but then relaxed a measure. "*Jackie?*"

Ember smiled. "I used to babysit for him when he was little. His mom's a Seer, lives uptown now in a nice condo. She works here too, I think."

That was a bit of a surprise. I glanced at Jonathan again. He was young, with dark curly hair, medium-brown skin and an aquiline nose. Couldn't be more than twenty-three, probably.

"Hard to imagine you as a babysitter," I joked. I never joked. *Why was I joking?* I suppressed the urge to cringe.

Ember glanced at me sidelong. "Turns out I had a lot of time on my hands when my house got burned down and all my best friends moved away."

Jonathan looked up and simply shook his head. She stuck her tongue out at him. He wanted to stick his tongue out, right back at her, I could tell. People liked Ember. That was something I'd noticed over the years, but hadn't ever processed. She seemed to have trouble in her close relationships, but people who didn't know her well loved her.

What would that be like?

The question ricocheted through me for long enough to make my stomach churn. Luckily, before I had the chance to do something about it, Lola Carmichael came out of the door next to Jonathan's window. She was a tall, willowy woman with dark brown skin and eyes that noticed everything about a person. It helped that she was one of the Cognoscenti, an Intuit, if I wasn't mistaken—someone whose pattern recognition was preternaturally super-charged.

"Mr. Necroline, Ms. Verona. I can see you now."

Today, Lola's hair was combed out in a puffy halo around her head, and she wore a trim suit in emerald green. Ember and I followed her through a long, narrow hallway flanked with heavy paneled doors. Above our heads, the electricity flickered in the chandeliers. When we reached Lola's office, she pushed the door open and gestured for us to sit in two leather wingback chairs opposite her desk.

As one of the Clerical Directors for the Consulate, Lola worried about the business of parapsychs operating outside the law. The technicalities of things. The business of keeping the Consulate's extra-legal activities in line with what the Authority would tolerate, or worse, what it wanted from us in the shadows.

She'd helped me out of a jam before, about forty years ago, when I'd wanted to relocate some Necroline charges to the farming districts. They were orphans, and I'd wanted them out of Orphium. The Consulate didn't like that kind of thing. They preferred to lure children into the life Eryx and I led now. Despite that, Lola helped me get them out.

As she sat, she locked the vast array of screens on her desk with a single button. "Your overlords command you to take charge of the child while we coordinate with the Authority to find their rogue agent."

Rogue agent, my ass. Mike Fairchild's actions were perfectly in concert with the Authority and it was a shame Lola felt the need to toe the Consulate line in such a way, but I understood it. We all did. There weren't any alternatives.

Ember sighed in her chair. "We're not *qualified* to do childcare."

Lola Carmichael smiled. It was a devious kind of smile. She was used to games like this. "Ah, yes." She pushed two clipboards towards us. "I anticipated you might make such a claim.

We shall do a reconciliation to determine whether you are fit to take care of the girl."

Ember groaned, and I let out a huff of frustration. It had been nearly fifteen years since I completed a reconciliation for the Consulate. They were such pains in the ass. Ember snatched the clipboard with her documentation on it off the table. Unlike my paperwork, hers was just a few sheets long. She was here more than I was, after all, to bring in the tithe. She'd probably done one recently.

I glanced at Ember's list, and she frowned at me. "Keep your eyes on your own paper, Necroline."

I chuckled again as I picked up the thick stack of paperwork and the pen Lola provided and began to move through it. A reconciliation was an accounting of known work done for the Consulate and… other actions that were unconfirmed. My jaw tightened as I began checking boxes. The years after burning the Maere's mansion to the ground had been difficult. Getting the Necroline operation back in line after my adoptive uncle's corruption had been a monstrous project. The blood on my hands would never come clean.

A Shade in the corner of Lola's office shook her head. She'd been an admin here when Roman adopted Eryx and me. She appeared next to me, a short, round-faced, pale woman with eyes the size of saucers. Neither Ember nor Lola saw her. "Look at all that death, child."

I glanced at her but did not respond.

"So much murder," she growled. "Was it worth it?"

There was no point in answering her. I flipped the page.

The Shade bent closer to me, her skin beginning to peel from her flesh. "All those Necroline deaths. Roman Necroline took you in, gave you his name, and this is how you repaid him?"

I closed my eyes and breathed deep.

The spirit's cold fingers closed around my wrist. Though she could not move me or truly touch me, I felt the chill of her. "Traitor. You are a traitor, boy."

My pen stopped. I looked up, into the spirit's now ghoulish face. Oddly enough, I recognized her from somewhere other than this office. She had been one of my uncle's staunchest supporters. "I did what was necessary to bring honor back to the Necroline Dynasty. *Did you?*"

Lola and Ember had both stopped what they were doing to watch me. Lola drew a pair of spectacles from next to her desk. Likely, they were equipped with spirit glass, which was nearly impossible to come by these days. She put them on and frowned.

The spirit drew back from me, her skin no longer melting off her. She was prim once more, her permed hair vibrating with rage. I shook my head. "Did you support my uncle murdering Roman? Destroying everything he'd worked so hard to build?"

"Magnus was a good man," the spirit said with a sneer. "He didn't kill Roman. *You did.*"

Lola cleared her throat, a sharp sound. "That will be quite enough of that, Fran." The spirit looked instantly chastened, but Lola did not stop speaking. "You know very well that the inquest into Roman Necroline's death was definitive, despite your interference."

Lola stood, and turned a switch next to her desk that activated an old television in the back corner of the office. "Though I cannot for the life of me banish you, I will play the videos again if you don't bugger off to wherever your kind go when they're not harassing people."

It was the most I'd ever heard Lola say at once, but the spirit instantly disappeared. Lola sighed and sat back down. "You'd think being executed for her interference in the inquest would have been enough," she muttered.

Ember stared at me, arching one eyebrow, almost playful. "What were you going to play on that television?"

Lola smirked and flipped another switch. An old children's program started, the one with the animatronic rabbit. Even the opening credits were enough to elicit a shudder from both of us. The show had been rated as one of the most unintentionally disturbing children's shows of all time, and it was obvious why.

Ember covered her face with her hands. "*Please.* Turn it off."

Lola laughed, but obliged. "It's the only thing I can do to get her out of my way some days."

I took a steadying breath. "Do people think I killed Roman?"

Ember placed a hand on my arm. "No, Ares. Reasonable people know it was Magnus. The only ones who say such things were your uncle's supporters."

Lola nodded, apparently agreeing. Somewhere in the distance, I could still hear the golden oldies playing in the waiting room. It was a disconcerting juxtaposition. "Please continue your reconciliation."

I flipped through the pages, reading as quickly as I could. "Most of this seems correct. Do I actually have to check this all off?"

Lola and Ember shared a look. Finally, Lola held out her hand, wiggling her fingers at me. "Give it."

She took it, and I sighed. "Surely you don't think the two of us are qualified to take care of a teenage girl after all that."

Lola pulled a stamp from a drawer and thumped it onto several pieces of paper spread out on her desk. Each read "APPROVED" in large crimson letters. "On the contrary," Lola replied. "It makes you both uniquely qualified to care for the girl. Keep her safe, please."

Ember and I both sat staring at Lola. What she was saying was inconceivable, even for the Consulate. What did Lola Carmichael know that we didn't? Ember's head tilted to the side in a way that was both charming and threatening at the same time.

After several moments of uncomfortable silence, she spoke.

"What is going on here, Lola? With Mike Fairchild and his operation? What aren't you telling us?"

Lola raised her eyebrows, opened her mouth, closed it, and simply smiled. "You've been approved. Please feel free to attend the training seminar happening in the auditorium right now."

Ember stood. "*Feel free?*"

Lola nodded. "By which I mean: you are required to attend. Get going. It starts in ten."

CHAPTER 18

EMBER

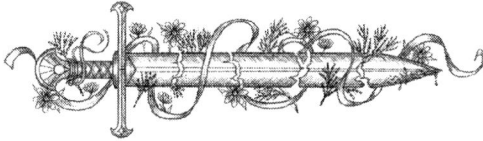

THE SEMINAR WAS BORING, as expected. Stuff anyone would know, but no actual advice about how to take care of a teenage girl in this day and age. Ares refused to sit next to me, and in the car on the way back to the Carlyle he was silent.

It wasn't until we reached the elevator that he spoke to me. "I need to go get Avaline's laptop, and then I'll be up."

There was no doubt he was uncomfortable about what had happened at the Suzerain, though I couldn't parse out what was making him so itchy. "Was it the reconciliation that did it?" I asked on impulse as he turned to go. "All that bloodshed and violence?"

He spun, his eyes wild with some emotion I couldn't gauge. My breath quickened as he stalked towards me. He stopped a hair's breadth from my face. "Do you think that's something I should be *proud* of?"

I thought about it for a few moments. There was, of course, talk about how dangerous Ares Necroline was, that he was a brutal head of the Dynasty. But Roman had been worse by far. The man had believed in governing through fear, after all. When he was king of Orphium, this place had been a bloody mess. He'd made the newly-forming Authority look gentle in comparison.

But Ares had changed things. He'd killed a lot of his uncle's cronies, and tortured even more of them if his reconciliation was accurate. But his dynasty had come to heel. They'd improved under his rule and things were changing, if slowly.

"Yes," I finally answered. "I do. Changing things takes a terribly long time and brutal effort. You've done your best."

Ares breathed deep, his chest grazing mine. Our encounter in the laundromat thrummed in my bones, the memory a living thing. His pale green eyes narrowed as he bent over me, bringing his lips to my ears. "No, Ember, I've done my *worst*."

Shivers ran through me, straight to the base of my spine, then lower. He straightened, his face a mask of intimidation. A Necroline prince, through and through—no, *a king*. It was wild how different the public version of him could be from the man I'd seen in private.

"And I would do it all again, if given the chance." A cruel smile played at his lips as he turned away from me, his words haunting me as he walked towards the long back hallway that led to the business wing of the Carlyle.

Watching him go, my knees turned to jelly, relieved he couldn't see the slump in my shoulders or hear the way my heart raced for him. The way he spoke had shaken something loose in me. Something I wanted to put firmly back in its place. Something I could not have, could not even dare to want. I closed my eyes against the storm of emotions brewing within me and waited for the elevator.

U pstairs, I found everyone waiting awkwardly for me in the parlor, which meant I had to pull myself together on the double. I shooed them all away, motioning for Lara to follow me with the girl. The child was still asleep as I showed Lara the room I'd made up for Sera, decorated in the soft silvery tones she'd always loved, with tiny little stars on the ceiling that glowed softly in the dark.

Lara set the girl down on the bed, pulling the fuzzy lavender blanket up over the girl's feet. "Do you think she'll be okay?"

I didn't know much about teenage girls, so I shrugged. "I have no idea."

Lara frowned as she left the room, leaving me to shut the door. "You did a nice job with the flat," she said as we walked down the hall. After all her bluster from before, that was rich coming from her now. The praise still warmed me, though. I couldn't deny that. "Can I see my room?"

My heart thumped with nerves as I pushed open the door across the hall. Lara touched the brass light switch and several lamps cast their golden glow around the deep emerald tones of the room. Lara walked to the wall of bookshelves that surrounded the windows, her mouth falling open. "These are my books…"

"They're not," I interrupted, not wanting her to get her hopes up. Lara was the type to annotate all her books with her deepest feelings and reactions. "Your books burned with everything else, but I did my best to replace them. I tried to find replacements for everyone's treasures."

Lara smiled, a soft and fragile thing. The first time I saw her, she'd given me that exact same look. She'd been stuck in a pillory in her village square, the people she loved most in the world throwing rotting vegetation at her. When we sensed her ascension, we came for her, but they'd already found her out.

The second she saw us, she knew we were there to be her family. To be the ones who would never leave her behind. Who would accept her for who she was. Or at least that was how it was supposed to work. My chest ached. Without Max and Sera, both Lara and Rhi coming home felt temporary.

It hurt too much to think of them leaving me again. As Lara flopped down on the giant bed, I backed away, whispering, "I am glad you like it."

I turned before I could hear her respond. I found Rhi and Avaline Reyes in the sitting room. Rhiannon sat at the writing desk by the arched floor-to-ceiling windows, scribbling away in her journal, while Avaline sat on the floor, eyes closed. I sat down in the green velvet wingback next to the writing desk and watched the necromancer for clues about what she might be doing.

Rhiannon set her pen down, sighing as she closed her journal. "Avaline is summoning spirits to safeguard the flat from surveillance tech."

I nodded, but said nothing.

Avaline opened one eye, then grimaced. "Would it be possible for the two of you to go elsewhere? You're making me nervous."

Rhiannon placed her journal in her bag and nodded, rising out of the desk chair in a motion so fluid and graceful that I couldn't take my eyes off her. Avaline had a similar reaction. Her cheeks flushed a tiny bit as she looked away.

I sighed as I followed Rhi out of the room. "Do you have to do that to people?"

She looked over her shoulder as she walked towards the kitchen. I don't know how she knew the layout of the flat already, but it didn't surprise me. "Do what?"

"Be all irresistible like that. You've got everyone under your spell," I hissed as we entered the kitchen.

Rhiannon slid out of her jacket, revealing creamy pale skin. She moved around the kitchen with that same preternatural grace as she ground beans for coffee. Watching her was witnessing art in motion. I sighed deeply, envying the way she moved through the world with such ease, utterly captivating anyone who came in contact with her. It was a skill I did not possess. Rhiannon was a generous bolt of the finest silk, and I was as smooth as a cheese grater.

"Have you ever thought about why it is necessary for me to present this way?" Rhiannon replied as she dumped coffee grounds into the wildly expensive coffee maker I'd purchased with her in mind.

Her words snagged, catching on the corners of my perception of her. Rhi had always been like this, as far as I knew, and yet something in her words suggested it was a cultivated state.

She gestured to me. "You are messy. Irritating. Wild."

A part of me wanted to argue, but her tone wasn't insulting. Rather, it was tired, deeply, deeply tired. And nothing she said was untrue, so I nodded. She opened the refrigerator and took milk out, bringing it to the frother and measuring out enough for both of us to have generous helpings.

When the milk was going, she placed a perfectly manicured hand on her pristine decolletage. "And no one questions if you are elegant, intelligent, or capable."

A sinking feeling went through me. I wasn't sure what she meant, but I knew when my perception had failed me, and now was one such time. "In this life, I have always been different," she said. "Even before I ascended. I was… *bigger* than everyone in my village."

Humans had been smaller in size when we all ascended. I had been tall as well, but I'd never been as large as Rhi. Being different, in any way, when we were born invited scrutiny. I nodded, slowly starting to understand.

"I was too big, too loud, too beautiful."

I smiled at the last phrase. Rhiannon would never go so far as to deny that she was, indeed, too beautiful. But my smile fell away, quickly, remembering what life had been like for Sera when we found her. Though she was a tiny thing, and did not have the same issue of size that Rhi had, she was, by society's standards, the most beautiful among us. Ethereal, really.

And it had almost ruined her. If she had not ascended, it might have. It took her years to want to stay, to not mourn the death she anticipated as a release from all that had happened to her. I had never thought about what Rhi might have endured. She never talked about it.

Any visible difference, on top of what set us apart as parapsychs, had always been dangerous. And before we'd ascended, we were vulnerable. Far, far too vulnerable. Each of us carried those scars, but Sera and Rhiannon most of all.

"There is no use in looking backward, Ember. But my grace is not a joke. It's how I survived." Her eyes averted as she turned from me.

I rushed around the kitchen island before she could lift the pitcher off the frother, my arms going around her. She smelled, as she always did, expensive. Heavenly. Ever so slowly, one of her silken arms hugged me back.

"You are not a joke to me," I whispered. "You're a marvel. You always have been."

She nodded once, a single tear sparkling in her left eye. When she blinked, it was gone, disappearing inside the most beautiful assassin I'd ever known. "I am so glad you're here," I said, my voice cracking. "To smooth out my rough edges."

"Oh, Ember," she breathed as I pulled away from her. She sighed, bringing down mugs. "I know this has been hard."

I couldn't voice the fears I had about what might happen next. From inside her jacket, her phone rang. She was in the middle of making a beautiful froth of foam in my mug, so I fetched her phone for her. When she answered, cradling the phone between her cheek and shoulder, she sounded different: Sharp, capable, and confident. "Yes, I understand."

There was a long pause as the person on the phone talked. I had tried, early on when she left, to find out who she worked with at the Consulate. But the entire organization above the bureaucratic levels was so opaque as to be a complete mystery. Humans assumed that the Maere and those in Trinity leadership knew much more than we did about how things were run.

"They had hex boxes."

Another pause.

"Four."

Yet another pause.

The truth was that the Consulate was run, at the highest levels, by parapsychs who went practically unnoticed in mundane life. And to folks like me, they were simply voices on the other end of the line. People who called to tell me my mistakes, and who I called to complain. To be perfectly honest, it was all a lot of bitching and moaning.

"Destroyed now. Ember crushed them."

A longer pause this time.

"Thank you, I will tell her."

Rhiannon hung up. Checked twice to make sure she'd *actually* hung up. Then turned her phone off entirely. As it shut off, her shoulders slumped, her hand flying to her forehead, her thumb and index fingers pinching the bridge of her nose. She blew out a tightly held breath. "Your approval went through. You and Ares are the girl's official guardians. She's to stay with you, though, wherever you choose to reside."

I breathed a sigh of relief, which surprised me a little. I hadn't known I'd wanted the girl to stay with us until just this moment. "What about the Necrolines?"

She shook her head as she leaned against the kitchen counter. "They said nothing about punishing them." She was visibly shaken. I wondered for the thousandth time who she'd worked for, and why she feared them so deeply.

My jaw clenched. "Then it's confirmed. That Fairchild person was working outside the Authority's official channels."

"They know what he's up to," a voice said from the kitchen door. I turned to find Ares Necroline. "But he's definitely running his own operation."

CHAPTER 19

ARES

THE MAERE'S penthouse apartment was beautiful—all heavy stone walls and arched windows with leaded glass. This part of the Carlyle was older than the wing our offices were in. The architecture was gothic, sweeping and mysterious in a way that lent an almost castle-like feel to each of the penthouse's various rooms.

As we entered, Brontë and Verona turned, and it was clear I'd interrupted a moment between them, but Av was still in the cozy little parlor calling spirits, and she'd scolded Eryx and me for interrupting her. I'd just followed the voices into the kitchen, which was a haven of state-of-the-art appliances, a lot of white marble, and painted white cabinetry.

Rhiannon Brontë glanced behind me and her expression shifted, but I couldn't tell why. I looked over my shoulder to find Eryx standing in the doorway, his mouth practically hanging open, staring at her. Her nostrils flared slightly, and I recognized it for what it was, frustration.

I smacked my brother's burly chest, frowning at him in disapproval. We needed the Maere. He couldn't be gawking at Rhiannon like she was some sort of goddess, just stepped out of the clouds.

His mouth closed as his brow furrowed. "Apologies," he said, his usually deep voice a bit higher than I expected. He cleared his throat, his eyes on the floor. "Truly, Ms. Brontë. My apologies. It's just that you were… amazing tonight."

One of the assassin's eyebrows lifted. "Are you complimenting my *skills*?"

Ember bit her bottom lip, her long, spindly fingers covering a smile. She averted her eyes from the awkward scene before us, pretending to examine some invisible speck of dust on some dimly glowing glass light fixtures. The room was bright by design, but the overhead lighting had been carefully chosen not to exacerbate the light sensitivity that most parapsychs experienced.

Eryx struggled behind me. "I… Yes." He glanced at me, practically helpless. Usually, he was very good with women. Smooth, even. But Rhiannon Brontë had reduced him to a nervous wreck. "You are also very beautiful," he blurted out. "But of course, you know that."

It took everything I had not to groan aloud. I had never seen or heard my brother so awkward before. I joined Ember in her examination of the seeded glass globes that hung over the island.

"Yes," Rhiannon agreed, taking up her mug of coffee. "Please excuse me. I need a bath."

As she swept out of the room, Eryx's cheeks flushed red, probably at the image conjured in his head of her in the bath. He hadn't the nerve, apparently, to watch her leave, but his mouth pressed into a grim line. "Where is your office?" he asked Ember. "If you don't mind, I'd like to get our tech set up before we determine what our next move should be."

Ember nodded, her face completely serious, telling him where to find the office and the codes he needed to bypass her security. My brother's shoulders squared off, and he seemed himself again as he left.

When his footsteps faded away, Ember dissolved into bubbly laughter. "Rhi'll destroy him," she whispered.

The words were harsh, but the delivery was not unkind. In fact, it was conspiratorial—like a secret between us. Nor was she wrong. I'd never seen someone so unaffected by my brother as Rhiannon Brontë. Typically, people fell at his feet, practically begging to be admired by him, though he rarely indulged in such attention. He might have finally met his match.

A low laugh rose from my belly, twining with the musical sound of her laughter. Ember's eyes caught mine. "You have a nice smile."

My heart fell victim to her soft expression and crinkled eyes. In my mind, I took three steps across the kitchen and pushed her onto the counter, kissing her so hard she couldn't breathe. In my mind, her arms twined around my neck as her back arched, pushing those perfect breasts into me. In reality, I stood stock still, the smile falling from my face as I tried not to act on every instinct in me that told me to claim this woman as my own.

She frowned. "Did I say something wrong?"

I shook my head. "No. You're perfect." It wasn't what I'd meant to say, but it was true. To me, for me, Ember Verona was perfect. I couldn't keep denying it to myself, even if I could never have her the way I wanted to.

"Ares," she breathed, setting her mug down. "You can't *say* things like that to me."

I nodded, solemn. I couldn't. *We couldn't.* She was right. I glanced at the clock that hung on the wall next to the refrigerator. "It's late. Where do you want everyone to sleep?"

She took a deep breath, as though showing me to a bedroom would take immense effort. "So, we're just going to talk about everything tomorrow, then?"

I nodded. "I think that's best, don't you?"

"Why not?" she replied, motioning for me to follow her.

A n hour later, Av was done with the spirit-warding, and we were settled in our rooms. The penthouse was huge, with many more bedrooms than necessary, which wasn't that surprising. The Consulate owed the Maere plenty, the least of which was lavish accommodations.

My bedroom was small, but handsomely appointed in midnight blue, with a giant bed that nearly took up the entire room. The worst thing about it was that it shared a wall with Ember. Imagining her, just feet away from me, tangled up in her bedsheets, was more than I could handle. I tossed and turned for an hour, trying not to think of her, my cock almost painfully hard.

I got up to go to the bathroom, thinking a dousing of cold water might help. Just as I was about to turn the shower on, I heard the sound of my bedroom door opening, and soft footsteps creeping across the room. My heart beat faster as I turned the shower on.

Slowly, I moved towards the door, hoping to catch the intruder unawares. But when I burst out of the bathroom, all I found was Ember, eyes wide. "Hi," she squeaked. "I was just checking on you. You've been tossing and turning for what feels like hours."

"You can hear me?" I growled.

Her eyes locked on my bare chest, sliding down to my still-present erection. She wore nothing but a thin, white t-shirt that barely covered her hips, and as she stared at my cock, her nipples hardened.

"No," she whispered. "But every time you toss or turn, you send a little vibration through the wall. My headboard shares a wall with yours."

"Oh," I replied, unsure about what to say or do next. My

cock was so hard it ached, made worse by the sight of her body through the thin fabric of the t-shirt.

"But… you're fine. So, I'll go."

She said the words, but didn't move. The HVAC in the Carlyle was shit, so the room was far colder than it might be otherwise, but my skin heated as she stared at me. It was like she was stuck. Her eyes were wide and desperate, but she didn't move a muscle to leave.

I couldn't stand this a moment longer. I took the three steps toward her that I regretted not taking in the kitchen and tipped her chin up towards my face. "What do you want, Ember?"

She pulled away from me, so much pain in her eyes that it nearly broke me. "Something no one can give me," she said, finally backing away.

Ember sank onto the bed, cradling her head in her hands. All thoughts I'd had about what might happen next flew out of my head—she was upset. I pulled an upholstered stool from next to the wardrobe up to the edge of the bed and sat directly in front of her. Our knees touched.

"Talk to me," I said, keeping my voice soft. This felt like a moment for gentleness, which was not my forte, but for her I would try. "Tell me what's on your mind."

Slowly, her eyes raised to mine. In the dim light from the bathroom, I could just make out the surprise written in the invisible lines of her face. "I am lonely."

Those three words sank deep into every wound I had, right into my soul. It wasn't just the words, but the hollow sound of each syllable, the ache in the silence between us. It was the knowledge that no matter what, or who, I wanted for myself, that I would always find myself alone at some point, making the decisions no one else would or could.

This had to be why I was so drawn to her. Maybe if I acknowledged it, it would have less power over me. So I nodded. "Me too."

She narrowed her eyes at me. "How could you be? You have your brother and Avaline."

I sighed, resting my elbow on my knee, and my chin in my hand. Our faces were so close I might kiss her. It felt good to be close like this, but not touch. There was an intimacy in it better than fucking, though I was certain there were few things in the world that might feel better than burying my cock in her.

But this. This was something else. Her kaleidoscope eyes locked on mine, searching for the answer to my question. "They're best friends," I explained. "And I love them dearly… But I am always…" I trailed off, searching for the right words.

"On the outside," she murmured, her breath grazing my face.

"Yes," I answered.

She held my gaze for a long moment, her chin tipping upward, so slowly it hurt to watch. When her mouth grazed mine, she was hesitant, but I did not pull back. Nor did I rush in the way my body screamed at me to do. Instead, I opened for her slowly, letting her tongue drift into my mouth.

She tasted like fresh air and a long-forgotten mountain stream. My fingers grazed her jaw, and she moaned in my mouth as they trailed down the silken column of her neck. I deepened the kiss, pulling her forward so gently it gave her every opportunity to say no.

Ember slid, in one fluid motion, onto my lap. Her t-shirt went up above her hips as she straddled me. "Keep me company tonight, Ares," she breathed as she pushed her shirt above her head, exposing those perfect breasts to the cool night air. "Help me not to be so lonely."

All thoughts of lessening the power she seemed to have over me flew out of my head. I nodded, my lips closing around one of her nipples, my hands palming her breasts as she arched into me, her hips rocking slowly over the hard length of my erection.

Here, alone with her in the quiet of this bedroom, I could be honest with myself. There was almost no one in the world I allowed to have power over me. As much as I loved my brother and Av, even they did not compel me the way that Ember did. For her, it seemed I would lose all my hard-won control. I slid my hands down her sides, luxuriating in every inch of her soft skin, then pulled her tight against me as I rose.

She clung to me so tightly I groaned with the pleasure of feeling her damp nipples press against my chest. Over the years, I'd refused to think of her, though every time I saw her, my cock twitched with this same pulsing need. And now, I had her in my arms. Had her in my grasp.

There was no way I would rush through this. I lowered her slowly to the bed. She pulled me down on her, her mouth meeting mine with desperation as she raised her hips, grinding against me.

Her need drove me, as I slid my hand between us, playing with the waistband of her panties as she worked herself against me. My cock strained against my pants, and the thin fabric between us felt like miles. I rolled off her, and she whimpered beneath me, arching her back off the bed, and spreading her legs just a little.

I stroked my fingers down the center of her panties, until I found the damp spot between her legs. Her legs spread wider as I circled her clit so lightly I hardly knew if I'd touched her until she moaned my name. Her arms went around my neck as she kissed me harder.

"Touch me," she begged in my mouth. "Please touch me."

My previous resolve to go slow shattered into a thousand pieces with those pleas. There was no mistaking what was between us now. Anything she wanted, I would have to give to her. And besides, I wanted to know how wet she was, to feel the evidence of how I affected her. I pulled her panties aside, exposing her pussy to the cool air of the bedroom.

"Yes," she hissed, her knees falling open.

So slowly it nearly drove me wild, I pushed one finger inside her. I couldn't wait to taste her, but I wouldn't rush. I wanted her begging for my tongue. Her eyelids fluttered, a whimper eking from her lips in slow, sultry tones. The deeper I pushed inside her, the more she lost control beneath my hands.

"More," she whispered. "Please, Ares—"

Whatever she was going to say was cut off by a bloodcurdling scream. Both of us startled, uncharacteristically slow to react, as she yanked back from my touch. Her breath heaved as she pulled her t-shirt down, her eyes wide and dazed, as though maybe we'd both hallucinated the scream.

In moments, there was rustling in the hallway. Voices. Ember's eyes fell closed in obvious frustration, and she shook her head. "Go," she whispered. "I'll follow."

I nodded, grabbing my sweater off the bench at the end of the bed. When I glanced back at her, she was gone.

CHAPTER 20

EMBER

I SLID through the secret door between the bedrooms and grabbed a robe from off the bench at the end of my bed. My breath hitched, my heart still beating. Had I really just had Ares Necroline's fingers inside me? I was fucking this whole thing up, wildly. I dreaded what Rhiannon would say when she found out.

Another truly wretched scream broke through the haze of lust I'd stumbled into. It was the girl. I rushed out of my bedroom, finding all the lights on in the hallway. Avaline and Eryx both stood outside the girl's door with Lara. Ares stood at the doorway to the girl's room. Rhiannon was inside.

That figured. The child needed someone comforting to talk to and none of us filled the bill. I stayed back, afraid to get too close to Ares right now. He nodded, as though having been asked something, and turned. When he saw me, the only indication that we'd been wrapped up in each other only moments ago was the way his eyes dragged over me as he passed by.

"Brontë's asking for you," he said, his voice gruff as he disappeared down the hall.

"It's all right," I said to the others. "Go back to bed."

I didn't wait to see what they would do next; I just walked into the bedroom. Inside, one of the silver mercury glass lamps next to the bed was lit. Rhiannon, dressed in a matching set of camel-colored cashmere sweats, sat on the edge of the bed, speaking softly to the teenage girl.

The girl had dark brown hair that was nearly the same color as her skin, and she was pretty, but far, far too thin and badly bruised from where Fairchild's torturer had hit her. "Hello," I said, keeping my voice as gentle as I could.

Even old as I was, I still remembered what it meant to be a terrified child. Those who have been one never forget the feeling, and this girl would be no different. I whispered a prayer to Paloma for a miracle. That time might heal this child, rather than exacerbate her wounds. Prayer did fuck all, but it seemed worth a shot.

"What is your name?" I asked as I sat down on the clear lucite desk chair I'd bought for Sera.

"This is Briony," Rhi explained. "Briony Rathbourne."

I nodded. "It is nice to meet you, Briony." Rhiannon stared at me for a long moment, as though there was something I should say or do, but I didn't know what it was. "I am Ember," I said, finally.

The girl nodded, then winced as she spoke. Her bottom lip was split open. "You're Ember Verona. Leader of the Orphium Maere. I know."

As she spoke, something shifted around her. I realized, with an appropriate amount of wonder, that I saw her aura. Just the shadow of it, as I hadn't touched my sword in two hundred years. But there was something familiar about it. I glanced at Rhiannon, who nodded.

Ares returned with a glass of water. "For you, Briony," he said. "Do you remember me?"

The girl took a careful sip of water and nodded, holding it in her lap. She looked like every inch of her body hurt. "Yes. I remember you pulling the spirit from me. Thank you. It wanted to help me, but…" Tears filled her eyes. "My father was a bad man… I know that…"

Rhi touched her arm, her fingers featherlight on the girl's bruised skin, the movement tender and comforting. "But you didn't want him to die."

The girl shook her head. "He was horrible, but he was all I had."

"It will take time to heal," Ares said, with the wisdom of someone who had been there. Curiosity about who he'd been before Roman Necroline found him itched at the back of my mind. I knew the stories about what had happened to his parents, but they were just that. Stories.

Ares' voice was uncharacteristically tender as he said, "It'll take time to find peace again, but you will. You are safe now."

Rhiannon nodded. "Yes, we will keep you safe." She gave me another pointed look as Briony turned her attention to me. She hadn't even been back a day, and she was already getting judgy about how I operated. I wished to all Saints that she'd been born first, that she could lead the Maere.

She wanted to do this kind of work. I just wanted my family back. To be a part of something bigger than me again.

"Yes," I agreed. "They're right. We'll keep you safe." Rhi shook her head, as though I'd disappointed her. But that was no surprise. I stood. "I will let you get some rest."

Lara was in the hallway, a bottle of heavy duty painkillers in her hand. "Can she take these?"

"Ask Rhiannon," I replied, not knowing anything about what a human child her size might need in terms of dose.

Suddenly, the apartment felt too small. Too close. How was I supposed to know what to do with a kid? That familiar note in her aura haunted me, driving me to near-panic. Ares followed me through the apartment and onto the terrace. The night air was cold, but it had stopped raining.

He could see auric energy. I had to ask. "What did you see in her aura?"

Ares shut the door to the terrace, staring out at the city. "She is Maere."

My breath caught. This was either a very good thing, or possibly the worst thing that could have happened to me. My cowardice won, at least for the moment. "You can't know that. She's barely even seventeen. She can't have ascended."

He shrugged. "She hasn't." He leaned against the balustrade, his jaw clenched in a way that I now recognized was him thinking, not frustration or anger. "It resembles your aura, or Lara's or Rhiannon's, but...I just thought she was a medium..." he shook his head a little, as though he couldn't quite find the words. But I knew what he was trying to puzzle out. The Maere were supposed to be born as humans, not parapsychs.

My heart beat faster as he continued, wondering how close he might come to the truth of things. He squinted a little, thinking hard. "I couldn't see it before. Not until she was with the rest of you. It's not that the Maere signature is weaker in her. It is strong. But more like, it hasn't matured."

But it would. And then she would be locked into a life just like mine. My heart pounded in my ears. At least he hadn't gotten to the heart of things. Not yet, anyway.

"Well," I snapped. "She *is* a child."

He stared at me, those gorgeous light green eyes roving over me, like he knew what it felt like to be inside me. Technically, he did, but the way he looked at me scared me half to death. If only that were possible.

I wrapped my arms tight around my body. "Sorry. This is all just... a lot."

He nodded, seeming to wait for me to say more. A frigid wind howled over the city, but on the terrace, we were protected enough that it didn't so much as lift my hair. Still, it got colder by the moment. The sky was clear enough tonight that I could see all the way to the seawall. Lightning struck over the water, illuminating a gargantuan tail as it sank back into the ocean.

"They're getting bold," Ares breathed at the sight of the

scaled tail sinking beneath the enormous waves. "It's been ages since the Ceti came so close."

I shivered, but not because of the wind. The seas were not for us. They were for the monsters. Another web of lightning crossed the night sky, showing the raging sea, threatening as any of the Ceti. We stared at it for a long time. It was rare that the cloud cover lifted enough to see the ocean, even when it stopped raining.

Most of the time, that was well enough. No one in Orphium wanted to think of the sea. Of what lurked beyond the seawall. As one of the few who'd traversed those waters, I certainly did not. I ran my eyes over the city, watching as people went to their windows, stared at the seething masses of water and Ceti. The eldritch horrors of what lay beyond were captivating, if terrifying. It was impossible to look away.

"What does all of this mean?" I whispered, leaning on the balustrade, my arm pressing into Ares.

Though he didn't jerk away, I felt his absence acutely as he carefully sidestepped my touch. My heart sank. Whatever that was in his bedroom earlier, it was not what I'd thought it had been. It was not the start of anything between us. It was a lapse in his perfectly calculated exterior. I had never once seen Ares Necroline deviate from his mission to help his own people.

There were rumors about him, of course. About what the proclivities of Orphium's most dangerous necromancer might be—that he might enjoy the strange and unusual when it came to sex. But I'd never found evidence of anything violent. Mostly, it seemed he hurt feelings, not lovers. The man fucked, and rather often, to be honest. But he never darkened a lover's door twice.

If that held true, then he and I were done. I couldn't let that affect me. Couldn't let it show that it hurt. I hadn't been with anyone in years. Hadn't been in love in centuries. But I knew myself well enough to know that the resentment that was merely a kernel of emotion in me now would germinate and spread like an invasive vine.

This was why everyone always left me. Because the mess inside me always leaked out onto those I loved. There was no way to keep it in. No way to keep me from ruining anything good that ever happened to me.

"Maybe it doesn't mean anything at all," Ares mused from his new spot, a few feet away from me. He stared at the sea, watching the confluence of sea creatures as they feasted, just beyond the city. "Maybe it's all just a coincidence."

"Do you actually believe that?" I couldn't believe that he would ignore this. The Ceti hadn't been seen in numbers this great for centuries—not this close to the city. They were deep water creatures, and only surfaced to breed in summer, and never so close to land. He knew that as well as any child. "Or are you just being an asshole?"

Ares pushed off the balustrade, obviously annoyed. His tone was loathsome, laced with superiority. "I think it's unwise to connect too many dots at once." Here was the Ares Necroline I'd always disliked. There was something comforting about being back on opposite sides of things.

Perhaps that was why he did it. To put me back in my place. Two could play that game. I scoffed, giving him my worst glare. "And that's that, right?"

I had his hackles up, and loved every moment of it. If he wanted to be horrible, we could be horrible. He positively glowered. "What the fuck is that supposed to mean?"

I shook my head, pushing past him with the unmistakable thrill of having riled him. The feeling was nearly as delicious as his touch. And if I could not have that, this would suffice. "You're the only one who is ever allowed to be right, Necroline. Have you ever noticed that?"

It was an unfair thing to say. He didn't always have to be right. In fact, he was quite a good listener. But I wanted to hurt him, and the way he flinched at my words was enough to show me I had. Had I gone too far? That would be like me.

"Are you sure you're not talking about yourself?" he hissed as I brushed past him. "Because the only arrogant asshole I see is you."

Yes, I'd gone too far. I stopped short, my heart in my throat, then turned slowly to face him. "Is that really what you think of me, or is this all just foreplay?"

Ares took a deep breath, and I wasn't sure if he wanted to punch me or kiss me. I knew the feeling well. He was a dick and I was an insufferable bitch. We'd be perfect for one another if we weren't both emotionally constipated, immortal fools. So much the worse for both of us then.

When he failed to find a good answer, I stalked back inside. There was no reason to keep on with this nonsense. I was an ancient immortal. Perhaps it was time I grew the fuck up.

CHAPTER 21

ARES

THINGS WERE tense between Ember and I for the next week, but we fell easily into our antagonistic relationship. I hated it, but at the very least, it was familiar. We made no headway on learning more about Briony, and the girl needed rest.

Those who'd been possessed often needed months of recovery. The stronger the Rider, the more time the possessed needed. And, of course, she'd been injured. Now that we knew what she would become, it was easy to see the way her body already prepared for ascension and immortality. She healed faster than humans did, though not so much that it would be noticeable to people in her everyday life. I wondered if her stepmother had noticed—if she'd been the one to report her own child to Fairchild.

We came up with very little there as well. Whatever Fairchild's covert operations were, he'd gone deep underground. He would resurface, I had no doubt. As a result, despite the way things were developing with me and Ember, my commitment to helping the Maere deepened. We'd uncovered something dangerous about the Authority, and we would need the protection. Stealing the Maere's swords back would be complicated, but it was more important than ever.

We'd done several recon missions to the National Gallery, with Avaline on point. She was the least recognizable of the six of us, and with the power of her spirits on her side, she was able to move in near invisibility. It was little more than misdirection, but the vast wealth of talent it took to manage so many souls at once was remarkable.

The five of us waited for her return in the kitchen, Lara making breakfast, and the rest of us sitting quietly, practically ignoring one another. Briony was still sound asleep, and would not wake even if we shouted at one another. And yet, the kitchen was perfectly silent, but for the sound of bacon sizzling in the pan.

Eryx, Brontë, and I sat on rustic stools at the marble kitchen island, while Ember sat at the small bistro table placed under the only window in the kitchen, sipping her coffee. Every few minutes, I stole a glance at her. She was beautiful as ever, in a long silk robe. It was emerald green, with aubergine lining and hand-painted peonies. Her hair was messy, and there were mascara smudges under her eyes, as though she hadn't removed her makeup the night before.

To be fair, she had been up half the night watching footage of the human guards in the National Gallery. We had the basics on their movements, but Ember insisted we also do real-time surveillance to see what the outliers might be. Right now, the plan was to steal the swords before the night of the auction.

Especially as a group, we were too recognizable to attend the actual auction and expect to make it out without consequences. So we had to learn as much about the security teams the Gallery employed as we could. Ember and Brontë began trading off night watches after they'd managed, with Avaline's help, to hack into the CCTV feed. Since they needed less sleep than the rest of us, it was logical. Lara spent her evenings on watch, with Eryx and myself to cover her. We weren't becoming friends, certainly, but the six of us worked well together.

Brontë glanced at me, raising an eyebrow as she followed

my gaze. She shook her head slightly as she sipped her latte. It was obvious she would not approve of any relationship between Ember and myself, which was fine. The mistake we'd made the night we arrived was just that, a mistake. There wouldn't be another. At least, that was what I told myself about a thousand times a day.

Eryx, who watched the news on his phone in tandem with his usual newspaper, drew a sharp breath in. Brontë glanced over his shoulder to look at the screen. I watched as my brother tensed with anticipation. It was so obvious to me that he admired Rhiannon Brontë on some level I couldn't quite understand, but she didn't appear affected in the slightest.

Not that I expected her to. She was one of the coldest creatures I'd ever met in my life, rarely showing even a hint of emotion. And yet, her actions were deeply thoughtful, sublimely considerate of others, and almost altruistic. She was a bit of an enigma.

"Play it aloud," she murmured to Eryx. Her face was very close to his ear, and he flushed as she breathed on him. I did my best to stifle a laugh. My little brother was so far gone for this woman, it would be funny in any other circumstance.

"You all need to hear this," Brontë said.

Eryx dragged his finger across the screen to back the news report up, then took out his headphones, switching to the phone's speakers. A familiar news-anchor's voice played. The man had been dead for nearly thirty years, but he'd been a favorite, so the Corps had simply replicated him with AI tech. It was, to say the least, disturbing. I tried to ignore the unsettled feeling in my gut that appeared any time the dead were replicated and focus on the message.

…waves cresting at a usual forty to fifty meters may reach the height of one hundred meters before the end of the week. If conditions continue, the seawall will be breached by the increasing wave height by the end of the month.

The Senate-approved evacuations of the Center for Oceanic Vigilance have begun, and will continue remote observance of both Ceti and Krakenic movement as wave height increases. The Authority has set a restriction of movement order along the coast until such time as the waves decrease...

Brontë shook her head as Eryx shut his phone's screen off. "This hasn't happened since..."

Lara murmured, "Since I ascended."

Ember made a soft humming noise before speaking. "There was one after you, of course."

Lara shrugged. "The last of the Aradios Maere."

"Calypso Montague," Brontë murmured absently, sipping her coffee again.

Eryx frowned. Clearly, he was trying to puzzle out the significance of all this, as I was. "Are you suggesting that more Maere are ascending?"

Ember sighed. "They're not *suggesting* anything."

I turned quickly in my seat. Her tone was serious, not mocking. "Do you mean to tell me that there are *more* Maere somewhere?"

Rhiannon Brontë looked as though she might explode with frustration. "Have you never wondered why there are so few of us, and so many of..." she gestured elegantly at Eryx and myself. "*You.*"

My heart beat faster. This wasn't something I'd ever considered. There were only three known territories on Kraitos, the three cities—Orphium, Aradios, and Palladiere. It was a little odd that out of millions of people, only fifteen were ever Maere, or ever had been Maere.

Parapsychs had always existed in the margins of history, and yet, these fifteen were the only Maere we'd ever actually known. There were historical accounts of others, of course, of ancient predecessors, but that did not make much sense, when I really thought about it, since the Maere could not die.

Where had they all gone?

Ember's laugh as she set down her mug on the stone bistro

table was irreverent, dry. "Ah, you're puzzling it out, aren't you?"

Lara rolled her eyes. "No one ever gives it much thought."

Rhiannon pursed her full lips. "Don't be so hard on them. They've been conditioned not to ask where our forebears skittered off to." Though her tone was even, her words were sharp.

"So where are they?" I asked. "If there are others, where are they?" Both Rhiannon and Lara's faces were carefully neutral. I turned to Ember. "Well?"

She shrugged, suddenly casual. "Who knows?"

Briony appeared in the doorway to the kitchen, her eyes glassy, as though she still slept. "There is an island. A land of hope."

The kitchen went so silent I could hear the electricity running through the veins of the building. My heartbeat turned erratic, only for a moment, before correcting course.

Ember got up from her chair to place her arms on the girl's shoulders. "Yes, love. That is what the lore tells us."

I might not know much about the Maere's origins, but I knew an obvious lie when I heard one.

Briony blinked a few times, her eyes clearing. "Was I sleep-walking?"

"Not exactly," Ember said, in a tone so soothing it surprised me. The hard edges of her personality were gone.

On instinct, I glanced back at Lara Achilles. There was a soft look in her eyes that was mirrored in Rhiannon's. Ember had been the first of them. She was the eldest, and if I understood timelines correctly, had been alone for what probably felt like a long while when she first ascended. They all had nearly a thousand years on me, and usually, with such long lives, these differences didn't matter so much. After long enough, any age over a few hundred years just felt similar.

But now, given what we'd just discussed, I wondered what it had been like for Ember to be alone. To be without people like her. She'd grown up as a human, believing she would have a human life, and then one day, she ascended outside of the Aradios and Palladiere territories, where there were other Maere establishing their cohorts. She had been alone, hadn't she?

"Were there Maere here when you ascended?" I asked. The question was impulsive, rather unlike me, but curiosity took over. "In Orphium?"

Ember glared at me. "This is not the time."

Rhiannon's attention flicked to Ember. The change in her countenance was small, but significant, as I'd come to expect very little variation in her outward emotional state. *She was worried for her.*

Briony frowned up at Ember. "Are you trying to hide something from me?"

Ember sighed. "No. We just…"

"Don't talk about these things in front of civilians," Lara finished for her—she too looked towards Ember with concern. Or some other emotion I couldn't quite understand. The sense that the Maere were having some sort of interaction with one another outside what I could perceive strengthened.

Eryx snorted, breaking my train of thought. "*We* aren't exactly civilians."

I held my hand out to Eryx, stopping him from speaking further. The three Maere had changed in the span of a breath. He was far too comfortable here, but I saw the shift. The way Lara Achilles set down her spatula and ignored the bacon burning. Rhiannon Brontë might look collected, but somehow she stood between us and Briony, while Ember shifted into a defensive stance.

They were ready for us to attack them. Whatever secrets they protected, not even our loose alliance here afforded us safety. Though only a moment had passed, it felt like an eternity. Eryx finally noticed what I did.

Slowly, he set his phone down and raised his palms. "I apologize for whatever offense I've caused," he said, his deep voice soft. He turned to Rhiannon, speaking to her directly. "This is not something we have to discuss. I promise, I won't press further."

She nodded once to him, and once to Ember, who glanced back at her, seeming to need Rhiannon's confirmation before she could back down. For her part, Briony's eyes contained a fierce light that I hadn't noticed before. The Maere had told her what I'd sensed within her right away, and had been monitoring her closely. It was clear the girl felt more aligned with them than with us.

Briony had mentioned an island. I tucked that away for later. It would be too noticeable if I whipped out my notebook and started writing in it.

The scrape of Lara's metal spatula broke the tension. "The bacon is fucked."

Rhiannon picked up the wired house phone. "I'll call down to Delicia's for pastries."

Only Ember did not return to her relaxed state. Instead, she perched uncomfortably in her chair, watching closely as Rhiannon made Briony tea. I wasn't sure exactly what had just happened, but we'd tread too close to some essential secret of the Maere. My senses were heightened from the near miss we'd had with a true confrontation, and I heard the soft noise of the front door opening. Av had returned.

I called down the back hallway to her. "We're in the kitchen."

She smiled at all of us as she entered, all sunshine and ferocity. Briony grinned at her. The teenage girl could see all of Av's spirits as well as any medium could, and she especially liked Stanley, who was playing the part of a giant alley cat today, a black tom with a notch carved out of his right ear and a missing left eye. He rubbed against the girl's ankle as he raced past Av, purring loudly.

Briony reached down to pet the Poltergeist, and I nearly warned her that he was about to do something disgusting, but the spirit cat simply accepted ear scritches. My brow furrowed as I watched the two of them together.

Av slapped my arm. "I told you Stanley was a good boy."

My fear that the Poltergeist would do something horrendous wasn't going to die down so easily. The thing had been with us for years and it never failed to do something awful eventually, though I'd seen it use its cat form most frequently when alone with Av. Perhaps Stanley was only cute with people he liked.

At least I knew where I stood.

CHAPTER 22

EMBER

THOUGH I SENSED THE POLTERGEIST, I could not see it clearly. But I heard its purrs, and Briony smiled as she pet the spirit. The confrontation with the Necrolines had been tense. I was glad Avaline was back. Her personality was a delightful mix of cheer and lethal acuity, and it tempered the brothers somewhat. I liked the way she smoothed things over.

Eryx got up, leaving his seat for Avaline. "I have to get to the gym today, or our people will suspect something's up."

"Can I come?" Lara asked.

Eryx shrugged. "Sure. Ready in five?"

They left the kitchen. Ares settled back into his seat and Rhiannon left to pick up the pastries. We were left with Briony and Avaline, who stared longingly at Eryx's empty latte mug. I smiled at the girl. Avaline was only forty, barely out of her teenage years by immortal standards.

Avaline watched for a moment as I made it clear I was going to make her a latte of her own, then launched into what she'd learned over her past few days of surveillance. "The spirits told me something odd about the guardians in the traps…" she began, her delicate brow wrinkling as she looked at Briony.

I turned from measuring out beans to look over my shoulder. "They say they are Maere who didn't ascend."

Briony's jaw tightened, but she did not flinch. The girl was stronger than I thought. Ares had argued against telling her the truth of things, but the three of us had vehemently disagreed. To be one of us and not break meant developing a very thick skin early on.

The way Rhi, Lara, and I saw it, the girl had a head start on things. She had years to understand the way things would be when she ascended—and she had us. She wasn't alone with the heightened senses and lightning fast healing, the dreams of the island, the strange occurrences that grew increasingly difficult to explain.

Briony would know who she was, and why those things happened to her. And she would be freer for it. Those dead girls hadn't had the same luck, and very likely, that's what got them killed.

Avaline breathed a sigh of relief. "So you know then."

I nodded. "Yes. I am sorry we didn't tell you."

Avaline grinned. "Actually, I'm glad you didn't. If I'd known, I would have gone in differently, and I think I may have learned more this way."

She waited while I finished making her drink. Rhiannon returned from Delicia's with pastries, and Ares made a pot of tea. When we were settled once more, and Briony munched happily on a croissant nearly the size of her head, Avaline continued.

"So, I have good news and bad news. The good news is that the guardians are not helping willingly. If we can disable the spirit traps, we'll be able to take the swords without a problem. In fact, I think they'll help us."

Rhiannon nodded. "Were you able to speak with them?"

Avaline shook her head. "No, the traps don't allow for that, but the other spirits can hear their thoughts, and enough of them told me similar things that I believe this to be true."

Ares glanced at me. "Spirits have a difficult time lying to Avaline. Most of the time, they simply don't want to. They like her. But the ones who don't… they still struggle to manage it."

The young medium nodded. "That's true. It's because *I* can trap them."

"What?" I breathed.

Ares' mouth quirked up at the corner as Avaline answered. "Oh, I am a living spirit trap. That's why they're so attracted to me. Why they do what I say. It's not just my sparkling personality."

"That's incredible," Rhi said, her eyes shining with admiration.

"It sounds sad to me," Briony added between mouthfuls of croissant.

Avaline smiled at them both. "It is. I never know if they like me for me, or because of what I am."

Briony glanced down at Stanley, seeming to listen for a long moment. "He genuinely likes you."

Avaline's smile widened, tears pricking the corners of her eyes. "That is very nice to know. Thank you, Briony." She didn't ask how Briony knew—she simply trusted the child. Avaline Reyes was singular. A ray of sunshine in a raincloud's package. I understood why Ares liked her so much.

"So," I said, breaking the syrupy sweetness of the moment. "It sounds like we'll need to find a way to disable the spirit traps."

Avaline nodded. "Trouble is doing it without hurting the girls."

Ares drew a sharp breath in. "Destroying a spirit trap annihilates the souls."

That was always the problem with spirit traps, and precisely why whoever was baiting us had done this. They knew we wouldn't just pull a smash and grab. They knew full well that we could pull off the heist with raw strength and speed, but that to do it we'd have to eradicate our sistren from not only the planet, but existence. That we'd be forced to destroy their souls—and that we wouldn't.

Whoever was behind all this knew about the island. Knew the truth of our origins. It was a disturbing thought. There hadn't been an unaffiliated Maere in the territories for eons. A vague suspicion grew in my mind, stress chewing at my stomach. I'd avoided making contact for so long… but it might be time.

"We'll have to find a way to disable the spirit traps," I said slowly.

Ares nodded, standing. "I have a contact who may be able to help us."

Rhiannon smiled, serene as always. "As do I. Will you be all right without me?"

I nodded. Hex boxes, spirit traps, the Ceti, and Fairchild's weird mission, all coming out of the woodwork at the same time that our swords went up for auction… I had things I wanted to look into without all of them around, and Avaline had been up all night. She would need sleep soon. Briony, for her part, looked exhausted from her short time up.

"Do you want to get back in bed?" I asked the child as Avaline yawned.

She nodded. "Would Stanley come with me?"

Avaline smiled at her. "If you ask him kindly, I think he would."

Briony slid off her stool and crouched on the ground, whispering to the ghost cat. She smiled. "He says he will come with me."

Avaline held out a hand to her and the three of them left the kitchen, Ares following close behind.

Rhiannon's eyes locked on mine. "Be careful poking around."

I nodded. So we were on the same wavelength. It was time to make the call I'd been dreading. I wondered if she knew more than she was saying from her time at the Consulate. "Anything I should watch out for?"

Slowly, she shook her head. "Nothing we haven't watched out for a thousand times. If all this is connected to the island, all bets are off."

As she left the kitchen, the vise around my heart tightened. *All bets are off.* That's exactly what I was afraid of.

W hen everyone had gotten off to where they needed to be, I went to my bedroom and shut the door, curling up in the back of my closet on the floor. I took several deep breaths before sliding open the panel behind my evening-wear.

There was no getting around this. I chided myself with the fact that I should've done this the second I saw the spirit traps, and if not then, when I realized what Briony was. At this point, it wasn't wise to proceed on our own. The Authority had gone too far, though of course, it could be the Consulate. Or even some new threat.

The point was that there were too many possibilities to keep this to ourselves any longer. I dialed the number I'd had memorized for nearly fifty years, my breath stalling in my throat as the phone rang and rang. When it had rung more times than I could count, I sighed, about to give up.

"Hello?" a voice said at the other end of the line, sounding tinny and faraway.

I gave my identifying data, though of course, the island knew exactly where the call was coming from. When the answering voice gave me the go ahead, my voice went weak.

"We have a problem," I whispered.

"You're not supposed to call this number unless it is an

emergency," the faraway voice replied. "It is not time for your check-in."

"This is an emergency," I replied, my heart racing. "Or at least it's going to turn into one if someone doesn't do something quickly... And there's a child involved... One of the unascended. I thought she'd want to know."

There was a long silence. So long I thought I might have lost them.

"Hold, please. I'll transfer you to the top."

CHAPTER 23

ARES

RHIANNON and I rode the elevator down together. She didn't seem inclined to chat, and neither was I. When we reached the lobby, she walked beside me, matching my strides exactly. As I hailed a cab, she waited next to me.

"I'm going downtown," she murmured.

I nodded. "As am I."

"I am going to the Library of Amarante," she said.

That piqued my interest. The Library of Amarante was a private institution. "Do you have a card?"

She smiled. "I do. And I am able to bring one guest per visit. Would you like to come with me?"

My heart slowed. Rhiannon's question was so mundane, nearly friendly. But the woman did nothing by chance, nothing without meaning. I'd known her peripherally for years, and that was enough to make such an assumption, but one week in an apartment together and I knew now, without a doubt, that she was the other side to Ember's coin.

Both were vastly intelligent, strategic even. While Ember operated on instinct, and a good heap of chaos, Rhiannon Brontë was sheer calculation. They made a good team. I did have a contact or two I wanted to speak to, but I could send Av later. She'd get more out of them than I would, anyway. I was mostly getting out of the house to escape the tension between Ember and myself.

"I'd love to come along." I had the sneaking suspicion I'd learn more with Rhiannon than going my own way.

The cab pulled up, Rhiannon gave the address for the library, and we rode across town in perfect silence. Far from being uncomfortable, the two of us seemed relieved to be out of the crowded flat at the Carlyle. She stared out the window, watching rain drip down the window in the gray-blue light of the morning. I didn't need to watch the world go by, so I caught up on email.

T he Library of Amarante was silent, smelling of books and cold stone. Everything in this place was clean, bright marble and highly polished crystal chandeliers. Giant statues of the Saints towered over us in the lobby. Rhiannon signed in, then motioned silently for me to follow her up an enormous spiral staircase.

We climbed six stories. On the sixth floor, Rhiannon motioned for me to follow her into a honeycomb of passages, making a sharp left turn down a narrow hallway. The walls here were close, but the brightly painted white wood panels and embedded shell-shaped sconces made things feel less claustrophobic. Each door had a brass figurine affixed to the front, like a door knocker.

Rhiannon stopped in front of a door with a swan. But not the usual placid creature depicted in so much art, its curved neck making an elegant S. This swan faced us, beak open in a scream, wings raised in aggression. It was, to be frank, a bit disturbing, but it fit Rhiannon Brontë perfectly.

She gestured to the door. "After you." I tried the crystal

knob, and though it turned, I could not open it. I frowned, but Rhiannon smiled. "Watch."

She pressed her hand to the door, just under the angry swan. The door knob turned, and the door swung on silent hinges. This area of the library was so quiet my ears rang with the rush of blood in my veins. Far from being calm, this place vibrated with alien energy.

"Would it have opened for me?" I asked as I followed Rhiannon into what appeared to be an empty room, but for a marble plinth at its center, risen out of the floor itself. The entire room appeared to be constructed from the same piece of stone, almost as if it had been hollowed out from an enormous rock.

She shook her head. "No, none but myself may enter here." Then she smiled. "My guests, of course, are also welcome. Please place your hand on the plinth."

My heart beat faster at her request. Was this some sort of trick? I suddenly realized how very alone I was with an immortal capable of ending my life in mere seconds. I wouldn't even have time to scream at Rhiannon Brontë's hands.

"I don't want to hurt you, Ares Necroline," Rhiannon said. "I will show the truth of who you are. Who we all are. It is a gift. A sacred gift—a burden, really—but a gift all the same."

"All right," I agreed, placing my hand on the plinth.

"If you tell anyone what you saw here, you will forget it instantly. The same will happen should the person you tell attempt to speak of what they learned."

My eyebrows raised, as I thought through the logic. "Would that happen to you if you tried to tell someone?"

She nodded. "Yes, the only way to know this is to be shown. The only way to retain the knowledge is to keep it secret."

That sounded like magic to me. The Authority had taken so many pains to paint parapsychism as preternatural prowess. As an abomination of humanity, rather than magic. Magic, according to the Authority, did not exist. But what Rhiannon spoke of was a spell. Something that not even a Thaumas could manage.

My curiosity was far, far too piqued. "All right," I said. "I want to know."

She stood directly across from me, placing her hand on the plinth, next to mine, but facing the opposite direction. "Close your eyes."

I did as she asked, and though nothing in the room moved or changed, as far as I could tell, now there was noise: The sound of crashing waves and seabirds crying far above.

"You can open them now," Rhiannon said.

When I did, I found myself somewhere else entirely, high above the raging sea, at the edge of a rocky cliff. I gasped, stepping backwards, right into Rhiannon. "Careful," she cautioned. "This is real. You can be hurt here, just as in the open world."

"*The open world?*" I stammered, still staring out at the sea. "Where am I now?"

"Oh, still on Kraitos, you haven't traveled so far as that." Rhiannon smiled as she slipped out of her high heels. "And though you can be hurt here, we are not *exactly* here."

She turned away from the cliff, beckoning me to follow her as she picked her way through lush, tall grass that undulated in the wind. We stood at the bottom of an enormous forested hillside. Everywhere I turned, there were spirits. But they were like none in Orphium. They fit none of the usual classifications. These spirits were at rest, in harmony with the land, blinking in and out, obviously curious about me, but barely taking note of Rhiannon.

And what was more, here I felt that same sensation as in the library. The vibration of some alien power. Only here it felt less strange. In fact, it spun out in concert with the whisper of the wind through the trees. Was this what magic felt like?

My heart felt as though it might swell out of my chest when a flight of herons swept across the field, upward towards some unknown location. Tears slid down my cheeks, though I could not fathom why—why this place felt like home.

Rhiannon turned to me, a wistful smile on her ethereal face. "I am sorry, Ares. That feeling you have now? You will carry it with you all your life. Homesickness for a place you may never come to, a world we are not meant for."

"Where are we?" I asked, desperate to know why I felt this way.

"Otrera," Rhiannon said, as though I might glean some essential knowledge from the name.

It *was* familiar. There was lore about this, wasn't there? "Otrera was the first of the Maere?"

Rhiannon nodded. "Yes. She was Amarante and Tanith's child."

I sensed she might say something else, that she had something to add about Otrera, but she stayed silent, so I asked the first of many questions that came up. "The Saints?"

"The gods," Rhiannon replied, sinking down into the grass, wrapping her arms around her legs as an enormous reptile crept shyly out of the trees far above us. It had scales, as well as a silky green ruff around its neck. It took a few delicate bites of a treetop, then paused to look at us. Rhiannon raised her hand to it, bowing her head as she slapped my thigh.

I mimicked her motions, and when I raised my head again, the creature was gone. "What is this place?"

Rhiannon sighed, though it was something between a deep breath and a powerful exhalation. "This is where all parapsych power originates from. It is the heart of our planet, the one place the Corps and the Authority cannot touch."

"What about the Consulate?" I asked, though I thought I already knew the answer.

"Nor them," Rhiannon said, her wistful expression turning sour. "The Consulate has done their best, but they are a corrupt organization. You know this. And they can never know this place exists."

"What does it all mean?" I asked. "I mean, why am I here?"

Rhiannon shrugged. "You've been trying to sort out your place in things all your life, right?"

I nodded. She'd cut to the quick of me so easily.

"This is it," she murmured, gesturing around her. "*This* is our place. *This* is our origin."

"But what does it *mean*?" I asked again.

Rhiannon sighed. "It would be easier to show you. Are you up for a walk?"

❧

We walked up the hillside, along a stone path, passing the place where the giant reptile had appeared. Everywhere there was birdsong and the sound of the sea. As wind flowed through the trees, a symphony of natural noise filled my ears. There were no cars here, no factories.

The smell of green things and fresh water filled my nose. Tears pricked endlessly in my eyes, emotion filling me to the brim with a bittersweet longing that had, perhaps, lived inside me all my long life. The trees here were so large it would be impossible to wrap my arms around them.

In all my life, I had never seen such a place. When we crested the hilltop, we found a clearing that looked out onto a small range of mountains. Dotting the terraced hills and valleys were the types of structures I had been taught to believe were built by humans in the ancient world. But now I saw that those humans had only been copying this place, whatever this was.

"Sit," Rhiannon said, gesturing to a large outcropping of huge black boulders. She climbed them effortlessly, though I struggled a bit.

When I found a place next to her, she smiled, pointing to a cluster of columned buildings in the distance. "Those are

Amarante's temples." Her arm moved, sweeping over the valley to the opposite side. "And those are Tanith's."

My eyes followed as she explained where the rest of the Saints' temples were, but again, she spoke of them as gods. There had always been those among us who posited that the Authority had turned our gods into Saints to drain them of their power. But here, in this place of magic, it was obvious to me that we had been right. It was not a tall tale, but the truth.

One temple was no longer intact. It appeared to have been burned. "What about that one?"

Rhiannon followed my gaze. "That is Chiore's temple." She paused, waiting to see if I knew my lore. I did, of course. In *The Saints Tales*, Chiore had stood against Amarante, Tanith, and the others, and spoken up for the humans. I nodded, to show I recognized the name. "Long ago, when the island closed, Chiore's temple was destroyed."

"Why?" I asked.

The question was casual, but Rhiannon nearly flinched to hear it. For a moment, her ultra-calm mask fell, and I saw fear behind her eyes. The moment passed quickly, the mercurial immortal's face going smooth as glass.

"I don't know, to be honest," she said. Rhiannon lied, but I understood why. Some secrets were simply too dangerous to tell, and whatever the true story behind Chiore's betrayal of the rest of the gods was, it might very well be dangerous. Perhaps it was better I didn't know. "By that time, I'd already been sent to the wider world. I was being reborn as a human."

My heart raced. So the Maere were reincarnated somehow. They'd lived other lives before the ones we knew. Bells rang in the distance, and people flooded out of the temples. They looked tiny from here, wearing a style of dress that had been ancient when I was a child.

"Has time stood still here?" I asked, in awe.

Rhiannon smiled, watching her people. "In some ways, yes."

"Who are you, Rhiannon?" I gestured to the temples, the people in the distance. "In all this, who are you?"

Her smile faded. "If I had stayed, I would be their queen someday."

"And Ember?" I asked, shifting my position on the rock.

"Eventually, their General, or Admiral. The Maere are a bit of a mix between warriors, mages, and scholars. She wasn't meant for academic life. Ember has always been a fighter." That much I could believe. "Though, of course, there's been nothing much to fight here since my mother drew the mists down and hid Otrera from the world."

I nodded, but I was still full of questions. She said this was all our origin, but what did that mean? "What are we?"

Again, she smiled. "That is a good question." She took a long breath. "We, the Maere I mean, are demigods. We are the direct descendants of the Saints and what were once the magical people of this world."

I nodded. That explained their rather sturdier bodies, and the things Maere could do when in possession of their swords. "And parapsychs?"

Rhiannon looked at me. "Distant children of the gods' couplings with early humanity. We are your protectors, but really, we're not so different from you. Just more… eternal."

I laughed, though I wasn't sure why. The whole thing both made all the sense in the world, and felt completely unreal. "Why did you bring me here?"

Her long arm extended, pointing to the scene before us. In the distance, I made out people bustling between temples in each of the various complexes. "Because Ember never would have brought you here. She is too respectful of our rules. And you need to know who she is, and the burden she carries."

I frowned, and started to open my mouth, but Rhiannon shook her head, interrupting me before I could say another word. "I see the way you look at her. The way she looks at you.

She needs you, Ares. But she needs the version of you who knows this place exists."

Again, I frowned. I wasn't sure exactly what she meant. Of course, I understood the part about me and Ember... Apparently, we were not as covert as we thought ourselves to be. "What do you mean by that?"

Rhiannon sighed. "Ember thinks that she shouldn't have been made leader. Since the swords were stolen, she's blamed herself for all that's gone wrong. And when we all left her, she deteriorated significantly. Surely you've noticed."

Now that she mentioned it, I had. There was a time, years ago, that Ember had been different. More vibrant somehow. But the past twenty years had changed her. She was a shadow of who she had been. So much sadness weighed her down now. And so much loneliness. I nodded.

"She needs you to know that she is the child of gods. That she is magic and stardust, and the most legendary warrior this island ever knew, though she'd likely call herself a soldier if you asked her."

The surprise I felt must have shown on my face. Rhiannon laughed. "You thought it was Lara? Or maybe the Palladiere Maere?"

If I was honest, I'd never given it much thought, but now that she asked, yes, those would have been my assumptions. I shrugged. For most of my life, the Orphium Maere had been without their swords. It was hard to imagine them any other way.

"She was grace embodied as a child," Rhiannon breathed. "Pure kinetic energy. No one was faster, no one better in a fight than her. She was Amarante and Tanith combined. She even looks like Tanith. Did you know that?"

I swallowed. I hadn't even imagined that the Saints had real bodies or faces. I shook my head.

Rhiannon grinned. "I wish we had time to go to the temples, and I could show you. They are too far, though, and we should get you back. Being here for too long would be bad for you."

I looked behind me, back to the path. The enormous reptile from before had returned and munched on the treetops. It turned opalescent eyes my way. *Hello, little necromancer*, a voice said in my head.

"Did… it just speak to me?" I whispered.

"She," Rhiannon prompted. "She just spoke to you."

"Hello," I murmured, unable to find my full voice, or more words. The creature was so large. So large and magnificent.

"Do we have to leave?" I asked.

"Yes," Rhiannon said, her eyes darkening. "Pull your hand off the plinth, Ares. It's time."

I wasn't sure how to do that.

"Think hard," she said, an edge in her voice I didn't like. "Remember the library."

I tried, but could not. *And wouldn't it be easier to stay here?*

"Ares," Rhiannon hissed. "Ember needs you. Pull your hand off the plinth."

CHAPTER 24

EMBER

CALLING the island had been a mistake. I'd known it the moment I dialed, and yet, I let the phone ring and ring. Maybe it was the homesickness that would never abate, or the feeling that I needed someone on my side, someone to tell me definitively what to do in this situation.

Myrine had not been happy to hear my voice. That much was clear with her sharp hello, and the way she'd launched into the middle of our situation, rather than asking what I was calling for. I'd curled in on myself like a small child, hiding in Amarante's temple, rather than the grown woman I was.

"She brought the Necroline boy here," the ancient voice on the other end of a very secure line said.

Why didn't that surprise me? Rhiannon had always done as she pleased, consequences for me be damned. Did she even *think* about how I might be affected by such a choice? I let out my held breath as quietly as I could so it wouldn't sound like petulance. "Of course she did."

Apparently, my attempt at stifling my irritation had been useless. It slipped out in my words instead. I went ahead and sighed. Why not, at this point?

My superior took a long pause, the years and history

between us spiraling out into a web of potential responses... All of which I already resented. This was simply what was asked of those devoted to the Temple, and I had pledged my immortality to the Maere. There was no use in saying it wasn't fair, but it wasn't.

Finally, Myrine spoke, her voice calm as ever. Never was she outwardly bothered or disappointed in me, and yet, I knew I worried her. "You cannot blame her, Ember. She is trying to help you. She has only ever been trying to help."

I fiddled with the sequins on a gown I'd worn to a ball seventy years ago, resting my head against the wall of my closet. There was no use in arguing with Myrine. "I am fucking all of this up."

"My child." Myrine's voice was smooth and comforting. This was the true reason I called. I'd wanted to hear her voice. To talk to the one person in the world who knew the whole of me, who'd known me all my lives, and who loved me still. Myrine was more than a friend, more than a parent. She was my lifeline and mentor. The blueprint for all I wanted to be. So, when she spoke, I tried to let her words sink into me. "That is part of things. Amarante gave you different gifts than she did Rhiannon. Do not fight your nature."

I understood full well that the goddess had given us all different gifts. It was so hard to trust myself and mine, when it felt like everything I tried backfired on me. I closed my eyes, throwing my head a little too hard against the closet wall. Everything felt too small, too constrained. I knew better than to ask to come home. But I needed help.

"The swords, though..." I faltered. "How am I supposed to fix things without them?"

Myrine hummed a little, as though thinking about her next words carefully. Slow, steady Myrine. This was helpful, even if not directly so. "The swords are important, but they are not all. Balance, child. Balance."

Her expectation was that I would figure these things out on

my own. That we would figure them out as a team. The trouble was that my sistren had left me high and dry. They lied, they went behind my back, they were disloyal. And according to Myrine, I was capable of handling all that on my own.

"Stop grinding your teeth, beloved. Get to work." The Admiral's trust in me was comforting, and utterly unhelpful at the same time.

"How am I supposed to do that without all of them?" I growled. "Without more help?"

Myrine was silent for a long time. "Ember, we sent you to Orphium for a reason. We sent your sistren with you for a reason. Are you questioning the Temple's vision?"

I swallowed hard. In all my long life, since I ascended and remembered the truth about where I came from and what my purpose was, I had not questioned it. I'd believed, as all Maere did, that it was our calling to be here. To protect the gods' children. To find a way forward for the last splinters of magic in this dangerous world.

But more and more, it felt like a losing battle. That humanity would never accept us. But then, that was not the mission. The mission was to protect. To help mitigate the harm that the Consulate might do as an entity that had very little choice but to corrupt itself, to make unsavory deals to inch progress forward, little by little.

"No," I answered. "But I am worried about the way things are coming together here. I could use some guidance."

I'd already explained, in painful detail, about the swords, all that had happened with Lara and Rhi, the situation with Briony, Fairchild's actions, and the Ceti. She'd been remarkably quiet throughout the whole thing. Her mentorship had always been based on her mentees thinking for themselves. She'd rarely had patience for too many questions, preferring that we find things out on our own.

But I'd called for real help and I was determined to get it. "Is the one Rhiannon and Lara know as 'Mother' one of us?"

To my surprise, Myrine answered immediately. "No. We haven't sent another since Calypso. She was the last of you."

"Are you sure?" I asked, something stirring in my gut. It didn't make sense.

It was Myrine's turn to sigh. She was quiet, but that didn't worry me. Myrine had seen me through eons and lifetimes. When she took the time to consider a question, it wasn't hedging. It was because it took time to sift through thousands of years of information. I could be patient.

"There was a group who left the island before the mists drew closed. Do you remember?"

When the Temple had finally seen that humanity was unable to accept us, the island had taken in as many parapsychs as wanted to stay safe, as wanted to stay cloistered for all eternity. Some had chosen to leave. For the most part, the Maere had stayed, though in those days we were priestesses. Our vows to the Temple were clear. We did as the gods asked. We did as the Temple decreed.

But a handful had, and rightly so, argued that their vows had not included reincarnating into the dangerous world we left behind, risking our immortality to be human for twenty-eight years. They saw it as a breach of contract, a violation of trust— a coercion. I had not seen it as such at the time. I was young then, and the group that made such arguments was older. I had not thought of them in an eternity.

"I remember the ones who left," I answered. "How many were there?"

"But a few," Myrine answered, vague in that way that told me this information was above my pay-grade. Not that I was being paid by the island, in any way, shape, or form. "Have you ever come in contact with them?"

"No," I replied. "But that doesn't mean much. As I remember it, they were not allowed to take their swords."

Myrine laughed. "As though being swordless has slowed you down."

She had no idea what it was like here. What it was like to be cut off from the full range of my power. From the gifts that now, only those on the island could use without a sword as a conduit to the Temple's power. There was no use in arguing, no use in explanation.

So I stayed silent. But Myrine would have the last word. "This was *not* an emergency."

I nearly sputtered with frustration. This wasn't an emergency? Our swords were held by an unknown foe, we were being baited into getting them back, my cohort refused to fully assemble—and some unknown entity had been interfering in our mission here for years. What *was* an emergency then?

Bitterness seeped through me like poison. My words were petty, sharp as the sword I simply didn't have. "Is *she* going to get in trouble for visiting?"

It was forbidden for us to use our doors unless severely injured. Even Sera had not used hers when she'd been burned beyond recognition. But Rhiannon waltzed through with a guest. Myrine did not respond to that, of course.

My temper boiled over. "Fucking princess gets her way every time without so much as a scolding."

"Princess or not, *you* are her superior officer." Myrine's voice was low and deadly. If I were at home, she'd take me to the mat and work me til I regretted my insubordination. "Perhaps *you* should give her a scolding."

Myrine was about to hang up. I'd let my temper get the better of me, but I still needed her help. "Wait," I breathed. "Wait."

Myrine did not answer, but nor did the line go dead.

"What about the spirit traps? Do you know of a good way to disable them without destroying the Maere's souls?"

Myrine sighed. "You have use of the Necroline boy, I assume?"

"Yes," I agreed. It was a bit funny to hear her call Ares a "boy," but of course, we were all children to the Admiral.

"Tell him to use one of your auras as a lens to amplify his power. If he does, it should help him calibrate his natural talent to the auric energy of the unascended. It will loosen the hold the traps have enough for them to escape. He will need time, though. Time to get it right."

Relief flooded me, making me bold. "Thank you. Just one more thing…" Myrine didn't jump in to stop me, so I continued, "Let Sera use her door. Let Max go with her. We need them at their best."

"Fine," Myrine assented immediately. My head spun with the ease of the past few moments. *Should I have called sooner?* "Do not call again."

The line went dead, and I had two choices. Either let my feelings be hurt by the Admiral's brusqueness, or laugh. I chose laughter. The whole thing was so utterly ridiculous. My life felt like a parody of what it was supposed to be. Still snickering, I crawled out of my closet to find my phone. It was on the floor next to my bedside table.

First, I sent a text to both Max and Sera, telling them I was going to call them. Telling them it was important. I dialed Sera first, but there was no answer. Then Max. The same, but this time, the phone only rang twice. They were there. They were screening me out.

"Fuck," I swore at my phone. I so desperately wanted to tell them this in real time, to hear the gratitude in their voices when they thanked me. It was selfish, and I knew it.

I licked my lips, staring at the ceiling. I had my selfishness and pride, but I loved Sera more than just about any person on this godsforsaken planet. My phone was heavy in my hands as I sent the next text.

Sera is approved to use her door. Take her home for healing.

I waited, heart in my throat. The seconds ticked by so slowly. One hot tear fell on my cheek, then another. When my phone vibrated with an answer, it was Max, not Sera. My hand clapped over my mouth to quiet my sobs.

Took you long enough to ask them. Don't think about using this as leverage for anything. We're not coming back.

I shook with anger, but also sadness. I couldn't deny that I'd made mistakes. Too many to count. I'd never wanted to be my cohort's leader, and when the plan to send the Maere into the open world was conceived, I believed Rhiannon would be chosen.

She was a princess, after all, and I was a mere soldier. But her mother had not seen fit for her to lead. Silea had always been concerned with nepotism, forcing her children to earn their way, no matter how hard that was for them.

I wrapped my arms around my knees, hugging them to my chest, and sobbed. Years of resentment seeped out in my tears. I had to let it go. Accept what was, not what I wished things could be. My body rocked back and forth, soothing the harsh edges of my mind.

There was no way out of destiny. Only through. I would get our swords back, and then, when Sera was well, I would get her and Max back, too. Amarante had deemed me the leader of my cohort, and I could no longer choose against the goddess herself.

Relief flooded my body as I accepted my place in this. My eyelids drooped and my limbs were heavy as I pulled myself off the floor and into bed. My phone buzzed with some alarm, but all I wanted to do was close my eyes, just for a few moments.

CHAPTER 25

ARES

MY PALM BURNED, agonizing in its intensity. It was as though the plinth meant to devour me whole. I was back in the library, in the little room. But I was alone this time. Rhiannon was not here, and my hand was stuck to the plinth. I tried to yank it away, but it would not come. Somewhere within the library, there was a noise—an alarm of some kind—but it sounded very far away.

The burning sensation in my palm intensified, and the horrific smell of burning flesh filled the room. I pulled harder, but my hand was stuck tight. "Fuck," I snarled, trying again. *Where was Rhiannon?*

The door burst open, cracking down the center. On the other side stood Ember Verona, dressed in a three piece, emerald green velvet suit, carrying a godsdamn labrys. With one lovely, lethal motion, she embedded one side of the axe's double-headed blade into the door, right underneath the swan.

"Stay calm," she cautioned.

I nodded as she approached.

"You're not calm," she whispered as her hands closed around mine. "Be calm, Ares. I am here to help."

I looked down into her hazel eyes. There was no emotion

but pure confidence in them. I saw what Rhiannon had revealed to me now, a warrior through and through. I was panicking, if just a little. She took an exaggerated deep breath, ducking beneath my outstretched arms and between them, sliding her slender body between the plinth and my chest, wrapping her arms around my neck.

"Be calm," she breathed, pressing her long fingers to my chest.

She wasn't wearing a blouse underneath her waistcoat. I swallowed hard, forgetting for a moment about the fact that my hands were searing with pain as she pressed her body to mine. Her head tipped up, her eyes hooded with either desire or fear, I could not tell, but as her lips parted, she raised up on her tiptoes. "If you can't breathe deeply on your own, maybe it would help if we shared breath."

I lowered my head to hers, the pain of my hands all but forgotten as her mouth met mine. We shared breath for one long inhalation, followed by an exhalation before her tongue slid past mine, her arms tightening around my neck as her long body pressed against me.

A soft whimper passed from her mouth into mine as I deepened the kiss, every throbbing beat of my heart sending unbearably lovely heat through my body, mixing with the pain in my hands as the plinth consumed them. I wanted nothing more than to touch her, to run my hands over her body.

And then they were free.

She smiled against my mouth as I tentatively pressed my palms into her back. They did not sting as though they were burned. They didn't even hurt. I didn't know what to make of the moment, but Ember seemed pleased as she pulled away from me. I glanced over her shoulder at my palms. They showed no evidence of having been injured, but I had no doubt of the danger I'd been in. Rhiannon appeared behind us, skin pale, eyes haunted.

"Wonderful," she muttered. "You're making out."

"Hi, Rhi," Ember said as she stepped away from me. Her movement was casual. It wasn't a jump away, trying to hide what we'd been doing. In fact, she still stood so close to me that if she leaned back, even slightly, her back would press into my chest.

Visions of wrapping my arms around her waist and exploring her body danced through my head, distracting me from all that had happened. The mere heat of her was enough to send me beyond reason or good sense. I had to get this under control, and fast.

"I took him to the island," Rhiannon said as she crossed her arms, glaring at the labrys. "And you broke my door."

Ember shrugged. She was different in some small, but significant way. The set of her shoulders was stronger somehow, her spine a little straighter. "I'll get him home. You can go." Rhiannon rolled her eyes at Ember's imperious tone as she stalked out, but Ember called to her. "Sunrise, Brontë. I'll see you at sunrise for penance. You and Achilles both."

A delicious chill ran down my spine, remembering what Rhiannon had said about their life on the island. Ember Verona was not just a legendary fighter, she was a true leader. Somewhere under all of the bullshit she'd been through for centuries, there was a commander. And it seemed she was emerging once more.

Something stirred deep within me, and the desire to pin her against my chest and make her scream with pleasure returned. She was all messy heat and imperfect glory, and I had the distinct feeling that I wanted to drink her in, absorb as much of her as I could. She felt like a part of me that had been missing for my entire life, and now that I found her, I didn't want to let her go.

I stepped back, my breath catching. These were dangerous thoughts. Thoughts that no matter how attractive, I could not make good on. I would always be loyal to the Necroline

Dynasty first. And the way I wanted this woman threatened that.

A soft groan in the hallway brought me back to the moment, then the click of Rhiannon's heels as she walked away. Ember stood with her back to me, still. I watched as some of the bravado of the previous moment melted away.

"What did you think of the island?" she asked, her eyes tired and haunted when she glanced back at me. I frowned, not wanting to forget the place I'd just been. "You can talk about it to other people you're sure know about it."

I watched as she went to the door and pulled the labrys from the wood, alternating between watching her and staring at my hands. I had been so sure they were burning. "It was beautiful. Rhiannon seemed to think that showing me would help me help you, though I don't know how."

She made a small noise, non-committal, but an acknowledgment all the same. "Maybe it'll come to you later."

I nodded, still staring at my hands. "How was I still here, but Rhiannon had actually disappeared?"

Ember sighed. "Those are secrets that aren't mine to tell. You can never actually visit the island, while we are able to return via the plinths." She motioned for me to follow her as she slung the labrys over her shoulder.

I followed her into the hallway. "Do you have a door here as well?"

She nodded, walking a few steps deeper into the hallway, before stopping a few doors down. When I caught up to her, she smiled up at me, the bittersweet sadness in her eyes almost unbearable to witness. "This is my door." She swallowed hard before turning back towards the stairs Rhiannon and I had come up.

I stared at the brass serpent on the door, a vibrant symbol of both chaos and renewal. A small smile found my lips. It was like finding a gift, a secret about her that I might never have known otherwise. Hope budded up within me, a fragile bloom that would need to be nurtured carefully, but I already saw the tattoo in my mind, a serpent twining through blooms of hemlock on my chest. On the place over my heart.

Ember's sharp breath broke my reverie. The fragile bloom, the serpent in the hemlock, the vision of something better for my future—all dissolved in an instant, as though I'd never had the audacity to think of it.

At the end of the hallway stood a woman with umber skin and a shaved head. Her eyes were smudged with elegant kohl liner, and she was dressed in sturdy, close-fitting pants, heavy combat boots, and a leather jacket. Standing next to her, leaning on her, cloaked in an ankle-length black wool coat with the collar flipped up around her face, was a silver-haired beauty with the saddest eyes I'd ever seen.

My heart crushed under the violence of my own mistakes. This was retribution for the errors I had made. For my lack of experience and vigilance. For my trust in the wrong people. Now I would pay for all I'd done.

Max Vela and Serafine DuVal.

"What the *fuck* is this?" Max snarled. In an instant, she stepped in front of Serafine, her movements lightning quick as the sound of metal brought Ember and I both to attention. Max Vela had her sword. Her *true* sword. The air in the library contracted with its power.

"Max," Serafine whispered, her long fingers closing over her friend's shoulder. "Max."

"No," Max barked in return. "Explain this, Verona. Is this a trap?"

Ember shook her head, her face smoothing into a strange mask of neutrality I'd never seen her use before. "No. It's a bad coincidence. Rhiannon brought him here."

"She wouldn't do that," Max shot back. She moved into a defensive stance. "He tried to kill Sera."

I opened my mouth to speak, but Ember shook her head

once. "He did not, and you know that. We've seen the evidence. It was a terrible mistake."

"Let us pass," Serafine said. "Please. We don't want trouble."

Ember made a noise that sounded like choking. "I would never stop you from getting the help you need. I am sorry." Her voice broke over the apology. "I am so sorry."

Every ounce of pain that flowed between the three of them was my fault. My negligence. My mistakes. I pushed past Ember, my hands raised to show that I was unarmed. I took several steps forward slowly, bowing my head as I did.

"My intentions did not matter," I said as I knelt before Serafine DuVal. "All that matters is that I harmed you. I would never beg your forgiveness, but I do ask for peace between us." I paused, breathing deep. "For the sake of my people. Please, let me help your sistren regain their swords. If, after that, you wish for my life, it is forfeit."

Cool fingers tipped my chin up to stare into the violet eyes that looked down on me. Serafine's heart-shaped face was framed by loose silvery-white waves and unruly bangs. Her rosebud mouth turned down. "I know you meant me no harm, Ares Necroline."

Behind her, Max scoffed. Serafine shook her head. "Max cannot forgive you. But I do. Help my sistren. Find my sword, and all will be right between us."

I nodded as she held out her hand. This was an old tradition. One from her homeland, just outside of Orphium, consumed by the wastelands now. I took her hand, pressing a chaste kiss to it. "I promise it will be done."

She lowered her head to kiss the top of mine, and as she did she whispered in a voice so soft I barely heard her, "And when you do, you shall have my blessing. Now, rise."

I glanced up at her as I stood. Serafine's periwinkle eyes sparkled with elven mischief. What had she read in me the moment I placed my hand in hers? There were rumors about her, about the things she could do. Some called her a witch, with that silver hair and translucent skin, with eyes like the rarest of jewels.

"I will take my leave," I said, continuing on with formality. It seemed best. "You have much to talk about."

Ember nodded, still standing where I left her. The three of them stood silent, staring at one another, ancient sentinels, awash with power. As I made my way to the stairs, I heard the click of Ember's heels, and the hissed question. "Where the fuck did you get that sword, Vela?"

This was a conversation I wanted nothing to do with. I pulled my phone from my pocket and dialed. I still had an informant to talk to. If I was going to make good on my pledge to Serafine DuVal, I should start immediately. There was no turning back now. We had swords to steal.

CHAPTER 26

EMBER

ARES DISAPPEARED DOWN THE STAIRS. I wondered if he knew how serious the pledge he'd made to Serafine was. It was his to make, and I did not begrudge him the chance to make amends, but the danger of it all worried me far more than I liked to admit. Fucking Ares Necroline. A pain in my ass to the last.

My lips burned with the brand of his kiss, of the touch that saved him from the plinth. His ignorance was evident in the fact that he'd trusted Rhiannon so implicitly. That he'd given the plinth a part of him without knowing what it might ask for in return.

Rhiannon and I would have words later for this. Now I had to deal with Max and that sword. She guided Sera, who moved well, but slowly, past me, towards her own door. I touched Max's arm. "Before you go, I need to know where you got that, and why you thought it was all right not to tell me you had it."

Sera shook her head, as though she were disappointed. She looked too tired for this. "Let her go on," I bit out. "They know she's coming, and she doesn't need you to get through the portal."

Max opened her mouth to argue, but I held up a hand. "I have given you nearly twenty years, Vela. I have respected your devotion to Sera. I have been more than kind. You will stay and report out."

Sera pushed Max gently from supporting her. "She's right, and you know it."

I touched her arm lightly. "I am happy to see you looking so well."

She bowed her head. So she was still angry with me, despite that ethereal calm that came over her. I deserved that. She had to wait too long for this, and I could own that. "I made many mistakes, Sera. But I must ask before you go through. Do you also have your sword?"

I knew the answer. If she had, she would be healed already. She wouldn't need to go home. "No," she whispered. "Please. Find it for me."

"We will," I promised, before pressing a kiss of my own to her pale cheek. "Go get well."

As she moved slowly towards her door, I turned back to Max. It was an effort, but I kept every bit of fury and resentment I held deep within me. If I wanted things to go my way, I could not show my feelings. "Report out."

Max glared at me.

"Please, Max."

Her jaw tightened. "On one condition."

I sighed. "You can give it, but I do not have to accept it. You owe me your report, regardless."

Still, she glared. Max and I had never been close. It was a bit of a surprise when she'd been assigned to my cohort, as she'd always been closer with the Aradios Maere. But the key had always been Sera. They'd been friends since they were children. Best friends—and until I understood more about Max, at one time I'd wondered if they would be more.

Finally, Max sighed. "When she's well, I want a trade to Aradios. Out of your unit, away from this hole."

My head tilted to the side. "Why?"

Her eyes fell as the rosiness in her cheeks deepened. "I'm not doing her any good. I make everything worse for her…"

A hollow in my chest that I tried desperately to ignore ached in response to her words. The loneliness in her statement. That they could spend an eternity together, but it would never be enough. They could love one another to the greatest of their capacity, and it would still be wrong for both of them. My heart broke to think of it.

Max stared at her sword. "I can't give her what she needs… I can't love her the way she wants me to. And she—"

Max practically choked on the words she could not speak. There was nothing in the world that would make her speak ill of Sera, not even the fact that Sera would always want things from Max that Max couldn't give her.

It was easy to be angry with them when they were gone. When they were not so real, so whole, so complicated. All my resentment washed away. If I'd ever fantasized about punishing the two of them, that made no sense now. All I wanted was peace, for all of us.

I pressed a hand to her shoulder. "Max." She looked up at me, her lovely brown eyes full of pain as she finally made eye contact with me. "You shouldn't have to change for anyone—and Sera wouldn't want that, would she?"

Tears welled in the other Maere's eyes. She shook her head. "She's told me a thousand times she understands that I am not built the way she is—that she doesn't expect me to fuck her, or love her the way she loves me." The words spilled out of her along with her tears. "But she won't move on either. I love her more than anyone… but it hurts me too."

I drew Max to me, letting her sob against my shoulder. She might want to leave us—might *need* to leave us—but we had spent lifetimes together. Eons. I would miss her. But this wasn't about me.

"I will arrange things," I murmured. "But you've spoken to her about it, haven't you?"

As she pulled away, Max nodded. "Yes, she knows. We agree that it is best. I wouldn't do anything without her knowing and consenting first. When she is well—and not before."

I cupped Max's face in my hands, emotion drawing my vocal cords tight. "I will miss you so much."

She mirrored the movement, an old gesture between the Maere. It signaled equal footing, even within hierarchy. "I will miss you too. Despite how I've acted these past years." She sighed deeply, her spine straightening—a warrior's stance. "Shortly after we left Orphium, the sword appeared on our kitchen table with the promise that if we never came back here, they would return her sword, in time."

Max was a terrible liar. She had been since she was a child, and had a thousand tells. Not one of them showed in this moment. I searched her face, then nodded, my hands falling to my sides. I couldn't blame her for taking the opportunity. They were both angry with me—and the sword gave Max the power she'd needed to protect Sera while she recovered.

If I'd requested healing for Sera sooner—if I hadn't been so afraid of Myrine saying no—they might not have been so vulnerable to the bribery of the sword. Not that I'd ever have expected them to reject it, but my clever sistren would have found a way to double cross whoever did this to us.

"If I'd been better all along, this would not have happened," I said, my voice soft as Max's eyes widened. "All I'm asking now is that you stay with her until she's well again—and until we get the rest of the swords back."

Max nodded. "I wouldn't leave her until she's strong enough to defend herself. Surely you know that."

"I do," I said, drawing Max in for one more hug. Her arms went around me. "Go," I said, pushing her away before tears could spring up and show how much this moment meant to me. I'd put more than enough of my feelings on display for today.

As she disappeared inside her own door, resolve hardened in me. I turned back to Rhiannon's door. It was whole again, the magic of the library mending what even immortal hands could not. I stared at my own door for a long moment, wondering what it would be like to go through it. To arrive back on the island, unannounced and unplanned.

Would they force me back here? Could Myrine be so cruel? My heart weighed heavy in my chest as I moved towards the stairs. I knew the answer to that, and now was not the time to contemplate this. With so little time until the auction, we needed to find out as much as we could about the Maere who'd been exiled from the island. If there was any possibility they were behind all of this, I needed to know why.

I opened my phone and sent Kara Asterion, leader of the Aradios Maere, my first communication in over twenty years. *We need to talk.*

CHAPTER 27

ARES

THE AUTOMAT WAS EMPTY, but for the spirits. Dozens of flickering fluorescents gave off an erratic buzz that set my teeth on edge. The mac'n'cheese wasn't nearly as good as mine, but it was decent enough. When I arrived, the spirits had congratulated me—on finding the Angel, on rescuing the child. It was odd. They seemed almost singularly interested in the two of them, and once they'd confirmed that those tasks had been taken care of, they lost interest in me completely.

In fact, they'd lost interest in almost everything. It was as though they were all *tired*. But that was impossible. Fatigue was for the living. The dead never tired. When Eli Cabot pushed through the door, his mood dark as the thunderstorm brewing in the late afternoon air, the Automat's spirits simply left.

That was the funny thing about the Thaumas—spirits were naturally repelled by them, even when they were as serious as Eli. Avaline always joked that Eli was the only one of the Thaumas that truly belonged with us. In many ways, she was right. Most thaumaturges had a sunnier outlook than he did.

Today, the big miracle worker wore jeans, work boots, and a fisherman's sweater. He hadn't bothered with a coat, because apparently rain hardly dared touch him. His perfectly tousled brown hair wasn't even wet. He didn't get anything to eat, but sat down across from me with a scowl on his face.

"What now?" he demanded. "I thought we were done."

I raised an eyebrow and got right to the point. "I know you know something you're not telling me. What has Lux told you?"

Eli's square jaw tightened. He was the kind of handsome that the Authority loved. Clean cut, dependable. Even his grumpy demeanor was something they ate up. He was what humans considered "classically handsome"—and when we were young, he used that advantage to protect both Lux and I when he could. It's what had bonded us as children.

And he was the reason, I was certain of it, that Roman Necroline had found Eryx and I in the nick of time, though Eli had never admitted to performing a miracle for us. I kept eating my mac'n'cheese while Eli decided what to tell me and what to keep back. I hated asking him for this information now. But after having been to the island—after understanding more about who we were, *what* we were… I was more determined than ever to help Orphium's Maere regain their swords and their power.

Too many forces were coalescing against us. It felt as though a storm was coming for this city. We needed our protectors to do what they did best, with all the tools at their disposal. Eli and I always seemed to follow the same train of thought. He leaned back in his chair, folding his arms over his chest.

"There's other players on the board," he said, finally. "Lux can't see who, but they are connected somehow. Standing between you and what you want."

"The swords?" I asked point blank. There was no need to dance around things. Eli wouldn't rat me out.

He shrugged. "It's more than that, but yeah."

"What's that mean?" I snapped back.

He shrugged. "If you wanted to know what Lux knows, you should've talked to her."

I sighed. That much was true. But if the Maere were being

set up, the Cognoscenti were being watched. There was no doubt in my mind about that. "Thanks, anyway… it was worth the ask."

I went back to my food. There was more. I knew there was more. Lux wouldn't have sent him without what I needed. Whether Eli was being difficult for a reason, or because he was an insufferable crosspatch, I'd never know.

He slid a piece of paper across the table. It was an address uptown, and a name. I raised an eyebrow. "This one's awfully high up in the Authority."

Eli shook his head. "Don't dig into this, man."

"Has Lux seen something?" I asked. I needed to know if there was something to be suspicious of.

He sighed. "No. The road goes dark after I give this to you. Whatever happens next is Saints-touched."

Not Saints-touched. Gods-touched. The Saints were gods.

My heart nearly stilled as I contemplated the multi-faceted idea of truth in all its myriad forms. Did it matter that the Saints were gods? From some angles, yes. In others, no. Pulling apart these kinds of knots was tricky, especially when it came to visions.

Typically, a Seer as powerful as Lux Medios saw infinite possibilities if fate hadn't been decided yet. Or what they saw changed rapidly, moving too fast or too erratically to read. If the road went dark—well, there were a lot of interpretations for that.

Some thought it meant Fate herself had intervened. Others thought it meant the Saints had drawn a curtain over the rest to let Fate sort herself out in private. But it was not good. It meant that whatever this was, it was as big as I feared it might be.

Eli stood. "I hope I see you alive again, Ares."

His words were ominous, but they were pure Eli. The man was nothing if not a pessimistic optimist. And then he was gone. I stared at the address for a long moment, before calling my snitch in the notorious building's security. I smiled as the information I wanted came through, then texted Ember the address, asking her to meet me there. We could search the Senator's apartment together.

CHAPTER 28

EMBER

DENSE FOG HUNG low over the city, permeating every atom of air from the street to the sky. The Authority had a lot of locations where their precious pets lived—locked behind heavy iron gates to keep the rabble out—and the Valnord was one such place.

I watched the building from a perch three blocks away, behind one of LimonCo's subtler "daylight" screens. In neighborhoods like the Valnord's there wasn't so much as a hint of flashing neon or bright digiscreens. This was where all the managerial class Corps employees had homes. They hated the aesthetic of neon and flashing lights.

My phone buzzed in my pocket. I glanced at it for a long moment, digesting the paragraphs upon paragraphs of words—a veritable lecture on my poor performance—then shot back a one-liner. The heart of Kara Asterion's response was what I expected. Calypso Montague wanted out of Aradios. It was all worked out, but for the timing. Obviously, we'd have to wait until Sera was well and Max could go to Aradios for good.

I rolled my eyes a little, but it was fine. Kara was as condescending as ever, but she had the upper hand here, so she could afford to be. The digiscreen I hid behind shifted images, showing a snow-white unicorn galloping across colorful fields of wild-flowers. Such nonsense—everyone knew unicorns were waste-land creatures and the beasts certainly weren't white and fluffy.

The digiscreens showed nothing but artificially generated bullshit that didn't exist anywhere and glorified evil creatures like unicorns. My lip curled in disgust. Unicorns ate humans alive, after all, if given the chance. But the images were quiet. Beautiful to the untrained eye of the corporate and government bourgeoisie, but not *actual* art.

Much like the Valnord itself. It was a forty story limestone behemoth, guarded by enormous gothic renditions of the Saints. I checked my phone, re-reading Ares' text to make sure I was in the right place.

Another text appeared below the address. *I'm here. Are you close?*

I searched the Valnord's rooftop. At first glance, all was calm, empty, serene. Near the stained glass dome that covered the atrium, there was the merest hint of movement. Had I not known exactly where Ares was meant to be, I might have missed it. I watched the guards at the Valnord's gates for a few moments before making my way across LimonCo's roof and onto the next building.

Far in the distance, sirens blared, muffled by the thick, soupy fog that thickened by the second. I hated these bougie neighbor-hoods. They were too quiet, too empty at night. I got the reasons why Lara hated the Carlyle, but at least it was in a lively neighborhood. Right now, across town, I knew for certain the streets were full of people, rushing back and forth in the neon-soaked fog, from the bars and noodle shops or late night seances.

There was life in our neighborhood. This one was sterile. Nearly every window in the Valnord was dark. Everyone was either still at work, or at posh dinners further uptown. My jaw ached as I leapt onto the Valnord's roof, my feet stinging with impact when I landed, though they did not make a sound.

I didn't have Rhiannon's talent for moving in pure silence, but I still had a warrior's ability to move quickly and quietly, and I stole over to where I knew Ares waited. He stood leaning against the rooftop door, dressed in slim-fitting black trousers and a black turtleneck sweater that showed off the lean, lanky muscles in his arms and chest.

"Aren't you cold without a coat?" I murmured as I approached.

Ares' eyes narrowed a bit. "I'm fine. You ready?"

I nodded.

He picked the lock to the rooftop door. They didn't use electronics up here, but real keys still. It was a boon. The less we depended on any kind of spiritual energy, the less likely we were to be tracked. I was certain Ares could summon a spirit to pick the lock for us, but the fact that he didn't was yet another mark in my growing list of things I found impressive about him.

The door clicked open, and Ares pocketed his picks. Silently, I followed him down the stairs and through the hallways of the uppermost floor of the building. He closed his eyes for a moment, his lips moving in silent communication with the dead, I assumed. When those green eyes opened back up, he nodded once before picking the lock on the Senator's door.

As I waited, watching his back, listening carefully for anyone approaching, it occurred to me that when he texted me I came without question. Of course, I looked up the address and found out who it belonged to, but I hadn't dug deeper. I didn't trust myself, but for whatever reason, I trusted him. That alone felt like I'd leapt into a yawning abyss, with no guarantee of safety.

The door to the Senator's apartment swung softly open behind me, just as Ares' fingertips brushed mine. When I turned, he pulled lightly on my hand, his skin barely touching me. It was enough to send shivers up my arms.

"Stanley is blocking the CCTV," he said, as the door closed

behind us, sealing us into the Senator's apartment. "And there are two Shades on this floor. The Senator is out for the evening, and they've agreed to keep watch while we search."

I nodded. Aside from the Poltergeist's blocking of the security cameras, it was such ambient spirit activity that we shouldn't draw much attention. I still didn't know why we were here. "What are we looking for?"

We still stood in the narrow front hall, which was all black marble, cold and reflective. Ares shook his head. "To be honest, I don't know. Eli Cabot is my go-between with Lux right now and he passed this address onto me without context."

I drew a sharp breath in, impressed yet again that Ares had both been so careful, and that he had strong enough connections with both the Cognoscenti leader and Eli Cabot, who was one of the most talented Thaumas in the city, that he received such favors. I'd never paid Ares Necroline as much respect as I should have, busy as I'd been being furious with him for burning my house down.

My impulsive mouth got ahead of my good sense. "We should have been working together all this time."

His serious expression deepened, the planes of his gorgeous face honing fiercely. "Things would be better if we could. For our people."

The way he said "our people" sent a slow, delicious warmth creeping down my spine and through my abdomen. My breath picked up pace. Ares stepped closer to me, backing me against the wall, his eyes burning with emotion. We were alone. Really alone. Not just alone in my room, in an apartment full of people who could hear every move we made if they listened hard enough. But truly alone.

The heat of his body warmed the chill off mine. "We don't have a lot of time," he murmured as his head lowered to mine. "We should get started searching."

My back arched away from the cold marble, my body skimming his, the space between us nonexistent as I pressed into him. "Right."

His arm snaked around my waist, his hand spreading over my back as he pulled me into his chest. "You are infuriating," he murmured. But it didn't sound like an insult. It sounded like yearning's end—like finally giving into the magnetic pull between us.

"You're a dick," I replied.

His thigh slid between mine as he backed me up against the wall, giving me a full expression of just how hard he already was for me. My arms flew around his neck and I pulled his mouth against mine.

Ares Necroline kissed me like he knew death intimately. Like he was mortal and understood just how close he was to perishing. Like I was the only thing standing between him and Tanith's peaceful promise. I had no choice but to be the answer to Tanith's dark call—Amarante's endless loop of light.

He pulled me harder against him as we moved against one another, a writhing tangle of breath, tongues, and limbs, of heat mounting and desire finally about to be met. Stanley wound around my leg, materializing in his form as a two-headed black cat with bat wings. I was surprised he allowed me to see him. Ares growled with frustration at the interruption.

"What?" he snarled to the ghost cat.

Though I could not hear the answer, Ares nodded. "The Senator has moved onto the opera from dinner. We have about three hours, unless he has parties to attend afterwards."

Neither of us moved, but Stanley disappeared, back to his monitoring of the security cameras, and apparently the CCTV system. Ares didn't let go of me. In fact, he pulled me harder against him. "The next person who interrupts me when I'm kissing you gets their aura twisted into knots."

The hard length of him pressed into my core with his words. He nipped at my bottom lip, kissing me again, as though he couldn't bear not to, before his grip on me slowly loosened.

"I want you so fucking much," he murmured, his gaze lowered, as though in prayer. "This isn't…" he trailed off, worry clouding his eyes.

Was Ares Necroline worried that *I* didn't want him the way he did me?

My hands went to his face, my thumbs grazing over his cheekbones until his eyes met mine. "I want you too."

He still wouldn't meet my eyes. I felt him flinch, as though he might pull away. I pulled gently on the sleeve of his sweater to keep him from going. And then slowly, so he wouldn't try to walk away, I turned in his arms, dragging his arms around my waist as I leaned hard against his chest.

"Touch me," I whispered, bringing his hands to the waistband of the leggings I'd worn this evening. I'd dressed practically for quick movement and there were no buttons, zippers, or even undergarments to deal with.

"Ember," he breathed into my ear as I guided his hand beneath the waistband of my pants.

His hand slid lower, sending heat cascading through me. His opposite hand pinned me to his chest, tightening around me so possessively that I nearly blacked out. The man held me like doing so would absolve him of his immortal sins. I spread wider for him as his fingers wound through the hair at the apex of my legs.

"Touch me." I begged this time. "Feel how much I want you." His fingers slid so easily inside me.

"Fuck," he breathed.

He added a third finger, using the palm of his hand to make a slow, rhythmic pulse against my clit. I moaned, trying to keep my voice soft, but unable to stay completely quiet. Ares' tongue swept across the lobe of my ear, letting me hear the increase in his breath as he fucked me with his hand. The hand on my abdomen slid upward to cup my breast.

"Can you come like this?" he asked.

The question itself was nearly enough to send me over the

edge. It was beyond considerate, free of any ego. Just a simple ask after my pleasure. I nodded, suddenly unable to speak. I was overcome with emotion.

That one question reverberated in my mind as he continued to pulse his fingers into me, harder as I pushed my hips against him, his breath still hot in my ear. "You feel so fucking good."

I bit my bottom lip to keep from crying out, but Ares' free hand gripped my chin, bringing his mouth to mine as his speed and pressure increased just enough to push me over the edge. As I came, his mouth closed around mine. He swallowed my cries with kiss after kiss, refusing to stop touching me, even after the first wave of my release began to relent.

Another built in its place and his mouth was back at my ear. "Yes," he urged me on. "Again."

My head flung back on his shoulder and I caught sight of his face for the briefest moment before my eyes squeezed shut, my walls clamping down hard around the fingers inside me as I came harder. I'd never seen him look like that, so open, so enraptured by something.

Was that what Ares Necroline looked like in love?

The thought was so forbidden, so unreal, that wet heat rushed through me, white light flashing behind my eyes as I rode Ares' hand as hard as I could. When my body went limp, he caught me, holding me against him as I shuddered with the aftershocks of pleasure.

I had no idea what to say. If that was what happened when he fingered me, what could he do with his cock? I laughed against him, at myself, for the smallest of moments, until he drew his hand out of my pants and sucked his fingers clean. That had me panting again.

"Stop distracting me," he muttered, but there was more than a little bit of amusement in his eyes, and when he kissed me again, tasting myself on his lips, I felt a way I never had with any other lover… Safe.

"Find what we're looking for in under an hour and I'll return the favor," I said when he finally pulled away from me.

He held onto me so tight I thought his fingers might bruise me. "I don't want a favor," he whispered. "Just you. All of you."

His eyes burned with that possessive light again. To be possessed by Ares Necroline would not be about control or dramatics, but about belonging. And every part of me wanted it. Even my pathetic, shriveled heart.

Ares pulled me into the Senator's apartment. The two of us stood staring at the minimalist atrocity before us. There was a hard, white couch sitting in the center of an enormous room, and no other furniture.

"Ugly," Ares remarked as we walked past the kitchen.

He opened a cabinet, his brows pulling into a frown. He opened every one in succession. They were all empty. The refrigerator had nothing in it but booze and a few protein drinks. Ares kept looking at the empty kitchen, shaking his head, as I walked further into the living room. There was only one piece of art in the living room, an enormous black and white photograph of an empty lot. Most people wouldn't recognize it. But I did, and my blood ran cold.

Who was Senator Cromvale?

I swallowed hard as I stared at it, my gaze sliding to Ares, who was still shaking his head at the bare cabinets. "Not even a junk drawer," he muttered, half to himself.

When he looked up, he read the look on my face first. Then his jaw clenched as he stared at the photograph. "That is—"

Everyone knew about what had happened to Ares and Eryx's parents, but no one ever talked about it. What was the use? Their story was a common one. The Authority had them eliminated for being too talented, and so painted them as criminals, when in reality they'd owned a little flower shop back in the ancient days of Orphium. The place in the photograph, the empty lot, was the place the shop once stood. They'd been killed on a raid, executed on trumped-up charges everyone knew were false.

It was obvious he couldn't finish the sentence, that he was as sick as I was. "What is he doing with that?"

I shook my head. The photograph was enormous. Its scale alone was an indication that the Senator had some sinister perspective. I didn't know much about Chance Cromvale. Only that he was relatively young. "Let's split up," I said. "You take the bedroom."

Ares nodded. "There's an office, I think. You wanna try that?"

"Sure," I said.

As we passed one another, my fingers brushed his. He held on tight, just for a second, his eyes shifting slightly away from mine. I paused, listening for any increase in his breath, any outward sign that he was upset by the photograph. Some might try to rationalize it as a coincidence. Ares and I were both old enough to know those didn't exist. Especially not with these types.

When I heard him in the bedroom, calmly opening and closing drawers, I moved on to the office. I didn't even bother with the computer. There wouldn't be anything there, or in the file cabinet. The minimalist decor and sadistic photograph told me all I needed to know about Chance Cromvale. I went right for the painting of a single red balloon and pulled it off the wall.

Sure enough, there was a safe behind it. The thing was a Sentry Vault, the best safe in the world. There was no way for me to crack it. I sighed, about to sit down at Cromvale's hideous glass desk, when movement out of the corner of my eye startled me. For half a second, I saw a beautiful woman with dark sepia skin, and a mass of ebony hair that fell past her waist. She was dressed in a stola that draped around her sturdy frame. Her eyes were wide and haunted. She walked across the room, weeping, paying me absolutely no mind.

As soon as she reached the door of the office, she disappeared, then reappeared in the exact same spot and made the journey across the room again. Every time, she started right next to the safe, and then crossed the room to the door, weeping in exactly the same way. I tried to get her attention, but she was an Echo.

I stepped out into the hallway, calling softly for Ares. He appeared faster than necessary, concern in his eyes. "Are you all right?"

"Yes," I said softly. Echoes were sometimes scared off by loud noises, or sudden changes. "We have a looper."

CHAPTER 29

ARES

I FELT the Echo before Ember said anything, so I stood at the threshold of Cromvale's office when she called out. The spirit whose path across the office repeated was familiar to me as my own mother's face.

All of the blood rushed out of my head as I watched the ghost. "Amanita?" Ember followed me as I walked into the office. "Amanita?" I said again, hoping that by saying her name, she might hear me, might recognize my voice.

I had only been a child when my parents were killed, but Amanita had been my mother's best friend. She'd been visiting the shop the day my parents were executed, same as she did dozens of times a month. Just passing time gossiping with my mother, arranging flowers and laughing.

"Amanita," I pleaded again.

This time, she flickered halfway across the room. I didn't want to yank on her aura. That could be disorienting for spirits, and the way she looked, locked in grief like this... I couldn't cause her more harm. She was repeating something in that voiceless way that so many Echoes had.

"Can you read her lips?" I asked, looking back at Ember.

Her kaleidoscope eyes were heavily hooded with grief,

perhaps for me, but mostly, I thought, for Amanita. She nodded, swallowing hard before choking out, "She's saying, *the safe is a decoy. It's under the rug.*" Ember shook her head. "I don't understand, Ares. This isn't where she died, is it?"

"No," I murmured. "She died in the flower shop with my parents."

"Amanita Erebis," she whispered, surprising me with her knowledge. "But how... why is she here? Loopers tend to stay near something important from their lives, or their deaths, right? Cromvale's ancestors probably weren't even born when your parents and Amanita died."

I inhaled deeply. This was what came of keeping secrets. Of keeping the Trinity's knowledge siloed within each dynasty. "That's not exactly true. Echoes don't always start out as loopers. Sometimes they start out as Shades, going where they please, and sometimes even seeking out aspects of their old lives."

Ember drew in a slow breath. "Are you saying she might have found out something so disturbing she got stuck like this?"

She was so smart, so quick, I didn't even have to try to explain things further to her. I loved it. "Yes."

"But what rug?" she asked. "There's not a rug in this place; not that I've seen, anyway. Is there one in the bedroom?"

I shook my head, then drew a sharp breath in. "But I didn't get to the closet yet."

I spun on my heel, running through the apartment, Ember close behind. There was no telling how little time we had left, and we'd come up empty thus far. When we got to the closet, it was there. A plain black rug in the middle of the walk-in closet, with an incredibly heavy-looking stone table standing atop it. We glanced at one another and then worked to move the marble table.

For mortals, it likely would have been too heavy to move. But for Ember and me, it took just a little effort. When the table was off the rug, we pulled it back, working in perfect time with one another. Below the rug, there was a trapdoor.

Ember stared at me for a long moment before bending down to open it. Both of us were silent, my pounding heart and the trapdoor creaking open the only sound in the apartment. I glanced up as the door opened, movement distracting me. Amanita stood opposite me, behind Ember, her tear-stained face full of relief. A smile stretched her heart-shaped face into an exhausted, but happy expression.

You found it, she said before she started to fade.

There wasn't enough time. There was never enough time. My emotions hadn't caught up yet. I hadn't had time to process this, to try to pull the feelings I'd had to abandon, along the long road of my life, up from the depths. Amanita would be here and gone before I had a chance to say what I needed to— to *feel* what I needed to.

"Tell my parents I love them," I whispered, dredging as much feeling as I could into my voice. Numbness threatened to pin me down in this moment, but I staved it off the only way I knew how: By talking about the one person I always trusted, that I knew as well as I knew myself. "When you see them, tell them that Eryx is just like Papa. I tried my best to make sure he would be a good man. That he would be strong enough to withstand this world, and all its horrors. Everyone who knows him loves him."

Ember's hand clapped over her mouth as I spoke. Tears welled in her hazel eyes, clinging to her long lashes. Amanita nodded, then looked down at Ember, whose focus was so closely narrowed on me.

And what about you, Ares? Amanita asked. The tears had disappeared, and she was translucent—the way spirits whose business on the mortal plane always looked when they were not long for the world. *What shall I tell them of you?*

I shook my head. "There is nothing to tell. Eryx is my greatest accomplishment. Roman will have told them the rest."

Ember's breath shuddered through her as she listened to me. The tears in her eyes fell onto her cheeks in streams now. She shook her head at Amanita, but could not seem to form words as her fingers stretched toward the spirit.

My mother's best friend seemed to understand something of her intention though, because she smiled gently at Ember, a comforting expression that seemed to soothe her, at least a little. *I will tell them you found the love of a good woman,* Amanita said, placing her fingers under Ember's chin. *It will please your mother to know it.*

Amanita's relief was palpable in the closet as she dissolved into thousands of glowing particles, breaking apart and then faded into nothing. She would be at peace now; whatever was behind the trapdoor was the thing that tied her to this place. I looked down to see only one thing in the space below: a manilla file folder. Ember glanced at me, wiping tears from her eyes, before pulling a set of rubber gloves out of her jacket pocket.

Ember Verona was everything I'd hoped for. I had no idea how long I'd been falling in love with her, but now that I saw myself through Amanita's eyes, I knew it had been longer than the past few days. *Years.* I'd been watching her, longing for her, since the inquest into the fire.

Since I pulled my head out of my ass and realized the harm I'd done. The mistakes I'd made in service of my people. For the past twenty years, I'd been searching out ways to make things better, and she'd been here all along. Right by my side, annoying the shit out of me—the answer to everything.

The love of a good woman. Yes. That, but also a partner in this lonely life. The chaotic complement to all my desire for order.

Ember pulled another pair of gloves from her pocket and handed them to me, before bending down to lift the folder out of its shallow hiding place. She placed the folder on the marble table we'd just moved, and opened it. I went to stand next to her. The harsh overhead light in the closet was unpleasant, its dull whine making my ears ring.

There were several photographs inside the folder. Some were old, over a hundred years old, by the looks of things. The photograph from the wall—of the lot where the old florist shop had been—was among them. There was also a document, a single piece of paper that showed a web of dates. Ember pressed her gloved finger to the day my parents died, her eyes flicking over the other dates on the web.

She touched several that had black slashes through them, her eyes narrowing. "All of these are days after Lara's kills."

"Days after…" My mind raced. "These are the dates the murders she prevented were supposed to occur?"

Ember nodded, frowning deeply as she pointed to one of the earliest dates on the web. "This is when the swords were stolen."

I looked through the photographs again. They were all from different, empty locations. None were familiar to me but the one where my parents' shop had stood. As Ember looked at them, she began to shake her head. "No…"

"What?" I asked.

"Someone is playing a very long game," she murmured.

"Ember," I insisted, suddenly desperate to know what my parents had to do with any of this. "What do you know?"

She held up a finger, then took her phone from her pocket. She snapped several photos, then closed the folder. "We have to get out of here. *Now.*"

Just after she spoke, Stanley appeared again, still in his two-headed, bat-wing cat form. He sent several images to me telepathically—CCTV footage of the Senator in a cab.

"There's no cameras in this place, but we've tripped an alarm," Ember hissed. "Senator Cromvale is a devotee of Chiore."

My blood ran cold at the name. On the island, Rhiannon had reacted badly to my question about the destruction of Chiore's temple. "What is the truth about Chiore, Ember? What did she do to the other gods?"

Ember swallowed hard. "She forged a weapon that could end a true immortal's life. She swore it was to keep balance, but she wielded it like a threat."

"How do you know Cromvale is devoted to her?" I asked, desperate to see what she did.

Ember let out a frustrated noise, something between a growl and a squeal. "These places. In Orphium's ancient past, before you were born, before the Consulate or the Authority, they were all her temples. Humans sacrificed parapsychs to her. Fed them to her flames for favors. She was the only god who did not create parapsych children. She created the monsters."

The monsters. The Ceti. The Kraken. The multitudes of creatures that inhabited the vast wastelands between the three territories. If they were her children, what did that mean? And why would anyone worship such a god?

I remembered the fire in the flower shop after my parents had been murdered. Fury mounted in my veins—had they been a *sacrifice*? "What did they hope to accomplish by this?"

Ember leaned forward, taking my hands in hers, pushing me towards the door. "Do you remember the way that Fairchild moved the night we rescued Briony?"

I nodded, but pulled back, reluctant to leave until I understood what we were dealing with.

"That wasn't a Thaumas-made miracle," she hissed. "He sacrificed something, some*one* to Chiore for the power, and he obviously meant to do the same to Briony. There have always been rumors that the Chiorics liked to sacrifice young parapsychs because Chiore liked the taste of potential best."

That was impossible. Or at least I'd been led to believe it was impossible to reach the Saints, let alone gods. I shook my head. "Are you saying what I think you are?"

Ember placed the folder back in the shallow divot in the floor, then closed the trapdoor. "Do you think I'm suggesting that some sect of the Authority worships Chiore?"

Truly, I hadn't gotten quite that far, but that was the gist of what I'd been thinking, so I nodded. Ember kicked the rug back over the trapdoor, moving quickly to the table. We moved it back into position together.

I touched her arm. "Is the story about Chiore's weapon true?"

Ember sighed. "No one knows. A group of Maere left the island before the mists descended. They were supposed to hunt the weapon down. No one's heard from them since." That didn't make me feel any better, but it also didn't make me feel worse. Her forehead shone with a gleam of sweat. "Cromvale will know someone was here."

I nodded, then glanced up. Several baseball bats hung on the wall, and vaguely I remembered that Cromvale had played in college. I grabbed one, tossing it to Ember, then pulled down another for myself. "Then I think we need to make it difficult to tell what we meant to do here."

A slow smile spread over her face. "Let's go."

CHAPTER 30

EMBER

I THREW the slugger over my shoulder as I marched into the living room. I glanced back at Ares, who followed me with the kind of purpose that made every part of me tingle. "How long have we got?"

"About thirty minutes," he replied. "Why?"

"Lock the door," I said, my body heating with anticipation.

As Ares locked the door, I stared at Cromvale's impressive sound system, flicking through the flat screen until I found a playlist one of my favorite DJs at the Odyssey made. It was titled "Angry Girls." And as the first notes of one of my favorite songs played over the Senator's most excellent speakers, I turned it up all the way.

Ares stalked back into the living room, watching me carefully, expression quizzical. He was both amused by me, and probably a little confused about why, after trying to be so quiet, I was now insistent on making a shit-ton of noise. The way he moved was unfair, the fluid roll of his muscles, the dangerous grace in his hands. As the drumbeat pounded through me, the cold apartment was suddenly too warm. My skin flushed, remembering how Ares had touched me when we first entered this wretched place.

If we slunk out now, he would leave feeling exactly the way I did now: afraid and discouraged. Neither of us had room to feel like that. Neither of us could fold, or back down. Sneaking out, like we'd never been here, wasn't the move. Well, it was the *smart* move, but no one had ever accused me of making wise choices.

No, not only did we need a diversion from what we'd been here for, but we needed to feel better. We needed to feel powerful again. The Authority had run our people into the ground for nearly two thousand years. It was time for us to take at least some of our power back.

And if we couldn't get it back in this second, we could do the next best thing—create an unhinged amount of chaos. I grinned as I rolled my shoulders back. Then I smashed the fuck out of the horrendous photograph of where his parents died. "Fuck Chase Cromvale," I howled as I moved through the room, hitting every breakable object I could.

Ares watched me closely, jaw clenched tight. The way he looked at me sent shivers along my spine, tingling straight through to my core. My body ached for him, too hollow, needing desperately to be filled, fucked, and Saints-forbid, worshipped. The way he'd sucked his fingers clean of me earlier let me know that fucking Ares Necroline would be more than good—it would be a religious experience.

If the humans wanted a dark god to worship, I could give them an entire selection. My gods were braver than Chiore. Better than a god who sought only to destroy. Death was one thing, destruction another. I had not lived this long only to see the people I was meant to protect suffer further at the hands of the Authority.

When I moved to the office, Ares followed, his movements matching mine with a heated fury that mounted as the seconds ticked by. Time seemed to slow as we laid waste to Cromvale's perfect, minimalist world. Neither of us bothered to leash our strength or speed. We moved in concentric circles, using the bats to smash through the entire apartment, each broken object sending a rush of euphoria through my body.

It didn't take long before we stood in the shattered remains of Chase Cromvale's insufferable apartment, standing chest to chest, breathing hard.

"How much time left?" I shouted over the music.

Ares' chest rose and fell as he moved closer to me, his lips parting with only slightly labored breath. We'd worked hard to move so quickly, but it wasn't the physical exertion of destroying Cromvale's apartment that had us both panting. Wet heat pooled between my legs. This was foreplay, plain and simple.

I wanted Ares Necroline inside me. I wanted to fuck the sadness and fear out of him. Because it was still there, lurking in me, just as it was behind the desire in his eyes.

"We have twenty-five minutes," he shouted back.

I pressed my hand to his chest. "Set fire to it, Ares. You're good at that." He flinched away from me, almost hurt by my words. But I grabbed his arms, yanking him back towards me. I needed him angry, annoyed by me—anything but afraid. I was willing to say anything, do anything to banish the fear from both our hearts. "I hated you for so long."

His eyes narrowed dangerously, his head tilting in that predatory way he had, his upper lip curling slightly. There was the expression that I'd secretly loved every month for years. That irritation with me that made me want to fuck the disdain right off his face. He pushed me against the wall. I shoved my hands into his pants' pocket. Just lock picks in this one, so I moved to the other, where I found a lighter and the head of his cock, poking into his pocket.

I let my fingers graze his erection, feeling him tense against me, his eyes falling shut as I pressed my body harder against his, creating more friction between us as I pulled the lighter from his pocket and stuck it between his lips. He bared his teeth to me as he accepted it. His hips thrust against mine as I wrapped my legs around his waist.

I tossed my bat towards the windows. The force of my throw smashed them instantly, the bat rolling onto the terrace, but my eyes didn't leave Ares' face. "How long have I been pissing you off?"

He removed the lighter from his mouth with his free hand, his pretty mouth going from a sneer to a smirk. "At least a hundred years. Probably more."

"Show me," I growled, bucking my hips against the hard length of his erection. "Show me just how much I annoy you."

For a wild moment, I thought he might turn me down, or hesitate. But he tossed his bat aside as well, smashing the mirror over the vanity in the bathroom. And then he lit the lighter, tossing it into Cromvale's full wastebasket in the bathroom. It went in like he was a pro ball-player, the trash going immediately up in flames.

"You're infuriating," he said as he pulled me away from the wall and turned me around. "Hands against the wall."

I gasped with pleasure as I obeyed, watching the flames in the wastepaper basket explode from some chemical Cromvale had discarded, and climb up the wall to where dry towels hung. This place was going to go up in flames, and I didn't give a flying fuck.

All I wanted was to feel Ares inside me. Behind me, he fussed with his pants, and I couldn't help but wiggle my ass against him, making it more difficult. He pulled me hard against his chest, one hand sliding fast underneath my jacket and the light sports bra I wore underneath to pinch my nipple, hard.

"You can't wait for this place to go up in smoke, can you?" he said with a laugh, then trailed his lips down my neck.

He pinched my nipple again, and I gasped at the mix of pleasure and pain. The song had changed, moving to something darker, with a pulsing beat that seemed to move in time to the throbbing between my legs.

"Irresponsible." He pushed my pants down. "Disrespectful." My back arched as I felt the head of his cock push at my entrance. "With a smart mouth," he hissed before turning my head to capture my mouth with his.

The kiss was frenzied as he slid into me, stretching me open with ease. He had me pinned against him as I braced myself against the wall, thrusting into me at a relentless pace that took my breath away.

"You feel so good," I moaned into his mouth.

This moment was everything I'd wanted for years. Someone who knew the ways I needed to be protected and possessed. That I needed my lover to respect my power in all places but this one. That in this, I needed release from making decisions, from knowing what to do. And that I wanted a mix of pleasure and pain that kept my attention, that didn't allow space for my anxious mind to take over.

As if he could hear my thoughts, Ares slapped my ass hard. I cried out, the bit of pain spiking my pleasure even more. He paused for half a second, and I wondered if a spirit spoke to him. Being watched by the building's spirits should probably bother me, but it didn't. In fact, if possible, it just made this better.

I wished I could see what we looked like. What I looked like from behind, being railed by Orphium's most dangerous necromancer. A man people crossed the street to avoid—that humans were terrified of. A man who scared the dead. Whose cock was so hard inside me, I knew he was close to coming.

"Touch yourself," he said as he took my hand in his, bringing it to my mound and pressing it into me. I moaned as he pressed harder, bucking my hips against the pressure of our combined hands. He didn't allow me the dexterity to pleasure myself further just yet, his mouth grazing my ear so he could whisper into it. "Cromvale sent cops ahead. The spirits shut the elevators down, but his people just got the stairwell open."

The thought of being caught here, of the cops storming in while Ares Necroline fucked me silly in the Senator's smashed up apartment, made me unspeakably hot. As he thrust harder into me, I rubbed my clit in hard, fast circles.

"Come for me, Ember," he commanded. "We can't leave until you come for me."

I let out a feral cry, white light blurring at the edges of my vision as I rubbed faster, harder, loving the feeling of him stretching me open and fucking me deep and hard, all at once. It was so much stimulation, so much energy that I couldn't possibly focus on anything but us. "Harder," I begged. "Come inside me."

He obliged on both counts and as he roared with his release, the swelling burst of white light exploding behind my eyes. From the front of the apartment, I could hear them trying to break down the door. We were in danger of being caught, and honestly, Ares felt so good I didn't care.

"Fuck," he snarled as he thrust into me one final time. His movements were lightning fast as he pulled my pants back up. By the time I turned, he had his pants back in place. Neither of us had taken our rubber gloves off.

The sight of us, sex-addled and rubber-gloved, struck me as funny. I laughed at us as he kissed me. "You are terrible," he said as he pulled away.

I pushed him towards the broken window. "I think you love it."

He stepped up onto the balustrade, pulling me up next to him. Inside the apartment, the door cracked. The cops were going to get through in seconds. Ares smiled at me as he stepped off the stone terrace and into the night.

His words echoed in my ears as I followed him.

"Damn right."

CHAPTER 31

ARES

EMBER WAS SO light on her feet that she hardly winced as we touched down. My feet and knees stung, but she pulled me into a sprint away from the Valnord before I could think much about it. The cops were gathered around the other side of the building, near the more traditional entrances and exits.

We, however, were racing down back alleys, skirting trash and scuttling rats as we left the scene of our crime. I didn't have time to think about the wisdom of what we'd done back there, destroying Cromvale's apartment that way, but I knew there might be consequences.

Ember finally slowed down enough that I was able to start to piece things together. If we were going to cover our asses, I was going to have to wrangle some top notch shit, and fast. As I pulled my phone from my back pocket, I breathed a sigh of relief.

I had a text from Eli Cabot. It was just the address of an exclusive club uptown that Lourdes Thaumas owned, called the Rosewood, with the words, *Come in through the back door*. I showed my phone to Ember, whose lips were still swollen from kissing me. Her eyes were glazed over with lust, fear still chasing her as it did me, but she nodded.

We moved as one, continuing to skirt through back alleys and rooftops, staying out of sight. She didn't ask me if I trusted Cabot. She just followed, her body moving in perfect time with mine. It was as though we were still connected, as though I was still inside her. It was a trial not to pull her against me and taste every inch of her.

Now that I'd given in to what I wanted most, I was starving for her. When a squad car screamed by us, and I pulled her against me in a dark alley, just a block from the Rosewood, my cock hardened in an instant.

"Do you know what kind of place the Rosewood is?" I asked. She couldn't go into this ignorant.

Her response was a laugh, low and sultry. "I've heard it described as a den of iniquity." Her back bowed slightly, and the little moan that whispered through the alley had me burying my face in her neck, drinking in the soft, warm scent of her skin. "It's perfect for a cover."

"You're sure?" I asked. "The best way to make sure our alibi is solid is to make... a scene."

She grinned up at me, fisting my sweater in her hands. "Fuck me on a table six ways from Tuesday, while the entire Authority watches, if it pleases you."

My mouth slid down her neck, one hand covering her lips so she wouldn't make a sound as I slid my free hand into her pants. She was still wet from our encounter in the Senator's apartment. Her eyes fell closed as she leaned against me. It began to rain, soaking us both as I pushed two fingers inside her.

"We should go," she moaned against my hand.

"I know," I breathed in her ear. "But that was too fast back there. I need more time with you."

The truth was, my brain was sex-hazed. I was desperate to be alone with her, to taste her, to find out every way I could touch her that would elicit the delicious noises she made right now. Such soft, sweet sounds from a creature as vicious as

Ember Verona. I wanted her pussy clenched around my cock as she rode me into oblivion.

The way her hips moved to take me deeper was too much, and her ass ground against my cock, making me harder than I'd been in my whole life. She turned in my arms, my fingers sliding out of her. Her eyes were wide.

"We need to get to the Rosewood," she whispered. "You can fuck me there, and then again at home, if you still want to."

If I still wanted to. I laughed, a rough noise I was unused to making. "You don't have to worry about that. I'm in no danger of tiring of you."

The relief in her eyes pained me. I'd meant it as a joke, but I hadn't lied. There was no way I would fuck her once and then ignore her. Why would she think that? My long history of one-night stands surfaced in my memory. So she had been paying attention to me, as I had to her. But surely she knew that she was different. That the way I wanted her was about more than my physical needs being met.

"We should go," she said again.

I caught her hand. "You understand the way I want you, don't you?"

She looked back at me, suddenly vulnerable and small. "Sure." Her teeth sank into her lip and she averted her eyes. "Now."

"No," I said, voice insistent. "Not just now. Before now. For a long, long time. And for more than just sex, Ember."

She blinked a few times, as though she might be welling up, but her head was turned far enough away from me that I couldn't see clearly. I pulled her back against me, stroking the back of her hair. "I don't just want to fuck you. Despite the games we play, I do actually like you."

It was more than that—more than like. But I couldn't say that without scaring her, that much I knew. If she could hardly believe I wanted to fuck her, she would shy away from hearing just how hard I'd fallen. That the way I needed her wasn't just bone deep. It went through to my soul.

These were declarations for another time—when she'd had more time to think through what she wanted. We were different in thousands of ways, but the way we saw the world, the way we processed things? That was the same. I'd just gotten a head start on loving her.

Loving. Her.

The words sputtered in my mind. Did I actually love Ember Verona?

Her arms went around me, and she buried her face in my chest. Could she hear the way my heart pounded? Could she feel the emotions coursing through me as I clung to her?

I could feel the shuddering breath go through her as she tried not to cry. "I like you too," she said into my chest. When she looked up at me, her eyes were bright. "Now, take me to the Rosewood and have your way with me."

Her voice was light, but I saw the seriousness in her eyes. She needed to keep going. The fear that nearly struck us both down in Cromvale's apartment chased us both. We needed this. Needed to feel something we could trust tonight.

So I didn't say anything else about how I felt about her. No matter what I said, she wouldn't believe it right now any more than I would. So I just nodded. She slipped out of my arms and I followed her as she hurried down the alley.

We made it the next few blocks unseen and slipped through the unlocked back door of the club. There, in the storeroom, Lux Medios sat waiting. So this was a full-on Trinity operation now. Something in me shifted, past the fear I'd felt earlier and straight through to hope. Lux, Eli, Lourdes… the Maere. Me. We were all in this together, and whatever came next, this was progress. This was us changing things.

When we entered, Lux locked the door securely behind us, using an enormous deadbolt. Tonight she wore a silver sequined jumpsuit that contrasted beautifully with her rich brown skin.

Her hair was bright pink, and her makeup was relatively subdued, despite the fact that it sparkled like a disco-ball.

"Took you long enough," she whispered, handing us each a garment bag. "Right now, the two of you are in the bathroom. Presumably fucking each other's brains out. Make sure to come out looking… well-used."

Ember frowned slightly, but took the garment bag.

"Eli?" I asked. He was the only Thaumas I knew that had such mastery over illusion.

Lux nodded as I took my bag, and turned to walk away, but Ember interrupted her. "Was my hair up?"

Lux smiled, stroking Ember's face with her long fingers. "Yes, but I doubt it will be when you come out. *Well. Used.*" Lux brushed a kiss to Ember's cheek and whispered. "Be the dirty little slut I know you are, love. Or at least look like one."

Ember laughed, a soft, sexy noise, then saluted Lux, an irreverent expression on her flushed face. "Will do."

"Leave your clothes in the garment bags," Lux replied. "Just stick them in the closet and I'll send them to the incinerator. Lourdes will take care of the rest."

"Thank you," I said, catching hold of Lux's arm as she made to leave. "Really."

She nodded, her mouth tightening with emotion. I knew when Lux Medios might cry, and this was one of those moments. "I'm sorry you had to see all that, Ares. But I'm glad Amanita is at peace now."

She'd seen it all. Whether before or after I'd found out was of no consequence. Lux never held anything back that she didn't have to. We had enough history for me to trust that. We'd grown up in the same neighborhood and she was only a little older than I was. She'd known Amanita and my parents. Everyone knew each other in those days. I swallowed the pain that threatened to lodge itself in my throat and choke me.

Lux squeezed my arm, and said. "You be a dirty slut too,

Ares. Don't let this chance to fuck Verona's brains out pass you by."

Ember snorted as Lux left me wide-eyed and slightly shocked. When the Seer was gone, Ember stripped naked, and I nearly followed Lux's command on the spot. But Ember shook her head, her honey-colored hair damp from the rain.

I watched her lithe body as she slid into the slinky red dress Lux left her, and a pair of stilettos with straps around the ankles. There was lingerie in the bag, but Ember left it behind. Her nipples were hard, poking through the thin fabric of the dress. A low growl rumbled through my chest.

"Get dressed," Ember hissed. "So I can be your dirty little slut." She smiled while she said it, but her voice had dropped into a husky register that told me she had no intention of pretending.

I stripped quickly, changing into the suit Lux left for me. I zipped up the bag and grabbed Ember's hand. Her fingers closed around mine, squeezing hard as I pulled her down the hall, towards the bathroom. There was a line outside the door, but no one seemed to see us. Ember glanced back at me, wonder in her eyes.

We were invisible.

From inside the bathroom, I heard her moaning my name. I made every effort not to make a noise. I wasn't sure what might break the illusion Eli had conjured, but I saw him at the end of the hall, ostensibly in line to use the bathroom like everyone else. He nodded once to me.

I pushed the bathroom door open, pulling Ember inside. The second we were in the bathroom, the noises stopped, but Ember picked up right where her illusory doppelganger left off. Her mouth fell open as she slid back onto the vanity.

"Ares," she moaned. "Yes, yes, just like that."

She spread her legs, pulling her dress up to show me how wet and swollen she still was. The sight of her nearly stopped my heart. There was only one choice. I fell to my knees, pushing her thighs open further so I could bury my face in her pussy.

"Yes," she moaned louder as I slid two fingers inside her. She was so wet and I could taste myself mixed with her fluids as I rolled her clit between my lips.

"I need your cock," she moaned.

Someone pounded on the door, but I ignored them. I glanced up at her and she smiled, before whispering. "They've been waiting so long to take a piss… let's give them a show."

She winked once, then raised the volume of her voice so the line outside could hear her plea. "Give me your cock. I need you inside me. Now."

"Beg for it," I snarled back, not knowing if anyone could hear me, and frankly, not caring. If she wanted to play this game, I'd play my way, and we'd both love it.

I unbuttoned my pants, fisting my cock. "Is this what you want?"

The laughter had gone out of her eyes now, replaced with feral hunger. "Yes," she hissed. "Fuck me, baby. Fuck me so hard."

She reached out for me, her opalescent nails elegant in the dim light of the bathroom. I moved towards her, fitting the head of my cock at her slick entrance. Outside the door, all had gone quiet. The crowd was most definitely paying attention to us.

I leaned towards her and whispered. "You know what they think of me, what they say about me."

Her face turned towards mine, and she kissed me. Her lips were sweet, so tender, as her tongue slipped into my mouth. She slid forward to take me in. She was so tight, and my cock was almost too big for her. Even as wet as she was, I could feel her stretch to accommodate me.

"I know what they say about you," she murmured. "Put on a show, Ares. Give them the terrifying necromancer they want."

"Are you sure?" I asked, stroking her hair back from her

face. It was almost dry now, waving around her face in wild, untamed curls.

She smiled, her eyes bright and wicked. "Claim me, Necroline. Tell me who I belong to."

I pulled out of her, then pushed back in with a loud, wet slap. "Whose pussy is this?" I growled, increasing the volume of my voice.

"Yours," she moaned as I rubbed my thumb in slow, wet circles around her clit, staring into her hazel eyes as she panted.

"Who do you belong to, Ember?"

"You," she cried out as I thrust harder into her, increasing my pressure on her clit as I filled her. "You. I belong to you."

"That's right," I replied, louder again. I pulled out and thrust back in harder this time. "You belong to me."

"Yes," she screamed. "Ares. Fuck. I'm about to come."

I pulled her closer, yanking her dress down to expose her nipples. "Not yet," I murmured, slowing my movements inside her so I could bend over to take one pebbled nipple into my mouth. I pushed slowly into her as I sucked each of her nipples in turns, blowing on her wet flesh and nipping at them in tandem until she whimpered with need.

"You are so fucking perfect." It wasn't a show, or a lie. The people listening outside this door thought I was a monster. Master of the dead. Terrifying. And it would behoove me for them to think I was the kind of man who wanted to possess a woman fully, to continue to be frightened of me.

And I did want to possess her. But I wanted the same from her. I wanted to claim her in every way possible, and to be claimed in return. I wanted her to ache for me when I wasn't inside her. And I wanted to spend every moment I didn't have my face buried between her thighs, or my cock inside her, longing for it. I wanted to wake up to her mouth around my cock and to finger her in the backseat of a cab.

I wanted to spend the rest of my life listening to her wild ideas and watching her slaughter her enemies. I wanted to fuck her on her moon, and have my cock painted with her blood. I wanted her in my lap while I manipulated spreadsheets and on her knees under my desk.

"I belong to you," I murmured. It was too soft for the people outside the door to hear. This wasn't for show. "I am yours, Ember."

"Ares," she breathed as I fucked her so slowly, pushing as deep inside her as I could. "Deeper," she moaned as she tilted her hips to take me. "I am yours, Ares Necroline. Take me as hard as you can."

I pushed harder into her; pulsing, rather than thrusting, so her clit rubbed against my pelvic bone. I moved my hands to her lower back, helping as she lifted her hips to meet each powerful thrust of mine. She leaned back against the mirror, her back bowing as her breasts bounced.

At this angle, I could fuck her deep and hard without moving much. The view was incredible. Wet fluid seeped out of her slit as I pulsed inside her, her fingers slick with desire as she traced circles around her swollen, flushed clit.

When she screamed my name, her walls clenched around me, sending me over the edge. She clung to me as our movements slowed, raising up from her reclined position to kiss me. I was still buried in her, our combined desire dripping out of her onto the countertop as her mouth met mine.

"We'd better go," she said when she pulled away.

CHAPTER 32

EMBER

THERE WERE a few low whistles as we left the bathroom, but nobody paid us much mind. This was the Rosewood, after all. Plenty of people fucked in the bathroom. Ares pressed a kiss to my hair as he slid his arm around my waist. I felt his phone buzz in his jacket pocket as we walked into the bar.

There were enormous murals on the walls, lit by soft red light. As we moved towards a booth, I noticed that the light itself wasn't actually red, but the lamps on each table and the sconces on the walls all had red shades. The murals were beautifully done, depicting one of the most gorgeous orgies I'd ever seen painted. Every sex act possible was elegantly portrayed.

And despite the fact that I'd been fucked twice in the last hour, I ached for more. I glanced around Lourdes' bar, and noticed that plenty of people were engaged in various phases of coitus. Some were simply dancing provocatively on the dance-floor down below, but in each of the alcoves on the mezzanine level people clustered together, kissing and touching.

I had heard stories about the Rosewood, but I hadn't ever been here. It was very exclusive, members only. There were several Authority officials here, at least one Senator, who appeared to be getting a blowjob from a gorgeous silver-haired necromancer. The man's head bobbed in the Senator's lap, taking his cock deeper and deeper into his throat.

I needed Ares back inside me as soon as possible.

"We're over here," he said, glancing down at his phone. In a semi-private corner, there was a large leather chair by the fire-place, angled so that whoever sat in it would be three-quarters of the way obscured from the rest of the room. A small table next to it had two fresh glasses of bourbon on it.

Ares pulled me towards the chair. He paused in front of it. "Are you up for this?" he murmured in my ear, his hand spreading over my abdomen. "Everyone who comes here loves to play. They're sworn to secrecy, but word will get out that we were here together."

I understood fully why we were here. Eli had orchestrated this perfectly. I read the text from Eli as Ares angled his phone towards me. *The two of you got here two hours ago, ate in back with Lux, and then headed to the bathroom to fuck. The whole bar has been talking about it, but you've hardly been seen.*

So we had to be seen now. Had to make an impression on the influential crowd up here, so that should anyone question where we were tonight, they'd remember the glimpse of us they'd been shown earlier in the night, and that memory would be cemented by whatever we did next.

Gently, playfully, I pushed Ares into the big chair by the fire. It was a cold night, and the old building the Rosewood was in was drafty. Anyone who bothered looking would know I was cold just by glancing at me, my nipples were so hard. I was grateful to be by the fire, but I couldn't just snuggle into the extra large chair with Ares and sip bourbon.

When he was seated, I stood before him, smiling sweetly. I watched as he lifted one glass of bourbon from the table and sipped, taking me in, his eyes lingering on my breasts. A few heads turned my way, including the Senator, who stroked the back of his lover's head fondly as he watched me.

I knew him. He was one of Cromvale's cronies, but I

couldn't quite remember his name. Just that he was one of the more severe Senators, who believed stronger sanctions against parapsychs were necessary. But here he was, getting blown by a necromancer in a parapsych sex club.

Hypocrite. They were all hypocrites. They wanted to oppress us while enjoying us. People like these Senators would never admit to loving us, or loving to fuck us, but would speak against us in public, then engage in whatever pleasure they wanted in private.

Hatred and righteous fury flowed through me, heating me as Ares' fingers grazed the skin behind my knees, pulling me closer between his legs as his hands moved higher. I glared at the Senator as Ares grazed my inner thighs.

The music from the dancefloor pulsed in a sensual beat. I met Ares' eyes and took his glass from him, bringing it to my lips as I drank the rest of it down. The bourbon slid down my throat, a mixture of hot and cold, warming my belly as I strad-dled Ares' lap, covering his mouth with mine while the Senator watched us.

The man was going to get off watching me fuck Ares, and sick as it was, I liked the idea. Liked that while he had what would probably be the best orgasm of his life, that he'd be giving us an alibi. There were other eyes on us as well, a few more recognizable members of the Consulate, a few lower-level Trinity leaders from Aradios and Palladiere—enough important people that this little show would be more than worth it.

Ares was already hard as I unbuckled his pants. My dress hid the particulars of what we did from view, but there was no mistaking what I was up to as I freed his cock and slid it into my still-wet pussy.

"Fuck," he breathed as he filled me.

His hands slid under my dress to grip my ass, pulling himself deeper inside me. That cold Necroline gaze locked onto me. "Eyes on me, Ember. They can watch you, but your eyes are *mine*."

"Yes," I breathed, doing as he commanded.

If he bossed me around in a fight, or while we were trying to do business, I would hate him. But this felt so fucking good. I didn't even know how much I wanted him to act this way until he did it. How much I wanted him to tell me over and over that I belonged to him, that I was his, for him to lay claim to me repeatedly and in public.

I had been so lonely. So sure I was the source of everything bad that had ever happened to me. Every time Ares Necroline called me his, I got a little piece of myself back. He pulled me closer to him, kissing my lips, then my cheeks, his tongue grazing my ear.

"Don't rush," he murmured. "I want to fuck you slow and deep. I want everyone here to see you come apart while I worship you." A wild little noise came out of me. His words were just for me and I loved them. "You deserve to be worshiped," he murmured. "Deserve to be fucked like the goddess you are. The embodiment of power."

"Ares," I moaned loudly. It wasn't an act. His words went deeper than his cock, filling me with succulent heat, so sweet I might burst. His hands caressed my ass, gripping hard one moment and gentle the next as I slowly moved on him. I leaned back, pulling my dress down to expose my breasts. If he wanted to worship me, he could do it properly.

"Fuck yes," Ares breathed. "I need a taste."

I brought one breast to his lips, and they closed around my nipple. There were no gentle kisses here. Ares sucked me hard as I rode him, taking him deeper with each thrust, rotating my hips in a circle to better stimulate my clit.

I reached behind me to take his balls in my hand, squeezing as he sucked my nipple even harder. He growled with pleasure as I did, sending vibrations through my breast. I glanced up for a moment when the Senator roared. His eyes met mine as he came, his fingers gripping the hair of the man whose mouth he fucked.

I smiled at Ares, who grinned wickedly back at me. He had a beautiful smile. I was glad I got to see it. This was the most fun I'd had in years. Wanton, sensual, absolutely filthy—and I loved every second of it. I loved being watched, loved being seen.

Around us, the mood in the room had shifted. More people were openly fucking now, fewer of them paying attention to us as they took their own pleasure. Neither Lux nor Eli were anywhere to be seen, but that was better in some ways. I looked back down at Ares and pulled my dress up over my thighs, a question on my face.

He nodded as I pulled the dress over my head. When it fell to the floor, there were eyes on me again. Ares' mouth closed around my nipple again for a brief moment, and then he pushed me back from his mouth, running his hands down my ribcage. One lingered on my belly and the other went to my clit.

I was on full display for anyone watching now. From a few angles, some people could probably see Ares' cock driving into me as I lifted slowly off him and slammed back down. It felt like he had grown two sizes inside me. I pressed my palm against the hand on my belly.

"Can you feel your cock inside me?" I asked, knowing that at least a few people in the room could hear me. "Can you feel how big you are, how full of you I am?"

Ares groaned as I rode him harder.

"You're so fucking big." The words fell from my mouth —a performance, but an honest one. "Fuck me so deep, Ares."

His mouth was back on my breast, his arms tight around me as he held me close, fucking me so hard it felt impossible from the angle he was at. But he was a man possessed now, his cock pulsing into me as he sucked my nipples in hard, wet turns, pulling them to stiff peaks.

One hand grabbed my ass, pulling me harder onto him with each thrust, while the other wound through the hair at the base of my neck. Ares pulled my hair as he came inside me, making me scream with the euphoria that broke over me in seemingly endless waves.

When my eyes opened, my breath still came in fast, hard pants. Ares gathered me close to him, pressing kisses to my cheeks and temples, before his lips met mine. Our kiss was long and sweet, and when we finally came up for air, I noticed a basket next to the chair. Someone had been by without my notice.

Ares lifted me off of him, and sat me gently in the chair. He buttoned himself up neatly, then knelt on the floor in front of me. I frowned, opening my mouth to protest, but he shook his head. The room still watched.

He bent between my legs, spreading my thighs wide as he buried his face in my pussy, lapping up the combined fluids of our encounter. His mouth was soft and warm on me, and though it felt good, he did not suck my clit or push fingers into me. This too was a show, but not just for them, for me too.

Ares Necroline was showing a side of himself the world rarely saw. He lifted the lid of the basket, drawing a warm washcloth from inside the steaming depths, and ran it up each of my thighs. With each sweep clean he kissed me again, his tongue gentle on my sensitive flesh.

It felt so good I could cry and though I already longed for his fingers, I knew I couldn't take them. But when he took my clit between his lips, rolling it so slowly and gently I couldn't possibly be hurt, tears slipped down my face as I came again.

Ares pulled me to him when the last of my cries died down, dragging a robe around my shoulders and wrapping me up in it. He gathered me into his arms and lifted me off the chair.

"It's time to get some rest," he said, softly. "Don't worry, I have your phone."

I nodded, my eyes heavy. "I want to go home, I think," I murmured.

"Of course," he whispered.

I buried my face in his shoulder. I wasn't ashamed of a thing we'd done, but the night had exhausted me. "I have to tell you something," I whispered. "I know how to get around the spirit traps."

"Tell me when we get outside," he murmured.

I nodded, resting against him until we were outside waiting for the cab. Then I whispered what Myrine had told me. He smiled, faintly. "That's good," he said. "I can work with that."

***

He held me in his lap the whole way home in the cab, watching over me as I dozed, pressing kisses to my lips every time I lifted my chin. I tasted myself on him each time his tongue swept mine. And when I fell asleep in my bed, he was naked at my back, holding me so tightly that for the first time in years I fell asleep feeling safe.

CHAPTER 33

ARES

Disorientation clouded my mind as I woke. It took a few heartbeats to remember where I was. The Carlyle. Ember's room. I turned over in bed, expecting to find her next to me, where I'd left her last night, but she was gone.

I glanced at the clock. It was only six, but if she was up, I should be up. My muscles felt heavy and overused as I pushed out of bed, dragging my hand over my face. I didn't bother with clothes. Ember had two robes that hung on hooks in her bathroom; I'd seen them last night. One was missing.

I took the one that was left, a silk, floor length number in aubergine, with a beautiful print of chrysanthemums. I wondered if she knew they stood for comfort in times of grief. If that was why she'd chosen this robe, to wrap comfort around her lonely heart.

If the previous night had taught me anything, it was that Ember Verona was as lonely as I was—probably lonelier. She thought everyone would leave her. Trusted no one to want her, or to stay. As I wrapped her robe tightly around my waist, the resolve within me strengthened. I wouldn't be the one to walk away.

It was all right if she decided she didn't want this or couldn't

ALLISON CARR WAECHTER

do it. But I wasn't going anywhere; I'd meant what I'd said to her. I'd wanted this for longer than I'd previously been able to admit. Now that I had even the smallest taste of what it might be like to have her for real, to truly partner with her, I wasn't going to give up my place by her side easily.

I padded down the hallway, making my way towards the office, where I could hear voices. From the snippets of conversation that I could make out, it was obvious that everyone already knew about the Rosewood, what we'd found at Cromvale's apartment, and how we planned to disable the spirit traps.

I made a detour and headed for the kitchen. This wasn't a conversation I wanted to have without coffee. Briony found me a few minutes later, as I finished pulling espresso shots.

"Hey," she said, so casual it was difficult to conjure up images of the way I'd found her.

The teenager wore an oversized sweatsuit with a label I recognized as an expensive clothing brand, which meant that she'd been allowed to shop. Or that someone had shopped for her. Rhiannon, if I had to guess. Her dark hair was pulled up into a messy knot atop her head, and she wore big fluffy slippers and a pair of glasses.

I watched as she poured herself a cup of coffee, dumped a shitload of milk and creamer into it, and then topped it with whipped cream from a bowl she pulled out of the fridge. Stanley trailed behind her, once again in tomcat form. He hissed once at me as he passed, but Briony hushed him, almost absentminded as she went about her business.

"Do you like it here?" I asked when she'd finished dumping chocolate sprinkles onto her whipped cream topping. There was enough sugar in the concoction to make my teeth ache, just looking at it.

She glanced up at me. "Yeah. I like the Maere. I'm excited to ascend... eventually."

I nodded. "And has anyone talked to you about what happens next?"

Briony sighed, like I was the most annoying person in the world to her. "Ares, get to the point, please."

I suppressed a laugh. This child *did* fit in with the Maere. But better than that, she seemed to be doing all right, despite all she'd been through. I needed to make sure she was okay, but I sensed asking outright might not be the move. "Do you want to stay with them? Do they want you to stay?"

She gave me an odd look, like my questions were ridiculous. "Yes. Ember asked me to stay the first night. They've all said I can live with them… wherever they go next."

Briony walked out of the kitchen. I grabbed my mug and followed her. "Wherever they go *next*?"

The teenager shrugged as she wandered back into the office. "Ask them yourself."

"Are you planning to move?" I asked as Briony took a seat on a couch next to a giant pinboard and Ember.

Clearly, plans were being made for a few different things. Lara sat on a matching leather chesterfield, directly opposite them. No one else was in the office.

Ember smiled at me, her cheeks flushing a little as she took in what I was wearing. "It's a possibility. Given what we've learned about the cult of Chiore, combined with some other factors… it feels like leaving official Consulate ground might be wise."

I nodded, glancing at the pinboard. There was an entire column devoted to the island, a group of missing Maere, and the mysterious "Mother." I knew what part she'd played in all this, so far, but…"Who is Mother?"

Lara took a big deep breath, but Briony was the one who answered. "We don't know. She's portrayed herself as a Consulate plant inside the Authority. Ember thinks she might be one of the missing Maere. They elected to leave the island, rather than remaining trapped there for eternity or reincarnating as guardians."

"Okay," I said slowly, unsure why Briony was answering me.

But Ember simply smiled and nodded. She was obviously proud of Briony for having absorbed so much of what was happening. Seeing her with the girl softened something inside me, much as it seemed to have softened her. Ember liked being a mentor. That much was clear.

Lara sat back, watching Briony carefully, as though assessing something about what she had said. Her posture was relaxed, but her expression was avid. Something bothered her.

Finally, she spoke, leaning forward to place her elbows on her knees, her chin resting in her hands as she stared at the board. "I don't think Mother is the one who stole the swords—I mean, I know that we suspect the Chiorics were the ones who orchestrated that, but I don't think Mother is affiliated with them."

I sipped my coffee, nodding to show that I understood. But from the way Ember and Briony had perked up, this wasn't information they'd already discussed. Lara was simply continuing the discussion.

It was comfortable the way they'd accepted that I was a part of this now. I didn't even mind that we'd gotten off topic, and no one had explained to me if they were planning to move out of this place.

Lara got up and took a big piece of paper from the printer by the windows. She pinned it to an empty spot on the pinboard. It was the same web of dates as what Ember and I had found the night before. But now, the dates had labels. I set my mug down on the coffee table and went to look at what she'd produced.

A few dates were crossed out, like the ones Ember had recognized as thwarted plans. Those had been labeled with both the perpetrator that Lara had eliminated, along with their intended victim, and whether they were alive or dead at this juncture. Everything else was a dizzying array of parapsych murders, but quite a few dates were empty.

"We're calling this web of atrocities *Project Hierophant*," Lara said. I liked the name. It fit. She tapped one of the empty dates. "These have to be events like stealing our swords."

From the couch, Briony added, "Rhi went back to the Library of Amarante to look for information on the Chiorics." She pulled a laptop out from under the couch and started typing quickly as she read the dates off the pinboard. I had no idea what she was doing, but the child was something of a genius with her computer.

I crossed my arms, staring at the pinboard for a little longer, willing some hidden piece of things to appear so that I could make an equal contribution. Behind me, Ember whispered, "I like your robe."

A laugh bubbled up from deep inside me. I turned to wink at her, but one of the more recent dates on the pinboard caught my eye. It was six months ago, and it seemed familiar.

"I'll be right back," I said, rushing back to Ember's bedroom to get my phone.

When I returned, I keyed in several codes to reach my calendar, scrolling back several months until I found the date. Sure enough, it matched. I set my phone down on the coffee table and thought hard. The women were quiet, clearly waiting for me to finish thinking.

"On this day, I met with an antiquities dealer in Midtown." My jaw clenched as I struggled to regain as much of the memory as I could. "Poor guy had an infestation of Poltergeists, attracted to objects that hadn't been properly cleared for sale." This was the part I was struggling with, though. It had been nothing to me at the time. "A man came in, plain, unremarkable in nearly every way… like Fairchild. He asked after something called a thry—"

"A thrysos?" Lara asked, her expression dark.

Ember gasped. "Surely not."

I shrugged. "That might have been it. I can't remember. The only reason I paid any attention was that the shop owner stopped speaking to me, and shook his head at the attendant who helped the man. When his attention returned to me, he was visibly upset, and asked if we could take our conversation to his office."

I paused again, remembering the rest. "When I left, the man was gone, but so was the attendant. I honestly just thought they didn't have whatever it was the guy was looking for."

Lara stood, taking up a footpath across the room, pacing. Briony watched, then turned her attention to Ember, expectation clear on her face. The teenager wanted an explanation.

Ember seemed to respond to her, patting her hand before answering. "The thrysos has been depicted in many different ways. Some say that Chiore carries one. That it is a weapon, a staff of sorts, that can kill a god... Or one of the Maere."

Lara paused in front of the arched, leaded glass window. Backlit by the late morning light, she looked rather like one of the statues of avenging angels that could be found around the city. I could see how she got her moniker. "Some have also called our swords by that name. The word has as many meanings as our name does."

"Maere?" I asked.

Now it was Briony's turn to answer a question, and she looked pleased as a schoolchild. "Maere has roots in lots of words. It can describe the sea, or nightmares... it even has roots in some of the names of the original factions of warriors who populated the island, right?"

Ember nodded. "Yes, all that is true. Thrysos is not a word we commonly use on the island. It's a human name for our tools, which is why it has an inconsistent meaning... much like the word Maere itself. But it could be referring to Chiore's weapon, certainly."

Rhiannon appeared in the doorway, dressed in a matching set of navy blue workout clothes, her hair pulled back tightly into a slick bun. "If the Chiorics are looking for a thrysos, it is because they want to cut us down." She stalked towards the pinboard, staring at the date in question in comparison to the others that had been identified. "I think we should assume they were successful."

"No," Briony answered. "They weren't... How to explain this... The dates are a pattern of some sort. A mix of moon phases, though not all *our* moon. They seem to be tracking a moon from a distant planet, Tyche. Some of these dates are when Tyche is in a kind of alignment with our moon... There has to be some significance here." She turned her screen. "Does this mean anything to you?"

Ember glanced at the screen, then shook her head. "That's not very precise, but you might be onto something. Rituals do typically follow an astrological pattern." She pointed to several of the alignments in the simulation Briony had seemingly conjured from nothing. "Look, each is several degrees off; they're all different."

Briony shrugged. "I'll keep working on it."

Both Rhiannon and Ember nodded, while Lara simply turned to stare out the window. When she spoke, her voice was flat. "This is a setup. Surely you see it. Someone's luring us in. Whether it's some Chioric faction or the missing Maere, this whole thing is a trap."

"Yes," Ember agreed, standing up from the couch. She stared at the pinboard, frowning at the list of dates. "But what else are we going to do? Just leave the swords?"

"We could try to buy them," I suggested. As soon as the words left my mouth, I wanted to take them back.

Ember leaned back on the arm of the sofa. "If they want us trapped, they're not going to allow us to simply buy them."

Rhiannon crossed her arms tightly over her chest. "So we have to be better than them. Faster. Get in, get out fast, before the auction even begins. That's been the plan all along."

Ember nodded, but as she did, she frowned. "The trouble is, if we assume this is a trap, then we have to assume they'll assume we plan to do this the safest way possible."

Rhiannon grimaced, then stared at the ceiling. "So, what do we do? *Go* to the auction?"

I drew a breath in. That would be dangerous, but it might also play to our advantage. Whoever was planning this would assume that we wouldn't risk doing this the hardest way possible. But if we waited until the very last moment to steal the swords, we might actually take them by surprise. I shook my head at Ember. It was a wild idea, but it might work.

Ember smiled when I finally shrugged, tossing my hands into the air. "Guess we're going to a party," she said with a grin.

Lara groaned in response, while Rhiannon simply glared at the pinboard. The only sound in the room was Briony's fingers clacking over her keyboard, drumming out an anxious rhythm.

Rhiannon moved towards the pinboard. "There's something about these dates I don't like…" She shook her head, as though frustrated, then glanced at Briony. "Any luck refining those numbers?"

Briony shook her head, her fingers still flying over the keyboard. "No, but it might help if you told me what you're thinking."

Rhiannon grimaced. "I can't put my finger on it. There's a pattern in them, like you said, but it's more than just some astrological event. The whole thing looks like *something*." It was the most imprecise I'd ever heard her be.

Briony stopped typing to stare at the pinboard. She nodded. "I see what you're saying. It's like there's a pattern behind the pattern. Like chess, almost. Like someone orchestrated all of this very carefully."

Ember grimaced. "The Cognoscenti they have working for them. That's gotta be it."

Lara sighed. "Is it possible Cromvale is the Cognoscenti, and that's why he has all this stuff? Or Fairchild? Both of them are way too deep into all this."

I shook my head. "They're human. We'd know if they weren't. It has to be someone else."

The silky fabric of Ember's robe trailed behind her, catching on the couch for a brief moment as she got up to stand closer to Lara, giving me a glimpse of her bare skin. Ember's arm went around Lara's waist. The two of them were the same height and Lara had to bend somewhat to lean her head on Ember's shoulder, her muscular arm snaking around Ember's waist as she hugged her tightly.

Rhiannon only watched the two of them, some unspoken pain in her eyes. Did she feel left out by their affection for one another? The look passed in the span of a heartbeat, and I feared I might have imagined it, but for the way the assassin now appeared to force her hands from fists, balled at her sides, to a more relaxed state.

The sound of the front door opening and closing was quickly followed by the sound of Eryx and Av talking at once. Both of them sounded excited, and I noted with some guilt, relieved. From the sound of things, they'd figured out a way to get the swords out of the case once we'd dealt with the spirit traps.

I heard the words "shape charges" and "targeted explosions" in the midst of their chatter. Lara's eyes lit up at the same words, and she slid out of Ember's arms to go join Eryx and Av in their discussion.

As Lara said, "so, we're blowing shit up, huh?" Ember turned to me. Her eyes met mine as a soft ray of sunshine broke through the clouds for a moment, before retreating, leaving her face in shadow. Her smile stretched into a grin, and for the first time in years, I no longer felt lonely.

CHAPTER 34

EMBER

Two DAYS LATER, and I was almost sure I understood the technical aspects of our plan, though it made me nervous that we still didn't know who'd stolen the swords. Rhiannon and I had both exhausted all our contacts and research methods, and so had Ares. There was no sign of the mysterious Maere that had sought out the Chioric threat so long ago.

That didn't worry me so much. If they were Maere, they'd know how to keep themselves hidden. It did further confirm my theory that the mysterious "Mother" was probably one of them, though, and I liked the idea that there might be someone out there on our side. The most likely answer now was that the Chiorics stole the swords and were baiting us, probably with the Authority's go-ahead, which would explain why no one had seen hide nor hair of Fairchild since we rescued Briony.

Too much was still unknown for my taste, but we had plenty going for us.

Ares understood what Myrine had meant by using one of our auras as a "lens" for his power, to create just enough of a disruption in the spirit traps to loosen their grip on the five imprisoned, unascended Maere. It had just been a hint, but he'd run with it, figuring out exactly how to maneuver his power to disrupt the spirit traps.

He said it was easy once he thought to look at it that way. I gave silent thanks to Amarante for Myrine's generosity. I wanted to be the one he used, but Lara made a godsdamn compelling argument against it, given that she was the explosives expert between us, and I was the best fighter. Someone had to watch her back while she set the targeted shape-explosives that would blow the bottom off the case and send the swords straight through the floor of the National Gallery after the others disabled the spirit traps.

All in all, it was a risky plan and we would get out of it by the skin of our teeth, if we were lucky. The morning was rainy, as per usual, and in the background of the office, Briony was watching the news. The Ceti had been sighted near shore again, causing another round of massive waves on the coast. Humans were uneasy. Rumors were already circulating that somehow parapsych groups were enticing the monsters to shore.

The Senate was meeting in a special council to go over a bill that would require parapsychs to have a special section on their identification keys, explaining what level of parapsychism they possessed. In my experience, the bill was unlikely to pass. The Senate met to discuss such measures any time humans drummed up hysteria over parapsychism, only to be wooed later by the Consulate in back room meetings—and, of course, with bribes.

Bribes paid for by our people's tithes to the Consulate. I tried to shut out the news, but couldn't stop listening to it. To distract myself, I found a pair of noise-canceling headphones in my desk drawer and put them on.

When it was quiet once more, I looked over the real estate listings Rhiannon had sent me again. The connecting properties downtown were in a neighborhood primarily inhabited by necromancers and cognoscenti. The two houses had most recently been for sale for nearly four years. Though both mansions were in lovely shape, the smaller of the two was considered to be the most haunted place in Orphium. The spirit activity there was especially malicious.

I didn't believe the neighborhood lore that there was treasure hidden somewhere between the two properties, but it was hard to deny that anyone who'd purchased them met a grisly end if they spent too much time in Oleander Cottage. And they always did. It was why the properties were tied to one another. Whoever owned Hemlock House always ended up in Oleander Cottage at some point, and they always died gruesome deaths. The most recent owners simply never moved in, having disappeared.

The two houses had been empty for fifty years at this point. No one wanted them. No one but Rhiannon, who was sure that if anyone could survive the most haunted houses in Orphium, we could. She and Lara both argued that once we got the swords back, we couldn't stay here. That if we wanted our power back, to be the force the island thought they were sending to Orphium eons ago, that we would have to leave the Carlyle and the Consulate's money behind.

I didn't disagree, but the houses troubled me a little, though I couldn't put my finger on why. If we had our swords back, we could ward off Oleander Cottage. That would be simple enough for us with access to the island's real magic, and then we could live in Hemlock House. The photos were lovely. It would make a good home for Briony.

Ares sat across from me, going over Avaline's morning EMF readings from the National Gallery, comparing them to the ones she'd taken before in a spreadsheet that hurt my head to look at. He wore a pair of horn-rimmed glasses as he entered more variables. I sighed happily, looking at him. I wanted to play professor and cute co-ed while he wore those glasses…

I let myself daydream a filthy little scene for a few moments before crossing my legs and dragging my brain out of the smut factory. I tried to remind myself that he was playing with spreadsheets, not my clit, but that didn't help much. According to him, he was testing the calculations of auric energy he would have to channel through Rhiannon's aura to reverse the aspects of the spirit boxes that trapped the unascended Maere inside.

Reminding myself of all that was enough to quiet my lust-ridden brain down a notch or two. It was all more than I could hope to understand, but Rhiannon seemed to, and that was all that mattered. They'd tested their theory several times this morning, having constructed several spirit traps of their own. I hated the thought of them doing any of it while Briony watched, but the girl was fascinated by it all.

"What do you know about Hemlock House and Oleander Cottage?" I asked Ares, keeping my voice soft as I took my headphones off.

He looked up, taking his glasses off so he could see me. Apparently, he only needed them for reading. "Hemlock House was the first official Necroline property in Orphium. Roman is actually the one who sold it."

Of course, I knew that already. It was why I asked. "Would you ever buy the property back?"

Ares sat back in his chair, narrowing his eyes at me. "Maybe. But Oleander Cottage is the real problem. Even I couldn't exorcize the spirits haunting that place. Roman had me try twice before he sold it."

Ares held my gaze for what might be an uncomfortably long amount of time for someone else, but simply lit a fire in my core that reopened the smut factory, as I imagined what we'd do together tonight. He was definitely going to wear those glasses while we did it.

"I always thought Eryx could do it, though. But Roman insisted that he go nowhere near the place," he continued. "I got the impression he had higher information on the matter."

"A spirit?" I asked.

Ares shook his head. "No, a Seer."

I made a noncommittal noise in reply. Without more information, it was futile to speculate on what a Seer might or might not have predicted.

"Why do you ask about the houses?"

I shrugged, turning my screen towards him. "Rhiannon wants to buy them. They're expensive, but we have more than enough, especially if we drain the last of the funds from the Consulate."

Explosives were expensive. The account that had once seemed like it would last forever was practically gone, and I wasn't the least bit sorry about it.

Ares nodded. "It would be a good buy. If anyone could survive Oleander Cottage, it would be you." His tone was clipped.

Fear rose up inside me, dousing the heat that had mounted in me only moments before. I knew I should ask what was wrong if I wanted to know, but like a coward, I couldn't seem to form the words.

All the sex we were having was divine, but the more he fucked me, the more fearful I became. We'd been screwing like wild hares every chance we got, but I thought it was leading to more. If it wasn't, I might die of shame, I wanted him so much. It would be just like me to let love finally be the thing that killed me.

Love? Terror dug its claws into me. I couldn't think like this.

Instead, I asked a less controversial question than "what's wrong?" "Did you want to buy them?"

He'd gone back to his spreadsheet and looked up again with a little sigh. He sounded so annoyed with me, but I truly couldn't say if it was in my head or if he actually was irritated with me. "Not at all. Have at it."

And with that, he went back to typing. I tried telling myself that he was in the middle of something important. That this very likely had nothing to do with me whatsoever and not to make everything about me. But rational thought wasn't actually helpful in moments like these. I was so used to rejection, so prepared for it, that I saw it everywhere I looked.

It wasn't that I didn't *know* that. It was that no matter how hard I thought about it logically, I couldn't make it go away. Tears filled my eyes, but I couldn't cry. Not here. Not in front of him, when he would soften at the sight of my sorrow and confuse me all the more.

I bit back my emotions, shoving them as far back inside myself as they would go. I didn't want to dwell, so I shot off several text messages and finished answering my emails. Now that Rhiannon and Lara were back, the Consulate wanted us on several new jobs. I was having trouble fending them off. We couldn't take any commissions from them right now. My phone buzzed back almost immediately, and I let myself become engrossed enough in my communications that the edgy feeling I had about Ares faded into the background.

Rhiannon and Avaline swept in. They'd spent the morning working on alterations for what everyone would wear to the Gala, and they had the invitations that Ares had procured for them. They were stolen from some human aristocrats who were vacationing in Palladiere this weekend, our only bit of cover for the night, as our group would be recognized immediately upon arrival.

I felt guilty for feeling jealous that I didn't get to dress up for my part in things, but such was life. Still, I wasn't keen on watching the fashion show they obviously had planned, so I excused myself to go to the training room to check my weapons for the thousandth time.

Lara was there already, weighing swords as though one of them might magically become the weapon she wanted most. "Hey," I said softly, not wanting to startle her, even though I was sure she heard me coming.

She replaced the sword on the rack and turned to me. Apparently, she and Briony had been shopping, because Lara wore the same brand of sweatsuit the teenager wore, just in black. I sat down on the floor, leaning against the floor-to-ceiling mirrors, and watched the rain fall outside the window.

"Are you going to leave after we get the swords back?" I asked Lara. It was so much easier to be straightforward with her than it was with Ares.

Lara sat next to me, leaning against the mirror. "No." I nodded, and we sat in silence for several long moments. "Sorry, I've been a bitch about pretty much everything since I got out of the Asylum."

"Me too," I replied. "Sorry you're such a bitch, I mean. I'm not sorry about anything."

Lara laughed, a sweet, rich sound. Her smile transformed her face from stoically handsome to absolutely dazzling.

"Do you want to talk about it?" I asked. "The Asylum, I mean. I haven't asked because I wanted to give you time, not because I don't care."

She shook her head, her mouth pressing into a grim line. "I can't talk about that place, Ember. Not ever... Unless it's necessary for something... I just..."

"It's okay," I replied as quickly as I could, so that I didn't interrupt her, but also so that she didn't feel she needed to keep speaking. "I get it."

There were plenty of Authority Hel-holes, and I'd seen the inside of more of them than I liked to think of. The years after I'd ascended, but before the rest of my sistren had, were dark holes in my memory. Places I didn't touch or return to. The island had a poor grasp on how the reincarnation rituals would actually work. Nothing had gone as planned and being a "new" kind of parapsych under the first waves of the Authority's power had been unending fear and torture.

I closed my eyes, breathing deeply, raising the walls I kept fortified within my mind to allow me to remain whole. Lara touched my hand, empathy in her eyes. She was the only person on the planet who knew a fraction of what I'd gone through. "I'm glad it's just you and me setting the bombs," she said, keeping her voice soft. "I'm glad we don't have to be up there with all those people watching us."

I hadn't thought about it that way. It was exactly what I needed to hear. "Yeah," I murmured. "I'm glad too."

It felt good to sit here with her, feeling the bonds we'd built over so many years thread between us, binding us to one another in the way I'd missed so much. It was a good reminder that no matter what happened with Ares, that in the end, Lara Achilles was my secret-keeper, the person who knew the whole of me. That even when I wanted to murder her out of existence, she was my true match in the depths of darkness.

I hoped things would turn out better than I expected with Ares, but if they didn't, I had Lara and Rhi… and hopefully Sera. If Calypso joined us, we would have new dynamics to navigate, but even with Briony, that was true. For the first time in years, it felt like there was more than just making it through the day or week ahead of me.

"Are you going to buy the houses?" Lara asked, her fingers closing around mine. "Rhi showed me the listing."

I showed her my phone and the evidence that the deal was already done. "Movers come tomorrow. I want us out before this all goes down."

"Shit," Lara swore with a grin. "You moved fast."

I shrugged. "You and Rhi were right. We need to depend less on the Consulate, *and* we need to get back into a neighborhood with our people. Regular people, not just the ones who live here." Lara's responding sigh was so full of relief, I was offended. "Did you think I lost my way?"

Lara swallowed hard. "It's not that, Ember."

I shook my head, frustrated. "Was I that bad a leader? Before you went in, I mean. Be honest."

Lara stared at her hands. "No. It wasn't ever that. But in some ways we were the leftovers, you know? The Aradios and Palladiere cohorts were tight from the start."

They had been. When we were children—the first time on

the island, anyway—they'd been the ones who always worked together, who always chose each other for every game, who went everywhere together. And Max had never been interested in the rest of us. She'd only been Sera's friend. Lara, Rhi and I had been loners, not even friends with each other.

That lifetime had never felt real to me, not after being reborn. I wasn't the woman I'd been on the island, and neither were Sera, Rhi, or Lara… But Max was still attached to who she was on Otrera, in many ways. When she ascended, she'd always thought of her past life as though it were a part of her present.

"Maybe it will help that Max plans to go back," I murmured. "To Aradios. They're trading Calypso out." Lara's silence was the stunned variety. I couldn't blame her.

"Sera fell in love," Lara finally replied. It wasn't a question, but a statement. We'd all seen it coming for years.

"Yes," I hissed, the sound of the one word slow and sibilant as I accepted that things would change. "I think she did. They're just hurting each other now. And for whatever reason, Calypso wants out too."

Lara blew air out her cheeks. "Well, that'll be a change. Calypso's good people though."

It was true, Calypso Montague was good people. I wondered what made her want to leave Aradios.

The muscles in Lara's shoulders tensed for a moment and then released with a long breath out. "You ever hear that rumor that the Aradios Maere can turn into mermaids?"

I laughed. "Yeah. Humans make up the weirdest shit."

Lara laughed too. "Makes sense though, what with the fancy beaches and all that."

I snickered. The City of Miracles was, by all stretches of the imagination, a lot nicer than Orphium—warmer, a giant bay with a better seawall than ours to keep the monsters out. Beaches. Lovely, white sand beaches. *Saints, I needed a vacation.*

"We'll get the swords back," Lara said, her voice low. "I

don't think the Chioric weapon is real. We're gonna make it out of this."

I nodded, blowing past the idea that there was a weapon out there that could kill us. Better not to think about that. *Ever*. I ran my mouth instead. "With the swords back, we can ward off Oleander Cottage and live in Hemlock House."

Lara nodded, glancing at me sidelong, mischief sparkling in her eyes. "Ares and the others would probably help us with that, if you asked. Might be good to have some advice on the wards from the best necromancer in the Three Cities. Would be like the old days."

The old days… My mind drifted back, further and further into memories I didn't particularly want to recall. I hadn't noticed Lara leaving, or returning with blueprints of the Gallery, or that Briony was with her now. The two of them plopped down on the floor across from me, in their matching sweatsuits, spreading the blueprints out on the floor.

"Let's talk about bomb placement," Briony said.

When I raised an eyebrow, Lara shook her head. "She's good at this stuff, Ember. She's got a lot of Cognoscenti in her. Amazing intuition."

"I'm also a hacker and a certified genius," Briony said proudly. "Rhiannon gave me a test yesterday."

"You are *sixteen*," I said, panic mounting in me.

Lara reached out to take my hand. "This is better for her than what happened to the rest of us when we were sixteen, isn't it?"

She knew the memories of what it had been like to be a human teenager were too dark to ruminate on for long. The world had been different, but not so different that Briony wouldn't experience the same thing on her own. Suppressing our natural talents had harmed all of us. At least Briony was with us.

"You are not coming with us to the Gallery," I said, keeping my voice as firm as possible and thinking fast. "You'll have to stay with a grownup."

Briony rolled her eyes. "You sound just like Ares. He said some miracle worker named Eli is going to watch me."

That was good. Eli Cabot was trustworthy, and despite how unsure I was about how Ares felt about me, I was certain I could trust him with Briony's safety. "Fine," I finally said. "Let's talk about explosives."

CHAPTER 35

ARES

THE MORNING OF THE GALA

EMBER CAME TO BED LATE, but at least she'd come to bed with me. I sensed that something had gone wrong between us, but I couldn't say what it was. The movers had come and gone, taking most of the Maere's personal things the day before. The tension between us had been mounting ever since. I'd stayed up half the night, listening to her toss and turn, before finally falling into a deep slumber in the wee hours of morning. I must have fallen asleep about the same time, because I didn't remember the sun rising.

When I woke, it was well after ten, and the apartment was quiet, everyone still deep in slumber. We'd agreed to get as much sleep as we could; after all, everything hinged on tonight. Maybe that was the problem. Perhaps Ember sensed that I expected too much. I stared at a hairline crack in the plaster ceiling, wondering what seismic shift over the years had caused it.

"I can *feel* you thinking," Ember whispered.

I turned onto my side. She faced away from me. Lightly, afraid she did not want my touch, I reached out to touch her shoulder. We were just inches apart, but this morning it felt like miles.

She leaned into me immediately, her back resting against my chest. Relief flooded me, her sigh transforming into the softest moan as her buttocks met my morning erection. She reached back to take the hand that rested on her shoulder, bringing it first to her breast.

Ember moaned again as I gently squeezed the place she brought my hand, her legs tangling with mine, hips angling precisely, until the head of my cock was fitted at her entrance. "Ember," I murmured.

"Shhh," she hushed me. "You'll wake them."

She dragged my hand down her ribcage, lower until my hand splayed across the silky skin on her belly. Ember was lean, but softer than I might have expected, a gentle curve, rather than flat, sculpted abs. It was a delicious surprise the first time I'd seen her naked, and a true pleasure every time since.

I teased her with my cock, pressing it into her wet slit, but not further. She arched against me, trying to take in more of me, but I refused to oblige her. I felt her frustration shudder through her and she flipped over, pushing me flat onto the bed as she straddled me in one quick movement.

Whenever she used her immortal speed or strength, it made me so hard I couldn't concentrate. And as she sank down on my cock, taking me in one smooth stroke, her naked body glorious in the gray light of morning, I'd never wanted her so much. She closed her eyes, leaning back to touch her clit as she moved on me.

I wanted to tell her I loved her.

Wanted to tell her that maybe I'd loved her for years and hadn't known it. But the words would not come. I pulled her down towards me, onto all fours, so that she had to look me straight in the face.

"Look at me," I whispered as she slid on and off my cock.

Her eyes met mine and fire lashed through my veins, my balls tightening with anticipation. Her walls clenched around me as she panted, her mouth falling open so that I could see her wet tongue. She ground her clit against me, milking every bit of tight friction and pleasure she could from me.

I slid my hands down her back until I had two firm handfuls of her ass cheeks and then pulled myself deeper into her. She was about to moan, so I captured her mouth with mine, kissing her as deep as I fucked her.

There was nothing like this in the world. It wasn't that our movements were new, or particularly creative. It was her, all her. We had human lifetimes' worth of history between us, and all of it should have kept us from wanting this. But it didn't. I had never wanted something like this for myself. I'd made the mistake of thinking that love—romantic love, at least—was not meant for me.

But here it was, blooming inside me like the flowers I'd always loved so much. And yet, I couldn't bring myself to say the words. If it was too soon, if she didn't love me the way I did her... I just couldn't know that today of all days.

Her movements took on a frenzied pace, her fingers winding through my hair as her tongue tangled with mine. The two of us were desperate, too many conflicting emotions racing through us. She shuddered against me, her back bowing as she raised up slightly, then pulled herself harder against me, her mouth falling open in a silent scream that sent me right over the edge behind her.

When her body finally stilled, I stroked her back, kissing her again. The way she returned my kiss was sad, as though she were saying goodbye. "What's wrong?"

"What will happen when we have our swords back?" she asked. Her voice was quieter than a whisper. So quiet I almost wondered if I'd imagined her speaking. "To us, I mean."

Her question scared the shit out of me. What I wanted might be miles apart from what she did. The thing I never wanted between us was a struggle for power, and she was just getting hers back.

"Oh," she said, pulling back.

I'd taken too long to answer—but that was me, a slow thinker—always wanting to say precisely what I meant, and not a word more or less. She tried to pull away from me, but I moved quickly, grabbing her arms as she sat up. "Stop," I breathed. "Please."

Ember paused, her pussy clenching around my cock, which was coming quickly back from half-mast as she moved on me. She must have felt the way I responded to her, because she rolled her hips a few times, touching her clit in slow, deliberate movements. Fluid seeped out of her, onto my thighs.

"Saints," I breathed. "You feel so fucking good. Stop moving so I can think."

"No," she answered, shaking her head in a stubborn way that should have frustrated me, but only made me harder. "I don't want you to think. I don't want you to answer. Not right now. I don't want to know."

I pulled her back down to me, fisting the hair at the nape of her neck with one hand, and grabbing a handful of her ass with the other. "You are assuming the worst of me, Verona," I hissed in her ear. "Stop telling yourself I don't want you."

I thrust hard into her, and she almost moaned, but bit her lip instead. I kept her pinned to me, my fingers digging into her hair and tightening on her ass as I tilted my hips to pulse inside her, to reach that spot that made her squirm.

When I hit it, she whimpered, so I mimicked the movement several more times, gently teasing her, keeping her still so she couldn't take me deeper and control her own pleasure. I had to make myself clear to her, even if now wasn't the time to profess my love.

"Feel how hard I am?" I growled in her ear. "The way I'm stretching you open, filling you up?"

She nodded, arching hard against me to take me deeper, but I kept her pinned in place. I wanted to fuck her as hard as she wanted me to, but I had to make this point, and make it in a way that would carry us through this difficult day. On the other side of this, when we had what we needed to create a new life for ourselves, we could talk about love.

"No one gets me hard like you, because no one challenges me like you do. I don't know what's next, but I know we need time to figure it out. To see where we fit into each other's lives."

"Okay," she replied, gasping for breath as I teased her.

"Do you understand, Ember? Do you understand that I am only this way for you? That I have only *ever* been this way for *you*?"

Her eyes widened, and I think she understood me. Something changed on her face, and she became liquid in my arms. "Yes," she moaned, my confession having sparked some new height of pleasure within her.

Good. It had done the same for me. My cock felt like it might erupt.

I pushed her back, releasing her hair. "Show me how I fit inside you," I commanded. "Ride me hard, Verona. Come all over me."

"Fuck," she swore, her lips swollen as she clenched me tight.

I reached forward to grab her ass with both hands.

"Fuck me as hard as you can," I growled. "Show me how good it feels to have me inside you."

She slid desperately against me now, her breasts bouncing as I pulled on her hips, thrusting as hard inside her as I could from this angle. "Touch yourself."

Ember's fingers went to her clit, and it was enough for us both. The sight of her body moving on me, writhing for me, her back bowing as she silently came all over me, our fluids mixing in hot waves of pleasure as I filled her. She fell boneless against me, entirely spent.

It was the right time to tell her how I felt, by all reasonable measures of that sort of thing. We were, essentially, going into battle. There was every possibility that tonight would go wrong somehow. With the possibility of Chiore's weapon on the table, anything could happen.

But neither of us spoke. Ember slid off me, kissing me as she went. "I need to get ready," she said. "Lara and I have to go in an hour."

"See you at Hemlock House after?"

She slid into her robe, nodding before she bent to kiss me again. "Sure."

I grabbed her hand when she tried to pull away, not liking the clipped end to that single word. "Don't disappear on me, Ember."

"I'm not," she said, her voice relaxing a little. "I just wish we had more time."

I brought her hand to my lips, kissing the back of it first, then pressing my lips to her palm, an intimate gesture. "We are immortal, Verona. We have all the time in the world."

Ember stared down at me, her hazel eyes sad and hopeful at the same time. "I hope you're right, Ares. See you tonight, when it's done."

"Promise?" I asked her.

"I'll be there," she replied, before slipping away to get ready. There would be no emotional goodbyes—neither of us could take it—but it felt like my heart was dissolving in my chest. Or maybe it was just the last walls of protection I had left for myself.

If anything happened to her, I wouldn't survive it. I let myself get in far too deep here, all for dreams of a future I wasn't sure was even possible. I sat up in bed, covering my face with my hands. Just a few more hours, and then we'd sort all this out. We just had to make it through the night.

CHAPTER 36

EMBER

THE AFTERNOON OF THE GALA

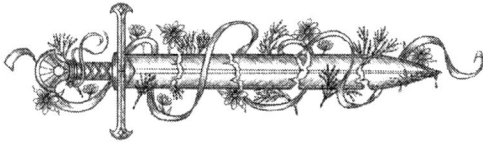

LARA and I left without saying goodbye. The Orphium Maere never said good luck, never said goodbye. There was no need, after all. We were eternal. But I could tell from the jittery way Lara tapped out a beat on the steering wheel of the Dodger that the Chioric weapon was on her mind, same as it was mine.

We were dressed similarly in close-fitting cargo pants, heavy combat boots, and warm sweaters. Lara wore a turtleneck, but I couldn't stand to have anything so close around my neck on a day like today. The tall collar of my sweater was less constricting due to the zipper that I'd left undone.

Lara raised an eyebrow as I got back into the car with our breakfast sammies. Two jumbo biscuit-egg-and-cheeses with bacon from Little Jimmie's on Fourth and triple shot lattes to go.

"Does Ares like it when you wear those pushup bras?" Lara joked, tweaking my zipper as I arranged our food.

I glared at her teasing face. "It's not a pushup bra. It's a sports bra." I gestured to my tits. "So they don't bounce all over the place while we blow up the National Gallery."

Lara snickered, taking a big bite of her sandwich. "I'm so fucking glad we don't have to dress up tonight."

I didn't answer her. I wouldn't have minded dressing up with Ares. It had seemed like he might say something emotional to me this morning, some profession of how he felt, or what he wanted from me. I'd wanted him to, but at the same time, a superstitious beast lived inside me. I avoided saying how I felt, because declarations felt like goodbye, like hedging. We could say what we needed to later.

Lara and I ate in silence. "You gonna choose the mixtape, or what?" she said as we tossed our wrappers into the to-go bag.

I flipped the glove box open, chose my favorite and threw it in the deck. Lara turned the volume up as a sick drumbeat pulsed through the car. Shivers skittered over my skin as I watched Lara drive. Hoofbeats of the past echoed through me. She shifted gears, the Dodger leaping forward as she wove through traffic. Her hand slid across the console.

Lara's fingers wove through mine, and I squeezed her hand. She drew it to her chest, letting me feel her heartbeat, which was strong and steady. "Sing it, Verona," she ordered me as the lyrics began.

Memories of our voices, lifted to Tanith and Amarante on an ancient battlefield, slipped through the atoms of the car, mixing past and present. Lara's heartbeat set the pace of my own. She let go of my hand to shift and the familiar music swelled, taking me through memories of all the victories we'd ever had.

And there had been many.

In this lifetime and the last.

The Authority could fuck with us forever. We had the time to wait them out. They took Lara from me. Tricked Max and Sera into betraying us. Separated us at every turn. But we were here now, making our way towards the swords that would set things right.

We were very likely walking right into a trap, but the three of us were about to take back what was ours. And tonight, after we had our swords back, I'd call Max and apologize one last time. I'd figure out where Sera's sword was, and whatever happened next, we would win. I wasn't going to let anyone keep us down from here on out.

Whoever did all this wasn't going to ruin us. *I wouldn't let them.*

Lara grinned at me as the song changed, biting her bottom lip, her pronounced canines gleaming viciously as rain splattered on the window. I laughed as she swayed to the guitar riff at the start of her favorite song, then unlocked my phone and sent Rhiannon the digital version I had saved of this mixtape with the note, *Blast the shit out of this while you get pretty, and keep the necromancers safe tonight.*

She sent back a positively filthy selfie, which I flashed at Lara, who shook her head. "I'll never get over her."

I laughed, tears pricking at the corner of my eyes. "You already are."

She shook her head. "You don't get over Rhiannon. She just lives inside you." Lara sighed. "Deep… inside."

I laughed so hard that I snorted. The two of them loved to make jokes about their breakup at the most inappropriate times. It felt like we were back. "We can do this," I said, before turning the music's volume up all the way.

As we crossed the bridge into uptown, strength filled me. I touched the medallions around my neck. One for Tanith. One for Amarante. I was sure about this. We could get the swords back.

A half hour later and we were in. The first bombs to set were the ones directly under the swords in the Auction Gallery. From all of Avaline's spying, we knew there would be guards on this level. But when we got there, the numbers were double what we'd anticipated.

The long hallway underneath the swords was packed with a dozen well-armed guards. To our advantage, there was no electricity on this level, so the hallway was dimly lit, only the glow of the guards' personal neons in the murky darkness.

As quietly as possible, we stashed the backpacks with the bombs and drew knives. I nodded to Lara. I wished to all the gods that Rhiannon was here instead of me. Her famous silence would be a boon right now. Lara brushed a kiss to my left cheek and disappeared, doubling back to come at the guards from the other direction.

I tried to channel Rhi's silent movement as I approached the first guard. My knife slid through his throat like his tendons were made of butter. I covered his mouth while he shuddered in my arms, before laying him silently to rest in the grid of hallways that intersected this part of the passage, and moving onto the next.

At the opposite end of the hallway, Lara took one out of her own before the guards noticed us. We disappeared into the grid. It was a labyrinth down here, but I hardly cared. Senses I hadn't used in years kicked in. I'd forgotten what it meant to be Maere.

Somehow I'd lost sight of the fact that while the swords gave us a fuller range of parapsych powers, I was not human—and never had been, in any lifetime. I'd let myself forget. But now, as my eyesight adjusted to the dark, I became the predator that Amarante and Tanith made me.

I slid through the darkness as though it were broad daylight, sensing the racing hearts of the human guards, and the steady heartbeat I knew was Lara's. One by one, the guards fell. Knives slicing through flesh in the cursed dark. Heartbeats silenced in a macabre ballet of death.

When I met Lara back in the hallway, she wore a neon headband from one of her victims. "Keep watch," she murmured as she unpacked the backpack she'd retrieved, setting up a folding step-ladder that she scrambled up to set the explosives.

I nodded, keeping my knives drawn, listening for movement elsewhere in the building. Above us, I sensed the kind of movement I expected, preparing for the Gala. I didn't watch Lara work. There was no need. She knew what she was doing, after all.

When she climbed down, we packed up, retrieved my backpack, and made our way to the next level down, where we repeated the process. This time, there were fewer guards to kill, at least. By the time we arrived in the catacombs to set up the net, there was no one left to kill.

Lara set up our harnesses and the explosives, while I worked to stretch the net across the columns that dug deep into the subterranean lake beneath the National Gallery. Long ago, the aquifer that fed the Erydanos River, which cut through the center of Orphium, had created this underground lake.

Why anyone had thought to build a giant museum on top of a subterranean lake was beyond me. Humans did make the oddest decisions. It made for an unsettling project, stretching the net above the dark water. But it would ensure that neither of us had to dive for the swords if we couldn't manage to catch them as they came through the floor. When the other four had dispatched with the spirit traps, we would set off the explosives. The swords would fall through the building and we'd have them back.

There was no need to hide who had done it. The swords were ours. The Authority could hardly punish us for taking them back, despite the fact that they would surely want to. With our swords back, Orphium would slowly return to balance. And when we had Sera's our cohort would be whole again. Nearly impossible to stop. As I climbed into my harness to wait, I wondered if there was a part of Ares that was threatened by that strength.

My fears dissolved at almost the same moment they appeared. The memory of him cleaning me, caring for me, after our public encounter at the Rosewood played in my mind.

It hadn't just been aftercare, or a performance. It had been a show of fealty. A way of understanding the push and pull of power between us that I hadn't understood until now.

We would always be in some ways at odds. Our power was different. Never equal. But we needed each other. Somehow, we finished one another. He filled in my rough edges and I loosened the rigidity with which he approached life.

I clenched my jaw as Lara climbed into her harness, almost afraid to ask her what she thought. But I'd played scared long enough. "If me and Ares got together for real, would that be okay with you?"

Lara laughed, and for once it was a joyful sound, not sardonic or suspicious in the slightest. "Why the fuck are you asking me permission, Ember?"

I shrugged. "I just—"

She interrupted me. "Do you love him?"

I stared up at the place the swords would come through the ceiling in just an hour and nodded. "I do."

She grinned, swinging gently towards me. "There you go, ya goose."

Her shoulder bumped mine, and I grabbed her harness, keeping her close. I kissed her cheek. "I'm so glad you're home."

Her arm snaked around my waist in a hug, her head on my shoulder as we swung together in the dark, suspended in space. "Glad to be back."

CHAPTER 37

ARES

THE EVENING OF THE GALA

ARES NECROLINE, who was seen at notorious sex club, the Rosewood, with Ember Verona, has been confirmed to be attending the National Gallery's annual auction and gala with his associate Avaline Reyes. We have no confirmation that Verona is attending at all…

"Turn that off, please," I said from the back seat of the cab. Avaline's sympathetic glance was enough to turn my stomach. I didn't want her pity tonight, so I shook my head once. Like the great friend that she was, her face smoothed instantly into a calm, neutral expression.

"You look lovely," I said, hoping I hadn't glared at her. And she did look lovely, in a simple, elegant black gown that was probably vintage couture of some kind.

Now she smiled a little, her red lipstick accentuating her mouth in a rather charming way. "Thank you, Ares. You look lovely, too."

For the briefest of moments, she took my hand in hers and squeezed it. We didn't hug or hold hands much, but her kindness was much appreciated. The cab driver glanced at us in the rearview window, and I just *knew* that this encounter would appear in the paper, or some magazine, in the next week.

Av caught the glance too, and squeezed my hand a tiny bit

harder. We just had to get through the next few hours, and then Orphium would be changed in ways I hoped would be better for our people. As the car pulled up at the National Gallery, Av and I slipped out before the cabbie could get into the line for the red carpet.

We made our way to the side door. Av checked her phone and then nodded. Rhiannon and Eryx were already in. We made our way inside, showing our invitation to the guard, a tall, thin human with dark brown skin and kind eyes. "Have a nice evening, Mr. Necroline," he said as we passed.

He'd seen the names on the invitations, recognized us, and let us through without question, even though they didn't match. I'd prepared about a dozen ways to get past this moment, and they were unnecessary. I held out my hand for him to shake, and to pass him a generous tip for his graciousness, but the man shook his head.

"That's not necessary," he said. And then, in a much softer volume, "My husband is one of yours, and we both appreciate that you mean to change things."

Surprise flickered over my face. This *human* was married to a necromancer. Av bit her cheek, raising her eyes to the ceiling in an attempt not to cry. Her chin quivered a bit with the emotion that ran through us both.

I nodded to the man, but Av gave him a dazzling smile, to which he bowed slightly. "Ms. Reyes, may I ask… is that vintage Velaine?"

"Yes," Av whispered, her voice still unsteady. "Thank you for noticing."

The guard dipped his head again. "It is lovely. We have an exhibit of Velaine's work on the fourth floor, in Textiles, if you are ever interested."

Av had seen it. She'd talked about it several times, but now she simply nodded. I knew my friend, and she wouldn't ruin the pure hope that ran through this moment for all the world. This was what she'd dreamed of since we were children. A world where it didn't matter if people were human or parapsych, and to her, I knew this conversation was evidence that such a world could exist.

"Thank you so much for letting me know," she said. "I would love to see it."

We walked through the quiet lower hall of the garden level. There was a bar set up on this floor, but there were not many guests down here. That was the thing about Orphium, about the class of people we were expected to rub elbows with. They cared little for peace, or even art for that matter. The garden level of the National Gallery housed some of the most forward-thinking sculptures of the past fifty years. But no one so much as paused to admire the way it had been lit for the evening.

I watched as Av's attention snagged on it. She longed to explore, the same as I did. To just be a guest at such a lavish event. I didn't pull her arm, but simply didn't move. When she stopped, her shoulders sagged a little. I bent low to whisper in her ear, knowing we were being closely watched.

If someone wanted something to gossip about, perhaps this would distract them from our actual purpose. I pushed Av's hair back from her ear, and I knew the eyes on us would read it as romantic affection, but in reality, I placed her earpiece.

"We make it through this," I whispered. "And I promise, we'll come for real another year."

Avaline smiled up at me, her hands cupping my face, her deft fingers inserting my earpiece in what probably looked like another romantic moment. "I would like that, Ares. But next time, bring Ember as your date, all right?"

I nodded as my earpiece came online. Right away, I heard Rhiannon. "We are at the mezzanine level bar. Meet us here. We're a go."

We made our way up the marble steps and onto the mezzanine level, where Eryx and Rhiannon waited. Each of them held an extra glass of sparkling wine, which they handed to both Av and me as we approached.

Ember's voice came through, soft in my ear, though there was a bit of static. "We're in position. Go now and we can use the commotion going on with Lourdes on the red carpet as cover."

Eryx turned his phone towards me. His news app was open and headlines flooded the feed:

Lourdes Thaumas Can't Remember Her Date's Name

Thaumas Dynasty Boss Dates So Much They 'All Look the Same'

Maybe Lourdes Thaumas Should Treat Dates Like Humans, Not Boytoys

Aradios' Bad Boy Leonidas Atrior Can Do Better Than Lourdes Thaumas.

I raised an eyebrow, but not at whatever stir Lourdes had caused. In all the photos that flew by in the feed, she had the smug look of someone who was getting her way. Whatever Lourdes was up to, she'd planned for it to go just like this. No, what caught my eye was that she'd brought Leo Atrior.

Eryx shook his head. "You wondering what he's doing in Orphium?"

I shrugged. "On another night, yes."

Rhiannon's perfectly groomed eyebrows raised. "Wasn't Atrior tapped to take over the Thaumas Dynasty in Aradios?"

We made our way through the crowd. Discussing this was safe territory. From the snippets I caught, many folks were having some version of the same conversation. One of the main reasons that Orphium's elite held the National Gallery Auction each year was for scenes such as this one. They invited prominent parapsychs and then mocked them mercilessly in the press.

"Yes," Eryx replied, drawing Rhiannon closer to him, angling her body behind his as he made way for her. I was surprised by the way she let him guide her, and how comfortable she seemed with Eryx's hands on her skin.

Had I missed something between them? Things to put a pin in for later, I supposed, as my brother continued, "Rumor has it that

Atrior used a few too many miracles for devious purposes. Roue Thaumas chose her second cousin's daughter as heir instead."

I noticed the way Rhiannon's breath caught when his hand slid lower onto the small of her back. Ember's idea that she would eat him alive echoed in the back of my mind. Av didn't participate in the conversation. Her eyes scanned the crowd for her spirit friends.

I'd seen the way she worked so many times, but this was particularly impressive. The Shades were directing paths of foot traffic, making it easier for us to move through the crowded gallery as the humans instinctively moved out of the spirits' way. We were in sight of the auction hall when Avaline tensed.

She raised up on her tiptoes, placing a hand on my chest, batting her lashes at me. I bent down, appreciating the way she'd added a little spring in her movements, like she was excited to tell me some trivial secret. I let myself smirk, the smug expression of the asshole everyone assumed I was covering my face.

A few sharp looks told me that my ruse was working. All anyone saw was a man who'd fuck one of the most powerful women in the city, in public no less, one week and bring another to a major society event the next. That was good.

Av whispered in my ear. "There's double the guards we expected, and they're wearing strange uniforms."

Ember responded immediately. "Down here as well."

Av whispered. "The Shades say they're closing in on us."

Rhiannon had stepped ahead of Eryx, and was now several paces ahead of the rest of us. When she turned swiftly on her heels, my heart began to race. The look on her perpetually calm face was one of panic. It was only a flash, only for a moment, but whatever she'd seen, it had spurred her to action.

"Get out," she hissed. "The swords are fake."

Eryx didn't ask her how she knew, he simply nodded, taking her hand in his. "We're going now," he said, keeping his voice low. "Av?"

Av nodded, turning to me with a petulant face. "Do we have to go so early? I wanted to bid."

I smiled at her. "Rhiannon has a headache, darling."

She buried her face in my arm, and I felt her lips moving in silent communication with the dead. A path opened up through the crowd and we took it. Shades materialized at our sides. I took a risk.

"Are you getting out, Verona?"

"Yes," came the staticky reply. "We're right behind you."

But I heard the sound of clashing metal in the background. Somewhere below us, Ember and Lara were being attacked. The plan had gone to shit. We'd known this was probably a trap and bet that we could make our play in time to win. I didn't have time to be devastated about being wrong.

We all had to get out, and fast. None of us were going to end up in the Asylum tonight. I squeezed Avaline's hand and pushed her forward through the crowd. I murmured a prayer to Paloma for a miracle, and one to Tanith for a swift end if Paloma did not see fit to answer.

CHAPTER 38

EMBER

THE SOLDIERS that streamed into the catacombs were not the caliber of the guards we'd dispatched earlier. These were warriors, through and through. As soon as Lara and I heard their footsteps, quiet and calculated, we shimmied up the ropes attached to our harnesses and into the shadowed archways of the watery room.

A soft crackle came through my earpiece, then Briony's voice filled my ear. "Lara? Ember?"

Elsewhere on the comm line, faintly, I heard noises that I hoped meant our friends were escaping. Lara and I could make it out of this. We'd certainly fought our way out of worse. She held up her hands. *Eight.* She'd counted eight of them.

We could handle eight easily. I wasn't worried, but neither did I want to give up the element of surprise. I made a soft noise, hoping Briony understood that we could not answer her.

"Okay," she replied. "I take it you're not in a position to answer. That's fine." The teenager sounded a little out of breath, like she might be pacing, or at the very least, pretty hyped up. It was probably the latter, and I wanted to know how much coffee Eli'd let her have, but of course now was not the time to ask.

For a moment, I watched as the soldiers fanned out, then I followed Lara onto a narrow passageway atop the catacombs' arches. I nearly stumbled as something below caught my attention. When I paused to look, nothing was there, but I could have sworn I saw movement in the water below.

Please let me be wrong, I prayed to Paloma. Gargantuan sea monsters had never really been my thing. Not Kraken, not Ceti, not sweet blue whales. *Respect the sea* had always been my motto, and by that I meant, *stay the fuck out of it*.

The water rippled, a menacing movement and my heart sank. Unlike the soldiers, what might be in the water worried me, but we had to keep moving. Lara silently counted us down through long-established hand signals, giving me tactical directions so I could listen to Briony over the comm line. I nodded to Lara to show I read her clearly.

Three.

"Two things…"

Two.

"One: I found the swords. The real ones."

One.

As I dropped to the floor, movement in the water caught my attention again. Something huge lurked beneath the surface of the dark water, and it was rising fast. One of the Ceti had made its way here.

Fuck my immortal life. Godsdamn sea creatures. How'd it get here?

It didn't matter how the thing got here. We had to get out, as soon as we could. If it wrapped the tentacles that it could eject from its terrible mouth around the stone columns that held the National Gallery up, it could easily pull the entire building down. And despite what the lore said about them being devious creatures, they were mostly just giant destructive assholes.

We were lucky it wasn't one of the Kraken. Now there was a creature to fear. Smart, enormous and mean as fuck. But the Ceti just liked ruining things. Inwardly, I winced, thinking of all the art that would be lost if the creature did what was most natural to it. I motioned to the water, and though the creature had descended far enough that it could not yet be seen, Lara nodded. She'd spotted it too.

Briony kept talking as we moved faster. "The swords are moving. They're in a truck going north. If you can get to a boat, you can intercept them at the Midtown bridge."

Fucking, fuck, fuck. This was a mess.

Voices on the comm line spoke all at once. We weren't going to make it there on time. "Go without us," I murmured, hoping someone would hear. "There's too many of them. Get the swords."

Lara signaled to me: *split up*. I nodded, and we parted ways. She'd drawn two short swords, ones I bought in hopes that she would like them. It made my heart sing to hear her quick movements.

She was killing our opponents rather quickly, and there was nothing like the sound of victory to motivate me. I stalked the nearest soldier, slashing his throat from behind before he could make a sound. Like the guards before, he went down easily, but the next was on me, quicker and better prepared.

As I met each of the hooded soldier's blows with one of my own, Briony began to speak again. "Ember… Lara… You have to get out. This is the second thing… After you pointed out that Tyche's alignment was wrong, I wrote an algorithm…"

She kept talking, but I couldn't concentrate on killing the soldier I fought, as well as the second that had arrived, *and* listen to her at the same time, so I tuned her out to focus on elbowing the first in the gut as he tried to get behind me, then twisting to knee him in the groin and sink my knife between his ribs to get to the heart. It was a precision hit, but it went home.

They were like sad babies. Their training was good, but mine was better.

My second attacker got me in the kidney, once, but lacked the skill to keep up with me as I twisted away. I jumped atop a small pile of discarded crates as the remaining soldier ran at me, my vision clarifying my target as he moved. I leapt into the air, my knife delving into the space between his armor, near his collarbone, my knife piercing his meaty flesh, severing his subclavian artery.

I abandoned him as he fell. As I ran toward the sound of Lara fighting, I remembered Briony was still talking, still telling me about how she'd gotten her algorithm to track Tyche's orbit, or some such information.

Would she please *just get to the point?* I'd grown to love the kid, but she was prone to over-explaining at the *worst* times.

I drove my knives into flesh, moving in a gruesome dance in time with Lara as we cut down the rest of the soldiers. More were on the way. "Bottom line this for me, babe," I said finally. "What're you trying to tell me?"

The sound of Briony's little squeak hit me right in the heart. She was just a kid doing her best. I regretted being snappish, immediately, but she did as I asked. "There was a thrysos at the exhibit, Ember. This was all a ritual... They've imbued it with Chiore's power."

Motherfucking Chiorics, of course they did some gross little ritual. Why wouldn't they? Everything I thought I'd figured out about who might have stolen the swords went out the window. If this was all for the Chiorics to imbue some random thrysos with the goddess' power, then who the fuck had stolen the swords in the first place?

"Fuck," Lara swore. "This just keeps getting worse."

"You have to get out of there," Briony pleaded.

"We do," I said, nodding towards the water.

While we'd been fighting, the Ceti had emerged. Its great mouth opened and closed, showing rows upon rows of razor sharp teeth, and those dangerous tentacles that shot out from the back of its throat. Typically, it used them to pull prey, like sea dragons, down to the bottom of the ocean. Or ships. Right now, it had two tentacles wrapped around the columns that held the building up.

"Great, it smells the blood," I murmured. The Ceti might have drifted in here out of curiosity. It was rare they traveled into fresh water sources, but not unheard of, especially during a mating season, which this was not.

But when they did, they were almost always looking for food, and we'd killed enough soldiers in the past few minutes to convince the creature that we'd prepared a feast. And yet, despite that, the Ceti preferred a live kill. To hunt their prey and snap its neck... We were in danger if it saw us.

"Move slowly until I tell you to run."

Lara nodded. Slowly, slowly, we backed further away from the water. The Ceti could leave the water, of course, for short periods of time. And if it chose to do so, we were well and truly fucked, because in short bursts it was much, much faster than we were.

But its attention was elsewhere, on the stream of soldiers that flooded the catacombs from all possible entrances within the building. "Go," I shouted.

Lara ran, and as I turned to follow her, my stomach dropped out of my body, cold sweat breaking out on my neck and back. Senator Cromvale followed the soldiers, walking behind them, gazing lovingly at the thrysos in his hands. It was essentially a glorified glaive, ordinary enough, but for the fact that it glowed with sickly green power. I turned to follow Lara, cursing the luck that had kept our swords from us.

Thank all that was holy, Lara ran like she had a homing beacon inside her. It was like she innately knew the way, but I knew her practically photographic memory probably traced the path out inside her incredible mind. Joy filled me as I realized that she would make it out. Behind us, I heard the rumble before I felt it. And chanting. *So. Much. Chanting.*

The Chiorics were drawing the Ceti out. Beckoning it to do something. To pull the Gallery down? To chase us? Who fucking knew what they were up to? It was bad, that much was certain. They had the thrysos and a sea monster. Things couldn't get much worse.

I pumped my legs harder, forcing myself to run faster. We had to get out before the building came down. We took two corners at high speed, nearly skidding as we went, but up ahead there was a door labeled 'EXIT.' Lara made it through first. Ahead of us, tied to the dock on the river, there was a boat.

"See the boat?" Briony asked. "The fancy wood one with the red flag?"

"Yeah," Lara answered, nearly out of breath.

"Get on it," Briony breathed, her voice raspy. "It has a remote start. I'm hacking in now."

Lara ran for the boat, assuming I was right behind her. It wasn't until she was on board that she turned back. When she didn't hear my footsteps on deck. "What are you doing?" she shouted.

My throat ached, all the things I wanted to say burning me up inside. There wasn't time. We'd gauged this whole thing wrong. There was only one thing left to do.

"She's staying to fight," Briony whispered. "Ember, no."

Somewhere on the line, I heard Ares and Rhiannon, arguing. I took my earpiece out, but spoke into it. "Lara, you go. Help the rest of them get the swords. If you have time, bring mine back to me." I took a deep breath, watching Cromvale walk calmly out the National Gallery door, just as the building began to creak.

The Ceti *was* going to pull it down. And he was going to try to kill me, but I wasn't going to let him. This wasn't over, but I knew my odds against a godkilling weapon, a throng of cultist and a sea monster weren't superb, by any means.

"I love you," I said. *To Rhi. To Lara. To Briony. To Ares.* "I'll hold him off to give you time. Don't forget about my tree, Rhiannon. You know the place I want to rest."

Through the earpiece, I heard her screaming my name. I held a hand up to Lara in goodbye, then pressed it to my lips and my heart. "I love you," I shouted to her, as I dropped the earpiece and crushed it with my boot. "Go."

I could see the tears on her face from here, as she shook her head. "Go," I screamed. "Help them."

I didn't wait to see if she would do as I ordered, but turned to meet Cromvale. If tonight was to be my end, then I would go with honor, protecting the people I loved.

CHAPTER 39

ARES

When Ember's comm line went dead, I didn't realize I was screaming. That Eryx was trying to keep me from launching myself out the backseat of the car. It took five full heartbeats to come back to myself. When I did, the boy from the metro tunnel sat between me and Eli, pale and gaunt.

"You got the Angel back," the boy said. "You did what we wanted."

Eryx stared at the boy and then at me. "What is he talking about?"

"Lara," I replied, practically desolate. Now was not the time for this bullshit. My heart raced as I thought of ways I could get away from Eryx, back to Ember. "I think."

Eryx rolled his eyes. Apparently, I'd misunderstood the trajectory of his question. "Obviously. When did Hypatos Bielke find you?"

Hypatos Bielke. Hypatos Bielke. The kid's face finally registered in my mind. "You lived behind the shop."

The child nodded. "You always talked a big game. Thought when you became boss, things would change, but you got the Angel hauled off."

Rain pounded down the car windows, and it was nearly

impossible to see where we were going, but I trusted Avaline. She had us headed to meet Lara on the boat, no doubt. I had to get my head straight. Much as every instinct in me told me to get back to Ember, no matter the cost, if I went without her sword, I would only distract her.

What I had to do now was focus on getting her that sword. It was her best chance of surviving a weapon that had been imbued with a god's power. There were few secrets in Necroline history about gods, as even our own lore had been tainted by the Authority's rewriting, but there were serious cautions against objects that had no power on their own, but were blessed by gods.

They were to be avoided at all costs. Though vague, I could only imagine that the warning had survived all other attempts to suppress our knowledge of the gods because it was important. Rhiannon twisted in her seat to look at us.

"Are you talking to a ghost right now?" she asked, directing her question to my brother. "At a time like this?"

Eryx sighed. "Yes. There's a kid here. He wouldn't be if he didn't have something important to say, *would he?*" My brother raised an eyebrow to the kid who'd died in the fire that destroyed our parents' flower shop, when the blaze traveled to the building behind us.

"Yeah, yeah, yeah," Hypatos said, twisting his mouth into a knot. "I came to say thanks, and that we'll help your girl if you keep helping us."

"What does that mean?" Eryx asked, using the voice he always used with children, low and calming. Rhiannon frowned at him, but it was a look of confusion, not anger.

I kept my mouth shut. Anything I would say would make everything worse. Every part of me still wanted to launch myself out of this car and fly in the opposite direction, even knowing that wasn't what she wanted.

Hypatos watched me. "You have to get the swords, Ares.

We'll help her fight the godkiller 'til you get there." The little ghost boy's chin quivered. "Will you help us, if we help her?"

I had no idea what I was agreeing to, but Eryx touched the boy's arm. It was an odd part of his talent. Sometimes he could make physical contact with the dead. The little boy looked up into my brother's eyes.

"You need help, little man?"

The boy nodded, then smiled. "Awww, I got it wrong. 'S'you who's to help us. Will you? If we help his girl, will you help us?"

Rhiannon's eyes pleaded. Eryx held her gaze for a long moment. Whatever passed between them, I wanted to stop it, much as I wanted *anyone* to help Ember. Making deals with spirits was a dangerous business. I shook my head.

"Yes," Eryx agreed, his eyes not leaving Rhiannon's. "But you'll help her fight until we get her the sword, right?"

Hypatos nodded. "We will. For the Angel's sake as well. Tell her that when she crosses them over, we'll make sure they get what's coming to them. We won't spare them one bit of suffering."

Something deeper than a chill went through me. Spirits could be vengeful, that was a simple fact, but whatever this child spoke of, it was not normal. Not how spirits usually spoke or behaved. I didn't like it, but the child disappeared before I could argue.

Before I even had a chance to say another word, Avaline slammed on the brakes. "We're here," she said. "Lara's half a minute away."

We jumped out of the car and ran towards the river.

In what felt like moments, we were aboard the speedboat Briony had helped Lara commandeer. The child was an utter menace to society, but she was our menace. As we raced towards the Midtown bridge, I shut my worries about Ember out as much as I could, but I was losing my shit.

A warm hand on my back brought me out of the haze of panic I'd sunk into. Rhiannon's beautiful face came level with mine. Behind her, Eryx stood looming, watching. Somehow, in the past few hours, the two of them had become a team. I didn't understand how it happened, or what it meant, but they seemed determined to work together.

"Ares," Rhiannon said, tipping my chin up to meet her eyes. She spoke slowly, like she might to a toddler. "Ares, to help her, you have to help us."

I nodded, swallowing hard. My brother stepped forward. "Av's tracking the spirits—the spirit traps are still attached to the swords—and since we don't have explosives, or any way to get them out on our own, you've gotta get those girls free fast so that she can talk them into helping us."

Rhiannon raised an eyebrow. "I need you not to fuck this up, Necroline. For my sake and Ember's."

The task was nearly impossible, but I nodded anyway, rising from the seat in the bow I'd sunk into when we boarded. The boat slowed as we reached the bridge.

Av stood beside Lara, making eye contact with me as she nodded. "The truck is on the bridge, at the first stoplight. I have the spirits' attention, but I still can't speak to them."

Rhiannon stood in front of me, her aura pulsing with light and immortal energy, and I reached through it, trying to make contact with the spirits' essential nature. The idea here was that the traps would sense Rhiannon's aura first, and would ignore it because she was Maere, like the girls, thus making it easier to disentangle the unascended from the spirit traps.

If I did that successfully, Av might be able to communicate

with them. It was all a lot of mights and maybes, but it was the only shot we had. The traps stopped that right now, as they operated under the same principle that governed Echoes: repeating a past trauma over and over, so the spirit no longer saw the outside world or the call to the netherworld.

In short, it was torture. Even filtered through Rhiannon's aura, I heard the pain the young women trapped inside the truck were in. "Please," I whispered as I worked, using Rhiannon's aura to coat all of my movements so that the traps would not push me out. "Let me help you."

Even if the girls couldn't hear me, I spoke to them, reassuring them I was here to help. It was impossible to know when they would be free enough to hear one of us, or who they might be predisposed to make contact with first. Av was their best bet, but we had no real way of knowing. Perhaps Eryx or I would remind them of a brother, a father, a friend...

The bottom line was that we didn't know them. We had to approach with kindness. They had been harmed for long enough.

My fingers moved, trying to untangle their auras from the traps. Sweat beaded on my brow and the back of my neck with the effort. It was difficult to do remotely, but Rhiannon's aura helped to steady and focus my power.

In this case, like did reach like. But every time I had a knot undone, instead of releasing, it tightened. It was like one of the finger traps that were party favors at the high holy days. The harder I pulled, the tighter the traps became.

My heart raced. There wasn't enough time and I was failing.

"Ares Necroline," many voices spoke at once through my brother. His eyes had gone milky white, glowing with faint light from the spirits that spoke through him. "You cannot free us this way. There is a trick to this trap. You must rip and tear."

"No," Lara breathed, staring at my brother, as though she

could see the spirits of the young women trapped inside the vehicle above us. "You'll be destroyed."

The truck was on the move. I had it in my sights now. Traffic moved slowly, but if I didn't move quickly, the reverse-engineered charge would not release the swords. Sweat broke out on my back, causing my dress shirt to stick to my skin.

"We will become vengeance incarnate," the spirits of the unascended Maere responded. "We will become dark matter, beautiful and terrible."

I wasn't going to be the one to explain to a bunch of dead teenage girls what dark matter actually was, especially because it was something of a natural miracle that they were speaking to us at all.

I took a deep breath. "If you hurt people you should not, I will have to destroy you."

The truck had moved past the midpoint of the bridge. We'd already missed our window, but if this was the only way, I would do it.

"We understand," they responded, through Eryx. "Do it now."

My hands moved quickly; though the work I did was with my mind, it helped to focus my power as I took each of the girls' auras in my hand and pulled, hard—with a violence I didn't feel towards them, but towards their captors. Towards the people who would use younglings in such a way for their own gain.

When their souls ripped free from the traps, I felt them change. Felt their essences howl into the dark night, as they were torn asunder from their prisons. Eryx crumpled to the deck. Rhiannon dove after him, keeping him from hitting his head. When I was sure he was all right, I turned my attention back to the bridge.

The truck had skidded to a stop. Everything was still for a few moments, the air thickening as the mist over the river rose in dark clouds. The truck doors blew open, the driver and guards tossed out. They were dead. I could see that much from here; the blood and gore were overwhelming in scope and scale.

I'd seen hundreds of scenes just like it. Most Poltergeists were simply irritating, like Stanley, but those who were vengeful were pure, unadulterated destruction. Goosebumps raised over my skin as a chill slid deep into the base of my spine. *What had I done?*

I had turned six young women's spirits that were destined for unimaginable power into vengeful entities with the power to destroy. Bile rose in my throat, and as it did, the spirits appeared on deck.

Their eyes were dark hollows, glowing with powerful red light, as were each of the four swords they carried. Deep in the indigo dark of this autumn evening, the Maere's swords shone with power. Rhiannon took her sword and Sera's, going to her knees in gratitude as Lara stepped forward to take the sword offered to her.

"Thank you," the two of them whispered.

"Come with us, Ares Necroline," the spirits whispered as one, an eerie amalgamation of all their voices. Like Stanley, they had the power to change forms, and they did so now, melding together to become a six-headed sea dragon, a creature of legend, with eyes that glowed with the same crimson light as the swords.

Upriver, two boats sped towards us with purpose. Ember's sword was in my hand before I could reach for it, and the spirit dragon had slid into the water. "Come with us, Necroline King. We shall aid the Queen together."

Before Av or my brother could argue, I was astride the spirit dragon, holding onto Ember's sword, and the reptilian spirit, for dear life. I struggled to tap my earpiece back into the "on" position as we raced through the water.

"Come as soon as you can," I pleaded. "We'll need all the help we can get."

CHAPTER 40

EMBER

RAIN PELTED my body as I stumbled a little in the puddles that were forming on the Gallery's manicured lawn. Cromvale was surprisingly good with the thrysos. If I had to guess how he got that good, it would be expensive LARPing camps. The other option, fencing, wouldn't have given him skills with a long weapon. Had to be LARPing camps.

I was tempted to say something about it, to see if he was sensitive about it, but he was keeping me on my toes. If that thing got me one more time, it might kill me. Already, my strength was waning. He'd kept me on the move for at least ten minutes, striking me not one, but three times. Once in the shoulder, rendering my dominant arm useless. And twice in the abdomen. I was bleeding profusely, but I was still moving.

If he got me again, I would go down. It hadn't been long enough for them to get the swords. I had to keep going. I staggered, but kept moving. Typically, the wounds he'd inflicted would hardly slow me down, but something about the thrysos drained me. Every time he nicked me with it, I felt worse.

And he was just so damn *calm*. In fact, he smiled now as I tried to regroup, my vision blurring. "You're wondering how I got so good at this," he purred.

"Not really," I quipped, sounding better than I felt. "Just wondering if LARPing camp ever got you any ass."

Cromvale smiled, undeterred by my petty comments as lunged forward again, narrowly missing my left arm as I ducked him. "Haven't you been wondering how I knew all those dates? How I'm beating you now?"

I shrugged, dodging another of his strikes, but he was getting closer every time. Was he playing with me? "To be honest, Chad, I haven't spent much time thinking about you."

"*Chase*," he hissed, nicking me again, this time in the thigh.

"Whatever." My brain struggled to find some sort of nasty remark. Something that would bother a man like Cromvale enough to slow him down. But it felt like I was moving through a sea of thick honey. Every movement I tried to make was slow and sticky.

Suddenly, he was standing closer to me. Too close. "I know every move you make before you make it. I've seen the way this ends."

His words weren't enough to scare me, but the shift in his aura was. Chase Cromvale's mask of humanity fell away, suddenly, revealing something much, much worse. He was Cognoscenti. The Cognoscenti.

Cromvale was the one who'd been helping the Authority. The one who'd predicted the powerful parapsychs. And he was a Chioric. This all made a horrible kind of sense. His smile stretched over his face. It was odd how non-descript he was. How mildly handsome. How forgettable and trustworthy he looked.

Shock ricocheted through me. Not because I couldn't believe it, but because I hadn't even considered he might not be what he seemed. That was the trick of that brand of slippery *goodness* the Authority loved. The way what they called "normal" acted as a mask for evil. A mask that had fooled even me.

"Why?" I breathed. "Why would you betray your people?"

Cromvale chuckled. "My *people*? What people? Parapsychs are weak. Losers. I'd rather win for once."

He was one of those. There was no way to argue with his type, no way to reason with them or change their minds. Speaking was a waste of energy, so I stayed quiet, trying my best to see a way out of this that could surprise him. Without knowing exactly how his power worked, I had no way to fight back.

But I knew enough about seeing the future to know that there were infinite possibilities. That no Cognoscenti, no matter how powerful, ever really knew what would transpire. Lux had always said that the worst quality a Seer could have was hubris —that keeping humble made it easier to trace the threads of what might come to pass.

But how could I use that against Cromvale?

"There's nothing you can do," he said, his voice syrupy sweet now. "Nowhere to run that I won't find you, your cohort, and that sweet little girl. She's going to make the best sacrifice, Ember."

Bile rose in my throat at his words as I ducked away from him. It was time to run. But before I could gather the strength to move, a frigid wind cut straight to my bones, driving me to my knees. No, not wind. A murder of spirits. Spirits of all kinds. Shades, Poltergeists, Riders. Even a few Echoes, though they lagged a bit behind.

Though I could barely see them, the spirits were impossible to miss. Most were Shades, unable to affect anything physical, but their mere presence seemed to distract Cromvale. And then they began to drain him. The process was slow, but as they became more visible, they fed off whatever power the thrysos gave him.

It wasn't much, but it was enough. I got up off the ground and stumbled away from him, using the last of the energy I had. I was too used to my wounds healing fast enough that there was no risk of bleeding out. But even non-fatal wounds from the thrysos were different—they simply did not close, nor did my blood begin to clot at even a normal human rate. The weapon was utter destruction.

The more energy he had to use to fight the spirits, the better off I would be. Right now, I was just buying myself and my friends more time. I had no real hope of living through this, but audacity thrummed through me, a drumbeat of delusion that said I could make it. That I would see my sistren again, and feel Ares' arms around me before the night was through. I just had to make it long enough for him to find me.

Because if there was one thing I knew for certain, it was that somewhere, no matter what complications there were, Ares was trying to get here. To get to me. He wouldn't leave me here to die alone. That much I knew. I just had to live long enough for him to get here, for my friends to arrive and end Cromvale together.

I moved as quickly as I could towards the darker part of the river, hiding in the thick brush along the steep banks further down. I peeked back at the National Gallery to survey the damage the Ceti had done. The building was stronger than I'd assumed it to be, but it was most definitely caved in at its center.

That would take millions to fix. I was spiraling, losing my grip on reality. There was a pool of blood growing around me that should probably concern me, but I was too lightheaded and dizzy to really grasp what was happening.

Ares, get here faster.

It was difficult to stay conscious, but I was grateful for the dark, grateful for the fog that descended on this cold autumn night, obscuring the blood I most certainly trailed behind me. A spirit appeared at my side, a young man dressed in a tunic, perhaps nightclothes.

He was a Shade, but there was something odd about him, something almost solid as he pressed his hand into mine. Spirits usually drained the living of energy, but apparently this one had found a way to give some back, because I immediately felt clearer, more conscious.

Ares is on his way, the boy said, not aloud, but in my head.

I smiled. Some spirits could read the surface thoughts in your mind, and this one was kind and had obviously read my plea for my lover. It was a kind thing to say, but it hadn't been long enough. Ares couldn't be on his way. Not yet, anyway. The spirit smiled again, before fading from sight.

Above me, Cromvale screamed, frustrated with my disappearance. *Why couldn't he predict where I was?* The ghost child... Had it done more than pass energy along to me?

The thick, heavy feeling of the spirits disappeared in a flash of sickly green light. "That was cute," Cromvale called down to me. "Getting spirits to help you. But I have tricks of my own."

Obviously, I wasn't going to respond. I could never figure out what it was about the despotic types that made them want to talk so bloody much while they tried to kill you, but it was practically a stereotype at this point. Those that lived to oppress also seemed to have a desperate, fucked up need to tell you their plans as well. In fact, Cromvale was blathering on still.

Rhi would be so annoyed with me. He was giving away all the secrets of Project Hierophant. Something about the way power was more important than parapsychs or humans, and that he was going to usher in a new age of something-or-other... It wasn't altogether that tough to understand. Just the usual selfish bullshit I'd come to expect from the Authority.

His type were all the same: bullies with very little imagination, but a shitload of energy for their bizarrely oppressive passions. It wasn't worth paying attention to with my last bit of life and energy. I wasn't going to fade out of existence while absorbing that hogwash.

Besides, I'd been distracted by what might be a hallucination. I'd never been injured like this before. Maybe hallucinating was a part of things. But I was certain that something was moving in the river. Was it the Ceti? It would make sense that it might be in the river now, looking for me.

If I could lure it onto the riverbank, it might be able to distract Cromvale long enough for me to get away for real. I glanced at my phone. It had been nearly twenty minutes. If they didn't have the swords by now, something had gone very wrong, and I'd be better off finding my people and helping them than dying here like a godsdamned martyr.

I dragged myself down to the river and waited. A great reptilian head emerged from the water, not one of the Ceti, but a sea dragon. The hallucination was beautiful, a dream, really. I'd longed to see a dragon again since I left the island. Four more heads followed, and then finally, Ares Necroline strode off the beast's back, carrying my sword.

Yes, this was most definitely a hallucination. It had to be. Sea dragons no longer existed near the Three Cities. These were Ceti waters and the two species were mortal enemies, the sea dragons ending up as food more often than not. Still, I smiled at Ares as my vision blurred at the edges.

"Hi," I murmured as I stumbled towards the water. "So glad you could make it."

Ares rushed off the dragon's back, which sank back into the water, out of sight. Only the heads remained, creating a ring of safety around us. Yes, this was a divine hallucination. The best my brain could conjure up, I reckoned. Might as well say what was on my heart. I was surely about to die if I was seeing my sword, sea dragons, and Ares Necroline.

I stumbled into his arms, getting blood all over his wet dress clothes. "Didn't get a chance to tell you earlier," I blabbered. "But I am stupid in love with you."

"Verona," he breathed as he drew me close, his body warm, though his skin was chilled from the water. "Shut the fuck up and let me help you."

"She has lost much blood," one of the dragon heads said.

"Press her sword to her back, where she would carry a sheath in the days of old," another added.

Was this *not* a hallucination? Or had the blood loss addled my brain into the kind of creative storytelling that typically only happened in dreams? "Ares?" I whispered, as he held me to him, pressing cold metal to my back. "Are you really here?"

"Yes," he murmured, awe in his voice as warm red light engulfed me. "And I am so fucking in love with you, too."

My eyes locked on Ares' as warmth went through me. I had been so cold moments ago. Colder than I realized, now that I was warm. The pain of my wounds faded, and the feeling that I was drained dry receded as something greater flowed into me. This was not just my sword returning, but more. Ares' face was open, innocent in its awe as I rose into the air and floated above him.

"Tanith," he breathed in a voice I didn't recognize, so full of love that tears flowed from my eyes.

I was myself and not. He was himself and not. We were both who we had always been, and more. So, so much more. Memories that were not mine flooded me, of a home I'd never known, an archipelago that included my island, but that did not exist, of a race of divine beings I'd never known.

And the face below me was the one I'd been missing for all eternity. I reached towards Amarante, smiling. "My darling. You came."

"I will always come," Ares-and-Amarante responded. "But you must destroy our enemy. Chiore's weapon must be disabled."

"Yes," I replied. I was both myself and Tanith. Death and immortal life, entwined in one as I floated up over the riverbank.

Soldiers rushed out from behind the ruins of the National Gallery. Ares-as Amarante rode the sea-dragon, now a hydrae, into battle. I smiled as Cromvale approached me, brandishing the thrysos.

The weapon struck fear into me, but I was more than my fear now. More than a lonely immortal. I had the love of a good man, the surety of a good weapon, and the power of two gods rushing through my veins. As my body finished healing, I felt it as Tanith left, watching as she and Amarante rose together into the night, forever entwined, forever in love.

And as I fell to the ground, I drew my sword.

CHAPTER 41

ARES

THE NATIONAL GALLERY had caved in. Fires burned everywhere throughout the building, and in the distance, sirens finally blared. It was difficult to believe that little more than an hour ago we had been inside the building, thinking we were about to steal the swords.

My heartbeat regulated. I had done what I came to. I'd saved Ember, set her back on the path towards her destiny, and now all that was left was for me to help her meet it. Soldiers in the tactical uniform that I now recognized as associated with the Chioric sect headed my way. The hydrae spit infernal fire at the approaching soldiers. It didn't need my help.

"Remember what I said," I cautioned as I slid off its back.

"We remember, Ares Necroline. See to your Queen," the creature replied.

As we parted ways, I honed in on the auric energy of the soldiers streaming onto the lawn, headed for Ember, just waiting for her to fall. I twisted a dozen or so auras in my grip and ripped hard. They died almost immediately, but the effort drained me. This wasn't how my power was meant to be used, but I didn't care.

My eternal soul might be damned, but I would protect her

as well as I could. She still levitated in the air. My queen, as the spirits had called her. As Tanith left her body, she watched the spirit of the divine entities that humans insisted upon calling Saints rise into the air.

I only had eyes and attention for her, as I moved through our enemies, picking up discarded weapons as I went. I would drain myself too quickly if I manipulated aura, and besides, I was not above some good old fashioned slaying.

Cromvale was headed straight towards Ember with the thrysos. The thing glowed a terrifying green, so obviously hungry for destruction. I had to keep him from Ember before she fell from her encounter with our gods. I paused, a grin spreading over my face. Perhaps she didn't need my help after all.

As Tanith rose into the air with Amarante, Ember drew the sword that had disappeared into her spine when I pressed it to her back. Though I knew the Maere's swords were a literal part of their bodies, it had been a long time since I saw that truth played out in person.

My heart beat faster as I fended off a few more soldiers, keeping one eye on Ember. A very real sword was in her hands as she fell, angling with a precision that came from thousands of years of battle, training, and innate talent.

Whatever Cromvale's deal was, he'd gravely misjudged her. He didn't even bother to move out of the way as she fell, moving at what felt like light speed. It all happened so fast.

She landed just before him, her blade dripping with blood.

For half a moment, I didn't comprehend what had happened.

Had she missed?

No, her blade was slick with blood.

Ember, my vicious, chaotic Ember, smiled brightly. "Good-bye," she said, her voice soft and sweet as a lullaby while her arms moved lightning fast, drawing down on the thrysos as Cromvale's head slid neatly from his body.

The thrysos exploded as Ember's blade sliced through it. She whispered something inscrutable as her blade completed its arc, the hydrae disappearing from sight, sucked directly into Ember's sword—into some void that opened within it, through it. What I saw was beyond understanding. I hardly knew what I saw.

I watched, wide-eyed, as the energy of the combined Poltergeists drew in upon itself, imploding like a dark star. Perhaps the girls had been right; perhaps they were dark matter incarnate, because as they went through the void the sword had created, they sucked the thrysos in with them.

"Where did you send them?" I murmured as I rushed towards her.

Ember shrugged as she stepped over Cromvale's body. "Who knows?"

That was my girl. I didn't have time to hug her, or to tell her all the things I felt. As she rushed to my side, we moved forward together, as one, to meet the last of the Chioric soldiers. We moved together, my body a mirror of hers as we dealt death across the National Gallery's lawn.

There were so many of them, and there was a part of me that wondered if we could be overwhelmed. If I could even be killed. Amarante's touch had changed something within me. I could feel it in the way I moved, the way I felt stronger by the moment, instead of more drained.

I was willing to die here, with Ember at my side, but that small kernel of power glowed within me, growing by the moment. I moved faster than I was typically able, the soldiers I fought falling in a blur of golden light.

Ember too, was wrapped in some divine light, though it was a dark light, hard as that was to comprehend. I barely registered the motions my body went through, all on its own. *Slash, stab, kick, duck, fight, kill.* There was no room in my mind to think; everything moved far, far too fast.

The glow around us both… it was divinity. Amarante and

Tanith had come, for whatever reason, and what they'd left behind was just enough godhood to make this moment impossible to understand. The Chioric weapon had been destruction embodied, and now Ember and I were both death's sweet kiss and immortality's divine power, all in one. By reversing which of their children they embodied, the gods had given us the power to be more than we were.

But it was temporary, I felt that acutely. And though we fought well, more soldiers streamed onto the lawn. Were the Chiorics so prolific? Standing at the edge of the lawn, near the burning Gallery, I caught a flash of a familiar face. Fairchild. His face was drawn in rage.

He spoke into a walkie talkie, though I couldn't make out what he was saying. More soldiers appeared behind him before he blinked out of sight. We were going to be overrun. I grabbed Ember's free hand.

"Stay still as you can," I shouted. She'd managed to cut down enough of the soldiers that we had the briefest of moments before the onslaught of new blood arrived. Ember nodded, trusting me implicitly.

I pulled the last of Tanith's power from her aura, whispering a prayer for forgiveness. With fleeting godhood flowing through me, I took hold of every aura but Ember's on the Gallery lawn and tore them free in one fell motion. Then I shoved hard, sending them all to the other side.

For a brief moment it was the same as when Ember sliced through Cromvale. I wasn't certain it had worked. Ember squeezed my hand hard, keeping me tied to this plane. And then they crumpled, all at once. As the last soldier died, the divine light faded from both our forms.

We were left as we had been before, though I had to admit that Ember was obviously much improved with the return of her sword. Her injuries had disappeared entirely.

"The spirits are gone too," Ember murmured as she looked around. "What *was* that?"

I looked around, trying to make sense of it all. "I think that Tanith and Amarante helped us, called the spirits to aid." For a long moment, I couldn't speak. It was too big to comprehend. "Is that *possible*?"

Ember swallowed hard. She too was processing all of this. The destruction around us. The gods and monsters that had walked this plane, only moments ago. "Yes. It's possible." She stared at the river, then sheathed her sword. I marveled as it disappeared back into her.

"The Ceti were drawn by the Chioric's summoning rituals. They must have been working on them for weeks, if not months… On the island…" she hesitated, as though worried to expose some essential secret of her people.

"You don't have to tell me," I said, squeezing her hand. "It's all right."

She shook her head, smiling. "It's not that. I'm just trying to put all the pieces together."

I nodded, waiting for her to find her words. We were both a bit overstimulated and overwhelmed. She gazed up at the sliver of night sky that had appeared above us, a dazzling array of stars beyond the clouds.

"We are told, as children, that the gods exist in another realm from us. One that abuts our own, but that is not easily accessed in either direction. Long ago, there were sects, like the Chiorics, who were obsessed with getting the gods' attention. Maybe that's what all this was."

I nodded. "If they cracked open a portal to the divine realm, perhaps Amarante and Tanith were able to slip through as well." I thought of how Briony's stepmother had been so careless as to not protect herself against spirits like the one she'd called to possess her stepchild. Maybe it was something like that.

The sound of a speedboat broke my concentration. I touched Ember's arm. "Look, our friends."

I held out a hand to her. She didn't need my help up, but she took my hand anyway and let me pull her into my arms.

"You came," she whispered, more than an echo of Tanith, but the full measure of her heart behind her words.

"I will always come when you need me," I replied.

She smiled up at me. Lara was calling to us from the boat. She screamed that they were being pursued. Ember took my hand, and we raced for the boat. There would be time for catching up later. Now, we had work to finish.

CHAPTER 42

EMBER

IT MIGHT TAKE the rest of my eternal life to understand what had happened on the shore of the Erydanos. Or perhaps I would never understand, would never be able to put all the pieces of what had happened together in the right order. All I knew was that I had my sword back, and the people I loved most in the world were all right.

As we sped away from shore, a tear slipped from Lara's eyes. First, I pressed a kiss to Ares' hand and then went to Lara, pulling Rhiannon in as I went. The three of us clung to one another.

"We have her," Rhiannon murmured into her earpiece. "She's alive…"

I brought my lips to Rhi's ear, so that Briony could hear me. "I killed Cromvale, and destroyed the thrysos, I think… I mean, I sent it into what looked kind of like a mini black hole. You might want to run a search of some kind to find out if that's gonna turn out okay."

Faintly, I heard the teenager talking excitedly in the earpiece. Rhiannon shook her head. There was no relief on her face, though she and Lara looked significantly more relaxed than I'd seen them in hundreds of years. Both stood taller, their swords resting deep within them, as did mine.

Rhi and I kept an eye on our pursuers. They followed at almost the same pace as our boat. Gaining on us, but little by little. Their boats were certainly powerful enough to overtake ours. They were military grade. Stuff only the Authority had access to, though if the Authority followed us, they'd have overtaken us by now.

Something else was going on. I remembered, faintly, Ares telling me that Eli had said there were other players on the board. I had a feeling we were about to find out just how complex things actually were. On top of the night I'd already had, that seemed like a lot to take in.

Bird by bird. That was how we were going to get through this. I glanced back at Ares, who talked quietly with his brother and Avaline. He was making sure they were all right, just as I was with my people.

"How do you feel?" I asked Rhiannon, pulling her close to steal some of her heat.

"Good," Rhiannon breathed. "Not one hundred percent yet, but once Sera has her sword that should resolve itself."

Lara nodded as she glanced over at us. "Hopefully, anyway."

None of us knew if we could regain our full powers, given the situation with Max. Nothing like this had ever happened before, but at the very least, we were better off than we had been this morning.

I hugged them both again, careful not to distract Lara from driving the boat, but not wanting to let go. "Head for the Inland Sea," I said. "We'll face them at the delta."

Lara nodded. "Get seated so I can go full speed."

I took a seat in the bow between Ares and across from Rhiannon, who sat pressed against Eryx Necroline in a way that was just slightly more than friendly. For Rhi, that was practically the equivalent of public sex. I fought to keep the smirk off my face. Ares pulled on my braid, turning my face to his.

"Eyes on me, gorgeous," he whispered as his mouth met mine. I would take the reward, and the respite of his kiss, however brief.

When we reached the delta, Lara spun the boat so that we faced our pursuers. As the two fiberglass speedboats pulled up alongside us, my heart raced. I recognized the Maere inside.

Not only did they have Max and Sera with them, but about a dozen familiar faces. None of them had been reincarnated. Each was exactly as they had been on the island. Exactly as they had been when we were children. None of them even appeared to have aged much. *What were they doing here?*

A hopeful part of me thought they were here to help, that the island had taken my warnings seriously. But no one on the boat smiled. None raised a hand in greeting as a tall figure stepped forward, moving to the closest edge of their boat.

"Myrine," I breathed at the same time as Lara asked, "*You're* Mother?"

I glanced at Lara, who nodded toward the pin on Myrine's coat. "The only time I met with Mother, she wore a mask, and that pin."

The broach was a distinctive design, a cluster of silver dahlias, set with onyx centers. Ares stared at them as well. "Betrayal or commitment?" he whispered, obviously referencing his interest in floriography.

Myrine smiled. "Both, I suppose, depending on how you look at things."

A snarl caught in my throat as I saw that Max and Sera were bound. If Myrine was Mother, why were her people behaving as though they were our enemies? My heart sank. This was not what I'd hoped at all.

This was something I did not yet have words for.

I moved slowly to the edge of the boat, crossing my arms over my chest, feeling my sword's presence, snug against my spine. That at least was a reassurance of a kind. The storm clouds cleared above us, giving us a sliver of the moon. "Why have you restrained my people?"

Myrine was tall as ever, her translucent skin glowing in the moonlight, her eyes pools of mercurial light. She had always been a mystery to me, more goddess than earthly being.

The Admiral's voice was calm as she pushed back the hood of her anorak to reveal a silver crown of hair. "Your people fought us when we released them from the Chiorics' grip," Myrine replied. "They caught them coming out of the Library of Amarante. We were forced to bind them for their own safety."

Myrine's words sounded like a lie. Still, I nodded. She and her people were too powerful for us to fight with an incomplete cohort. "All right. But we are here now. Release them into my custody."

Myrine smiled again, this time at Lara and Rhiannon in turn. "Two of your cohort are already helping me, Ember. Why not join us?"

Rhiannon glared, lurching forward. "Does my mother know you're doing this?"

Myrine laughed as though we were all a bunch of sassy babies. Ares glanced at me, sidelong. He, Eryx and Avaline all tensed. They knew they couldn't survive a fight with this many Maere, but they were willing to stand with us. That meant more to me than they knew.

Myrine's gaze drifted, seeming to notice what I had. "You have done something unusual here," she said, her words careful. And smug. She was far too smug. Nausea crept over me as she continued speaking. "Without your swords, you changed."

This wasn't what someone who wanted to help me would say. This wasn't what the Myrine I knew would say. I shook with fear for what this really was, but I answered the Admiral. "Yes, Orphium will come back into balance, if I have to spend the rest of my life devoted to it."

"And what of the humans?" Myrine asked, obviously testing me. "What will you do with them?"

I wanted to throw the unholiest of fits. To leap across the small strip of river between us and throttle her into telling the truth, into shooting straight. Instead, I tried to word things the way that Rhiannon probably would. "There's a lot to be worked out, Myrine. And if you're working against the island, you are no longer my superior officer."

Myrine simply smiled. It was a knowing smile, one that I'd seen a thousand times. Usually when I was being taught a lesson of some sort. The kind that was hard won, after she'd pushed me just a measure too far. All my hope that this was better than it seemed died, shriveling into a cold, dead thing.

Rhiannon stepped closer to me, obviously understanding the conclusion I'd already come to. "It was you. You took the swords. My mother would never approve of this."

Myrine smiled again. "She didn't like the idea... at first. But she came around to my way of thinking." Rhi's face fell, and I hated Myrine. Hated the queen. Hated the whole damn island for fucking with us. "But we needed a way to prove your worth, to prove that your cohort wasn't the result of nepotism, and it worked."

Rhiannon's shoulders instantly slumped. "You did all of this because of *me?*" Tears slid down her cheeks. I would never forgive the entirety of Otrera for this. "Why? I could have just stayed home... Sera..."

Sobs choked my princess' words and in the other boat, Sera struggled against her bonds, her eyes wild with anger, and worry for Rhi. I pulled Rhiannon against me, beyond fury at this point.

Sera. No. They wouldn't have... Ares glanced at me, cold rage in his eyes. Was he thinking what I was? I shook my head, just once, just slightly, hoping he understood that timing was everything here.

Myrine kept talking, as though what she and the island had done wasn't an incredible betrayal. "You all did so well. And now all can be made right. You have passed our test of strength."

Anger simmered in my veins. I was tired of being buffeted about by all these groups scrapping for power. "No," I said, after a long moment of what I was sure Myrine read as contemplation. If that's what she assumed, she didn't know me as well as she obviously thought she did. I stared deep into the water, watching as a dim pair of crimson lights raced towards us. My heart leapt. If that was what I thought it was, we could still win this. "Give my people back and I will let you go."

I reached behind me, where Rhiannon still held Sera's sword, and took it from her. To her credit, she didn't so much as flinch. She simply released it into my hands.

They had stolen our swords for some arbitrary test of our resolve. And for what? To prove to the island that they had not sent Rhiannon here in some act of nepotism. It was ridiculous and cruel. Frankly, I didn't give a flying fuck why they'd done it.

"Come now," Myrine said, still infuriatingly calm. "Surely we can discuss all of this. I believe we want more of the same things than you imagine."

I shot back, immediately, "Did you kill those girls yourself? The potential Maere in the spirit traps?"

Myrine's eyes widened, as though I'd offended her. Her people tensed, ready to fight. "No, child. I stole their souls from the Asylum. Lara's job while she was inside paved the way for my people to grab them." Her gaze slid to Lara. Mine slid to the water. I sucked in a deep, steadying breath, certain now of what I saw. Myrine kept talking, unaware of what I now knew.

"Thank you for that, my dear. You executed my plan perfectly, causing the scene you did."

Lara looked as though she might vomit. She turned her head away, closing her eyes, before gritting out, "You didn't kill them, but you tortured them. Used them. Just like you used us."

Not everything could be solved by talking. My grip tightened on Sera's sword. I was tired, but if Myrine wanted a fight, I would give it to her. She had the numbers on us. That much was obvious. But she and her people were not a true cohort. They were not connected. Not the way we could be.

The way we *would* be in just a moment...

I held Sera's sword out over the edge of the boat as the Kraken rose out of the water, Calypso Montague riding it like it was a horse. She leapt into the air, her wet, coppery hair tossing a glorious spray of water over us all as the giant cephalopod sank beneath the river's surface. She landed on the deck of Myrine's boat, Sera's sword in hand.

"Hi," she said simply as she moved, lightning quick.

In mere seconds, she had Sera's bonds cut, and pressed her sword to her back. As she did, the connection between the five of us snapped into place. Our eyes glowed with the same crimson light. We were a cohort. Complete.

Myrine and her people simply watched. It was eerie, and somehow not unexpected. Awful as her methods had been, this was what she wanted. Us back together and stronger than ever. All my senses sharpened to a fine point. It was like taking a shot of my own immortality. Having my sword back was one thing, but the bond between a cohort of sistren was another altogether.

Calypso bowed her head to me, murmuring, "I am sorry it took me so long to get here. I had some trouble finding you."

Before I could respond or ask questions, she cut Max's bonds. Max drew her sword, pushing Myrine's guards away from Sera and Calypso. They stepped out of her way. Calypso had the wisdom to squint warily at them.

Whatever this was, it had to end. I had to end it. "This is not the fight you want, Myrine. It's not the fight I want either."

Myrine stared at me, not an ounce of shock on her face. None of her people had moved to fight back. They'd just let Calypso do what she meant to. The whole thing was terrifyingly odd, but I wasn't going to fight it. Not until Max and Sera were safe with us.

Myrine could keep the rest of her secrets. My desire to know why she'd stolen the swords from us to begin with wouldn't be satisfied with some story of ancient tests, meant to purify the heroes for their divine task. I was done with that sort of bullshit.

Lara moved the boat, sidling up to Myrine's vessel. Rhiannon and Avaline helped Max, Sera, and Calypso into our boat. Myrine's people tensed, as though they would like to attack, but she shook her head.

"No," she said. "Ember is right. This is not the fight we want. We have achieved what we set out to. We will celebrate tonight."

I let out a groan. "You're going to have a fucking party over this?"

Myrine shrugged. "My child, you have won the day. Why would we not celebrate your achievements?"

She made me sick. Our people suffered here in the outer world, under the thumb of the Authority, and her goals were to test us? But that was not exactly true, was it? What about the rest of the ones she took, the ones Lara had rescued?

As though she could hear my thoughts, Myrine smiled. "We will leave your new cohort in peace to regroup, Ember. But first, tell us where we can find the child. We must take Briony to the island."

I didn't wait so much as half a heartbeat to answer. "No."

Myrine raised an eyebrow. "That is not a wise choice, Ember. Give us her location."

"No," Ares said, taking my hand. "Briony is our family."

"She belongs on the island," one of Myrine's people said, their voice full of virtue and righteousness. "Where she will be safe."

"She belongs with us," Rhiannon said, having collected herself. "With people who won't treat her like a cruel experiment." Rhiannon straightened, every inch a princess. "You can tell my mother to come get Briony herself if she wants her."

Now Myrine's people did tense, all of them going for their swords. Ares stepped forward. "Which one of you infiltrated my organization?"

Everyone in our boat's head snapped towards Ares. My heart sank for them all. This was going to kill Rhiannon, though. And maybe Max too. I closed my eyes.

"Which one of you led me to believe we had the all clear to burn the mansion?" Ares asked. "Which one of you is to blame for Serafine's injuries?"

Anger flashed in Myrine's eyes now. "You are, Ares Necroline. You didn't check *yourself*."

I opened my eyes. Max looked as though she might leap back into Myrine's boat. Tears slid down Sera's too-pale cheeks. She reached out towards Ares, taking his hand. "Leave it," she murmured. "Your debt to me is repaid."

He nodded once at her, but turned back to Myrine. "Surely you cannot think to make further arguments that Briony belongs with you. Not after all the misguided choices you've made."

Myrine let out a little laugh, holding her hands up. "All right, all right. Keep the child. When she ascends, you will bring her to us."

Lara stepped forward now. "We will bring her *to the island* for the proper ceremonies. Not to *you*."

Myrine smiled, clearly pleased with herself. "Only think, if we had not interfered, you would all still be... so ordinary."

Max lurched forward now, a feral noise emanating from her chest. Calypso held her back, hugging her tightly, whispering something in her ear. I caught a bit of her vile language and worked to hide a smile. She was going to fit in perfectly with us. Max finally relaxed, slumping first against Calypso, then into Sera's arms, as they huddled together.

"Perhaps," I said as Myrine motioned for her second boat to move off. It was a lie, but I'd gotten my way and I had no further desire to argue tonight. "But leave my people out of your future plans. That includes Max."

"She is not yours anymore," Myrine said as her boat retreated into the mist. Why did she need to have the last word?

I smiled at Max. "She will always be mine," I promised my friend. "No matter who tries to come between us."

Max took my hand and pulled me into her and Sera's embrace as Myrine and her Maere disappeared. Our sistren crowded around us, tears streaming down their faces as our boat bobbed in the wake of Myrine leaving. Calypso stood wet and uncomfortable—apart. Sera's arm, pale as the moon, shot out to grab the redhead, yanking her into our group.

I made eye contact with her, smiling as gently as I knew how. "Thank you," I said as we released one another. "Lara, let's go home."

"I fear Briony has ordered like eighteen pizzas," Lara whispered to me as I sank into Ares' arms.

"That's perfect," I said as I leaned against him.

Calypso sighed. "I'm going to eat a minimum of two on my own. Riding a Kraken is no fucking joke."

Lara snickered. They were going to be friends, I could tell.

As our boast sped into the clouds of mist hanging over the delta, I listened as everyone listed the things they were going to eat. The delivery bill was going to be enormous. Ares pressed a kiss to my forehead as my heavy eyes fell closed.

CHAPTER 43

ARES

As I carried a deeply slumbering Ember into Hemlock House, I was mesmerized by the transformation. The mansion, which had fallen into deep disrepair over the years, practically glowed. The last time I'd been here it had looked like it might sink into the ground and simply cease to exist.

Now the herringbone pattern in the wood floors gleamed. New furniture, in deep jewel tones, graced the rooms I could see as we entered. Just off the entryway were a library and a small parlor, from what I could tell.

Plush rugs spread out over the floors—antiques, the quality of which were rarely seen in Orphium. The Orphium Maere could certainly afford this, but where had they gotten it all in such a short time? Everywhere I looked, there was precious art, glowing lamps, comfortable furniture, and *plants*?

Hemlock House looked as though it had been pulled from the pages of *City & County Magazine*. Many of the antiques I spotted on the shelves were occult in nature. Objects associated with each branch of the Trinity.

Briony came running down the sweeping staircase that filled the foyer, grinning. "It's great, isn't it?" she asked as I nearly maneuvered Ember's foot right into an enormous vase of expensive cut flowers. They stood on a gorgeous primitive table, carved from a dark marble at the center of the foyer. Each flower told a story on its own, but together... Together, they told a story of comfort, of loyalty. The flowers named this place *home*.

Briony had reached the bottom of the stairs. "Eli and Lux had people here all day. You should see my room.... Is Ember okay?"

It occurred to me that Briony's babbling was probably who she really was, not a scared, silent teenager, but one who talked. A lot. Something about that idea, combined with the story the flowers told, touched me deeper than I imagined possible. Perhaps it had been the stress of the day, in contrast with this place... I was overwhelmed by my emotions, unable to sort them out, tired as I was.

"She's all right," I explained as the rest of the Maere, Eryx, and Av streamed in behind me. "She just used a lot of power destroying the thrysos. Can you tell me where her room is?"

Briony grinned. "Sure can. Right this way."

I followed her through the house, which was decorated with such tasteful depth, it made sense that Lux was involved. Sure enough, as I followed Briony through a set of double doors, Lux Medios, dressed in a poppy-red three piece suit, stared out the floor-length windows that looked out onto the pool and the skeletons of a late autumn garden.

In summer, it would bloom with a riot of hydrangea, dahlias, and probably peonies, from what I could tell. But there was also foxglove amongst the flowers. Foxglove, datura, hellebore, and of course, plenty of hemlock. This was a Necroline house, originally, after all. Gray light filtered through the wavy glass in the double doors. The sun would be up soon.

Lux stepped forward as Ember woke up in my arms. "Hi there, baby girl."

"Hey Lux, this looks so pretty," Ember said in a somewhat uncharacteristically sweet, sleepy voice.

"You know I like a project without a budget," Lux purred. The Seer glanced up at me. "Leave us for a bit, so I can get your girl cleaned up, all right? There's a shower through those doors and another bedroom just beyond."

I frowned, was Ember going to be all right with Lux?

"I'll be all right. Go see the bedroom." Ember smiled at me as I set her down. "I hope you like it," she said through a yawn.

I was reluctant to leave her, but she and Lux were friends, and if she needed a few moments to herself, I could give them. The bathroom was on the smaller side, not as big as the one I'd seen through the doors in the primary bedroom, but luxuriously appointed. I closed the door to Ember's room to give her and Lux a little time.

Their soft voices drifted over me. Ember was telling her an abbreviated version of what had happened, from what I could tell, and Lux was running water in the shower. My girl would be all right. I pushed open the double doors that sat opposite the one I just closed. There was a smaller bedroom on the other side of the doors, and yet another set of doors opened up onto a small office.

On the desk that faced the window that looked out onto the garden and the pool, sat a note, written in Ember's hand. I frowned at it, wishing she was here beside me to explain. But when I opened the envelope, I understood. Her words were simply an invitation, one she wanted me to consider before saying yes.

There is room for all of us—stay if you like.

—E

I sank down into the comfortable desk chair and stared out at the rain, dropping into the crystalline emerald water of the pool. *Stay*, she said. She bought this enormous house that had once belonged to my Dynasty, renovated it with the treasure trove of money the Consulate had paid her with over the years, and invited all of us to stay.

I had no doubt that my brother and Av were being shown to

their own rooms as I sat here in my office. My office, which abutted a bedroom that was clearly for me. But it was not *hers*.

There was a line I'd missed in her note, a smaller one at the bottom of the card: *I sleep fitfully, but we can have sleepovers as much as you want.*

My heart swelled. She'd made room for me in her life in a way that finally accommodated her needs—that took how *she* wanted to live into account. And she did sleep fitfully. I knew that from the short time we'd spent sleeping in the same bed. If I had known she'd sleep better on her own, I would have left her to it.

But I was proud of her for speaking up for what she needed, the sting over having been given my own room fading as each moment passed, marked by another thump of my heart.

I set the card down and wandered back into the bathroom, showering and then dressing in a daze, choosing a pair of gray sweatpants and a black cashmere sweater—all in my size— before peeking through the door to Ember's room. She was tucked into her bed, her hair damp and cheeks rosy. She was fast asleep. Lux was curled up in an oversized velvet chair in the corner, reading her tablet.

She's fine, she mouthed to me. *Let her sleep.*

I nodded, then closed the door and wandered back through my bedroom and office. I stood staring at all the little details: a watercolor painting of a flower shop, a portrait of the breed of dog I'd had as a child. Countless pieces of me that Ember had collected in her mind over the years were evident here. I didn't understand how she'd done it, but she had. Her nimble mind had pulled all these disparate memories of me together and made them mean something.

The flowers in the foyer. When I'd mentioned the language of flowers to her, she'd acted as though she didn't know what it was. But she knew now. She knew that I would know what that combination of flowers meant, and she'd made sure it was right there, the first thing I'd see when I came through the door.

Had anyone ever considered me thus? I couldn't remember a single time in my life that anyone had ever paid such close attention to me. Ember Verona was chaos embodied, in so many ways, but I had underestimated her. I wouldn't do it again. My woman had range.

A goofy grin made its way across my face, unfamiliar to me as the feeling of being so *seen*. In the hallway, there was a bit of movement. I went to the door to find Briony coming out of the room across the hall.

She rolled her eyes at me. "Guess you're mom and dad now. Ember says my room *has* to be across from yours."

I snorted a laugh. Ember had thought of everything. "Show me," I said.

She opened the door wide, her smile brightening. Stanley, in his favorite tomcat form, wound around her feet, purring happily. The room was lovely, a richly patterned wallpaper that resembled an old tapestry of a unicorn hunt covering the walls. Briony's bed was canopied with midnight blue velvet curtains, and an enormous, sparkling chandelier cast a golden light throughout the room.

"It's more like a lamp than a big light," Briony explained. "Look, it's dimmable." She slid a switch up and down until she had it back at a cozy level. "Ember said I could have whatever I wanted. I'm getting tutors to help me get up to speed before I go back to school next spring."

I nodded as she showed me the little room that connected her bathroom and closet, where there was a neat little desk with a giant cork board behind it and a state of the art computer with several screens.

"She wants us all to stay," Briony said, sighing at the primo desk setup. "Are you going to?"

Briony's eyes were big, wide with worry that I was going to leave her hero. I touched her arm. "I am not certain yet, but know this, I will always be here if you need me."

"Don't you love her?" Briony asked. There was an edge of a

whine in her voice that I understood. In a short time, we had become *the* adults in her life.

"Yes," I answered honestly. I was deeply touched by all of this, but I wouldn't lie to the child. It wasn't that I didn't want to stay. I needed time to process. Time to be sure before I made promises I might break to people I cared for. "I just need to be sure that staying is the right thing for both of us."

Briony shook her head. "If you love her, I don't see what else there is to be sure of."

Briony might be a teenager, but wiser words were probably never spoken.

I wandered through the house, listening to Av talking with Eli, Lara, and Calypso in the hearth room off the kitchen. They were getting to know each other, telling the story of tonight, but also telling one another about themselves. As I made my way into the kitchen I noticed how carefully Eli watched Sera as she piled slices of pizza onto her plate. And the way Max watched Eli, giving him the stink-eye.

I was staying miles away from that. It was a mess waiting to happen. Rhiannon sat with my brother in a little alcove that looked out over the greater garden. The two of them stared wide-eyed at Oleander Cottage. Both seemed practically transfixed by the place.

"Hey," I said as I sat down with them. Neither had touched their food, though they both had full plates.

Eryx startled at my voice, as though he hadn't heard me sit down or seen me coming. It was utterly unlike him to be unaware of his surroundings. "Hey, big brother."

I frowned at Eryx, then felt for spirits. There were a few Shades wandering around the house, but their energy was curious, happy that there were inhabitants in Hemlock House once more. Nothing malicious. But under that, I *felt* Oleander Cottage. It was as I remembered it, a whispering mess of malefic energy. The sooner we warded it off, the better.

Slowly, Rhiannon turned away from the bank of leaded glass windows in the alcove. "Is Ember all right?"

I nodded. "She's resting."

Rhiannon took a deep breath, expelling air from her lungs like she was banishing something else. Was there something she sensed about Oleander Cottage that I didn't? Before I could ask, she spoke. "This all turned out well, didn't it?"

I hummed my agreement.

"Well," Eryx said, drawing the word out slowly. "Are we staying?"

I listened as Av talked in the hearth room, her voice bright and animated. A fire crackled merrily in the background, mixing with the sound of my friend talking. She was deep in conversation with the others, and she sounded happy. I watched as Briony snuggled in next to her, the necromancer's arm hugging the teenager close before pressing a light kiss to the top of the girl's head.

"I am," I said, feeling as though this was a conversation I should be having with Ember first. Still, I knew it in my bones now that I'd had a bit of time to sort through the events of the evening, of the past weeks. "But whatever you want is fine."

Eryx nodded. "I am not sure just yet. But I'm staying for a few days, no matter what."

I nodded absently, as Lux wandered down the hall, on her way back from Ember's bedroom. "Excuse me, please," I said, getting up. "I am tired. I think I'll go lay down for a while."

A small smile played on Rhiannon's lips as I walked away. My brother would stay. I knew it in my guts, the way I knew I'd never leave Ember or the family we'd build here—bit by bit, in a new world.

CHAPTER 44

EMBER

A HEAVY WEIGHT sank into the bed next to me. I rolled over to find Ares pulling a black cashmere sweater off. His muscled back was covered in the most beautiful floral tattoos and he was wearing a pair of thin gray sweatpants.

I reached out to snap the waistband of his pants. "Hey there."

Ares twisted as he climbed into bed, sliding under the covers first and then on top of me. He brushed a soft kiss to my lips, as he cradled my head in his hands. Like the needy, wanton girl I was, I pushed his sweatpants down.

The night had been long and terrifying, but here, in Hemlock House, where all the dreams I'd saved over the years had come to fruition in such a short time, I wanted my happy ending. I wanted my family, the family I chose, and I wanted *him*. Now.

Ares slipped out of his pants, kicking them onto the floor, deepening the kiss as he pulled me closer. "This place is incredible," he said as he settled against me. "You are incredible."

Though habit told me to deny it, I just nodded. Fear had me in its grip. What I wanted wasn't the only factor here. Everyone else still got to choose what they wanted to do. "I wanted us to stay together—but if no one else does, that's okay…"

"Stop," he said, his voice rumbling through me. "I don't know what the rest of them are doing, but I'm not leaving."

The smallest of smiles quirked at my lips, a rush of joy mixing with the particular pleasure of having Ares' hard body pressed against mine. His erection grew harder by the moment, distracting me as I said, "You can keep your place, of course. And you don't have to—"

Ares' mouth was on mine. "Shut up," he said, his lips moving on mine. "I'm staying. With you. No hedging."

"All in?"

He pulled back from me to look into my eyes, pushing hair back from my face. The gray light of a new day dawning filtered through the sheer curtains Lux had drawn before she left. In this light, and in my arms, there was no one but Ares. No sound but his words as he made his pledge to me. "All in."

His cock hardened against my belly with his words. My back arched at the feeling. "Ares," I breathed.

I hadn't known it, but this was what I had waited for. This, right here, right now. The peace of being chosen. The feeling of finally being home. Not just with a place, but with people. With *my* people. With *my* person.

Ares licked his fingers, then slipped them between us, between my legs as he kissed me. Gently, they slid against my clit, parting my inner lips until they sank deep within me. As he curved his two fingers inside me, wet heat bloomed between my legs.

"I love you, Ember," he breathed against my mouth. Blood sang in my veins at his declaration, a smile on my lips as he chided me. "Don't try to give me another out again."

I nodded as he added a finger, my body responding to his slow, but intense attention. My breath quickened as he strummed like a lyre, picking out a song my heart recognized.

The one we had been playing together for longer than I realized.

"I belong wherever you are," he said, his voice a low rumble. "And you belong to *me*."

I moaned at his words. At the claim he held on me. This was what I'd searched for, all my long life. A place to belong.

"Say it, Ember," he ordered me as he pulled out of me. I could feel him grip his cock with his wet fingers, sliding my slick desire down his shaft as he fit himself against me.

I took the head of his cock, spreading my legs wider, loving the way it felt as he stretched me open. But even more, I loved the promise he made to me with his words. With every reassertion of his claim on me, I sank deeper into the safety and love he offered me.

I had always been afraid of this. Afraid to give myself too fully to someone, knowing that someday, they would be disappointed by me. Disappointed by the power I possessed that they would never have. But Ares had proven time and again that would not be a problem between us. That he was more than secure enough to appreciate what and who I was.

This possession was not a balancing, but a fulfillment of my need to be assured that there was somewhere in *my* life that I was safe and protected. That for all the ways I'd committed to protecting others, that someone would do the same for me.

"I belong to you," I purred.

"Yes," he agreed as he pushed deeper into me. "Yes, you fucking do."

Swiftly, he kissed me, moving faster and deeper inside me. He broke the kiss to meet my eyes. My back arched up off the bed as my hips raised to meet his powerful thrusts.

"Mine," he growled. "You are mine."

"Yes," I hissed, bucking against him, grabbing two handfuls of his ass. "Yes, I fucking am."

"Saints," he snarled. "That feels too good."

"Come," I pleaded. "Show me you belong to me."

His release sent me over an edge I hadn't known existed. One where love and comfort ruled alongside pleasure and pain. With Ares, I was finally home, and so was he. I closed my eyes as I pulled him closer to me. We had eternity together, and that was finally enough time.

I finally had all I needed.

CHAPTER 45

ARES

SIX WEEKS LATER

A FRIGID WIND rattled the dry stems and leaves of the barren winter garden. It would snow soon. The Almanac swore up and down every news feed in existence that it was about to be the darkest, snowiest winter in years. Ember and I agreed that before the snow set in, we had to ward off Oleander Cottage.

The whispers had started the very first night on the property. At first, it was just that we'd find ourselves stuck in the kitchen, staring at the back of the cottage. Slowly, it had turned into more.

A week ago, Av found Briony at the garden gate, just about to walk through. That had spurred Ember into action. Calypso was a remarkable researcher, and she'd managed to dig up a rather clever warding that Ember and I could weave together now that she had her sword back.

The copper-haired Maere still hadn't told us why she wanted to leave Aradios so badly, but at least from my perspective, it looked like she was fitting in well with the other Maere. Even Max, who still had not left. She was expected to replace Calypso in Aradios before winter set in, but showed no signs of leaving.

And neither did we. While Oleander Cottage was certainly

a problem, Hemlock House was the seat of Necroline power. The spirits here were Roman's people, and they respected me, liked Eryx, and were happy to have Av around. It looked like we were moving in. There was space in the carriage house that we made into official Necroline offices and it was remarkable how happy our people seemed to come and go.

The necromancers of Orphium had never liked our offices in the Carlyle. They were rightfully suspicious of the Consulate, and all its trappings. But now that we resided here, that our headquarters were on neutral ground, they came and went frequently. Sometimes just to say hello, other times to ask for help, which I found much easier to give these days without the Consulate ever-present, looking over my shoulder in the bureau-cratic wing of the Carlyle.

I hadn't known how much being there had stifled all of us until we were gone. And even though winter approached, it felt like a kind of spring within the house. It felt like we were grow-ing, changing in ways that I probably wouldn't understand for years. And for the first time, that felt good. It felt right, after so many years of feeling stagnant and hopeless.

But good as things were in Hemlock House, everyone was rightfully wary of the cottage and the lingering concern about Fairchild. He'd gotten away, and between my network and the Maere's there was no sign of him, or whatever remained of the Chioric sect. It was as though they'd disappeared into thin air.

All we could do was keep an eye out for them at this point. Remain vigilant and try to understand the ritual they'd performed, and figure out whether they could do it again. There were questions left open, and I hated that, but we were doing what we could.

At least Oleander Cottage and its alluring evil whispers were problems I could more easily solve. I crossed my arms over my chest, waiting for Ember. I'd already laid down the salt. I was just waiting for my coffee now.

Ember came out of the house, bundled up in a matching

sweatsuit, a puffer and fluffy-looking booties. Her honey-colored hair was plaited into two braids and her cheeks were flushed with the cold. She looked like she'd let Briony pick out her outfit, which was probably accurate. The teenager had more influence on us than anyone else these days.

"Ready to seal this bad boy up?" she asked, scowling at the haunted cottage.

Even now, the pull to enter it was strong, and I'd whispered the words Calypso had found for us as I salted. That should have quieted things down until we finished the wards. We had to find a more complete solution to the problem of the cottage, but until we did, this was a good temporary one.

Ember smiled a lot more these days, and as time went on, I saw her deepening into a trust that the people she loved could come and go, but that they did actually love her in return. Whenever I found her with Briony, my heart swelled with love. Somehow, I'd ended up with a family.

Ember shook the mug she'd brought out for me, her movements jerky and impatient. Something was irritating her this morning.

I took the travel mug that Ember offered me and took a long drink of warm coffee. "What's wrong?"

Her eyes moved back towards the house, though her body stayed still. "Rhi got a call from her mysterious superior at the Consulate this morning."

A low growl rumbled in my chest. They'd been bothering all of us since finding out that we'd moved out of the Carlyle completely. I had a theory that we'd made things worse by moving in *together*. And not just me and Ember, but all of us.

And Briony. The Consulate offered again and again to find her a different family. But when we presented that idea to Briony herself, she'd thrown a very mundane teenage fit, screaming at us that we couldn't get rid of her so easily. It took two days to convince her that we didn't want to get rid of her, just to respect her choices. And, of course, both of us had told the Consulate to fuck off with their offers.

If Briony wanted us, then she was already ours.

I didn't like that they were coming after Rhiannon next. I glanced back at the house. My brother wasn't going to like it either. He was hooked on the assassin in a way I feared would end in him getting hurt. I'd never seen him so interested in a woman. Typically, he had short flings with people who understood that he wasn't in it for the long haul. I'd never once seen him pine for anyone, but all that had changed.

I took another long drink of my coffee then set it down outside the circle of salt, taking Ember's mug from her fingers. "Let's get this done, and then we can go sort Rhiannon out."

"No one needs to sort me out," the assassin in question said.

Both Ember and I nearly jumped out of our skin, twisting to find that Rhiannon had appeared behind us, as though by magic, a pile of luggage at her feet. It was still a complete mystery to me how she did that, and it had only gotten worse since she got her sword back.

"What are you doing?" Ember shouted, panic edging her voice. Her eyes were locked on the luggage.

"Eight weeks," Rhiannon said. "They've called every day for eight weeks. I've told them *and told them* that I quit, that *this* is my job, but they insist I can do both. I can't. And more importantly, I don't want to."

My brother came barreling out the back door of Hemlock House, an overnight bag slung over his shoulders. "You don't have to," he said.

Rhiannon stared at him. "What are you *doing*?"

He grinned. Eryx Necroline *grinned*. My brother was such a goner. "You're going to have them lock you in when they ward, right?"

Rhiannon blinked a few times, as though she couldn't believe he'd ferreted out her brilliant plan so easily. "Yes."

"Then I'm coming with you. The spirits like me."

It was true. The whispers from the house were still whispering, but they were more pleasant now, sweetly beckoning, rather ominously so, but still... less threatening. The difference was subtle, but it was there.

"No," Ember replied, looking at Rhiannon. Then she glared at my brother, rather more severely. "No."

Rhiannon tilted her head to one side. "Ember. Please. You can't just lock that monstrosity up and expect for things to be okay. That's not how warding works and you know it."

Ember's jaw clenched. We'd talked about this, and that's why the warding was to be temporary. There was, technically, a risk that we could make things worse by trapping the malefic entities inside the wards.

"Let me go in and solve this. I can survive that place." Rhiannon's tone and words were so reasonable, so calm. It was easy to forget that she was talking about going into the most deadly, haunted place in Orphium. Immortal as she was, there were things worse than death, and I was fairly certain all of them were possible inside Oleander Cottage.

Eryx picked up several of her bags. "Not alone. You need a clairsentient, and I'm the best pick."

Rhiannon rolled her eyes. And then, to my surprise, shrugged. "Fine." She brushed a kiss to Ember's cheek. "See you when spring comes. I'll have this solved by then."

"Do you... have your phone?" Ember asked.

Rhiannon shook her head. "No. It won't work in there anyway. EMF and all that."

Eryx, who was still piling luggage onto his back, nodded. "She's right. But there's a landline. It's connected to the house. We tried it yesterday."

"*We?*" Ember demanded. "The two of you have been planning this?"

Rhiannon rolled her eyes again. "No. We just..." she glanced at Eryx and frowned, almost as though she were a bit confused, "keep ending up there together."

"Absolutely not," Ember said, shaking her head. "No. And no again a trillion times over in eight dead languages."

"Technically there are only—" my brother began.

Ember interrupted him. "Kindly shut the fuck up."

Rhi pulled on Ember's sleeve. "I'll be okay. I need some time to process everything. Some space."

"Great," Ember said. "Take a vacation to Aradios, visit the beach."

"Ember," Rhiannon said, her voice soft. "They'll find me anywhere I go, harass me til I come back. I need quiet."

For a long moment, Ember was still. I knew she was considering how hard the truth of the island's involvement in all that had happened was on Rhiannon. We'd talked about it every night since the Gallery and Myrine's awful revelations.

Finally, Ember sighed. "Did you talk to Briony?"

Rhiannon nodded. "She's going to dig up some Cottage history for me. I gave her all my best Consulate hacks."

Ember groaned. "Rhi... she is a *child*."

Rhiannon shrugged. "She is a genius. Let her be a genius."

Eryx carried the rest of Rhiannon's luggage over the line of salt. They barely disturbed it, but I reinforced it all the same. Ember's eyes were worried as she looked up at me, but I took her hand. "They will be all right together. If anyone can solve Oleander Cottage's problem, it's them."

"We can still hear you," Rhiannon said with a sigh.

"Yes," I replied. I sketched a door into my salt barrier, using an old sigil my mother had once used. Both Ember and Rhiannon nodded, smiling at one another. "I know. This should allow you to take things like groceries in, but you'll have to perform the ritual in reverse if you want out."

Eryx reached across the barrier to hug me. "See you soon," he murmured. "We'll be okay."

Again, I nodded. They *would* be okay. We'd all dealt with worse, after all.

"Call as much as you can," Ember said.

Rhiannon agreed and then she and Eryx disappeared through the garden gate, and into the overgrown brush that was Oleander Cottage's garden. Ember took my hand again and we whispered the arcane words that would bring the ward up. It got quieter and quieter in the garden.

And then there was nothing but the sound of the wind, howling through the trees. There was a distinct scent in the air, one that spoke of crisp blankets of snow. Ember shivered, picking up our coffee mugs.

"That's that," she said, holding her free hand out to me.

I could tell she was putting a brave face on, so I took her hand, pressing a kiss to her cold fingers. "Let's get you warmed up."

CHAPTER 46

EMBER

INSIDE THE HOUSE, I found Max in the front hall, bags packed, by the front door. Sera sat hugging her knees on the staircase, looking for all the world like a lost little girl, she was so small. The two of them avoided each other's eyes so carefully. So today was to be a day of goodbyes.

Ares smiled at me, then kissed my hand again, taking the mugs from me. I watched as he walked towards the kitchen where Briony and Calypso were making cookies with Avaline. I wasn't ready to lose another friend to distance today. I hated that I thought that Oleander Cottage was a better solution for Rhi than a beach vacation, but I did actually believe her that it might be the only place she could avoid the Consulate.

But Max was another story altogether. I knew she had to go, but I wasn't ready to say goodbye. It was too much to ask. I needed more time. But glancing up at Sera, I knew Max had to go. Neither of them could manage even another day in the same house. They needed space and time to heal. Someday they would be all right, friends again even. But now, both their hearts needed time.

"So." It was the only word I could manage. There were too

many years between us. Too many things that should probably be said that would go unsaid.

Max nodded. "Yeah."

We stood awkwardly for a moment, each of us waiting for the other to know just what to say. Max spoke first. "Thank you for understanding why I need to do this."

On the stairs, Sera sniffed and took a shuddery breath, as though she suppressed a sob. I could feel her heart breaking from here. "Of course," I said, opening the door. "Let me walk you out."

Max glanced back up at Sera, her big brown eyes sad. "I—"

I touched her arm and shook my head, sensing what she was about to say. "Don't do that to her. You can't say those words right now. It won't help."

Behind me, I heard Sera get up and run up the stairs, her footsteps light on the carpet. When I turned back to Max, she looked as though her insides had been pulled outside her body. I pushed her gently out the door. Her motorcycle sat in the driveway, washed and ready for her journey south to Aradios.

I watched as she packed her bag in. The sun broke through the clouds. Probably the last of the autumn sunshine. The leaves had all fallen and the tree branches that danced above us were barren fingers, scraping at the sky. Once, it would have given me a lonely feeling to watch them, to say another goodbye.

Now, I knew that some goodbyes were new beginnings. "You both need a fresh start," I said, feeling careful with my words for once. "Give her some time to let her heart heal. To get over you."

Max smiled, her eyes watery. "Is it fucked up that I hate the idea of her finding someone else?"

I shook my head, dragging the Maere into my arms. "No. That's just the way love is. And she knows you love her, even if it can't be the love you both wish it was."

Max clung to me, shaking as her tears fell on my shoulder.

"Thank you for seeing me, Ember. I haven't given you enough credit over the years."

"Shhh," I breathed. "You don't have to say nice things just because you're leaving."

She pulled away from me, tears still streaming down her cheeks. "I mean it. None of us are perfect, but we all expected you to be and then we were mad when you couldn't…"

"Hush," I said, and not because I didn't believe her, but because it was true. It *was* true and I had let it go. I *had* to. I needed the room in my heart for whatever was growing inside Hemlock House. "We all made mistakes. That's immortality, babe."

Max laughed, wiping tears from her eyes. "Ember, I am going to miss you a lot." She looked up at the house. "Don't let her miss me, okay. When she finds someone else, tell her to go for it. Lie and tell her I said I wanted her to be happy."

I hugged Max again, pressing my forehead to hers. "Someday, you *will* be happy for her. And you will be happy too, in your own way. This is just the hard part."

Max hugged me tight. "You know a lot about the hard parts, don't you?"

"Sure do," I replied before letting her go. "Ride safe, okay?"

She brushed a quick kiss to each of my cheeks as an answer. I sat down on the front steps and watched as she drove away. Ares came out first, sitting behind me on the steps, his arms encircling me. "Cookies are in the oven," he said, kissing the top of my head.

He was wearing a black and red plaid shirt, rolled up to his elbows, which let me run my fingernails down his tattooed skin. Briony was out next, with mugs of hot chocolate on a tray. She carried one to me then left the tray on a table on the wrap-around front porch.

When she'd found a quilt, she curled into one of the wicker rocking chairs on the porch. Calypso came next, with a book in hand. Then Av and Stanley. A few more clouds cleared off and jazzy music drifted out of the house—an old love song from years and years ago.

"Who left the stereo on?" I asked. "I love this song."

No one answered me, so I turned around. Briony shook her head. Calypso and Av both shrugged. Ares was the only one who didn't move a muscle. He just hugged me tighter.

"The house is happy," he whispered. "And so are we."

I hugged his arms as tightly as I could, a grin spreading over my face. "Yes," I agreed. "We are."

<hr />

T hank you for reading *The Consulate*! All bonus content for this book, is available to my newsletter. Links to join my newsletter and my reader group can all be found on my website: www.allisoncarrwaechter.com

Printed in Great Britain
by Amazon